Penguin Books

Ita Buttrose always wanted to write, and *What is Love?* marks a natural progression in her long and distinguished career, which began when she was fifteen. During this time she has worked for Australia's major newspaper and magazine companies as writer, editor, editor-in-chief and publisher. She has also run her own publishing company and edited its flagship title, *ITA* magazine, for six years. Ita happily admits to being a 'magazine junkie' so perhaps it's hardly surprising that *What is Love?* is set in her much-loved media world.

Ita's success has made her a household name in Australia. She is equally at home on television and radio, where she has hosted prime-time radio shows on Sydney's leading talkback stations. Currently she is a panelist on the popular show *Beauty and the Beast*, on Foxtel and Network Ten, and a columnist with *The Australian Women's Weekly* and the Courier Group of newspapers.

Ita has two children and lives in Sydney.

ALSO BY ITA BUTTROSE

*Early Edition: My First Forty Years* (1985)
*Every Occasion: The Guide to Modern Etiquette* (1985)
*A Passionate Life* (1998)
*A Word to the Wise* (1999)

# ITA BUTTROSE

## What is love?

PENGUIN BOOKS

Penguin Books Australia Ltd
487 Maroondah Highway, PO Box 257
Ringwood, Victoria 3134, Australia
Penguin Books Ltd
Harmondsworth, Middlesex, England
Penguin Putnam Inc.
375 Hudson Street, New York, New York 10014, USA
Penguin Books Canada Limited
10 Alcorn Avenue, Toronto, Ontario, Canada M4V 3B2
Penguin Books (NZ) Ltd
Cnr Rosedale and Airborne Roads, Albany, Auckland, New Zealand
Penguin Books (South Africa) (Pty) Ltd
5 Watkins Street, Denver Ext 4, 2094, South Africa
Penguin Books India (P) Ltd
11, Community Centre, Panchsheel Park, New Delhi 110 017, India

First published by Penguin Books Australia Ltd 2000

10 9 8 7 6 5 4 3 2 1

Designed by Nikki Townsend, Penguin Design Studio
Author portrait by James Calderaro
Typeset in Berkeley Book 11.25/14.5 by Post Pre-press Group, Brisbane, Queensland
Printed and bound in Australia by Australian Print Group, Maryborough, Victoria

National Library of Australia
Cataloguing-in-Publication data:

Buttrose, Ita, 1942– .
What is love?

ISBN 0 14 029287 X.

I. Title.

A823.3

www.penguin.com.au

To my sensational nieces Elizabeth and Evie,
who so often asked me the question
that is the title of this book.

# Acknowledgements

This book might never have happened without the assistance of Nene King. I am most grateful to her for publishing my first fiction story in *The Australian Women's Weekly* when she was Editorial Director, because it led to a phone call from the Executive Publisher of Penguin, Julie Gibbs, and an offer that I couldn't refuse! Julie's enthusiastic support of this, my first novel, has been terrific.

I also want to thank my friend Jill Fraser for letting me use her as an occasional sounding board. Her excellent research skills have also been much appreciated.

Thanks to my brothers Will and Charles for their expert input, and a very special thank you to my dear chum Mel Clifford for being so generous with his time and knowledge.

I especially want to thank Fiona Daniels, one of the most considerate and sympathetic editors that it's been my good fortune to meet. It has been an absolute joy working with her.

Finally thank you to everyone at Penguin who are so brilliant at what they do.

*Each player must accept the cards life deals him or her. But once they are in hand, he or she alone must decide how to play the cards in order to win the game.*

VOLTAIRE

# Chapter One

Catherine Walker leant back in her chair and put her feet up on the desk. Kicking off her Ferragamo pumps, she closed her eyes. It had been another long day in a demanding year, but one that in spite of everything she'd enjoyed because of the way it had challenged her. Profits for her company, CW Publishing, were on target, and her expansion plans for next year would be able to go ahead as planned. Earlier that month, her success had been recognised by her peers, the ultimate accolade, when the World Association of Magazine Publishers had named Catherine Publisher of the Year and *MAUD International*, the magazine she'd created two years ago, had won the coveted Magazine of the Year award.

The awards had been presented in an impressive black tie ceremony at The Kennedy Center in Washington and Katharine Graham, the former publisher of the *Washington Post*, and one of Catherine's idols, was special guest presenter. Afterwards over dinner she had asked Catherine what her future plans were.

Catherine's reply had been confident. 'The timing's right for a woman – this woman,' she said, almost thumping her chest, 'to have a go at taking on the big boys. They think they're gods – invincible as well as infallible – but in reality they're dinosaurs.'

Catherine warmed to her theme. 'Not only am I fed up with the male slant that dominates world media, I'm bored witless with the misguided belief that the only way to do things is the male way. I intend to create a global media empire, one with influence that will make a difference – for the better – in the lives of others.

'And,' she added, 'if it means I have to go into battle with the male media barons, I will. What's more, I'll enjoy every moment of it!'

'I can see that,' Katharine Graham laughed. 'But it won't be easy,' she warned. 'Men like Rupert Murdoch, Kerry Packer, Conrad Black, Ted Turner and their set won't make you welcome. Even your impeccable connections won't open doors for you. Powerful men will resent your ambition, my dear, and your intrusion on what they consider their personal territory. Whatever you do, don't turn your back on them.'

'Don't worry, I won't.' Catherine's blue eyes shone with determination. When she was passionate about something she had the ability to sweep everyone up in her enthusiasm. Even Katharine Graham couldn't escape it.

'I wish I could join you,' the older woman said. 'You're making me excited. But, and forgive me for repeating myself, don't drop your guard because your opponents will be quick to put all kinds of obstacles in your way.'

'I know how ruthless they can be and if they force me to, I can play their game. I'm not my father's daughter for nothing, you know. I'm more than ready to take them on and to put my credentials on the line.'

'I'll watch your progress with interest. Good luck.' Katharine Graham kissed her on the cheek. 'I admire your ambition. If you ever think there's something I can do to help, call me. And remember, nothing is more fun than to love what you do and to feel that it matters.'

The conversation drifted through Catherine's mind as she sat trying to find the strength to get up and make her way to her private bathroom to freshen up for dinner. She was looking forward to Christmas next week and a few days off. My poor body is in need of some recharging, she thought. But in spite of her weariness she felt a wonderful sense of fulfilment. All her hard work had paid off. She'd made her critics, all those knockers who predicted she would fail, look like fools. Even her father, who'd been furious when she'd first told him she was leaving Walker Corp. (his huge media and entertainment company) to go out on her own, had had to admit that he'd been wrong and that she'd done better than he ever thought she would. It was something that gave her a great deal of pleasure.

*MAUD* was the thinking woman's magazine for the 21st century with an ever-increasing circulation in Australia, England and the United States. It covered politics and business, fashion and food, as well as lifestyle and design, and was considered the leader in the journalistic trend for what marketers described as 'adaptable information'.

The Christmas issue, the biggest Catherine had produced so far, had arrived from the printer that afternoon looking appropriately festive with its red and green cover lines. And it's fat and prosperous, as a successful magazine should be, she thought. Catherine smiled contentedly as she flicked through the magazine, admiring the abundance of advertising pages. She was more than happy with the way the issue had turned out and confident that it would sell well over the holiday period.

There was plenty to read, too – British Labour Prime Minister, Tony Blair, had allowed *MAUD* to take the first photographs of the newly renovated Number 10 Downing Street. At his wife's suggestion, he'd commissioned the noted British designer,

David, Viscount Linley, to create some exquisite furniture for the residence. Linley is so gifted, Catherine thought as she looked at the photographs. What style – and his line is superb. As one of Britain's most successful female lawyers, Cherie Blair knew that the Conservatives would grab at any reason to criticise her husband for refurbishing the official residence, even though it was long overdue. She'd cleverly invited Linley's aunt, Queen Elizabeth, to have the first look at the renovation and made sure the press was there to record the monarch's visit. The Queen had been so full of praise that it was difficult for the Tories to object about anything. A smart woman can go a long way, Catherine thought.

Jean-Paul Guerlain, the creative mastermind behind his eponymous French perfume company, had agreed to let *MAUD* carry the first samples of his newest fragrance, which had been eight years in the making. Catherine ripped open the strip on the double-page advertisement showing the new fragrance's stunning bottle, and sniffed it. The perfume was sensational, distinctive, wonderfully flowery and yet crisp. Catherine loved it.

She'd secured the first extract of Caroline Kennedy Schlossberg's book, *Flying with Eagles*, predicted to be one of the new year's biggest sellers. Just looking at the picture of Caroline with her late brother, John F. Kennedy Jnr, killed so tragically in

1999, and reading Caroline's thoughts on what his loss meant to her, brought tears to Catherine's eyes.

Germaine Greer had written a provocative piece on feminism in the 21st century and Lucy Turnbull, who everyone thought was aiming to go down in the history books as Sydney's first woman Lord Mayor, had given a one-to-one interview to Catherine on why she'd decided to throw her hat in the ring to be Australia's first female Prime Minister. Catherine reread the piece with satisfaction. Lucy's announcement would catch quite a few people unawares and its shock value would get plenty of publicity for the magazine and help boost sales.

Turning the pages, she stopped to admire the photographs illustrating the feature on Frances Henman, one of America's richest women. Catherine had met her through Katharine Graham, and was thrilled when the reclusive heiress had agreed to let *MAUD* exclusively photograph her priceless jewellery collection before she donated it to The Smithsonian in Washington.

The Henman collection was magnificent. Frances had been buying up Cartier creations for more than fifty years. The collection included a dazzling diamond necklace, from which hung three hexagonal diamond pendants with round and pear-shaped drops, that Cartier had created for Mrs Cornelius Vanderbilt in 1908. It was Frances's pride and joy. But Catherine's favourite piece was a diamond and tortoiseshell hair comb which had been made for Woolworth heiress, Barbara Hutton, to wear at one of her many weddings.

Catherine could have sat thumbing through her beloved *MAUD* for hours, she was so pleased with the Christmas issue, but she was also conscious that she had to keep an eye on the time. If she were late for dinner, her advertising director, Brenda Thompson, would be furious. Brenda organised these evenings every six weeks or so to give the magazine's principal advertisers what she liked to call a 'warm and fuzzy feeling'. Brenda insisted the mealtime get-togethers were important to the magazine's bottom line. 'You know as well as I do, Catherine,' she'd say, 'advertisers like to be seen to be appreciated at all times – and they're never happier than when they know someone else is going to pick up the tab.'

Sometimes the evenings were hard work but as a rule Catherine enjoyed them. They gave her the chance to speak with the people who made the decisions about allocating advertising budgets, and she often picked up useful information that she and Brenda turned to the magazine's benefit. She also took advantage of the opportunity to thank her advertisers for their support, something she assured them she never took for granted. When it came to wooing the advertising industry, as she and Brenda knew only too well, a little humility never went astray.

But not tonight, Catherine thought, excitedly. Tonight is going to be a lay-them-in-the-aisles, knock-them-for-a-six evening. I can't wait! I'll just check my e-mail and be off.

As she scrolled through her messages, one of them caught her attention because of its intriguing tag. It was titled *My Memorable Evening*.

She called it up. The message was simple and succinct. *Thanks for making my evening so memorable.*

Strange there's no name, she thought. Catherine was puzzled. It wasn't usual for her to receive anonymous e-mail. Whoever had sent it had put a block on their identity and address being revealed to the receiver. She shrugged. It's probably some idiot sending me junk mail. Bloody pest. She read the message again. I bet it's some kind of advertising gimmick. Oh well, I guess all will be clear in the passage of time.

At that moment Clare, Catherine's executive assistant, put her head round the door. 'Look what's just arrived for you. Aren't you the lucky one!' She was carrying a huge box of the most gorgeous red roses. 'There must be at least four dozen in here. Just smell them! They're heavenly.'

Catherine reached for the card to see who they were from. She couldn't believe it. *Thanks for making my evening so memorable.* Not again! This must be the in message of the moment! What's it all about? she wondered. And then she noticed the 'J' on the bottom right-hand corner of the card.

'Who or what on earth is "J"? Ring the florist would you please, Clare, and ask who sent them to me. They are impressive, aren't they?' Catherine couldn't resist smelling the roses – their perfume was overwhelming. She sat at her desk enjoying the fragrance, waiting for Clare to return, all thoughts of dinner momentarily forgotten.

'Well, the mystery's solved,' Clare announced triumphantly as she walked back into Catherine's office. 'They're from Jack Clement.'

'You're joking! Jack Clement. Are you sure?'

'Absolutely. The florist said he's one of their regular customers and she personally arranged your roses. I think he's trying to tell you something, Boss.'

Clare didn't wait for Catherine's reply. She knew that Catherine considered her private life exactly that and whatever the roses from Jack Clement signified she wasn't going to discuss it with Clare. 'If you don't need me for anything else I'm off. Bob's taking me out for dinner tonight for our wedding anniversary.'

'How romantic – have a wonderful evening.'

Catherine gazed at the roses. Why had Jack Clement sent them to her? It must be a joke of some kind. What memorable evening?

# Chapter Two

Catherine had seen Jack about a month ago at the Advertising Industry Floral Ball. The previous month they'd both taken part in the Prime Minister's Media Advisory Think Tank, examining cross-ownership of the media and looking at the links between the major media players and the rapidly growing Internet media groups. They'd met before socially at functions but had only ever exchanged pleasantries. The PM's Think Tank had provided an opportunity for her and Jack to get to know each other a little better, but only as business colleagues, nothing more.

With eight other businessmen and women, they'd spent the previous twelve months canvassing issues and topics that the Prime Minister had asked them to consider in preparation for what ultimately would form the basis for a major policy announcement. Think Tank sessions were held at four-thirty in one of their respective boardrooms and lasted around four to five hours. Afterwards they'd relax with a drink and a quick bite to eat at some nearby restaurant. On a couple of occasions, however, Jack and Catherine had eaten alone as the others had commitments. Their media backgrounds gave them much in common and they often chatted away until quite late. Catherine's sharp mind impressed Jack and he found it stimulating to debate issues with a woman of her intellect.

Catherine enjoyed sparring with Jack, too, and looked forward to their monthly meetings. In a way they were very much alike. Both no-nonsense people, they had the reputation for saying what they thought without pulling punches, as well as the all too rare ability to get to the point on whatever topic came up for discussion. When he thanked Catherine for contributing to the Think Tank's success, the PM had told her how refreshing it was to have such succinct opinions put to him, and not to have everything couched in bureaucratic mumbo jumbo. 'Sometimes,' he said, 'I have no idea what advice the bureaucrats are trying to give me because they simply can't express themselves in plain English.'

'Any time I can translate for you, Mr Prime Minister, you have only to ask.'

Jack, standing nearby, had overheard the conversation and laughed. 'Same goes for me, Prime Minister.'

Catherine had left not long after, for a deadline

back at the magazine. At the Floral Ball, though, something had sparked between her and Jack. She'd been aware of it and she knew he had been, too. But she'd put all thoughts of the evening out of her mind until now. Jack's cryptic message brought the memories rushing back.

It had been a magical night. Some bright person on the Advertising Ball Committee had come up with the concept of giving all the sponsors' tables a floral theme. Women guests were encouraged to wear flowers on their gowns, or in their hair. The men were asked to wear 'extravaganza' buttonholes. Everyone had entered into the spirit of the night and the ballroom looked like something out of Monet's flower garden.

Catherine had worn a long, sweeping gown of cornflower blue chiffon, cut to do all the right things for her body, by Perry Wolf, *MAUD*'s Designer of the Year. Perry had also come up with the brilliant idea of a plaited coil of fresh cornflowers, which he'd sewn on to the narrow shoulder straps of her gown and used as a medieval-style sash around her waist. It was feminine and supremely elegant. The dress made Catherine's eyes seem even bluer than usual and, with her shoulder-length chestnut hair and glowing milky white skin, she looked stunning. Heads turned when she passed by. She felt good about herself and had a feeling in her bones that it was going to be a night to remember.

Jack had asked her for a dance. And then another,

and another. 'You look sensational,' he said. 'I can't take my eyes off you.'

Something about the tone of his voice took her by surprise. She looked up at him. 'Why thank you,' she replied wonderingly.

If truth be known, Catherine could hardly take her eyes off Jack either. It was as if she were seeing him for the first time.

He was a man of presence and looked extraordinarily handsome in his beautifully tailored dinner suit. He was tall, which she liked – at least six foot three, she thought – and well built with a broad chest and slim hips. His hands, while big and capable looking, had long, tapered fingers with an artist's sensitivity about them. He wore his silvery grey hair short and brushed back from his face. Catherine thought it made him look distinguished. His eyes were the vivid blue of an Australian outback sky and when he looked down at her and smiled, Catherine felt as if she were the only woman in the room. She had never experienced such a sensation and found that it was very much to her liking.

'Look, why don't we leave and go somewhere quiet for a drink.'

'What?' Catherine had been so preoccupied with her thoughts about Jack, she wasn't sure she'd heard correctly.

'Let's leave,' he repeated. 'I want to talk to you. It's time we got to know each other properly.'

'Jack, I can't. I have to present the awards for the best tables. It's the price an editor has to pay – after all, most of the people here spend big money advertising in *MAUD*.' Bloody hell, she thought, I don't want to present awards. I want to go with Jack. I wonder if I could find someone to fill in for me. Catherine thought quickly but it was no use. She couldn't let everyone down.

'I really am sorry,' she said.

'Damn, you would have something official to do. What about tomorrow? How about having lunch with me?'

'Love to. I'll meet you at quarter to one at – where will we go?'

'How about Beppi's? I'll get Beppi to give us one of his little tables out the back where we can talk without being disturbed.'

'Perfect!' She smiled at him. 'I love Beppi's – and he does make the best pasta in Sydney.'

Jack swept her into another dance. Catherine could feel herself tingle as he held her. Oh my, she thought, as she moved a little closer to him, this man is turning me on. Desire crept through her body. She glanced up to find Jack's eyes on her. 'Having a good time?' he asked.

'Wonderful.' Catherine was sure she must have been blushing, that he could read her mind, sense her desire. They danced on in silence. She felt safe in his arms. She liked the feel of him and the way he smelt, too. She especially liked the way he looked at her. She was glad he couldn't read her mind. How nice he is, she thought.

But Jack Clement had plenty of enemies who thought otherwise. As one of Australia's most powerful men, he was well aware that hate and envy came with the territory. Before government regulations prohibited anyone from owning TV stations in the cities in which they also control newspapers, The Clement Group had owned newspapers, television and radio stations throughout Australia. All of them were outstandingly successful and made The Clement Group handsome profits. The flagship of the group, its morning newspaper, *The Sydney Morning Pictorial*, was often referred to as the 'River of Gold' because it carried millions of dollars' worth of classified advertising each week.

Jack liked the media business and was justifiably proud of The Clement Group's success but his newspapers were his pride and joy. He often sat in on *The Sydney Morning Pictorial*'s news conferences when the stories of the day were discussed and placed in the newspaper according to their importance. He made contributions to the stance the paper should take in its editorial, too, and sometimes, when it was an issue close to his heart, he would write the editorial himself.

Whenever he did, his critics accused him of 'interfering' in the newspaper. Jack wouldn't have a bar of it. 'How on earth can I be accused of "interfering" in a newspaper that I own? It's my bloody newspaper and if I want it to have an opinion about something, it will, and if I want to share it with our readers, that's my right as the owner. Anyone who doesn't agree needn't buy my newspaper.'

When Australia's media laws were changed in 1987 and it was a question of him keeping his newspapers and selling his TV stations, or vice versa, Jack decided to sell the lot. He didn't want his empire broken up – it was either his or it wasn't and he would never be satisfied with just a part of it. Fuck the government! Idiot politicians meddling in areas about which they knew nothing. Why didn't they just confine themselves to running the country and leave the running of the media to people who understood it?

Jack didn't waste time getting sentimental over what he planned to do. Business was business. He had no trouble finding willing buyers and at the end of the day, after he'd paid off some loans and entitlements for some of his key people who preferred taking redundancy packages rather than being sold to new owners, Jack had pocketed three and a half billion dollars. He was thirty-five years old and richer than he'd ever thought possible.

The Clement Group changed direction – it invested in property, commercial and residential, and tourism. Jack also served as director on the boards of six of Australia's top ten companies, including Rupert Murdoch's News Ltd. Canny Rupert knew how much Jack would miss his newspapers and figured that he'd welcome a directorship with News. He also knew that Jack understood the media business ('Almost as well as I do,' he'd told his son Lachlan) and that his knowledge would be beneficial to News Ltd's expansion plans.

What's more, Jack's connections were useful. He was on first name terms with Australia's influential people. His family was descended from the first settlers and had been successful in business right from the beginning as major breeders of Merino sheep. The Clement fortune had grown over the years. As the only son, Jack had inherited the lot when his father, James, died. He was just eighteen and simply went on making money like all the Clements before him.

His father had drummed the family success philosophy into him as a small boy: 'Making money is a family tradition and the only way to be successful and rich is to make money work for you and not the other way round.' Jack had learnt the lesson well. His reputation on the share market was the stuff of which legends are made. He was known as a man who always got what he wanted and there were many well-documented stories of his ruthlessness towards anyone who tried to stop him. But at the same time he was known for his wit and charm and, as Catherine had discovered, he had both in large quantities.

Jack also had a secret goal, which he'd only shared with Rupert Murdoch, whom he considered as a kind of surrogate father. He intended to establish another media group, but not one confined to Australia. The kind of global organisation he had in mind would give him a world presence – and power. How he missed it! The thought of power was like an aphrodisiac to him and drove Jack relentlessly on.

Lunch at Beppi's was excellent. Catherine was a bit tired after the Floral Ball and suffering from a slight hangover. (I knew I shouldn't have had that after-dinner cognac, she thought.) Jack confessed to feeling much the same way and there was nothing for it but to tell him her 'never-fail' hangover cure: a large bowl of Beppi's fabulous fettuccine gorgonzola, some crusty bread, a small rocket salad and a bottle of his specially imported Lacryma Christi, Catherine's favourite white wine.

'Works for me every time,' she told Jack.

'Every time? How often do you get hangovers?' he asked, laughing at her.

She laughed back. 'I don't mean that at all and you know it, but there are just times when . . . well, you know,' she said.

'I know exactly, which means I'm the perfect candidate for the Walker hangover cure.'

Beppi, who had been running his acclaimed Italian restaurant for more than forty years, served them himself. The fettuccine smelt marvellous and arrived steaming. Catherine liked her food served piping hot and Beppi knew it.

'Looks terrific, Beppi.'

'Thank you, Miss Walker. I hope you both enjoy it.'

'We will, Beppi. Thanks,' said Jack.

They both tucked in hungrily. The fettuccine was delicious.

'This is good,' Jack said in between mouthfuls.

'I was sure you'd like it.' Catherine smiled. 'Cheers,' she said, raising her wineglass.

'Cheers,' Jack responded, tilting his glass in her direction. He took a sip. 'Superb choice,' he said, leaning back in his chair.

They sat together comfortably, enjoying the wine and getting to know each other more intimately. They discovered they both liked classical music, especially Mahler and Mozart, as well as the music of the legendary rock group Cold Chisel. Even their palates were compatible – not only did they both enjoy Italian cuisine, they were devotees of Thai and Korean food, too. And Catherine was delighted to find that, like her, Jack was currently reading Katharine Graham's Pulitzer Prize-winning autobiography, *Personal History*.

'Amazing what she did with the *Washington Post*,' he said.

'It certainly was,' Catherine agreed, 'and especially given the fact that everyone told her she'd fail. Nobody realised just how determined she was to make a go of it. What a woman! In my book she is an absolute star.'

'Just like you,' Jack said, looking into her eyes. For a split second Catherine forgot where she was. All she could think of was how blue Jack's eyes were in the subdued light of the restaurant. She forced herself to concentrate. 'And how appropriate,' he was saying, 'that you both have the same name, even if you do spell it differently. I'm sure that's a good omen for your continued success.'

'That's what I think, too,' Catherine said, cheerfully. 'Katharine Graham is one of my heroes. I'm hoping to meet her when I go to Washington for the magazine awards in a few weeks.'

She couldn't believe the effect Jack was having on her or why it hadn't happened until now. She'd always found him charismatic and likeable, but something had changed in their relationship. She could feel herself falling for him. On your guard, Catherine, she warned herself, this man's almost too good to be true.

Jack, however, was seemingly oblivious to the impact he was having on her. He ordered coffee for them both and then changed the topic of conversation. 'How's your company going?'

'Never better. *MAUD* broke even in its first year, advertising revenue is healthy. We were Australia's top-selling monthly after only six months' operation and the circulation is still going up. Internationally the magazine has taken off, too. We're selling particularly well in New York and, after a slow start in London, we began to pick up after issue three and haven't looked back.'

There was no doubt that *MAUD International* had been an ambitious undertaking. No other Australian publisher had ever printed a magazine concurrently in three continents. But Catherine figured that in a global world there had to be a place for a truly global magazine. Her instincts, reinforced by some hefty market research, proved correct.

'I'm somewhat ashamed to admit that I didn't think you'd be able to do it,' Jack said.

'You weren't the only one. The knockers and doomsday merchants were out in droves.' Catherine's lovely face hardened at the memory of some of the battles she'd undergone. 'If I were a less confident person I might have given up before I began. There was so much negativity it was unbelievable. Mind you,' she gave a wry grin, 'it wasn't easy. The British press didn't welcome us. They've disliked Australian publishers ever since Rupert Murdoch bought *The Times* and gave it a touch of Australian pizzazz, so we got very little support for what we were planning. And funnily enough, Murdoch's London newspapers didn't go out of their way to say much about us either, which was disappointing. I'd hoped that the Aussie connection would be helpful.'

She leant forward enthusiastically. 'But you know, Jack, the harder it is, the more determined I am to succeed. I'm about to order a reprint of our first *MAUD Lifestyle* special, and soon I'm going to make a major announcement about something fantastic that we're doing with fashion and Perry Wolf. I've never been so busy and I love every minute of it.

'And,' she stopped to take a deep breath, 'I've never talked so much about myself either. I'm sorry, I'm monopolising the conversation.'

'Not at all. I'm interested. You're a fascinating woman, Catherine. Tell me,' Jack continued, 'how does your father feel about it all?'

Like most people in the media, Jack respected the reputation of media magnate Sydney Walker and found it difficult to believe the old man would have let someone of Catherine's ability go without putting up a strong fight.

For a moment Jack thought Catherine looked tense. She gave an almost imperceptible sigh before she began to speak again, choosing her words carefully.

'It's always difficult to let go,' she said slowly, 'to have to change your plans, and Dad's no different from anyone else in this regard. But I think he is genuinely pleased with how things have gone for me. Of course, initially he didn't want me to leave Walker Corp. but now he says he couldn't be happier about my success.'

'You're lucky your father is still alive. He must be very useful when you have a problem or want to talk through an idea.'

'Yes, he is.'

'I often wish my father hadn't died when I was so young. There have been times in my life when I could have done with some wise parental advice and the opportunity to talk things through with someone I could trust.'

'I know what you mean,' Catherine replied.

'More coffee?' he asked her.

'Love some.' She pushed her cup towards him.

'What prompted you to go out on your own?' he asked as he poured her coffee, and then filled his own cup.

'I wanted to see if I could do it. I admire my father enormously and he's built an incredible empire, but in the same way that he wanted to create something very much his own, so did I. Dad understood that when I explained it to him.

'It's worked out well anyway,' she went on, 'because my brother, Tom, will make an excellent successor to Dad. He's come into his own running the American division of Walker Corp. and I'm sure the day isn't all that far away before Dad tells Tom he has to come back to Australia and get ready to take on the top job. I know Tom can't wait – not that he wishes Dad ill, nothing like that, but he has lots of plans of his own for the company and is looking forward to implementing them. You know how it is.'

'I do indeed.' He finished his coffee. 'One day I'd like to meet your brother. Actually, that's another thing I envy you. As an only child I often wished for a brother – and before you declare me sexist – or a sister,' he laughed.

'You must have been very lonely at times,' Catherine said.

'Yes, I was. That's why I'm so pleased my wife and I had twins,' he went on. 'They're such great little girls. I just wish I could spend more time with them.' Jack reached into his pocket and pulled out his wallet. 'Would you like to see what they look like?'

'Of course.' Catherine held out her hand as he passed over a couple of photographs. 'Why Jack, they're absolutely adorable – and they've both got your eyes,' she exclaimed. 'Where do the girls live?' she asked, remembering that she'd heard him telling someone at a Think Tank meeting that since he and his wife had split, his family had made their home overseas.

'In Paris with their mother.' His cold, matter-of-fact reply and the steely glint in his eye made Catherine think it might be prudent to change the subject, but Jack beat her to it.

Putting the photographs back in his wallet, he said firmly, 'That's enough of my family. Tell me more about your brother. I hear he's a real mover and shaker.'

'He is that,' Catherine replied, 'and he's a very nice man as well, although I do admit to being biased. Tom and I always have been close and we're both very happy doing our own thing. When we need each other or have a problem that we want to discuss, or a creative approach that we want to bounce around, we're there for each other.'

'Sounds like the ideal arrangement.'

'I think it is.'

'You must do a lot of travelling. Do you like it?' Jack asked, and was pleased to see Catherine's radiant smile.

'Adore it,' she said, 'although it's usually on business and I'm so busy that my jet lag doesn't catch up with me until I'm home again.'

'What's your favourite country?'

'Italy. I'm mad about the place: its history, the scenery, the Italians themselves – they're the world's nicest people, and I love their style – and the shopping.' Her eyes glowed. 'My credit cards run amok when they're in Italy. *Mama mia!*'

'I can believe it!' Jack laughed. 'Isn't that a little Italian number you're wearing?'

'It is. Valentino. How observant of you.' Catherine's bright fuchsia pink silk suit was cut beautifully, a Valentino trademark.

'Is there anyone special in your life?' Jack asked, catching her off guard.

She felt herself redden. Why does this man have

the ability to reduce me to this state? She felt sure her cheeks were flaming. 'No, not really.'

'I'm pleased to hear it.'

His eyes were hypnotic. She couldn't look away. She found herself wondering what it would be like to kiss him. She might have blushed even more if she'd known that Jack was thinking exactly the same thing about her.

'Miss Walker, Mr Clement.' Beppi's voice brought them both back to earth at once. 'Would you like a fresh pot of coffee?' They shook their heads.

Looking down at her watch, Catherine couldn't believe the time. She'd have to leave but she didn't want to. Why did this keep happening to them? She'd have to do something about her timetable. She could have spent the entire afternoon talking to Jack.

'I'm so sorry,' she said, 'but I must go. I have a meeting with an anxious author who is hoping I'll publish an excerpt from her new book in MAUD. Thank you for lunch – I feel like a human being again and I know I'll be able to get through the afternoon now.'

'Me too.' They both stood up. Smiling down at her, Jack held her briefly before kissing her on the cheek. She felt a frisson of something wonderful run through her body.

'We must do this again,' he said, as they left the restaurant. Opening the door of Catherine's car for her, he held her hand for a moment and said, 'I'll call you.'

But he'd rung the next day only to say that he had to make a rush trip to China – there was a problem with some hospitals that his company was building there. He wasn't sure how long he'd be away but told Catherine he would call her when he returned.

She'd hoped to hear from him before she went to America but there had been no word. She had been disappointed but put Jack out of her mind, determined not to let anything distract her from enjoying her well-deserved moment of triumph at the magazine awards in Washington.

# Chapter Three

It was just so odd that after more than a month of silence he would send her roses. It must be a mistake of some kind. Catherine stared at the card again. Clare, always thinking ahead, had written The Clement Group's phone number on it. Catherine dialled the number.

'Mr Clement's office,' the receptionist answered.

'Is he there, please?'

'May I say who's calling?'

'This is Catherine Walker.'

'One moment please, Ms Walker.'

She felt strangely nervous as she waited for Jack to come to the phone.

'Good evening, Catherine. How are you?' came the familiar voice.

Much to her amazement, Catherine felt herself blushing yet again. She hoped her voice sounded its usual self. 'Fine thanks, Jack,' she replied calmly.

'I'm sorry I haven't been in touch with you sooner,' he said. 'My work in China took me longer to complete than I'd imagined it would. I only got back yesterday morning.'

'I understand – I know how work can get out of control.'

'But I did miss you,' Jack assured her.

'I'm glad.'

She couldn't bear the suspense a moment longer. She had to know. 'Did you send me some red roses?'

'Yes, I did.'

'But why? What memorable evening?'

'Come over and have a drink with me and I'll explain. I have a bottle of champagne chilling.'

'You mean now?'

'Why not? Do you have something else to do tonight?'

'As a matter of fact, I do. I'm having dinner with some major advertisers.' Bad timing again, she thought. 'Remember them, Jack? Don't tell me you've forgotten the importance of showing advertisers that you care!' She was surprised to find herself flirting with him. It had been a while since she'd done that with any man. 'They like to see us grovel from time to time – it makes them feel necessary.'

'I remember only too well,' he laughed. 'But what time's dinner?'

'They've gone to the International for a drink and I'm meeting them at Lucio's in Paddington at nine.'

29

'So you've plenty of time to have a drink with me at the office first.'

'It would be nice to have a relaxing drink before dinner,' she admitted. 'And you have definitely whetted my curiosity.' She hesitated for the merest second. 'Okay, I'll see you soon.'

Catherine quickly re-did her make-up and changed into her new Perry Wolf midnight blue soft crepe dinner dress. She usually went home to change before going out after work, but for some reason she'd decided to bring her dress to the office. Thank heavens I did, she thought as she brushed her hair, or I'd never have been able to have a drink with Jack. I can't wait to find out what's behind that mysterious note of his.

She gave herself a generous spray of Chanel's Allure before ringing down to the garage to ask them to bring her Saab convertible up to the front door. Within minutes she was driving across town to Jack's office in Macquarie Street. She wished she were out on the open road, driving under the star-filled sky with the hood down and the breeze blowing through her hair. Catherine loved the freedom of driving – strangely, she always felt anonymous when she was in her car, even though she knew she was often recognised.

But I bet there's no chance of any kind of anonymity tonight, she thought, as she drove up to the building where Jack's security man was waiting for her to arrive. Sure enough, he recognised her at once. 'Good evening, Ms Walker. I'll look after your car,' he said politely. 'Mr Clement is expecting you. Just take the lift to the top floor.'

As the lift doors opened Jack stepped forward to greet her. 'Glad you could make it.' He showed her into his office.

It was everything she imagined it would be. Large, masculine and quietly powerful, like the man himself. The walls were decorated with wonderful art – Catherine recognised a William Dobell (an artist she particularly admired), a memorable Arthur Boyd, a distinctive Brett Whiteley and a Van Gogh masterpiece. It was common knowledge that when it came to art, Jack Clement's purse was limitless.

One wall of his office was completely glass and looked out over Sydney Harbour. The sun had just set and the lights of the city gave off a halo of light that seemed to envelop Sydney in a kind of aura. The Opera House's shells appeared luminous and myriad craft were darting their way here, there and everywhere on the harbour.

Looking out, Catherine remembered how during lunch one day at Government House, Queen Elizabeth had told her how much she liked Sydney Harbour. 'It doesn't matter what time of the day or night, there is always something happening on it. I enjoy watching all the activity,' she had said. As Catherine admired Jack's spectacular view she could appreciate the Queen's remarks.

Just outside the Heads, there was a full moon rising above the ocean. Now that's a good omen, Catherine thought. She always wished for something when there was a full moon – it was a ritual that her mother had started when Catherine was a little girl and although she knew it was silly, she found herself making a wish.

This is a very interesting situation I've landed myself in. Everything about Jack appeals to me. Whatever the 'memorable evening' is all about, please let it be something fabulous. She gazed at the moon intently, willing it to grant her request.

'Here,' Jack's voice sounded behind her shoulder. Catherine jumped.

'Sorry, I didn't mean to startle you.'

'I was admiring your beautiful view.'

'It does tend to take your mind off things sometimes,' Jack said, as he handed her a chilled glass of Krug. 'Your health,' he said, raising his glass. Their eyes locked. Catherine was momentarily mesmerised by the intensity between them.

'And yours.' Her voice trembled as she spoke. Catherine felt as if she were standing on the edge of a precipice. She sat down quickly and took another sip of her champagne, then she looked at Jack, who was making himself comfortable in the opposite armchair. Suddenly the room seemed very quiet.

'Why did you send me the roses?' she asked again.

Jack threw back his head and laughed. 'I'm glad

you don't believe in beating around the bush, Catherine.' What a woman, he thought. He had liked the fact that she was so direct from the moment he'd first met her. Without taking his eyes off hers, he began to speak.

'As I told you, I got back from China yesterday. Last night, I was tired and decided to have a quiet meal by myself. As I sat there eating, I began to think about all the people I'd like to have dinner with and do you know what?'

She shook her head.

'The only person I wanted to be with was you.' He leant forward and put his glass on the coffee table between them. 'So I ate my dinner and thought about you, and it turned out to be a very memorable evening.'

'But why?'

'Because I realised something . . . I'm in love with you.'

Catherine didn't trust herself to speak. This can't be happening – and then she remembered something. Last night, after she'd gone to bed she'd dreamt that she was in Jack's arms and he was kissing her passionately. It had seemed so real that it had woken her up. She had got out of bed, walked over to her bedroom windows and, as she gazed out at the sea, Catherine could still feel Jack's lips on hers.

If he'd been thinking about her so deeply last night, perhaps her ESP had picked up on Jack's thoughts. Maybe it has something to do with that psychic ability Richard keeps insisting I have. Richard Sterling was *MAUD*'s astrologer, and he and Catherine had been friends for years.

Richard had often maintained that if she worked on her ESP she'd be able to tune into people's thoughts. 'But you're so psychic that sometimes it will happen to you without you doing a thing,' he'd told her once. 'It's a very special gift and you're lucky to have it.'

Catherine wasn't so sure – but there was no doubt that something unbelievable had happened to both her and Jack last night. Oddly enough, though, she didn't feel ready to share her ESP experience – or whatever it was – with him yet. She wanted to be absolutely sure of her feelings. After all, she'd been wrong about love before.

She was conscious that Jack was watching her closely. 'It's so sudden . . . so unexpected,' she stammered, almost bashfully.

'I know I've taken you by surprise. Don't say anything more,' he said. 'Think about what I've told you – there's no hurry. Why don't we just let events take their course?'

She nodded her head.

'Have dinner with me tomorrow night – I'm not safe eating alone, as you now know.'

'Yes, I'd like that. All right . . .' But Catherine couldn't bring herself to move. She'd felt her heart miss a beat when Jack had told her he loved her. Could it really be true? But what about her? How did she feel about him? She wasn't brave enough to explore that side of her emotions just yet. Jack sat silently, scrutinising her through half-shut eyes, and wished he could read her mind.

A loud sound from somewhere outside startled them. Catherine leapt to her feet. 'I must go – Brenda will never forgive me if I'm late for dinner. She's my advertising director,' she explained hurriedly, as she picked up her handbag. 'Thanks for the champagne.'

She tried to sound as normal as possible although she was sure she didn't. Her heart was fluttering so madly it made her feel giddy. At the same time, she had the overwhelming desire to throw herself into Jack's arms. The sensations she was experiencing stunned Catherine. Jack's words had touched a part of her that she'd thought safely locked away. She desperately wanted to be alone to think through the consequences of what he'd said. But as usual the clock was against her.

Afterwards, Catherine had no idea how she'd ever managed to get through the evening. It was as if she'd become two people – one of them was lost in the cosmos somewhere with Jack Clement; the other was the life of the party at the very trendy Lucio's. Much as she tried not to let it, her mind kept drifting back to her conversation with Jack.

Focus, focus, focus, Catherine, she told herself sternly during dinner. She talked about her editorial plans for *MAUD*. She outlined her ideas for maximising each advertiser's investment in the magazine. That's how she saw advertising, she told them, as an endorsement of and an investment in her product, and that's why she always believed in giving her advertisers the best possible return on their money. Anything she could do for them in *MAUD*, without compromising the magazine's editorial independence of course, was always on her agenda.

When the coffee had been served it was time for Catherine's big announcement. Her guests were looking at her with eager anticipation. As she got ready to speak, all thoughts of Jack were banished from Catherine's mind.

As usual, she didn't beat around the bush. 'For some time now, I've been of the view that fashion has been letting women down. It's almost as if most of the world's fashion designers haven't been able to keep up with women's progress – the way we work, the way we play, the way we live, even the size we are!

'I know that a great many people, including many of you here tonight, agree with me – after all, we've talked about it often enough. But now it's time for some action,' Catherine declared.

'I'm going to seize the moment and launch the *MAUD* 21st Century Fashion Collection, designed by Australia's one and only Perry Wolf. It will be shown simultaneously in Sydney, London and New York next year.' Her eyes flashed as she warmed to her topic. 'I'm fed up with Australia always being promoted as a place where all we do is put another prawn on the barbie or go for a surf after hugging a koala. It's almost as though we have a cultural cringe about ourselves. I intend to show the world that Australia has style.'

'Bravo!' someone on Catherine's left shouted. She had her audience in the palm of her hand.

'Going global worked for *MAUD International* and I'm convinced it will work for the collection, too,' she told them. 'I'm going to stage a spectacular event that will put Australian fashion on the world platform in a way no one has ever done before. Perry's clothes will be exactly what women have been clamouring for but haven't been able to get, because so many designers seem to have lost the plot.'

She looked at them with a bewildered expression on her face. 'It's almost as if some of them hate women, don't you think?'

One of the guests called out, 'I'm sure they do – the sillier they can make women look, the better.'

'Exactly!' Catherine responded. 'I don't know why women have allowed themselves to be dictated to in this way for so long. Well –' she held out her hands to them, 'and please remember you heard it here first – their rule is coming to an end and it's not before time.'

'Brilliant, Catherine, just brilliant. You're so right. The fashion industry certainly does need a shake-up. I'm sure everyone here will be keen to support you.' As he spoke, William Cheng looked confidently around the table. There were murmurs of agreement and a couple of the guests gave Catherine a round of applause. Everyone nodded enthusiastically. 'I'd like you to come and brief everyone at the agency so we can recommend *MAUD* to as many of our clients as possible,' he continued.

William Cheng ran Cheng & Farquhar, one of Australia's top advertising agencies. With annual billings in excess of $1.2 billion, the agency had offices in New York and London, and a reputation that was the envy of every other advertising agency in town. William's support had been crucial to Catherine's success in the early days because it had helped open influential doors for her in England and America.

'Thank you, William, and my sincere thanks to all of you here tonight.' Catherine turned to Brenda, who was sitting next to William, and gave her a knowing look. Brenda beamed back and gave her boss a discreet thumbs-up.

Catherine kept talking. 'I'm delighted you're so supportive about what we're planning – it's extremely encouraging – and I promise to keep you up to date on our progress. I'd be very pleased to do a special presentation for your agency, William. Just let me know when it suits you.' The evening broke up not long after and William and Brenda, who had been together for eighteen months, saw Catherine to her car before walking off arm in arm.

She locked the doors and sat quietly, trying to collect herself. What a night! Thank God I'm by myself at last. Jack, oh Jack – she ran her hand through her hair distractedly – what have you done to me? I'm going out of my mind thinking about you. The look on his face when he'd told Catherine of his love flashed before her.

So much for my vow never to let a man sidetrack me again, she thought wryly. She leant her head on the steering wheel. In no time at all, Jack had managed to turn her well-ordered and disciplined world upside down, and Catherine was both terrified and excited at the passion he'd stirred up in her, and the delightful state of suspended animation of her heart.

Peter Sheppard had told Catherine that eventually she'd find a man she could trust and love and she'd accepted that, but she had been sure it would be a serene kind of loving, not the disturbing ardour that Jack Clement had aroused in her.

Sheppard was a psychiatrist whom her mother had insisted Catherine consult after her disastrous marriage to Roger had ended two years ago. She'd assured Catherine that she'd find it helpful to talk about what had happened with someone who was objective, and to keep her mother happy, Catherine had taken her advice and met with him. She'd warmed to him at once when he told her that he didn't really think she needed counselling. 'You're such a positive person,' he said. 'I'm sure you've learnt to take the rough with the smooth.'

'Yes, of course,' she'd replied, nodding. 'Shit happens, doesn't it?'

'Exactly. But I know your mother wanted us to chat, so why don't we do that over a cup of tea? Sometimes talking allows a person to see things more clearly. It certainly won't hurt you.'

As it turned out, she'd enjoyed Peter's company and it had been cathartic to tell someone in confidence exactly how she felt. After all, she had been invaded and dumped and, deep down, she was bloody angry about it.

'I'm sure you feel that you've been let down by love,' the psychiatrist had said. 'You've probably even been asking yourself, what is love?'

'You'd better believe it,' she replied bitterly.

He ignored the tone in her voice. 'You'll know the answer to that one when you find love – real love, not lust. You mustn't fear love, Catherine, and you mustn't cut it out of your life. Everyone needs to love and be loved – it's good for you. I know that everyone has probably already told you that time is a great healer, but believe me, it is. In the meantime, indulge yourself – if you want to withdraw and sit in a darkened room listening to Bartok, just do it.'

'Well, Bartok's not quite my cup of tea but I might consider retreating with Mozart.'

But after one long, sleepless night listening to Mozart's clarinet concerto, Catherine knew exactly what she was going to do – concentrate on making her fortune. From that point, she had dedicated herself to her career and to making money. Wealth, she'd reasoned, would give her security and the freedom to do whatever she wanted.

So far her plan had worked well. She adored running her own publishing business and *MAUD* gave her great satisfaction – but she'd always considered the magazine as her stepping stone to the global media empire she wanted. Catherine was prepared to work as long and as hard as necessary to achieve that particular ambition.

She hadn't counted on meeting someone like Jack Clement quite so soon. Could she trust him? She wanted to, but the problem was that she was scared to love. She'd loved once before and her prince had turned out to be a frog. But what if Jack was the 'real love' that Peter Sheppard had promised her she'd meet one day? If she wasn't bold enough to venture down this particular fork in the road she might miss the most fabulous experience of her life, perhaps even the whole purpose of her existence.

She steeled herself. 'I will not be frightened to love Jack.' As soon as she'd voiced the words, the expectation of closing one door – and opening another – filled her with exhilaration.

Catherine had no idea how long she'd been sitting outside the restaurant and she might have stayed there longer still had the staff not begun to switch off the lights. She started the car and slowly drove home.

What a day, she thought with a sigh, as she let herself in the front door. I can't believe so much has happened. Never mind your memorable evening, Jack Clement, what about me? Because of you I've had the most amazing day. But right now all I intend to do is take a relaxing bath and go to bed – perchance to dream of you again. She sighed happily at the prospect.

But even in her wildest dreams Catherine could never have imagined the events that would follow.

# Chapter Four

Catherine's apartment was her pride and joy, and she always felt at peace the moment she put the key in the lock of her front door. She'd bought the place not long before the launch of *MAUD* and it was the first real home of her own.

Up until then, she had lived in the family mansion at Vaucluse, in Sydney's exclusive eastern suburbs. Ashburn had been the Walker family's home for three generations. It had huge, high-ceilinged rooms furnished with antiques, with sweeping views of the Sydney skyline and the city's spectacular harbour. Sydney Walker had bought the houses on either side and demolished them, putting a tennis court with a sauna and outdoor spa on one block, and an indoor pool complex on the other so he could swim all year round regardless of the weather. Ashburn also boasted a ten-car garage and a 5000-bottle wine cellar with an adjoining wine-tasting room, as well as a magnificent tropical garden, which Sydney particularly treasured. No expense had been spared.

Few people knew about his fondness for gardening. 'A man's entitled to some secrets,' he often remarked to Catherine, as they walked through it admiring his latest blooms. No matter how busy he was he always managed to put aside a few hours each week to spend in his garden. He employed a couple of gardeners but they weren't allowed to do anything without his approval. Catherine liked planting things as much as her father did and was never happier than when she was pottering about with him in his precious garden. When she was ten, Sydney had given her a patch in which to grow vegetables and she just about burst with pride one summer when he'd asked her to pick some of her tomatoes for the cook to make into salad for dinner. Her father was a different man when he was in his garden. Catherine liked this softer side of him and wished he showed it more often.

Ashburn's verandah was wide and long, and as a little girl Catherine had sat there with Sydney watching the yachts racing in front of the Harbour Bridge. Like her father, she never slept in and when she was older they often breakfasted together on the verandah – always early, as her father liked to be in his office by seven-thirty. They'd discuss the news of the day, the headlines, the lead stories and the general state of the publishing business. Catherine looked forward to these morning get-togethers – she was an eager and willing pupil and Sydney was a good teacher.

It was the only time Catherine felt she really had her father's attention. She wanted him to be proud of her, and she'd always try to ask intelligent questions to win his approval. Sometimes her independent spirit would break out and she'd argue a point of view with him. He'd listen for a minute or two and then talk her down.

Sydney Walker was a busy and hugely successful man. His group, Walker Corp., controlled the *Sydney Globe* and the *Melbourne Globe*, two important newspapers in Australia's two major cities, as well as the *London Globe*, a morning newspaper in England, and the *New York Daily Globe* and *Sunday Globe* in America. It also owned a chain of newspapers in Ireland – in Belfast, Dublin, Limerick, Galway and Clare.

Sydney was the first to admit that the latter were an indulgence. In fact, he often referred to his Irish newspapers as his 'folly' because they were not big money spinners for Walker Corp. However, they did give him an excuse to regularly visit the country he considered the prettiest in the world, as well as the opportunity to have a glass or two of draught Guinness, his favourite tipple. His great grandfather had come to Australia from County Clare in the early 1800s and whenever Sydney went to Ireland something stirred in his soul. It was a peculiar sensation, really, and he couldn't explain, even to himself, the mood that came over him but he felt at home there.

Sydney had always been fascinated with television but because of Australian government regulations, he was unable to indulge his obsession with the small screen. This had frustrated and angered him and had been instrumental in his decision to set up Walker World Channel in London, a satellite news and entertainment service that reached millions of homes throughout Europe. It had been a runaway success and had become a significant profit earner.

He'd been named Sydney after the city. His father, Oswald, always claimed that Sydney was the greatest city in the world and, as such, was the best name for his son and heir. Privately Catherine thought her father's name had gone to his head – sometimes he acted as though he owned Sydney and everyone in it. He certainly felt that way about the Opera House, which he funded generously through the Walker Foundation. Sydney Walker considered it most appropriate that his home had such an excellent view of Australia's most recognised icon.

The Walker Foundation had been started by his grandfather to help needy people, and had grown over the years to become one of the nation's largest philanthropic organisations. Like his grandfather and his father, Sydney believed in putting something back into the community and, as well as chairing the Foundation, he often gave generous personal donations to good causes on the proviso there was no publicity.

Ashburn also had its own wharf and several boats, including his prize-winning Sydney to Hobart Race yacht, *The Sarah Walker*. Whenever Catherine was going to a performance at the Opera House, she would ring down to Martin, the Ashburn butler, and ask him to get one of the boats ready, and Tony, their houseboy, would run her over to the Opera House wharf and pick her up after the performance. Sometimes she asked friends back to Ashburn for supper and champagne. On a warm summer evening, nothing could beat eating outdoors with the stunning Sydney skyline as a backdrop.

Catherine had her own living quarters at Ashburn, with a spacious bedroom, dressing room and ensuite, a sitting room with a wisteria-covered balcony, plus a home office. Her friends used to be envious of her luxurious lifestyle and Catherine was the first to admit that indeed it was privileged, but there was something they didn't know – her family life was anything but happy, and there were times when she felt very much alone.

If Catherine had ever told her friends that her family was a dysfunctional one, she doubted they'd have believed her anyway. But the fact was that

Sydney and Sarah Walker's marriage was not the stuff of which fairytales were made. Sometimes her parents didn't talk to each other for weeks. Other times they spoke to each other only through Catherine or her brother, something that upset them both. Their parents were such good actors that no one would have even suspected Sydney and Sarah had a problem in the world. Sometimes they almost fooled Catherine into believing everything was all right between them. But invariably there was tension in the air at Ashburn and the day finally came when Catherine decided she couldn't live with it any longer. She needed a place of her own.

It hadn't taken her long to find what she was looking for – it never did. Catherine Walker was a woman who always knew what she wanted, and once she'd made up her mind about something, she never delayed in bringing it to fruition. Her apartment, designed by Craig North, Australia's foremost architect, was one of three in a modern, low-slung block on a ridge overlooking Bondi Beach.

Each apartment occupied one floor. Catherine's was on the ground floor and had the advantage of a generous stone-paved outdoor area with a lap pool and barbecue for outdoor entertaining edged with bottle brush, grevillea, wattle trees and other native plants and bushes.

Below the ridge, and as far as the eye could see, was the magnificent Pacific Ocean, a sight that always stirred Catherine's heart. Sydney folk often debated the pros and cons of harbour versus ocean living. Catherine admired the beauty of the harbour, but somehow the ocean drew her to it. She loved its tempestuous nature and the way it could change colour so rapidly, often with very little warning, from dark navy blue, to shimmering turquoise, to its dramatic black and stormy look.

She could never get enough of it. The sea invigorated her. She would breathe it deeply into her lungs, feeling the sea's energy filling her body. There was nothing better than the sound of the breakers tumbling onto the beach as she lay in bed – they lulled her to sleep at night and welcomed her to the new day when she awoke in the morning. She often walked along the rocks around the oceanfront from her apartment to the neighbouring beach of Tamarama. Sometimes the sea was so wild that the foam would spray Catherine's face. She loved those mornings best of all.

The apartment was right out of the pages of *Architectural Digest* – sleek and modern with creamy white walls and polished floors. There was hardly an antique to be seen – she'd had enough antiques to last a lifetime at Ashburn. Her preference was for a pared-down look with synthetic suede upholstered sofas and sleek Italian armchairs in soft beige. Her only concession to the past were two grandfather clocks: one a plain oak Canterbury face clock which her grandmother had left her, the other a much more ornate Welsh clock in mahogany, with a magnificent chime, from her grandfather. Her friends told her she was mad to have two grandfather clocks but Catherine adored them. One was in the dining room, the other in the lounge, and every Saturday she went through the ritual of winding them. No one else was allowed to touch them.

Tonight as she walked in, the apartment smelt of tuberoses. Catherine always had bowls of scented fresh flowers throughout her home – she found that a pleasant-smelling fragrance was soothing after a hectic day. But I doubt anything could pacify me tonight, she thought as she tossed her bag onto a chair and slipped off her shoes. Jack Clement really turns me on and it feels fantastic! She danced down the hall, stopping at the table where Rosaria, her housekeeper, always left her messages.

Catherine checked through them. Good, nothing important. She walked through her bedroom and into the bathroom, where she turned on the taps and sprinkled some jasmine bath oil under the running water. She undressed and then studied her body in the bathroom mirror.

Looking good, girl, she told herself – that extra fifteen minutes of exercise each day is paying off. She was trim but well covered in a sexy, feminine way – a refreshing change, most of her admirers thought, from the 'I've been to the gym' muscular look flaunted by so many successful businesswomen. Catherine always watched what she ate but still enjoyed her food and wine. She walked every day, usually for an hour, or jogged for half an hour, swam laps for twenty minutes at least three days a week, had a weekly massage and a monthly facial. At thirty-six, she was in peak condition and had every intention of staying that way.

Catherine sighed with contentment as she soaked in the bath and felt herself relaxing. This is just what I needed. But later, as she tossed and turned in bed, sleep eluded her. Catherine's mind was on full alert, busily analysing everything Jack had said to her. Then she remembered the way she'd felt when they had danced together at the Floral Ball. All at once, she wanted him with a yearning that took her breath away.

At some point during the night she did doze off, and when the alarm went off in the morning she felt rested. But as soon as Catherine opened her eyes Jack commandeered her thoughts once more. It gave her pleasure just thinking about their next meeting. Then, unexpectedly, a sense of foreboding came over her.

She'd been so wrong about Roger. She had trusted him completely and revealed so much of herself to him, believing that he loved her in the way she loved him. It was all very well for Peter Sheppard to tell her not to be afraid to love but she was scared stiff. What if she was wrong again? What if Jack turned out to be another Roger?

No, she thought, that could never be. Jack is different. But even so, could we really have a successful relationship? We're both strong-minded, successful in what we do, committed to our work. Could we be happy together?

One thing she was sure of – Jack wasn't the kind of man who'd tell a woman he loved her if he didn't mean it. Why then did she have this premonition of fear? Maybe it was his past that made her cautious. But when they'd talked about his marriage nothing he'd said had made her doubt him.

'You're still married, aren't you?' she'd asked him.

'Yes, but Fleur and I have been separated for three – no, four years now. We've just never got around to getting a divorce. It's because of the twins, I suppose, but the girls seem to have adjusted well to our separation. As I told you at lunch, they live with their mother in Paris and they seem very happy. Fleur and I have an amicable arrangement that suits us both. I don't think she'll ever return to Australia, though. She's become more French than the French.'

Catherine decided to swim some laps to try to clear her head. She had a hectic day coming up. As she swam up and down her pool she thought through the things she had to do. The magazine had a couple of deadlines today and there would be colour proofs to check. There was a planning meeting for the *MAUD Lifestyle* specials, and she had a cover meeting scheduled with her creative director. Catherine had an idea, too, that she wanted to explore, using Elle Macpherson, Nicole Kidman and Kylie Minogue, three Australian women who had become major players on the world stage and were blazing new trails in entertainment and business and would be even bigger stars in the 21st century.

Catherine wanted them to model the *MAUD* 21st Century Fashion Collection and had put aside time today to ring them all – but they were incredibly busy women and first of all she had to find them. They could be anywhere in the world.

Just like *MAUD*, these women had successfully gone global. Catherine grinned: never underestimate the power of a woman – especially one from Down Under. Hey, that's not a bad cover line, she thought. I'd better write it down. Grabbing the notepad she'd left on the poolside table, she jotted it down. She kept notepads all over the house for this purpose. 'It's so easy to forget good ideas when the day gets going and meetings and other problems demand your attention,' she'd explained once to a journalist who was interviewing her on personal work practices.

As she dried herself, Catherine decided to put Jack Clement in a box. She visualised it – a large box, big enough for someone like Jack – then she mentally popped him in it and tied it up with red ribbon. Goodbye for a little while, Jack, until we meet later. She showered quickly, slipped into a Carla Zampatti hot pink and black patterned linen dress, sleeveless, short and cool, and strappy black sandals. On her way to the garage, she stopped in the kitchen to grab a tomato juice and to slice up an apple to eat in the car, called out goodbye to Rosaria, who was in the laundry, and drove to CW Publishing in Pyrmont. As she walked down the corridor towards her office, she could hear her phone ringing.

Catherine knew it was Jack. She had a knack of knowing such things and often picked up the phone and said hello to the caller by name before she'd even heard their voice. Richard Sterling had explained that it was just another example of her psychic ability. Catherine wasn't sure what it was but her friends were suitably impressed whenever she did it to them.

As she quickened her pace she could hear Clare answering, 'Catherine Walker's office, good morning.' She smiled a greeting as Catherine approached. 'Morning, Boss, it's Jack Clement. Will I transfer it through to your office?'

'Good morning and yes, thanks. How was your dinner?' she asked, as she walked towards her office.

'Absolutely perfect.' Clare beamed at her.

'Good.' Catherine closed the door of her office and went over to her desk to pick up the phone.

'You're up early, Jack,' she said, wishing he were standing beside her rather than down the end of the phone. So much for putting him into a box.

'Couldn't sleep, how about you?'

'I had the same problem.'

'I just rang to say that if you like, I'll pick you up from your office tonight. We could have a drink at my apartment and then go to Aria for dinner.'

'Do you think we'd get into Aria at such short notice? You know how popular it is at the moment.' Sydney's upwardly mobile and beautiful people were somewhat fickle when it came to dining out. They'd no sooner discovered a restaurant before they were moving on in search of a new trendy eatery.

'I have a permanent booking whether I go or not,' Jack replied.

'My, that is being prepared, isn't it?' she teased. 'In that case, I'd love to dine at Aria.'

'Fine, I'll pick you up at seven. Does that suit?'

'Perfectly.'

'See you later.' He hung up before Catherine could say goodbye.

Seeing her boss was off the phone, Clare came in, carrying coffee and the mail. 'I've transferred the names and numbers of the people you want to call through to your computer; there's some proofs that need an urgent okay in the green folder. William Cheng's assistant has e-mailed me about a meeting he wants to set up for you at the agency, and Richard

Sterling has rung with a cryptic message: "Neptune rules the house. Is it love or only fascination?" Now, what's that supposed to mean?'

'I'll let you know when I find out,' Catherine said. 'Remind me to call Richard later today. Now, let's go. I've got a million things to get through.'

She worked flat out for the rest of the day, successfully tracking down Elle on a film set in Berlin, and was delighted with her reaction to the proposal. After that she left a message for Kylie with her answering service and e-mailed Nicole.

What Catherine liked most about publishing was its unpredictability. When she got up in the morning she was never sure what her working day would bring. In between trying to track down Elle, Kylie and Nicole, she had counselled one of the sub-editors, who had begun drinking too much at lunchtime. Catherine was aware the woman had a problem but she'd been waiting for the right time to raise the matter. She had gone on her regular stroll around the magazine to see how everything was going and discovered the sub-editor dozing behind her computer.

'Barbara,' she said, after waking the woman, 'why don't you come into my office. We need to have a chat.'

Over a cup of tea and after a few sympathetic questions, Barbara told Catherine that her husband had left her for a girl young enough to be his daughter.

'You poor thing,' Catherine said, 'but I don't think drinking is going to help resolve things, do you?'

Barbara looked shamefaced. 'No, of course not. But it hasn't been easy to cope with the fact that after twenty years of marriage I'm alone.' She began to cry.

Catherine opened a drawer in her desk and pulled out a box of tissues. 'Help yourself,' she said, pushing the box over towards the other woman.

'What you need is a break,' she went on. 'We've been asked to send a reporter to Hawaii to do a travel piece on a new island cruise. Would you like to go? It would do you good.'

After Barbara had thanked her and left, Catherine had taken a call from the printer, who was concerned about the quality of one of the colour transparencies in the fashion pages.

'I don't think it will reproduce well enough for your high standards,' he told Catherine.

'I know what you mean, George,' Catherine said, 'and I appreciate your ringing me, but the creative director is trying for a special effect and promises me the result will be fantastic. It's a deliberate decision of ours to go with that transparency. Just follow her directions – I promise I won't hold you responsible for the result.'

She had a tuna sandwich and a glass of tomato juice at her desk while checking some layouts. This issue is coming together beautifully, she thought, but then she came to an opening spread for a feature on

Lachlan and Sarah Murdoch's new harbourside mansion in Sydney.

Picking up the layouts, she walked round to the art department. 'Who did this?' she called out, holding them up in the air. Max, one of *MAUD*'s newer artists, replied, 'I did.'

'Have you a problem with big photographs?' Catherine asked him.

'No.'

'Well then, what possessed you to use all these wonderful shots postage stamp size? The readers will need a pair of binoculars to see the bloody place.'

'I think my layouts are very effective,' Max protested.

'They're not!' Catherine replied tersely. 'Get all the colour trannies from the Murdoch shoot and let's go through them again to see what we've really got. I'm sure we can improve on this.

'What you have to remember,' she told Max in a softer tone, 'is that getting into Lachlan and Sarah's house is a major coup. The readers want to "see" the place – after all, it's probably the only chance they'll ever get to do so. That's why the photographs need to be blown up.'

When the layout had been redesigned to her satisfaction Catherine returned to her office to read submissions for articles. She disliked having to discourage any budding writer, but the truth was that a great many of the offerings were dreadful and didn't deserve to be published. However, every now and again she came across someone with talent, which was exciting and, as far as Catherine was concerned, made all the reading and evaluation worthwhile.

At five to seven, she left the office and took the lift to the ground floor. Through the glass doors she saw Jack drive up. He leant over and opened the passenger door. She got in. Without saying anything, he handed her a red carnation.

She smelt it. Then looked at him. 'Thank you.'

He put his hand over hers. 'How are you this evening?'

'Glad the day is over. It's been a long one.'

'Same for me. Still feel like a drink at my apartment before dinner?' he asked as they weaved their way through the heavy night traffic.

'Of course,' she said. 'A drink would go down very nicely right now, thank you!'

Jack's apartment was at East Circular Quay, next door to the Opera House. It was in 'The Toaster', the controversial building nicknamed thus by its many critics who had opposed the block's construction, saying it was a design eyesore that spoilt the Opera House. But surprisingly, once the building had been completed and the wonderful array of cafes and shops had opened on the streetscape level, people seemed to forget all about their earlier objections.

Jack drove into the building's car park, and they

walked across to the lift, where he used a special key for the Penthouse Only floor. The doors opened into the foyer of the apartment.

'Come in and sit down and let me get you something.' Catherine followed him into the living room. 'Champagne?' he asked.

'That's just what I feel like,' she said, settling back into the lounge. The room had a spectacular vista of the city skyscrapers and normally Catherine would have enjoyed taking it in but she had other things on her mind. Finally Jack reappeared and handed her a glass of champagne before sitting down at the other end of the lounge. He raised his glass and said: 'To you. To us.'

'To us,' Catherine repeated. They both took a sip. Catherine put down her glass. She felt tense and strangely unsure of herself – but there was no going back now. Taking a deep breath, she began to speak. 'I've thought about everything you said, and . . .' She stopped.

'Yes?'

'And . . .' Still she hesitated. 'Jack, I'm in love with you, too.'

He smiled at her and simply said, 'Good.'

They sat there, saying nothing. This must be the lull before the storm, Catherine thought.

Jack broke the silence. 'You are so lovely.' He got up and walked over to where she was sitting. 'I do love you.'

'I can hardly believe this is happening. It's incredible,' Catherine said. She looked worried. 'Jack, I'm nervous.'

'Why?'

'It's hard to explain, really, it's just a premonition I have. There's such a depth of feeling between us. You have your life, you're powerful and independent. I'm very independent, too. Maybe we're both too independent for each other's good?'

'I don't think that's such a bad thing,' Jack said. 'There's nothing wrong with independence, you know. It's just one of the many things we have in common. The more I get to know you, the more I realise how much alike we are.'

'There's something I'm longing to do,' Catherine said abruptly.

'What?'

'Kiss you.'

'Be my guest.' Jack held out his arms and pulled her up to face him.

For one fleeting moment they looked at each other before Jack's lips were on hers, and Catherine was swept away in a rush of desire that almost knocked her off her feet. She was grateful that Jack's arms were wrapped around her.

Worries about their future vanished from her mind as Catherine gave herself up to kissing and being kissed. Nothing else in the world mattered.

Jack's hands were on her breasts.

'Make love to me,' she said.

'No.'

'But why not?' she asked, puzzled.

'I made a promise to myself not to seduce you tonight. I don't want you to think I'm the kind of man who lures a woman to his apartment in order to get her to bed.'

'Jack, I know you're not like that but I also know that we're wild with longing for each other. Let's do something about it.'

'No. I promised myself that I wouldn't and I won't.' He kissed her again.

Catherine was on fire. She wanted to give herself to him, to feel his skin next to hers. She wanted him to explore every part of her, to reveal to him the innermost secrets of her body. Why was he insisting on being so noble?

'Darling,' she said, 'you've no idea how much I want you. I know you feel the same way . . .' She was pleading with him. She knew that, but she didn't care. She was shameless in her desire.

'You're the most desirable creature in the world but I have made a vow to myself and not even you, no matter how much I might want you, can make me break it.' He kissed her. 'Why don't we put on some music and dance?' he suggested.

'That won't help at all,' Catherine laughed. 'Dancing with you turns me on too.' She put her arms around him and kissed him passionately on the mouth again.

'Temptress,' he said. 'Stop trying to seduce me! Let's have another glass of champagne outside and see if that will cool us down.' He refilled their glasses and, holding out his hand, led her outside to the wrap-around balcony with its million-dollar view.

Where else in the world was there a city like Sydney? Catherine thought. It was just so beautiful. No wonder she loved the place – and thank heavens for the southerly that usually blows into Sydney in summer, cooling the city down after a hot day, as it was doing tonight. God, why on earth was she thinking about such things when the most desirable man in the world was standing right beside her? She was always so bloody practical. She drove herself nuts sometimes.

Jack had no idea such thoughts were running through her head. He'd never wanted a woman so much in his life. How he'd resisted her invitation to make love, he would never know. They stood close together leaning against the railing, taking in the city's activity, almost touching but not quite. Enjoying the intimacy.

'You're an exciting woman, Catherine Walker, just as I knew you would be.' Jack kissed her on the forehead.

Catherine couldn't bear his nearness a moment longer. 'I think it's time I went home,' she said.

Just as well, Jack thought, or I won't be able to keep my hands off her.

'What about dinner?' he asked nonetheless. 'You must be hungry.'

She'd completely forgotten they were going to Aria. 'I haven't thought of food since I got here.' She looked at her watch. 'Goodness, it's after ten!'

'Time flies when you're having fun,' Jack laughed. 'Let me get my car keys and I'll drive you home.'

As they drove to Bondi Beach, every now and then Jack would put his hand over hers and she'd pick it up and kiss it. Catherine felt calmer now but she knew, and so did Jack, that they were on the brink of something over which they had no control. They were pawns in some kind of wondrous game fate had decided to play with their destiny. Where would it take them?

'Would you like to come in?' she asked him when they reached her apartment.

'I would, but if I do I might not be able to leave.' He kissed her. 'Sleep well. I'll see you tomorrow night.'

They kissed again and as he drove down the road she stood watching until his car disappeared from view before going inside. She leant against the door.

Oh my, she thought. What a night it's been. I haven't felt as happy as this ever before. Catherine could feel the smile on her face as she made her way to her bedroom, where she slid open the doors leading to the deck. The ocean looked its night-time best, the rays of the moon darting in between the waves, catching the white foam of the breakers as they neared the shore. The southerly had blown itself out and the night had become humid. The air was now tinged with the smell of bushfire, always common during Sydney's long, hot summer months. She sat down on what she called her 'meditation chair', where she always went whenever she wanted to think without interruption.

Catherine breathed in deeply, letting the sea air fill her body. It's a perfect, good-to-be-alive night, she thought ecstatically, and at this very moment I haven't a worry in the world. She sat there for an hour or so, thinking about Jack.

She could have cheerfully spent the night under the stars, dreaming her dreams, and even contemplated making up a bed on the hammock. Don't be daft, Catherine, she told herself, go to bed! She went inside, locking the grill security doors, but leaving the glass doors open so she could still hear the sea. She undressed quickly, climbed into bed and was asleep almost as soon as her head touched the pillow, hardly moving all night.

# Chapter Five

Catherine only awoke at six because of the persistent beeping of her alarm clock. Automatically, she reached out to turn on the radio – she always started her day with the news; it was the way her father had trained her. She was just in time for the headlines.

. . . Further conflict in the Middle East; food rationing in Russia; a warning from the Australian Medical Association that the health care system is in crisis – again; another win for the Australian Cricket Team; and speculation that a bid for Webster Media is expected today from The Clement Group.

Catherine sat up, wide awake, as the newsreader went into more detail. What on earth is Jack up to with Webster Media? He never even mentioned it.

How could he be so damned secretive? Now Catherine, be reasonable, she tried to tell herself – you and Jack were hardly talking business last night. But what was going on? Her father considered Webster Media to be one of the world's best performing newspaper groups and he'd always thought highly of Oscar Webster. 'A man of principle and integrity', as he'd once described him to Catherine.

Catherine's first instinct was to ring her father, but at the moment that wasn't possible. Sydney Walker was currently holidaying in Monaco – that was all she knew. It was unheard of for her father to take holidays, yet he'd left Australia last week without telling anyone what his plans were. That wasn't like him either. He always left his itinerary and contact numbers behind, with instructions to be called at any time of the day if there was a problem or an important decision to be made at Walker Corp., and woe betide the executive who didn't follow through on this.

Catherine always received a copy of his itinerary as well, but not this time. She shook her head. Her father had been acting strangely lately, and just when she needed to talk to him, too. I'll send him an e-mail before I go for a run, she decided. Sydney always travelled with his laptop. She went into her home office and switched on her computer.

*Greetings Father.*

*How are you? Hope Monaco agrees with you and that you're having a good time, whatever it is you're doing. You've been very uncommunicative about this trip, Dad. What are you up to? Are you plotting some incredible business deal? I'm sure you're up to something! But in the meantime I thought you'd be interested in an item on this morning's news. The Sydney Stock Exchange has announced that trading in Webster Media has been suspended. The speculation is that The Clement Group is going to make a takeover bid. Funnily enough, I'm having dinner with Jack Clement tonight! I'll see if I can find out what's going on. If I discover anything interesting, I'll let you know. Must go. It's a gorgeous day and I want to have a run on the beach before going to the office.*

*Love, Catherine.*

As she got ready for her run, Catherine remembered that she had left her car at work. She'd forgotten all about it. What a pest, I'll have to get a cab to the office. I'd better get a move on; it's almost impossible to find a taxi at peak hour.

There were plenty of early morning keep-fit enthusiasts pounding the beach by the time Catherine reached the seashore. As she ran to one end of the beach, she snuck a look at her fellow joggers.

Most of them appeared to be enjoying themselves, appreciating the terrific day and the unique location, but there was always the odd one or two who looked as if they were going to collapse at any moment, usually middle-aged men who refused to acknowledge their age, and tried to act like boys. They always amused Catherine. Who were they trying to kid?

James Packer, the Chairman of Publishing and Broadcasting Ltd, approached, heading in the opposite direction. He does have a good body, Catherine thought appreciatively, as she said good morning to him.

He had passed before she wished she'd asked him what he thought about the rumours of The Clement Group's takeover bid. I'm sure Dad told me that James and his father, Kerry, had once expressed a desire to buy into Webster. I might give him a call. She gave herself a mental shake. That's enough of thinking about company matters. I am going to clear my mind and enjoy this sensational morning. She quickened her pace.

When she returned to her apartment, Catherine felt ready to face whatever the day would bring. Rosaria had breakfast waiting – grapefruit, multi-grain toast with Vegemite and sliced tomato, and a giant cup of tea. Catherine took a big sip. 'Ah, nectar of the gods! Thanks, Rosaria, I was longing for my cup of tea.' She ate quickly, reading the newspapers as she did. The business pages mentioned the takeover bid but provided little detail.

I can't wait to ask Jack about it . . . well, only if there's the right opportunity to do so. Maybe we won't want to talk about business tonight at all. Was Jack looking forward to this evening as much as she was? Catherine wondered. She stopped reading and closed her eyes, willing herself into Jack's mind. She ran her hands over her body, imagining Jack's hands on her breasts. Then she raised her hands to her mouth, cupped them and kissed them. Jack, wherever you are, feel these kisses coming from me to you.

Catherine felt so close to Jack that she didn't want to leave the imaginary world she'd created, but she forced herself back to reality. I won't place you in a box today, Jack, but I will banish you from my thoughts for a little while. It was something her friends always admired about Catherine – this ability to put everything out of her mind, and concentrate on her work. Even when she had been heartbroken about Roger, Catherine had still managed to hide her despair, and get on with her job as if she hadn't a care in the world.

Now, she thought, opening the door to her wardrobe, what will I wear that will make me extra alluring? She chose a sleeveless Armani sky blue silk dress with matching shoes. She liked wearing Armani because his designs suited her body shape. Catherine's innate sense of style gave her an elegance that other women craved. Satisfied that her outfit would do everything she wanted as far as Jack was concerned, she began fossicking in her jewellery drawer.

I'll wear Great Grandma Maud's four-leaf clover diamond brooch for luck, she decided. She looked at her reflection in the full-length mirror and was pleased with what she saw. He doesn't stand a chance against you today, Catherine. She grinned at the thought of Jack as putty in her hands.

She set off towards Bondi Beach promenade in search of a taxi and had walked only a few steps when one drew up to let off a passenger. The brooch is bringing me luck already! Getting in, she asked the driver to take her to the office, and sat back to continue reading the papers. There were four morning newspapers produced in Sydney and usually Catherine had read them all before she arrived at the office, another habit her father had instilled in her. 'You can't work in the media and not read, listen and watch the news. You have to know what is going on. Never forget that, Catherine.' She never had.

As usual, Clare was at her desk. 'Morning, Boss. Kylie Minogue rang. She's left a number where you can reach her if you call within the next hour.'

'Fantastic, I'll call her straight away.'

'And Boss . . .'

'Yes?'

'Perry Wolf has some sketches to show you and he says he knows you'll love them.'

'How's my diary looking?'

'Not too bad. You have lunchtime free.'

'No I don't, I want to get my hair done. Can you please ring Lloyd Lomas and see if he can fit me in? I want a trim and a blow-dry plus a manicure. Tell him I'm sorry to ring at such short notice, but something really important has come up.'

'Will do. What about seeing Perry after lunch? You've got me pencilled in there for dictation, but we could do that tomorrow.'

'Great. Do that. Thanks, Clare.'

Before she could call Kylie, however, Catherine's phone rang. Clare intercepted the call. 'Boss, it's Jack Clement.'

'Thanks.' Catherine picked up her phone. 'Good morning!'

'Morning, beautiful. Just confirming tonight. I've booked Aria again for eight and if you don't mind, I'll meet you there. I have to go to Canberra and won't be back before seven-thirty. Why don't I send my driver to collect you at ten to eight?'

'That's fine, Jack.'

'Okay, I must go. See you tonight.' Once again, he'd hung up before Catherine could say goodbye. She stared at the phone almost incredulously – that particularly annoying trait will have to go!

She rang the number Kylie had left. Like Elle, Kylie thought modelling Perry Wolf's 21st Century *MAUD* Collection would be 'excellent' and said she'd be thrilled to be a part of it.

Catherine beamed and continued her spiel. 'I'm planning to show the collection at the Sydney Opera House and then, on an Internet hook-up, we'll present it simultaneously on a giant screen at The Ritz in London and The Waldorf Astoria in New York. Walker Wide Screens have developed an amazing slim-line, but wide, digital screen, with the most extraordinary stereo-plus sound – well, that's what they call it – and they've agreed to let me use it at family rates, naturally, in return for the publicity, which I've guaranteed will be worldwide.

'If what I have in mind works, it will open exciting new doors via the Internet for the communication and film industry. I'm going to show everyone the impact of technology on the way we do business – not to mention entertainment – and at the same time blow their minds away!' Catherine was in full flight. 'Kylie, I promise you a cover and at least eight pages in *MAUD International*, a large part of which will be devoted to the fashion collection. You'll have to share the first cover with Elle and Nicole, but within the next twelve months I'll give you another cover of your own. My circulation people estimate that by the time we launch the collection, *MAUD* circulation should be around the six million mark, and I'll be happy to plug your new album or whatever else you want publicised.'

Catherine knew that Kylie, like Elle, would be thrilled with that sort of publicity. She continued with her sales pitch. 'Naturally, we'll pay you a fee for modelling – I don't expect you to work for nothing. Winston Broadbent of Saxton's Management handles that side of the business for me. I'll get him to give you a call and he'll work out your flights, accommodation and expenses, too. Anything you want, talk to Winston. He'll sort everything out for you. I'll be in London in a few weeks' time and we'll have dinner and discuss everything further.'

Fantastic, Catherine thought, as she hung up the phone, two down and one to go. When would she hear from Nicole? *Maybe she's sent me an e-mail.* She checked for messages. There was one from her father. Yes, he'd heard the rumours about The Clement Group's takeover bid but she could take it from him that it was unlikely to happen. *Now what does he know that I don't?* Catherine thought curiously. *Trust Dad to have been tipped off about whatever's going on at Webster Media. I wish I knew what he was up to.*

Returning to her mail, she found a message from Perry Wolf, with one sketch of an enchanting creation from the collection and the words: *Just wanted to get you excited about what you're going to see later today, darling. Love, Perry.*

And much to her surprise and delight there was one from Jack: *Grow old along with me, the best is yet to be.* For a minute she was tempted to daydream but fought the impulse. *Not now, Catherine, work must*

74

come first. There were other messages but nothing important and nothing from Nicole. Oh well, she's probably travelling somewhere with Tom and the kids.

The remainder of the morning was to be given over to forward planning. This was a locked-in-concrete, never-to-be-cancelled part of the way Catherine ran her business and another thing she'd learnt from her father. 'Business success doesn't just happen,' he would tell her, 'neither do good news-papers and magazines. You can be lucky, of course, and have a great news story breaking, a major disas-ter, or a scandal like that bloody fool President Clinton and Monica Lewinsky, but planning is the key to a successful publication. Plan, plan, plan . . . never leave anything to chance.

'You must always have something solid lined up for every issue, at least three good "meaty" features, a special food feature, a glamorous lifestyle piece, that kind of thing. Light and shade, Catherine, light and shade. And Catherine . . .'

She could almost hear her father giving his favourite lesson.

'Always read everything that goes in a magazine or a newspaper for which you are responsible, even the recipes. Make sure your food editor isn't "killing" your readers with too much cholesterol. It can happen. You must read every inch of every publica-tion for which you're responsible. It's what makes the difference between an editor who stands out in the crowd and one who's simply run of the mill.'

Forward planning involved *MAUD*'s key creative people. These included the creative director, Samantha James, who was responsible for the look of *MAUD* – the way the photographs were used, the layout of every page, the type, the illustrations. She was the best in the business and brilliant at creating the distinctive look that was known in the trade as 'the *MAUD* style'. A woman picking up the magazine knew at once that it was *MAUD* – it was different to every other magazine, most of which were identical clones of one another. No wonder so many of them were losing circulation. Sam's skill and talent were awesome.

The production editor, Jennifer Pickhaver, kept everyone and everything running on time, and was vital to the magazine's success. As Catherine knew only too well, it was no use having a great publication if it didn't get out on time. Magazines and newspapers that ran late missed out on vital sales and upset subscribers, the bread and butter of a magazine's circulation. Magazines that didn't keep to their schedules also upset advertisers and that was simply unforgivable. Advertisers and their agencies expected to be treated like gods and the gods punished late publications by withdrawing their money and putting it elsewhere. It was a stressful job and Jennifer could be temperamental sometimes but she was a wonder when it came to meeting deadlines.

Suzanne Stanton, *MAUD*'s deputy and features editor, had the best connections anyone could have. The daughter of a diplomat, she had an impressive list of contacts not only in Australia but also in Europe and America because she'd travelled the world with her father and had lived overseas when he served as Australia's High Commissioner in England and as Ambassador to Washington. 'I always told Dad he had his uses,' she'd say. Suzanne's father and Sydney were good friends, and Catherine and Suzanne had got to know each other at various parties and dinners as they were growing up. They'd been friends since they were fifteen, and had always kept in touch no matter where each was living.

Then there was Brenda who, as advertising director, had built up *MAUD*'s impressive multimillion-dollar revenue with what seemed like remarkable ease. But Catherine knew that Brenda burnt the midnight oil thinking through her presentations to key advertisers, working out their weaknesses and strengths, cultivating their decision makers with a skill that made other advertising directors look like amateurs. Australian Consolidated Press had tried to woo her away from Catherine with all sorts of tantalising offers of money and perks, an approach for which they were renowned, but Brenda wasn't interested. 'I'm with you,

Catherine, and I'm here for the long haul, wherever it will take me.'

The final member of the team was Fiona Wallace. She was the director of marketing and promotions and had the ability to come up with the most incredible publicity-making schemes. She could always make the most of Catherine's ideas, too. They often lunched in the boardroom and batted concepts around for a couple of hours. Then Fiona would take the lot away and work on them, fine-tuning them into reality with first-rate results.

Catherine had known Fiona since they were students together at the University of New South Wales, where Catherine had studied Organisational Psychology. Sydney had thought she was wasting her time when she told him of her plans. He had a very low opinion of universities, which he declared were 'full of unwashed, long-haired morons', and he certainly couldn't understand why Catherine wanted to study psychology.

'Dad, first of all I've always wanted to go to university – I enjoy learning. And secondly, when I'm in a position of power, as I intend to be, I want to understand people as well as possible. Organisational psychology deals with the full range of work behaviour. It looks at how you select people to ensure that they have the correct skills for the job, then how you motivate them, train them and empower them for the future. I think these would be useful skills to have.'

Nothing she had said would convince Sydney but he'd known better than to argue with Catherine once her mind was made up.

Fiona had studied Communications, Marketing and Media, while Brenda, also at New South Wales, had done an Advertising course followed by a post-graduate Business Administration degree. The three of them hadn't met until they'd gone for auditions for the annual university revue. They'd hit it off immediately and a great friendship had developed between them. They were inseparable, sharing clothes and jokes as well as all the details of their romances. Whenever one of them had a broken heart, the other two would include her on their dates and outings.

Once Catherine had fallen deeply for a medical student from India and declared she had found the love of her life. After twelve tempestuous months he'd told Catherine that once he'd completed his studies he was returning to his own country to marry a girl his parents had selected for him.

Catherine had declared that she'd never love again as she wept on her friends' sympathetic shoulders. 'Once you've met and lost the love of your life, you'll understand how I feel,' she said, somewhat dramatically. It wasn't long, however, before she'd met a new man, and Fiona and Brenda heaved a collective sigh of relief.

Their university days were a happy time, all in all, and after graduation, even though they'd pursued their respective careers they had remained close, keeping in touch with regular phone calls and lunches. When Catherine made the decision to go out on her own, Fiona and Brenda were the first people she'd called to offer a job.

Sam and Jennifer were friends from her school days. Like Catherine, they'd gone to the exclusive Hawthornden College, a private girls' school not far from Ashburn. In their senior years the three of them had produced the school newspaper and promised themselves that one day they'd make their fortune by running a magazine for intelligent, fun-loving women.

All of them had gained experience with other major publishers. Jennifer had joined Rupert Murdoch's News Ltd and worked in the production areas of his national newspaper *The Australian* at his Sydney headquarters, before being transferred to New York where she worked on his women's magazine, *Mirrabella*. Later she was sent to London to become production controller of Murdoch's *Sunday Times* colour magazine.

Sam had started her career at George Patterson, then Australia's leading advertising agency, where she'd worked with the renowned creative director Bryce Courtenay. Bryce, who had gone on to become one of Australia's most prolific and successful novelists, had been Sam's mentor. Something he'd said – 'People don't buy when the words you write don't appeal to their self-interest' – had impressed her so much that she'd had it printed and framed. Sam told Catherine that she never started work on a new sales pitch without reading Bryce's words.

Catherine and her team were the new breed of corporate women, thriving on the opportunity to run business their way, and making sure there was enough time to enjoy outside interests as well. They used to laugh about the older feminists who often grumbled about thirty-something women like themselves, accusing them of not being as committed to the advancement of women as they had been when they were their age.

But Catherine would argue that they were out of date. Women of her generation were just as committed and were breaking down barriers that had proved insurmountable for the older women. They knew that being successful didn't mean giving up their quality of life as so many of the feminists of the '60s and '70s had done. Women of her generation had plenty of energy and drive and, unlike the older women, they were actually having their cake and eating it, too.

Catherine and her contemporaries were happy to acknowledge the debt they owed to the feminist pioneers because they had paved the way and had been important role models for the women of the next generations. No one questioned a woman's right to work these days, although some women still encountered barriers in their bid to reach the top of their respective professions. It was an issue often canvassed in *MAUD* and a popular topic with the high achievers who made up a significant proportion of the magazine's readership.

Forward planning meetings took place in the boardroom where there was little likelihood of them being disturbed. Everyone was on time – it was well known that Catherine had little tolerance for people who ran late for meetings. Even her friends knew better than to keep her waiting.

'Morning everyone,' Catherine said as she walked purposefully into the boardroom and took her place at the centre of the table. 'Lovely day.'

'It certainly is,' said Sam, 'and you look mighty pleased with yourself. What have you been up to?'

'Kylie and Elle have both said yes! I'm just waiting for Nicole to respond to my e-mail.'

'That's great news,' said Fiona. 'I'm itching to get cracking on the promotional plan.'

'That's how I feel, too, but before we get onto the collection, I want to do some planning for *MAUD* for the next three months. Incidentally, the Christmas issue looks great. The feature we have on Kate Fischer has come up brilliantly. She looks sensational, doesn't she? It was a good thing she didn't marry James Packer after all. She'd never have had her fabulous career. I'm sure James wouldn't have allowed her to continue as an actor, although he doesn't seem to mind Jodie working, does he? Anyway, Kate's cover shot is just super and I'm really pleased with it. It's about time she showed people she had brains as well as beauty and a good set of boobs.'

'Thanks,' said Sam, 'I'm pleased with it, too. I'd like to use Franco Bruni again as the photographer for our next cover.' Franco was one of Sam's discoveries. He'd called to see her with his portfolio a few months ago and she'd been knocked out by his work. His photographs were like paintings. At the time she'd raved about his technique to her colleagues and insisted they try him for their Christmas issue.

'He's a great find, Sam,' Catherine said. 'Well done! I think we should put him under contract and use him for the *MAUD* Collection shoot, too. I'd hate Consolidated Press to get their hands on him.'

'Good one, Catherine,' Sam said. 'If we stitch up a deal with Franco now, before the Christmas issue goes on sale and before everyone finds out just how brilliant he is, we can have him to ourselves for the next twelve months. Our competitors will be green with envy.' She whacked the table with enthusiasm.

Catherine was excited, too. 'Call him as soon as we've finished here and remember, Sam,' she went on, 'don't pussyfoot. We want this man.'

'I have some good news, too, Catherine,' Suzanne chimed in. 'You remember that request you put to

Hillary Clinton for a one-to-one interview and pho-tographs? I've been talking with her executive assistant for weeks now and she thinks Hillary is going to say yes. Apparently she's now prepared to talk for the record about why she stood by Bill, through thick and thin – which sums up Monica Lewinsky pretty well, I think.' The others laughed. 'I never thought she'd lose all that weight. It's amazing!'

'It is – but who cares about Monica. That's bloody fantastic about Hillary. Her story will sell plenty of magazines for us, especially if she doesn't hold back. I think she has such guts – it's no wonder she's one of the world's most admired women.' There was a murmur of agreement from the others. 'How she has put up with that dickhead of a husband, God only knows.'

'Dickhead is right,' Brenda said. 'I wonder if I can write something compelling about dickheads for our advertisers.'

Clare, coming in with their morning coffees, was greeted with peals of laughter and wondered what the joke was.

They ran through the rest of the features list. Jen-nifer brought them up to date with some new production schedules and Brenda reported that advertising revenue for the next three issues was above budget and that projected figures for the remainder of the year were building nicely, except for what she described as 'one glitch'.

'I'm really pissed off about it,' she said tersely. 'The Barnes supermarket chain is now not sure it wants to advertise with us after all. Their bloody whiz kid media buyer – who looks young enough to be still wearing nappies, I might add – thinks that perhaps we're not quite right for them.'

'Damn!' Catherine exploded, flicking through the advertising schedules as she spoke. 'Damn,' she repeated. 'They were talking about spending a million dollars with us. We can't afford to lose their business. Is there no way we can change their minds?'

'I doubt it. I get the feeling the buyer wants to place their business in *Vogue*. I promise you, Catherine, I've been racking my brain for an idea that will change her mind,' Brenda said. 'But one thing I do know – the managing director is one of your greatest admirers. Maybe if you turned your charm on him you could persuade him that *MAUD* is the perfect vehicle for Barnes.'

Barnes was a new upmarket concept in supermarkets, offering its customers imported foods, a huge range of organic products and a bakery with the best breads, cakes, biscuits and other tempting delicacies. But it was Barnes' exclusive, quick and easy takeaway meals that had put the supermarket chain on the map. Its takeaway range compared more than favourably with meals served in the finest restaurants and included cuisine from around the world.

'I've got an idea,' Catherine said. 'Why don't we

put together a Barnes Supermarket Catalogue featuring those delicious takeaway meals of theirs, complete with prices and ideas for serving for lunch and dinner parties. We could give them eight pages, on heavier paper than we use in the rest of the magazine, so that the catalogue stands out. You know how much advertisers like that.' The others nodded.

'I'll work out a rough concept and then you and Sam can polish it up,' she said, looking at Brenda, 'and then we'll call on Barnes again. They won't be able to resist us when we present this idea to them.' Her eyes sparkled at the thought.

'Okay,' she continued, 'apart from our hiccup with Barnes everything else seems to be going ahead well on schedule, which is a relief because I have to go to London soon to sort out some distribution problems. We always knew this would be a formidable task and believe me, it is. We certainly have good people looking after our interests in both London and New York but getting such a massive distribution of magazines out each month is really testing us. I want to make sure everything is checked and double-checked so that there are no circulation upsets to mar the worldwide presentation of the *MAUD* Collection. It's not all that far away and it will be upon us before we know it.'

'Bit like giving birth to a baby, Catherine,' Fiona said.

'That's about the size of it – and I can tell you, it

sure will be a big baby!' Catherine laughed. 'I must go. I want to get my hair done before Perry monopolises me for the rest of the afternoon. He wants to show me sketches of his designs. I can't wait to see them. If you all have time tomorrow night, come and have a glass of champers with me at the end of the day and I'll fill you in.'

'Great,' said Brenda, 'it's a date.' The others were free, too, and said they'd be there. There was a knock on the door. It was Clare. 'Boss, you'll be late for Lloyd if you don't leave now.'

'I'm on my way.'

# Chapter Six

As she drove to the trendy harbourside suburb of Double Bay, where Lloyd Lomas had his salon, Catherine listened to the news to see if there were any further developments in the Webster Media takeover but it wasn't even mentioned.

Catherine enjoyed going to Lloyd's. She was always able to relax there even though it was a hive of gossip and activity – in fact, she frequently picked up a lot of useful information whenever she went there. She often had a coffee and networked with other women executives while waiting for her nails to dry. Business, however, was the last thing on her mind right now – she was intent on getting herself glamorous for Jack and she didn't feel like talking, not even to Lloyd.

He was familiar with the 'Don't talk to me, I'm preoccupied' look that many of his high-flying executive women wore from time to time. If

Catherine didn't want to chat he wasn't about to invade her space. Lloyd made sure she was out of the salon in record time and Catherine was back at her office in a little over ninety minutes, where Perry Wolf was nervously waiting for her.

'You're early,' Catherine said when she saw him, 'but it's good to see you.' They exchanged kisses on the cheek.

'I can't wait to show you my designs!'

Catherine and Perry had met when they were both in their twenties. She'd been in need of a gown for a Walker Corp. gala function and, with her usual couturier overseas on an extended holiday, someone had suggested she try Perry, who had just gone out on his own. Perry had made her a stunning creation, exactly what Catherine had wanted, and the pair had hit it off straight away. She had become one of Perry's biggest clients and, over time, they'd become close friends. Catherine knew she could trust him not only to dress her well but also to keep any secrets she shared with him. Perry felt the same about her.

It didn't take them long to discover that they shared similar personalities as well as the capacity to work hard. Both prided themselves on being well organised and on letting nothing divert them from their goals.

Perry was tall and lanky, and liked to dress in black – he usually wore well-cut trousers with a polo-neck top, adding a black cashmere jacket in winter. When summer was at its hottest, he'd trade in his polo-neck for a black knit T-shirt. 'Black takes you anywhere,' he'd proclaim.

He was proudly gay but never flaunted his homosexuality and as a rule was quietly spoken, except when he was enthusing about one of his new creations. Then his voice would rise to crescendo levels. It was one of his most endearing features. His only vanity was his eyes. They were brown – but Perry preferred to wear green contact lenses and, with his sandy-coloured hair and lightly tanned skin, he cut an elegant figure entirely appropriate for a man, Catherine liked to tell him, with his panache.

'Let's get on with it.' Catherine opened the door to her office. 'Why don't we sit over here?' she said, indicating a work table away from her desk. 'Then you can spread out.'

Perry undid the large black portfolio he was carrying. 'Before I show you the sketches, let me give you my thoughts on where I think fashion is heading, or rather what I believe the woman of the new millennium will want to wear, so you understand where I'm coming from.

'Fashion has new energy, a new freedom,' he began eagerly. 'There are no boundaries. The *MAUD* fashion decree is freedom of choice. That's what women want. You know, easy styles, comfortable, more feminine, still shaped to the body, but soft. Everything is soft – shoulders, pants and fabrics. I'm aiming for luxury as well as simplicity but because fashion has been somewhat basic and minimal for so long, I've included beading and embroidery for day and more opulent treatments for evening.' He laid his sketches out for Catherine to see.

She picked them up one by one, studying them closely before putting them down. 'Perry, you're a positive genius,' she said approvingly. 'I love them all and especially that medieval feeling in some of the styles.'

'I knew you'd be pleased,' he said triumphantly. 'They're some of the best I've ever designed.'

'I agree. How long before you'll have some samples made up?'

He laughed sheepishly. 'I've already had several made up – I can organise a model for a proper showing and be back in a few days. As for the rest, with the help of the extra seamstresses I've hired, everything should be just about finished in a couple of weeks.'

'Fine.' Catherine walked with him to the door. 'Perry darling,' she said, taking his hand. 'I'm absolutely delighted with what you've done. Thank you.'

Catherine was in high spirits as she completed the rest of the tasks she'd set herself for the day. She was still on cloud nine when the hire car collected her for dinner. When she arrived at Aria, Jack was waiting for her.

'I've missed you,' he said, kissing her on the cheek, 'and that diamond brooch you're wearing is exquisite.'

'It belonged to my great grandmother and it always brings me good fortune,' Catherine explained.

As they walked to their table by the window, people stopped to look at them. Not only did they make a striking couple but, as two of Australia's best-known people, they both attracted attention wherever they went. Catherine had trained herself not to notice. 'It's the only way I can live my life,' she'd explain to her friends.

'Would you like a glass of champagne?' Jack asked.

'I would.' She smiled at him.

They ordered their dinner and made small talk. Catherine was longing to ask him about Webster Media but decided that discretion would be a wiser option – she didn't want to spoil the chemistry between them by talking business. She was pretty confident it wasn't on Jack's mind at all. When their food arrived they ate it, but some weeks later neither of them could remember much about the meal.

'How about coffee at my place?' Jack suggested.

'All right.'

On the way back to his apartment they were both comfortably silent, happily anticipating what was yet to come. In the lift Jack put his arm around Catherine and she cuddled up to him, her head resting on his shoulder. This feels so good, so good, so good – the thought kept whirling around in her mind.

But once inside the door of Jack's apartment an unexpected burst of hesitation came over her. Now that the very thing she'd been longing for was about to happen, Catherine felt awkward and somewhat tentative about what to do next. Much to his astonishment Jack was experiencing a similar uncertainty.

'I'll go put the coffee on,' he said. Suddenly, having something to do seemed important.

Catherine walked restlessly around the room. She opened the balcony doors and took a deep breath of the night air. It's so quiet, she thought. 'What we need is some music,' she called out.

'The CDs are in the corner – you choose something,' Jack said, as he walked back into the room with the coffee. 'Do you take sugar?'

'No, thanks.' The romantic melodies of Cole Porter blared out.

'Shall we dance?' Jack asked, putting down the cups.

'Why not?' She put her arms around his shoulders and he held her to him. Time drifted by; their coffees grew cold. Even after the music ended they kept on dancing, their kisses growing more and more fervent. Prolonging their lovemaking had simply added to their excitement and Jack was finding the tension between them exquisitely painful. He nuzzled Catherine's ear and whispered, 'And now, shall we go to bed?'

Her eyes answered him hungrily. But he'd no sooner issued the invitation than his phone rang.

'Bugger! It's my private line. I'll have to take it. Sorry about this,' he said. 'Make yourself comfortable. I won't be long.' Pointing towards the bedroom, he disappeared in the direction of the phone.

A wickedly sexy nightgown of black French silk and lace lay on the bed, which, Catherine observed, had already been turned down. She undressed quickly and went to slip on the nightgown.

'You won't need that.' Jack strode across the room, pulling off his clothes as he did and letting them drop on the carpet. 'You are a phenomenal woman,' he said, admiring her neat waist and shapely hips, as they stood naked before each other. 'I knew you'd be beautiful but I had no idea you were such perfection.' He cupped her pert breasts in his hands and kissed them. 'Beautiful,' he repeated.

He pushed her down on the bed and began to expertly caress her body. 'Your skin is like silk,' he said huskily. It was only a matter of seconds before they both erupted, their pent-up desire making them frantic in their passion – kissing, loving, touching as if they could never get enough of each other. One minute Jack was on top of Catherine, the next she was lying on him. His hands were masterful and her body was tingling. As she felt herself coming her back began to arch.

'Put your legs around me,' Jack said, holding Catherine's buttocks firmly and pushing himself deeper and deeper into her. Their bodies began to move in rhythm together. Catherine gave a soft yelp of pleasure as Jack's movements became quicker and quicker. It seemed as if their bodies were one, and as their orgasms peaked Jack's bellow of triumph echoed in Catherine's heart.

It was some time before either of them moved. Panting and covered in sweat, they lay contentedly together. For the first time in a long while they both felt at peace. Jack finally broke the silence. 'I adore you.' He raised himself on his elbows and looked at her with such love in his eyes that Catherine could have burst into tears of joy.

'And I adore you, too, my darling,' she replied.

In the early hours of the morning she dozed, snuggled up against him, her feet tucked under his. Jack's mouth on hers woke her immediately. She put her arms around him. 'I think I'm purring.'

'You look a bit like the cat that swallowed the cream,' he teased, gently kissing the tip of her nose. He sighed. 'I wish I didn't have to go.'

'Go!' Catherine exclaimed. 'Go where?'

'London.'

'You're joking.'

'I wish I was but I'm not. I've got a meeting with Rupert Murdoch and my plane is waiting for me.'

'Surely you don't have to leave now?' Catherine couldn't believe it. Work was going to interrupt their first night together! 'Can't Rupert wait? What's so important that you have to leave right now?'

'I'm sorry, darling,' Jack said, 'but we're working on a big deal and it's imperative I go to London. That's what the phone call was about earlier. I've already delayed my departure because of you.'

'Well, thank you. I'm so grateful,' Catherine said sarcastically.

Jack laughed at her. 'I'd heard you had a fierce temper but I didn't expect you to bite off my head quite so soon. Catherine, you of all people should understand that sometimes work just can't be avoided. I'm not planning to be away long.'

'I do understand, Jack,' she said, getting out of bed, and looking around for her clothes. 'But your timing's lousy.'

He laughed again and went over and kissed her. 'Don't hold back, Catherine,' he ribbed her, 'tell me how you really feel.' Holding her face in his hands, he caressed her with his eyes. 'You are magnificent, Catherine Walker, and I've fallen for you in a big way.' He kissed her ardently – but with finality.

'I'll drive you home on my way to the airport.' They dressed and Jack quickly packed a few things in a suitcase.

As the lift took them down to the car park, Catherine was aware that one small alarm bell was ringing. Jack had put his work first, before her, at this heady stage of their relationship – bloody hell, it wasn't even a relationship yet – after their first night together. Not many, if any, other men would have behaved in such a way. Snap out of it, Catherine, she told herself sharply. Jack's not like other men and you wouldn't love him if he were.

They'd reached her apartment. Jack got out and opened the door, helping her out of the car. She put her arms around him and they kissed lingeringly.

'I love you – don't you forget that,' Jack said, kissing her one last time.

'Don't work too hard while I'm away,' he ordered. 'I'm sorry but I must go now. I'll call you from London.'

'Good night, Jack.'

As she got ready for bed Catherine began to wonder how Rupert fitted into Jack's takeover bid for Webster Media. Obviously he was up to his neck in it somehow. Jack wouldn't be flying to London at such an ungodly hour just to have lunch. It had to be something big to take him from her side. Was it going to be a joint venture between News Ltd and The Clement Group? But Rupert would have to get rid of some of his newspapers if he wanted News to be a part of whatever was being planned. How could they make the deal work?

She yawned. I am tired, Catherine thought. I'm not going to think about Webster Media now. She got undressed. She could smell Jack all over her. How wonderful! If only he were here life would be perfect.

'I've said it before and I'll say it again – there's no place like bed,' Catherine chanted, as she jumped in. She lay with her eyes open, too keyed up to sleep.

Normally that would have annoyed her, but she was in such a buoyant mood nothing could upset her equilibrium. Jack Clement had changed her life and nothing would ever be the same again. Just thinking about him aroused her.

She hoped she was having a similar effect on him, especially as it was his fault she had insomnia! Sleepless in Bondi, she laughed out loud. She got up, went to the bathroom and had a drink of water before climbing back into bed. Maybe if I count sheep . . . she reached one hundred but was as wide awake as ever. She looked at the clock by her bed – four a.m.!

What's the point of lying here feeling like this? I'm in the mood for love – she hummed a few bars of the song. She got up again and went outside. The sea was incredibly still, the air warm and balmy. How calm the sea looks, she thought. Everything is so peaceful – everything but me.

Did I feel like this about Roger? No, she answered her own question quickly, no I didn't. This is different. But you thought you loved Roger, she reminded herself. She shuddered at the memory of the man. Please God, don't let Jack turn out to be another Roger Rowland. No, that's just not possible. God wouldn't allow it to happen to her again. One Roger Rowland was enough in any woman's life. And so, she chuckled quietly to herself, was one Jack Clement.

Her love for him was the kind that would last a lifetime, she was sure of it. She wanted to have his children. Goodness, she thought, where did that sudden maternal urge spring from? The emotion took her by surprise but the more she thought about it the more she liked the idea. This must be what true love does to a woman. Of course, she'd always wanted to have children, but suddenly the idea seemed more of a priority.

She'd had her share of short-term loving and now she felt ready for the commitment of a long-term relationship. It was what Catherine had always wanted. Sam and Suzanne had often told her that such thinking was old-fashioned. 'Relationships don't have to be for life,' they'd say. 'Be happy for as long as happiness lasts, Catherine, whether it's ten years or five. Don't plan on being happy "until death you do part" in a relationship. It just isn't like that any more.

'Besides,' they'd argue, when she protested, 'it's boring – why would you want to spend the rest of your life with one man?' They would profess amazement that such an intelligent woman could be so romantically minded. 'No one cares about living happily ever after any more,' they'd insist.

'I do,' she'd reply defiantly. 'It's the only kind of love that interests me.' Sam and Suzanne would just shake their heads at her.

Not surprisingly, it was a topic that was often discussed at *MAUD*'s regular story conferences, and whenever the magazine ran a feature on the importance of love and what it really meant, it never failed to get a response from *MAUD*'s readers. Catherine found their comments fascinating and observed that one thing came through loud and strong – everyone, man and woman alike, was prepared to search for love. They wanted it just as much as she did.

At one memorable story conference Fiona had declared that Catherine was fixated on the thought of love. 'Why don't you do a story on love as an obsession?' she suggested.

'You're mad,' Catherine had replied, a little angrily. 'I am not obsessed with love – the only thing that obsesses me is *MAUD*. I want to run articles that will have people talking.'

'Love is not all that it's cracked up to be,' Fiona had said, her voice sharp. 'You shouldn't encourage our readers to believe in fairytales. Any minute now you'll tell me that you're expecting a prince on a white horse to gallop up and whisk you away in his arms. Very few people live happily ever after – and furthermore, the world doesn't come to an end if they don't!'

The story conference had become far too personal. Fiona was the one who had a problem with love, not her, Catherine thought, as she'd prudently changed the subject. 'That's enough of love. Let's discuss travel. What country will we feature in the next issue? Brenda, what do you think about Italy?'

But Fiona's words had got to her, and Catherine thought about them now. Was she obsessed with love?

She knew most people looked at her and automatically assumed that her life was not only successful but also happy. She led what others considered a privileged life; she'd never wanted for anything – anything material, that is; she'd lived in a beautiful home and had been well educated. She loved her work. Most people would consider she was a fortunate woman and probably envy her lifestyle. But even so, there was a part of her that felt empty.

It's my heart, she thought – it's been let down. All my heart can remember is the pain of love. A deep melancholy swept over her and suddenly she was close to tears.

Catherine wanted to be loved and needed – and to love someone in return. She knew she had love in abundance to give to the right man. The question was: was Jack that man? She'd had so many disasters, Catherine knew that if she hadn't been such an optimist she'd have thrown in the towel ages ago. Surely there was a man somewhere who was confident enough to accept her as his equal, willing to make a lifelong commitment and give her the security she was seeking – not the kind that money is supposed to bring with it, but the security of peace of mind. It was important to Catherine that someone care about her happiness – and it had to be a man on whose shoulder she could rest her head, whenever the mood took her.

In spite of her father's wealth and everything it

had provided, Catherine had never felt emotionally secure, not with her parents and certainly not with Roger. Her disastrous relationship with him had been a tremendous blow to her confidence. She'd been head over heels in love with him – well, at the time she'd thought it was love but later she realised that it had only been lust.

Yet in the beginning she'd been so certain that with Roger she would find the love she'd always sought. He was so sure of himself, so confident in the same way that her father was. Maybe that was one of the reasons she'd been attracted to him. Perhaps subconsciously she'd been drawn to Roger because he reminded her of Sydney.

Was there also something about Jack that smacked of her father? she mused. He's a powerful man, just like Dad, but power sits comfortably with him. It never did with Roger. Jack likes to have his own way, but I'm used to that kind of male thinking. I can handle that. He has his ego under control, too. Not like Roger, she thought. His ego was haywire and he was insecure with it. Why couldn't I realise that about him when we first met? It was there for all to see, but not you, Catherine Walker. What a bloody nitwit I was.

Could it be possible she was making another mistake with Jack? Never! She smiled to herself, shaking off the melancholy. This time I've got it right. Jack is different and nothing at all like Roger. We're going to be deliriously happy together.

# Chapter Seven

When she was growing up, Catherine used to tell herself that her parents loved her but in her heart she always felt unloved. They'd always been so preoccupied with themselves and their own interests that Catherine sometimes felt in the way. At first Sydney and Sarah were so infatuated with each other that neither of them had much love left to give to anyone else. Then gradually Sydney had become caught up with building his empire and the power that came with it. Left to her own devices, Sarah concentrated on her business and began to console herself with the occasional one drink too many.

Sydney Walker believed that children should be seen and not heard and Sarah went to great lengths to make sure Catherine and Tom never disturbed him. As soon as she knew she was pregnant with Catherine, Sarah had begun looking for a nanny and she soon hired Miss Berman, a woman with a warm, friendly but no-nonsense manner who came highly recommended by friends in the country. When Sarah came home from hospital with Catherine she handed the baby over to Miss Berman, who fitted into the routine at Ashburn as though she'd been born to it. When Sarah had Tom two years later, Miss Berman was waiting at the front door for her return.

Both children adored 'Ber Ber', as they called her. She taught them how to walk and talk, took them on outings to the zoo and for picnics at the beach. She made sure they knew their prayers, too, and was a stickler about the need for good manners. She read them stories and sat up with them at night whenever they were ill. She took them to school and when they got home in the afternoon she was eager to hear all about their day. Ber Ber was both mother and father to the children, who rarely spent much quality time with their parents at all – Sydney and Sarah's hectic schedules precluded that.

As children, Catherine and Tom often discussed their parents' shortcomings when they were alone together.

'Why did we get such peculiar parents?' Tom asked his sister one day. 'Everyone at school has normal parents who play with them and everything.'

'Beats me. Maybe God wanted to punish us.'

'Why? What have we done to upset Him?'

'Nothing as far as I know, but I can't think who else could have done it to us.'

When they were older they decided that there came a time in a person's life when you simply had to accept your parents the way they were. Sydney and Sarah hadn't beaten them or deprived them of anything and, as Catherine explained to Tom, 'Everyone loves differently and I guess parents are the same. Ma and Dad love us as much as they're able. No one's perfect, Tom.'

'That's for sure.'

They'd agreed that things could have been worse. They could have been poor, for instance.

'What would that have been like, Catherine?' Tom asked her. He always expected his big sister to have the answers to everything.

'I don't know,' she said, 'but I don't think we'd have liked it as much as we like being rich.'

Catherine couldn't help but laugh at the memory. She'd been so good at explaining their parents' failings to Tom, but she'd never quite been able to accept them herself.

When Tom was eight he was sent to boarding school. Sydney believed that boarding school was good for boys: 'It teaches you to stand on your own two feet and to get on with others,' he'd told his son. When Tom said he didn't want to go to boarding school, Sydney wouldn't have a bar of it. 'If it was good enough for me then it's good enough for you. The matter is not for discussion.' Tom was put on the train to Berkdale College in Armidale in the New

England countryside of New South Wales and told to get on with it.

Catherine had been lonely without her brother. She loved Tom and he in turn worshipped the ground Catherine walked on. Unlike his parents, she was always there for him. He and Catherine used to write to each other but it wasn't the same. They missed not being able to talk with each other. She could talk to Ber Ber, of course, but the nanny was no substitute for Tom. Miss Berman was a sensitive soul and knew exactly how Catherine felt. She wished Sarah would take more interest in the child.

Miss Berman didn't approve of what she considered Sarah's indifference to Catherine. Nor did she approve of Sarah's drinking. She was well aware of her employer's growing addiction to alcohol, often smelling it on her breath on the rare occasions Sarah deigned to inquire about Catherine's progress at school. If only the woman could stop thinking about herself and consider the emotional needs of her daughter. Miss Berman used to worry what effect Sarah's unmaternal ways would have on Catherine later in life. She could see the hurt in the little girl's eyes when her mother brushed her away.

There was just so much Catherine would have liked to talk about with Sarah – the usual mother–daughter matters, the sorts of things her friends were able to chat about with their mothers, like boys, new dresses, whether or not to have a new hairstyle – but

Catherine had to work all that out on her own. She'd long ago accepted the fact that she'd have to look after herself and make decisions about her life without relying on her mother.

But even so, as a child Catherine had always thought her mother was the most glamorous person in the world. She would look at Sarah when she was getting dressed to go out and think how feminine she was and wish she'd be as pretty as her mother when she grew up. Of course, Sarah took good care of her body and face. A beautician visited her at home twice a week and she never went out in the sun without sunblock and a hat. Joe, her personal trainer, called four times a week to help her with her exercise programme and each morning 'the wonderful Valerie', as Sarah called her, would arrive to do her hair and make-up before she left for the office.

She had the most gorgeous clothes, which Catherine would try on whenever her mother was out. Sarah had so many outfits that Catherine knew she wouldn't notice if things were not in their exact place. Sarah's penchant for shopping was a family joke – they all teased her about it, especially Sydney.

'Why do you like shopping so much?' he'd once asked her.

'Darling,' she'd said, 'I simply can't explain why I adore it so much. All I can tell you is that I can shop when I'm happy, I can shop when I'm sad. I can find something to buy no matter what country I'm in. Shopping is my hobby.'

'A bloody expensive one,' Sydney would protest half-heartedly. It didn't seem to bother him how she spent his money. At first it had given him pleasure to see his lovely wife well dressed and attractive, and when he was no longer interested in her, he wasn't much fussed about anything she did.

When she was grown up Catherine was saddened by what she considered her mother's meaningless life. She often tried to remember the good times she'd had with her mother but found this difficult – they'd been so few and far between. It was such a tragedy and it depressed Catherine to think about it. If only her mother hadn't let alcohol destroy her. She'd seen sporadic glimpses of a different Sarah, of course – especially when she was a little girl – and Catherine remembered how delightful her mother's fun and bubbly personality had been. No wonder her father had been so taken with her.

Sarah Lawton was only nineteen when she first met Sydney Walker at a polo match in the country not far from where she lived with her parents, who were well respected in the district. Sydney had thought Sarah pretty enough but he made no attempt to get to know her better. He was only interested in girls who would come to bed with him and he could tell that Sarah wasn't that kind of woman.

She knew all about him, of course. Every girl did. Sydney was a charismatic young man with a reputation for being wild and reckless. He was handsome and athletic-looking, with roguish hazel eyes that promised excitement. Most members of the opposite sex found him irresistible, especially when he turned on his extraordinary charm. Even then, Sydney had an air of power about him and it just added to his sex appeal. Unfazed by the ease with which things came his way, Sydney just thanked his lucky stars for his good fortune and bedded any woman who took his fancy. He rarely got a knock-back.

There had been Lawtons breeding sheep at Mountainholme in Bungendore, just outside Canberra, for as long as anyone could remember. Unlike a great many men on the land in Australia, Sarah's father, Matthew Lawton, had been well educated and had a shrewd business brain. In the early '60s, he had seen the growing acceptance of synthetics and knew that ultimately they'd threaten the future of woollen fabric. He had also predicted the big wool slump of 1968–71 and by the time it occurred he'd cleverly turned his historic property into an exclusive 'Life in the Outback' experience. Only the very best people came to Mountainholme. They were also well heeled – they had to be, to afford the experience.

Sarah Lawton was a gorgeous-looking girl, tall, blonde, blue-eyed, with what everyone agreed was a great body. Men took one look and were instantly enamoured with her. She knew the effect she had on the opposite sex and, not surprisingly, was an outrageous flirt. When she left school she announced she was going to become an actress. Her parents were horrified but sensibly said nothing.

Matthew thought a woman's place was in the home and his wife, Ruth, always agreed with him. He was one of Australia's richest men and a real man's man, like so many men of country stock. He always preferred the company of his own sex – he liked talking business, going to the races and playing golf at his men-only club. He didn't approve of working wives, a trend that in his opinion did not bode well for family life, and was steadfast in his belief that a man should be the breadwinner, with a wife to look after him and have his children.

'That's the only full-time job a woman needs,' he'd argue. 'What a mistake it was to have given women the vote. It simply gave them ideas. Women are all very well as long as they stay in their place.'

Ruth Lawton knew exactly where her place was and she didn't mind staying in it as long as she could spend Matthew's money. When Sarah was older and railed against what she called her father's 'antiquated beliefs', she'd often asked her mother how she tolerated her father's attitude to women.

'Mother, Dad is so out of date. Why haven't you tried to change him? What attracted you to him in the first place?' she'd demand. 'Was it really love?'

Ruth would just laugh. 'My dear, what is love? Love can be anything you want it to be. I understand your father and I enjoy my lifestyle. That's all that matters. When you're ready to settle down remember that love isn't all that it's cracked up to be. Money is, though – make sure the man you marry has money. Make it number one on your list. Put love second.'

Ruth was renowned for her style and people conceded that Sarah had inherited her flair. There was a collective sigh of relief when, after three months at acting school, Sarah admitted that she didn't have enough talent for a career on the stage and decided to join a public relations and marketing company run by a friend of her parents. She took to her new job like a duck to water and was an instant success.

Four years later, when she asked her father to set her up in a business of her own that specialised in putting on corporate events, he agreed to do so. She was now twenty-three and had a confidence and sophistication that made her more desirable than ever. In spite of what he thought about a woman's place, Matthew was very proud of her.

'She's good looking and brainy,' he said to Ruth. 'What a combination. She might as well enjoy herself, until she finds someone to marry.'

Before the year was out she met Sydney Walker again when she was hired to do a gala event at the

Chevron Hilton Hotel in Sydney's Kings Cross to mark the first ever showing of a collection from Italy's leading couturiers such as Veneziana, Simonetta and Emilio Pucci, whose designs Sarah adored.

*Mother,* she wrote home to Ruth, *he's the only designer in the world who combines striking contrasting colours like screaming yellows with blues and greens with such success. Dad would be horrified at the knitwear. There's not a scrap of wool to be seen. Everything is made in a new synthetic called Orlon. It certainly is a new world!*

Appropriately Sarah started the parade with a specially written arrangement of the music from Dvorak's *New World Symphony* and afterwards put on an Italian banquet the like of which Sydney society had not seen before. It was one of the year's most glamorous events – people rushed to get tickets. The night was a huge success and a big breakthrough for Sarah. This time, something did click between her and Sydney, who found her very desirable. He was twenty-nine now and he knew it was time for him to settle down and start a family. He wanted an heir. Sarah had breeding and class. Together they would produce a fine son.

He asked her to have dinner with him the following night and before they'd finished their meal he'd proposed to her.

'Mother, it was the most romantic thing you could ever imagine,' Sarah confided in Ruth later.

'He's so strong and powerful, and so charming. I'm head over heels in love with him. I know he's the only man I'll ever love – and Mother, you don't have to worry about a thing, because he has plenty of money!'

In the beginning they were deliriously happy and made a good team. Sarah was vivacious and an excellent hostess. Sydney was proud of her business success and didn't mind her continuing with it after their marriage. 'But,' he warned her, 'don't get too busy – your job is to run my home and make sure everything goes smoothly. Don't forget that, Sarah.'

Before Tom and Catherine were born, Sarah and Sydney were out several times a week. On weekends they went to the races or sailing on the harbour. They frequently entertained with lavish dinner parties at which Sydney cultivated his business prospects. After the children came along, however, things changed. Sarah no longer appealed to Sydney sexually. This didn't mean that he'd lost his interest in sex – in fact, he was never short of female companionship. Sarah might have tamed him for a while, but it was well known in business circles that, given the slightest encouragement, Sydney Walker would fuck anything in a skirt.

As Sydney put in long hours at the office, Sarah was often left at home alone during the evenings. She did her best to cope with her increasing loneliness and wished Sydney could find more time to do things together with her. By the time Catherine was eight, she and Tom seldom saw their father in the evening and because they ate their dinner early Sarah usually dined by herself. Some of the other wives of prominent businessmen around town would go to the opera or ballet with gay 'walkers' but when Sarah had suggested to Sydney that she do the same, because it would give her something to do in the evenings, he wouldn't even entertain the idea. 'My wife is not going out with a faggot. I don't want a poofter anywhere near my son.'

At first, it never occurred to Sarah that Sydney wasn't faithful, and he took advantage of her innocence, entertaining a variety of mistresses. More often than not, when she thought he was working, he was actually out wining, dining and making love to one of them. Sarah never suspected a thing, because Sydney was discreet and maintained apartments in Sydney and Melbourne, as well as London and New York. Increasingly, Sydney found he didn't have much in common with Sarah – in fact, she bored him. She had given him what he wanted, a son to carry on the Walker name, as well as a daughter. It surprised him how fond of Catherine he was, but she was such a bright little thing. There was something about her that reminded him of himself.

In spite of their marital problems, Sydney and Sarah were on the social A-list and invited to everything that mattered. No one dreamt of having a serious dinner party without them, although Sarah tended to arrive unescorted, with Sydney usually appearing in time to have coffee. This happened so frequently that no one ever expected Sydney to make it for the main course.

One night at a black tie dinner given by her good friend Susie Blackburn, Sarah found herself seated beside Arthur Jensen, a distinguished-looking man somewhat in the mould of the actor Roger Moore. He was a delightful dinner companion and conversationalist. He told Sarah he was a bachelor and was out here doing some work for his government at the British High Commission. They got on famously and Sarah had a pleasant evening.

The following week they were both invited – separately, of course – to another dinner, and once again they were seated together. Arthur entertained Sarah with amusing stories about his life on the diplomatic circuit; she in turn told him about some of her famous clients. It was obvious to everyone they enjoyed each other's company and soon it was accepted that if Sarah was invited to dinner, so was Arthur. He was the answer to every hostess's prayer: the perfect 'spare man' for an unaccompanied married woman. Sarah was delighted. She loved going out and she liked Arthur's company, too.

She'd never had a male friend before – she was such a one-man woman that the thought of any other kind of man in her life had never been an option for her. She knew that Arthur's feelings for her were strictly platonic and felt very relaxed in his company. He was thoughtful and kind, too, and interested in what she had to say. She used to look forward to seeing him. When she'd confided in him about how lonely she was he'd sympathised and suggested that perhaps travelling overseas would amuse her.

His last posting before coming to Australia had been Egypt, a country Sarah had always wanted to visit.

'You should,' he told her. 'It's wonderful.'

'Someone told me that it's unsafe.'

'No more than a great many other places. If you go with a reputable tour company and don't do anything silly you'll be fine. You should go. Everyone should see Egypt before they die.'

'Well, I'm not planning to pop off just yet,' Sarah laughed, 'but I've always wanted to sail down the Nile, see the pyramids, climb Mount Sinai, visit Tutankhamen's tomb . . . everything,' she said excitedly.

'So then do it,' Arthur urged her.

When Sarah mentioned to Sydney that she'd like to go to Egypt his first reaction was one of amazement. 'Why would you want to go there? Dirty, smelly place – and totally unsafe. Tourists often get mugged for their money and jewellery over there, you know.'

'It's as safe as a great many other places,' Sarah

protested, repeating Arthur's words. 'I've always loved history and I've always wanted to go to Egypt.'

'I'd rather you didn't,' Sydney said ominously.

But Sarah went on and on. 'I'll travel with Susie Blackburn – she'll be a perfect chaperone for me.' Sarah knew that if she offered to pay, Susie would go in a flash. Susie had expensive tastes but her income didn't quite live up to them. 'Darling, you're so busy, you won't even know I'm gone. Please, I do so want to see the pyramids.'

Her constant pestering annoyed Sydney. 'For Christ's sake, Sarah, you're driving me nuts. All right, go to Egypt if you must, but if anything goes wrong don't say I didn't warn you.'

Sarah was ecstatic. She made the bookings, planned the itinerary, first faxing it to Arthur for his approval, before sending it on to Susie. She worked out her wardrobe and counted the days until her departure. On the morning she was due to take off she went to say goodbye to Sydney. He was having breakfast on the verandah.

'Darling,' she said, bending down to kiss him goodbye, 'thank you for letting me go. I'll see you in a month.'

'No you won't.'

'Why, what do you mean?'

Sydney got up and walked to the front door. 'Did you really think I'd let you go to Egypt? I only said okay because your constant nagging was becoming unbearable. I told you I'd rather you stayed at home and I meant it. I've got your passport, Sarah.' He waved it at her. 'You won't be going anywhere.' He laughed nastily at her and walked out of the house looking very pleased with himself.

Sarah was distraught. She should have known better. When Sydney gave orders he expected them to be obeyed, and that included her. As far as he was concerned, marriage meant that the husband always had total control over the wife.

Officially, Sarah came down with a sudden bout of flu and stayed home for ten days. Only Susie knew the real reason why their trip to Egypt had been cancelled. When word got out that she was well again Sarah began receiving invitations for dinner.

Everyone was pleased to see her back on the social scene. At her first dinner party after her 'recovery' she was, as usual, seated next to Arthur but before the first course could be served, much to everyone's amazement, Sydney arrived. He insisted on sitting next to Sarah and didn't leave her side all night. Arthur was quietly moved to another place at the table.

Just before they left, Sarah went to look at a new painting the hostess had recently acquired. Sydney sidled up to Arthur, who was also about to depart.

'Keep away from my wife,' he muttered.

'I beg your pardon?'

'You heard me, keep away from my wife.'

Arthur was shocked. 'I'm only a friend of Sarah's, nothing more, you know. She's a very nice woman.'

'I know what she is and she's mine. Keep away from her or you'll regret it.'

'Are you threatening me?' Arthur asked.

'Yes, and if I were you I'd take it seriously.' Sydney turned on his heel and walked away. Two days later, when Sir Harold and Lady Thornhill asked Sarah to dinner to meet a princess from Italy she declined. She gave an excuse for the next dinner party, and the next. After a while people stopped asking her. At around the same time she began to drink more heavily in the evenings when she got home from the office.

The change in Sarah's personality began with her first drink, which was always champagne. It was a ritual. A half bottle of something good and French would be chilling in an ice bucket waiting to welcome her home. Once she'd drunk it, Sarah would move on to wine and usually finish up with a balloon of fine French brandy or a port. It all depended on her mood. Catherine would marvel at her mother's stamina and wonder how she could do it. During the day she ran her business brilliantly but at night, away from the office, Sarah was a different woman.

Alcohol turned her into a shrew. She became foul-mouthed, argumentative and aggressive. Catherine soon learnt to leave her mother alone with her demons. So did everyone else, especially Sydney. When he told Sarah that he thought it best if they had separate bedrooms she was deeply upset but she knew it was pointless arguing with him.

Sarah had finally found out about Sydney's mistresses when he'd had an affair with a much younger secretary at Walker Corp. and someone had sent her an anonymous note. When she'd confronted Sydney about it he told her not to be so bloody suburban. 'It's not unusual for a man in my position to have a mistress – it doesn't mean a thing.' Sarah was devastated and began to drink before breakfast. Sydney was the love of her life but he didn't give a damn about her. Sometimes, Catherine would hear her mother ranting in her bedroom, when she was drunk. 'You bastard,' she'd say, 'why couldn't you have been satisfied with me? Why did you always need to have a slut on the side?'

It always troubled Catherine to hear her mother going on in this way. She held her father responsible for the whole awful mess. He doesn't know the meaning of love or even care that he's broken Ma's heart. He can't even accept that her drinking is his fault, the young Catherine thought crossly. One day I'm going to tell him exactly what I think of him.

She wondered how her mother would have reacted if she'd been aware that Sydney brought his mistresses home when she wasn't there, something Catherine discovered by accident when she was thirteen. Sarah was staying with friends in the country at the time. Catherine had woken up in the middle of the night and, unable to get back to sleep, decided to get a glass of milk from the kitchen. As she passed her parents' bedroom she heard a woman laugh and thought her mother must have come home early and was back on good terms with her father. Catherine always dreamt of that happening.

She opened the door of the bedroom and stopped, horrified. Her father was naked and so was a woman she'd never seen before. They were so preoccupied with each other they hadn't heard the door open. The woman was kissing her father. 'What can I do to make you happy?' she asked him.

'I want to mount you . . . like a dog.'

The woman turned over and, kneeling, laughed. 'Woof woof, take me, hound dog, and do with me as you want.'

Catherine watched her father put his enormous – or so it seemed to her – penis into the creature, who yelled with pleasure as he entered her. As he began to hump the woman, Catherine closed the door. She was shaking and couldn't believe what she'd seen. She made her way back to her room, forgetting all about the glass of milk. She began to cry. Why weren't her parents like other parents? It was so unfair. When she finally fell asleep her pillow was damp with tears.

Next morning Catherine felt sure her eyes would

give her away. But when she arrived at the breakfast table her father was reading the papers and drinking his coffee as if nothing had happened. She couldn't believe it. What had he done with the woman, she wondered? She turned scarlet as she remembered what she'd seen. She couldn't talk to him. He was revolting. She ran from the room. Sydney looked up, idly wondered what she'd forgotten, and resumed reading his newspaper.

Catherine went to the kitchen and grabbed an apple and set off for school, telling no one what had happened. She didn't even tell Tom when he came home for the school holidays.

Life went on as it always did, but Catherine felt lonelier than ever. When she was sixteen, her beloved Ber Ber announced that she was going to retire. The news had shattered Catherine, who felt as if she was being abandoned. She loved her nanny deeply and the thought of Ashburn without her was unimaginable. Tom commiserated with his sister when he heard about it, but he was rarely home and usually caught up in sport and other activities of boarding school life.

'But why must you go?' Catherine had demanded, as she helped Miss Berman pack her belongings on the day she was due to leave.

'You're almost an adult – you don't need someone like me any more,' Ber Ber had told her kindly. 'It won't be long before you go to university and then get a job. Exciting times are ahead of you, my dear.'

'I don't care about that,' Catherine had sobbed. 'Who will I talk to when you're gone? I love you, Ber Ber. Please don't go. Change your mind and stay. Please.'

'I love you, too, Catherine,' Ber Ber said, putting her arms around the girl and comforting her. 'But I'm over sixty and it's time I made a home for myself. I can't live at Ashburn forever. You can come and see me whenever you want – and we can always talk on the phone, can't we?'

Catherine blew her nose. 'I suppose so.' But after the final goodbyes she went up to her room and cried. Ber Ber's departure was one of the unhappiest days of her life.

Now and then Sydney didn't bother coming home. He'd bought an apartment at Point Piper about ten minutes away from Ashburn and used it to entertain his woman friends and business acquaintances. As for Sarah, by the time Catherine had finished school she'd had her first facelift. She was still drinking her evenings away and had begun to take sleeping pills to help her sleep at night. She also started to miss the odd day at the office.

Sometimes Sarah would ask people over for dinner and although she tried to limit her drinks, inevitably she drank too much and embarrassed her guests with her behaviour. Catherine overheard a couple of women chattering one night when they went to powder their noses. 'She's getting worse,' said one. 'Yes,' the other replied. 'It's such a shame because she's so lovely and talented. When she's at the office you wouldn't have the faintest idea she had a drinking problem. If only she could give the stuff up. It turns Sarah into a kind of Jekyll and Hyde character.'

Catherine used to worry when she overheard such conversations. Was there something she should be doing to help her mother? Sometimes she felt so guilty. She'd tried once to get Michael Shipley, the family doctor, to talk to her mother – but he'd told her he couldn't interfere. 'She has to ask me for help,' he insisted.

'But she doesn't realise she needs it. You're a doctor. Surely you can do something,' Catherine had pleaded. 'My mother requires help desperately.' But he insisted there was nothing he could do.

Every so often she'd get cranky with Sarah. She didn't mean to but she couldn't help herself. Her mother was her own worst enemy. Sure, her father was a difficult and demanding man, but Sarah had looks, ability and money, and in Catherine's opinion, she could have done so much more with her life than frittering it away with her drinking. When she was younger it used to annoy Catherine that her mother couldn't 'snap out of it' even for an hour or two to pay some attention to her and Tom. But now she was old enough to understand that Sarah would never have been that kind of a mother. The fact that she wasn't really had nothing to do with her drinking. The truth was that the only person who mattered to Sarah was Sydney – he was her major addiction and she could never get enough of him. Her drinking was a secondary craving that she found impossible to give up because alcohol helped her to forget the heartache he'd caused her.

Catherine kept herself busy at school. She was happy there and popular with her classmates. She was a clever student – study came easily to her – and always topped her class in English. She'd leave her school reports at her father's place at the breakfast table and glowed when he praised her. She'd won her first English prize when she was just eleven and she could still remember what her father had said.

'I'm proud of you, Catherine. You've done very well indeed. Maybe you'll come into the business with me one day. How would you like that?' he'd asked.

Catherine beamed at him. 'Daddy, that's exactly what I'm going to do – how did you know?'

'Fathers know everything,' he'd laughed. 'Now, how about I treat you and some of your friends to a movie and supper at Twenty One as a reward?'

Catherine had asked Sam and Jennifer and after they'd seen the new Barbra Streisand movie, they'd felt very grown up ordering cappuccinos to have with their veal schnitzels and salads at Double Bay's in place of the moment. Catherine left a note for Sydney on the breakfast table the next day.

*We had a fabulous time, Dad, and Sam and Jennifer asked me to thank you very much. And thanks from me, too! Love, Catherine.*

Sydney had a little chortle when he saw it. He had great hopes for his daughter – and also for Tom, who was getting good scholastic results at Berkdale. Later, when Tom was in the senior school and he'd been made captain of the school's First XI Cricket Team, Sydney somehow found the time to watch his son play. A keen sportsman himself, he'd captained the First XI Cricket Team and First XV Rugby Team when he was a student at Berkdale and he was delighted Tom had followed his example. Tom was a champion bowler and Berkdale dominated school-boy cricket during his time as captain, which made him very popular with his classmates. He was dux of the school in his final year and topped his class in English and Maths. Like Catherine, he also found time to edit the school newspaper.

Not long before she was due to start at university, Catherine came home late one night and found her mother passed out in the main lounge room. She was surprised and upset – usually Sarah stayed in her own suite of rooms after dinner, and Catherine couldn't bear to think that this was the way her mother spent every night. She woke her with some difficulty. Not only did Sarah reek of alcohol, she had trouble speaking and slurred her words. Catherine helped her to her room.

'Get into bed, Ma, and have a good night's sleep.' She closed the door of Sarah's room and walked along the corridor to her own bedroom. I have to do something about her drinking, she thought. Things just can't go on the way they are. Everyone had tried to help Sarah – even Sydney had finally suggested she see the family doctor, after Catherine had told him she thought her mother was drinking more than usual. But Sarah was in a state of denial.

'Don't be silly,' she'd say. 'There's nothing wrong with me. I can stop drinking any time I want. I couldn't possibly run my business if I had the problem you all seem to think I have. Stop worrying. I just like to have a drink from time to time. I wish you'd all stop going on about it.'

Catherine got up early the next morning and made a pot of tea. Putting two cups on a tray plus some milk, she went upstairs to her mother's room. Sarah was already awake.

'Morning, darling,' she said. 'Tea in bed. How divine. Thank you.'

Catherine looked at her mother. It was hard to believe she was the same woman that Catherine had put to bed the night before. Her mother's recuperative powers never ceased to amaze her. She had the constitution of an ox. It was incredible.

'Ma, I need to talk to you,' Catherine said, as she poured the tea. 'Here, take this.' Sarah always had her morning cup of tea served in a large, bright pink

Limoges china cup with a matching saucer. 'Tea always tastes best in good china,' she'd insist.

Catherine poured herself a cup of tea and sat at the foot of her mother's bed. 'Ma, you must talk to a doctor about your drinking – you're overdoing it.'

'Nonsense,' Sarah replied stiffly. 'You always exaggerate things. I was just tired last night and I didn't eat much dinner. I had a couple of glasses of wine and it went straight to my head. That's all.'

'That's not true and you know it.' Catherine chose her words carefully. 'We're all worried about you – even Dad is.'

'My, that's a change, isn't it!' Sarah gave a sour little laugh. 'Do stop nagging me – it's most annoying. I can stop drinking whenever I want to. Pour me some more tea, Catherine, and for heaven's sake, talk about something else.'

And, for a couple of days, Sarah was all right. She told everyone that she was giving up alcohol because she wanted to lose a couple of kilos. But her resolution didn't see out the week. She returned to her old ways and after that it was all downhill. She began coming home early from the office so she could start drinking sooner than usual. Sometimes she didn't go to work for two or three days in a row.

The day before Catherine was due to begin at university Sydney decided he'd had enough. Catherine overheard him talking to his lawyer on the phone. 'Sarah is impossible to live with, Richard,' he said. 'Living with a drunk isn't pleasant. I want out.'

As he hung up Catherine stormed in and confronted him, all her pent-up anger and emotion erupting out of her. 'Never once have you stopped to consider that it's your fault Mother drinks. My God, you're selfish. Your indifferent attitude to Mother staggers me.'

Sydney stared at her in amazement – what was wrong with the girl? 'What the hell are you going on about?' he demanded.

'You,' Catherine snapped at him. 'You and your constant unfaithfulness and your endless parade of mistresses. Do you think Mother doesn't know about them? Or that Tom and I don't? Everybody knows about you and your affairs. Your behaviour is disgusting.'

'How dare you talk to me like that!' Sydney was livid.

But Catherine was too angry to care about that. 'Somebody has to – you seem to think that you've got nothing to do with Mother's drinking habit but it's entirely your bloody fault!'

Sydney was dumbfounded. He'd never seen his daughter like this before.

'She only drinks to forget, you know.' Catherine almost shouted the words at him. 'Don't you know how much she loves you and that you've broken her heart? Don't you care about her at all?'

'For God's sake, Catherine, sit down and stop

carrying on.' He could see she was genuinely upset and it rocked him. He forced himself to control his temper.

'Catherine,' he said gently, 'no one but the two people involved can really ever understand what goes on in a marriage. When things don't work out it's as sad for the couple as it is for their children, but if someone in a marriage is unhappy you have to let go and get on. And if there's the slightest possibility of happiness with someone else, then I think you have to take it.'

'You're not in love with another woman, are you?' Catherine asked quickly.

'No, of course not and that's not what I meant.' Sydney sighed. Women could be so bloody perverse at times. He lit a cigar and took a couple of deep puffs before continuing.

'I did love your mother once – very much, if you must know – but over the years feelings can change. I know she's given me the best years of her life and I'll always be grateful to her for giving me you and Tom. And I'll make sure that she'll never want for anything.'

'Except love,' Catherine said bitterly.

'I can't help that – life doesn't always turn out the way we want it to. There's no guarantee about love and happy endings, you know.' He puffed on his cigar again. 'Neither your mother nor I would inten-tionally distress you and I'm sorry that we have. But what goes on between us is our business, Catherine, not yours.'

He stood up and looked down at her. 'I'd ask you never to mention the subject again – do I make myself clear?'

'Perfectly.' Her voice was frosty. She got up and walked briskly from the room. Bastard, she thought angrily.

Alone with his ghosts, Sydney remembered some of the happier times he'd shared with Sarah. She'd always been besotted with him. In the beginning, he'd rather liked it, although he sometimes got the feeling that Sarah wanted to possess him. Originally, her dependence had given him a sense of power, but then he'd begun to find it intrusive. Sarah had to know everything he was doing. He had no privacy. In the end, that's why he'd encouraged her to keep running her business. He reasoned that now and again her work would take her interstate, which would give him some time to himself and, more importantly, the opportunity to enjoy other women.

He'd never expected Sarah to turn to the bottle for solace simply because he was having a fuck with someone who didn't mean a thing to him. Other men had mistresses but their wives didn't go to pieces. He was a good provider – why couldn't she be happy enjoying the lifestyle his money gave her?

Why couldn't she be proud of being Mrs Sydney Walker? After all, it was a name that carried considerable clout. Other women turned a blind eye to their husband's infidelities – why did his wife have to buck the status quo? It wasn't in a man's nature to remain faithful to one woman. Men were made for conquests. He'd tried to explain it to Sarah once but she couldn't understand. 'Darling,' she'd said, 'so why do men get married if they still want to play around? You're not like that, are you?'

'Of course not,' he'd lied without compunction.

If Sarah wanted to live in a fantasy world she could – but this particular leopard had no intention of changing his spots. Sydney Walker was proud of his conquests. His charm and sex appeal, which had only increased as he'd got older, attracted women to him like iron to a magnet. Power was a forceful attraction, too, and so was his considerable wealth. He was a lucky man and he knew it. He had only to touch a woman on her arm and he could feel her tremble – a sure-fire sign that if he wanted her, she'd be his before the night was over.

Sydney Walker took lovemaking seriously. As a young man, he'd practised on prostitutes and read books on satisfying women. He'd trained himself not to come so that he could prolong the sex act. Women often begged him to come. 'Not yet, not yet,' he'd say. Sometimes one would complain that he took so long to come he'd made her sore. Next time, he'd hold himself back even longer and then he'd drop her. How dare the woman have the nerve to complain? Most men were impossible fuckers. He was the greatest. She, and the other women he took to bed, should be eternally grateful. No man would ever satisfy them like he could!

Sarah had been a great fuck once and he used to enjoy having sex with her. She was a lusty woman – he'd always liked that about her. Once it had excited him, and sometimes he even admitted – but only to himself – that he missed sex with her. They'd had some good times together and she'd had a heart of gold before booze had tarnished it. Once when he'd unpacked his bags on a trip to New York he found a card from her tucked between his shirts: *Happy Anniversary, darling. Do you remember when we married and I told you I loved you to bits and pieces? Well, I still do. Yours forever, Sarah.*

He'd forgotten all about the anniversary but her note had touched him. That day he'd gone to Cartier's and bought her a diamond necklace and matching earrings. When he gave them to Sarah on his return, she'd put them on and then slowly undressed while he watched, before inviting him to bed still wearing the diamonds. It was a monumental night. Sydney had an erection just thinking about it.

Not for long, though. Thinking about Sarah now soon fixed that. Drink had changed her from a charming, competent hostess, loving wife and great sexual companion into a stinking shrew. He couldn't bear the smell of her when she'd been drinking – it was a big turn-off for him. She still looked attractive – his money helped with that – but her skin had lost its glow. Unbeknown to Sydney, Sarah was contemplating a second facelift as well as a tummy tuck.

As he sat in his study mulling over his past, Sydney made up his mind about what he was going to do. Later, he told Sarah he didn't wish to leave Ashburn but nor did he expect her to go. 'Divorce is a messy business, Sarah. I don't want one and I'm sure you don't either.' As far as the outside world was concerned they were Mr and Mrs Sydney Walker and always would be, but privately, he told her, he wanted them to lead separate lives. Coldly, Sydney explained his intentions to have Ashburn redesigned. His architect would create an apartment for Sarah on the top floor and one for himself on the ground floor with its own entrance.

Catherine would keep her rooms in the Western Wing, and Tom would remain in the Eastern Wing, both of them on the first floor. The current drawing room and reception areas would remain as they were for those occasions when it would be necessary for the family to come together.

If Sarah wanted to see him or if she needed anything, she'd have to contact him through Dot MacGregor, his personal assistant. 'I'll let you keep my name,' Sydney told Sarah, 'and the privileges that go with it, but I don't want to have anything to do with you unless it's an emergency. I'll give you a generous allowance and you can lead your usual lifestyle. As I said, I don't want a divorce and I advise you not to even think about initiating one yourself.

'You always wanted to go out with faggots – well, now you can. But don't cause a scandal or embarrass me or you'll regret it.' His tone was threatening. 'And don't for one moment entertain the idea that you could take me to the cleaners and get your hands on my money,' he warned her. 'I've had Richard Crosswaite on a retainer for years, just in case I ever needed him. I've told him everything about you and your drinking.'

Richard Crosswaite was Australia's top divorce lawyer with a track record others in his profession envied. He was held in such high regard that he could have made a fortune working permanently in America or England, where his clientele consisted of some of the world's best-known people. But he preferred to live in Australia, where he earnt more than enough money to keep him in the manner to which he was happy to be accustomed.

What's more, Richard Crosswaite had never lost a case, and Sydney Walker liked winners.

Sarah was shocked and it showed. What had she ever done to Sydney to make him treat her in this loathsome way? Surely he doesn't mean it, she thought. How had their relationship come to this?

God, she thought, I could do with a drink. She still loved Sydney but what was the use? He didn't care. She was a bloody fool – she knew that. Why oh why did she love him so much? Had he ever loved her? Or did he only choose her because he wanted children and she came from good stock. He'd pulled her leg about it once – or at least, that's what he'd claimed. Maybe he hadn't been joking after all.

'Fuck your money, Sydney, and fuck you too.' Sarah slammed the door of her bedroom and went over to her dressing room. She opened a drawer and considered the assortment of bottles before her – gin, brandy, scotch, vodka, even sherry. She selected the gin and poured a generous slug into the tumbler on her bedside table. 'You can go to hell, Sydney Walker. One day you'll be sorry for treating me this way.' She gulped down her drink and poured herself another one.

When Catherine looked in to say goodbye on her way out to buy a couple of books for university Sarah appeared to be sleeping. She had in fact passed out again. Catherine had no idea about the conversation that had taken place between her parents. But when she opened the front door she was surprised to run into a couple of builders taking measurements of Ashburn, under the supervision of Toni Harwood, an up and coming architect whom Catherine had met on the party circuit.

'Hi Toni, what are you doing here?'

'Just checking out the measurements for the new entrance for your father's apartment.'

'Of course,' Catherine replied after an uncomfortable pause, 'I'd forgotten all about it. See you later.' Her father's apartment? What on earth is that all about? As soon as she was in her car and out of Toni's earshot, Catherine called her father's office to make an appointment. She didn't particularly want to see him but she had to know what was going on.

'You must be a mind-reader, Catherine,' Dot MacGregor said. 'Your father just asked me to call you to see if you could lunch with him today.'

'That's not possible,' Catherine said brusquely. 'I'll only take up ten minutes of his time.' Dot was surprised at the tone of her voice. 'Why of course,' she said. 'Why don't you get here about twelve-thirty and go straight to the private boardroom.'

Sydney was there when she arrived. Catherine didn't beat around the bush. 'What are you up to now?' she asked. 'I bumped into Toni Harwood this morning and she told me she was measuring up for the new entrance to your apartment.'

'It's nothing for you to worry about. Your mother and I are going to separate but we'll continue to live at Ashburn.'

'You don't mean it?' Catherine was incredulous.

'I do. I'm having the place remodelled. Your mother and I will maintain individual apartments but under the same roof. It's impossible as it is for me to lead a normal married life with your mother. Our marriage is over.'

'It's all your fault –' she began.

'Don't start berating me again,' he said, interrupting her. 'You don't understand and you won't until you fall in love yourself.'

Catherine wasn't sure she ever wanted to do that. If what her mother and father had once had was love they could keep it. Their kind of loving was vile.

'But what will people say?' Catherine persisted.

'Nothing because they won't know, unless you or your mother tells them. The servants won't give the game away – I pay them too well for them to be loose-lipped about what goes on at Ashburn. It's nobody's business but ours. Your mother needs to be looked after and this way she'll be protected without anyone knowing she's an alcoholic.'

Sydney didn't bother mentioning his deal with Richard Crosswaite. It had nothing to do with his daughter.

'It's most unusual,' Catherine said icily.

'I couldn't care less,' her father retorted. 'It's what I want and quite frankly I wish you'd stop interrogating me.'

But, much to Catherine's astonishment, the arrangement worked out remarkably well. It coincided with Sarah's retirement. After she'd sold her public relations and events company she gave herself over to a life of leisure, which included regular drinking sessions. She spent her days being pampered at her favourite beauty salon and going lunching and shopping. Twice a year she went to Paris for the haute couture shows before going on to London to catch up with old friends. The second facelift had not been as successful as the first one. Catherine felt it made Sarah's face a little too taut, but Sarah was convinced that it made her look younger than ever and that was all that mattered.

Catherine, meanwhile, was enjoying her studies at university and doing well. Tom, having completed his schooling at Berkdale, had gone on to do a Law and Arts Degree at Queensland's Bond University. He majored in Journalism and did Communications as a minor, graduating in just three years.

He then declared that he wanted to go to America to study for a Master of Science in Journalism and Master of Business Administration Degree at Columbia University in New York. Sydney hadn't been at all happy, but he was placated when Tom took a job during the summer holidays as a general reporter on his father's *New York Daily Globe* newspaper. Tom loved America and wrote glowing reports to Catherine about the people he was meeting, the places he was visiting, and the shows he was seeing on and off Broadway. Tom wrote well and Catherine enjoyed reading his letters.

Unlike his sister, Tom had spent little time at home apart from school holidays. After graduating from Bond University he'd spent only three months at Ashburn before leaving for America and Columbia. He'd thought Catherine was mad to stay there as long as she had. 'It's so full of hate, I don't know how you can stand it,' he said.

During the university holidays Catherine worked for Sydney, too. The relationship between them was still strained, but both were able to put their personal problems aside when they were at Walker Corp. After her graduation, Catherine had asked her father for a job in the production department of his Sunday newspapers. 'I want to know about the nuts and bolts of the organisation,' she told him.

'I agree, that's important,' Sydney said, 'but I'd like you to start in the advertising department. In this business, revenue is crucial to success. Learn about that first, then you can transfer to production.' She'd agreed and the following day she was appointed deputy advertising manager.

For the next five years Catherine worked in every department that her father considered important to her training. Sydney felt it was essential that she have a good overall knowledge of the many divisions that made up Walker Corp. 'The only way for a boss to understand how the people he employs feel about their work is to have done it himself. My father made me do it and I'm sure it's one of the reasons why I've been so successful and why we've never had a major industrial dispute.'

After twelve months he'd invited her to join the board, an appointment of which she was very proud. It helped her to acquire an even better understanding of Walker Corp. and to know the key people important to the company's success.

By the time Catherine was twenty-eight she'd become deputy managing director. The day her appointment was announced, her father told her he was more than satisfied with her work performance and that she had a bright future ahead of her. He opened a bottle of champagne and toasted her success before going out to dinner with his current mistress.

Catherine went home to tell her mother, but Sarah was asleep. The housekeeper said she'd taken her sleeping pills earlier than usual and didn't want to be disturbed.

# Chapter Eight

The sounds of the clock chiming six startled Catherine. She'd been sitting on her verandah, lost in thought, for two hours and hadn't even noticed the early morning rays of the sun dancing across the gentle waves of Bondi Beach. I wish Tom were here now, she thought, I need someone to talk to. It's a while since I heard from him – I wonder what he's doing.

A couple of joggers caught her attention. Now they've got the right idea, she decided. It's a lovely morning. I'll go for a run along the beach and then have a surf. That will clear my head.

As she went inside to put on her swimming costume the phone rang.

'Sis?'

'Tom, is that you? I can't believe it! I was just thinking about you, wishing you were here. I need someone to talk to.'

'Me too.'

'There's nothing wrong, is there?'

'Nope, I just felt like hearing a friendly Aussie accent. And I have a brilliant idea. How about meeting me in Honolulu for Christmas? I really can't make it all the way back to Australia – I've an important meeting in San Francisco that I can't put off. But I could make it to Hawaii, and if you meet me halfway we could enjoy the festive season together. I've already booked the Presidential Suite in the old part of the Royal Hawaiian – remember how we used to love going there with Ma whenever possible for our school holidays? Can you make it?'

'Honolulu – what bliss. I can smell the frangipani already. Listen, if you promise me a Mai Tai cocktail with double cherries, under the trees of the Royal Hawaiian within an hour of my arrival, I'll be there.'

'It's a promise, Sis,' Tom laughed. 'I'll see you soon.'

'You certainly will.'

Catherine was humming as she walked down to the beach. It was only when she started to jog that it dawned on her that the tune was 'Jingle Bells'. She grinned at her choice of music. She'd actually been dreading Christmas, thinking she'd have to spend it by herself or with some other lonely friend.

By now she had reached the south end of the beach and she turned to run back the way she had come. The water was so inviting that once she reached the flagged area, she charged into the sea and dived under the first big breaker.

Not much surf, she thought, but oh boy doesn't the water feel sensational! This is just what I needed. And she dived under the waves again.

Catherine had arranged to spend the morning working at home, writing her editor's column for *MAUD*. Then she planned to read some features she'd commissioned, before looking through a couple of books that had been submitted for possible extracts. She needed uninterrupted thinking time, something that wasn't possible if she went into the office. Although Clare was good at protecting her, there was always someone with a problem that needed her attention 'immediately', and work that she should have been able to complete in a morning often had to be put aside.

Her home office was her sanctuary. It also had the most brilliant view and whenever Catherine needed inspiration all she had to do was look out across the beach to the Pacific Ocean and in no time her thoughts became as crystal clear as the water. Sometimes she wished she could always work from home – it was so peaceful and pleasant.

'One day that's what more and more people will do,' she'd tell Clare. 'With the speed that technology is progressing there'll be absolutely no need for people to go to an office every day to do their job. The way we know and understand work today will change forever and it will be sooner rather than later, just you wait and see.'

She showered, slipped on a pair of aqua cotton shorts and a matching top, and walked barefoot out into the garden, calling to Rosaria that she'd have breakfast there. It was going to be a hot day, she thought – the cicadas had started their noisy singing, a sure sign of the heat that was to come. Rosaria was out in seconds with tea, muffins and the morning papers. Catherine took a sip of tea and began to read *The Sydney Morning Pictorial*.

'Oh no!' she cried.

'Something wrong, Miss Walker?'

'No, Rosaria, it's okay.'

But Catherine had turned pale. She tried to continue drinking her tea but couldn't hold her cup properly because her hand was shaking. Roger was coming to Sydney! He'd been invited to speak at the New Millennium Communications Conference, which the Australian Government was organising as the highlight of its annual Business Expo. Catherine had also been asked to speak – she was to deliver the keynote address and had been looking forward to it. But not now, she thought. Damn, I won't be able to avoid him. Why the hell did he accept? She knew why – to make her feel exactly the way she was feeling right now. She'd hoped never to have to see Roger again and felt sick at the idea of even having to be in the same room with him. He hadn't always had that kind of effect on her. There was a time when he meant everything to her.

∽

They'd met in London when her father had sent Catherine to run World Channel, after her five-year 'apprenticeship' working in every department of Walker Corp.'s Australian operations. Sydney was delighted with the success of World Channel. He'd set it up in the early '80s and, with his usual impeccable timing, had managed to do so a couple of years before Rupert Murdoch started his Sky Channel satellite service. Sydney prided himself on the fact that he usually managed to keep one step ahead of Murdoch, much to the latter's frustration, although he was the first to acknowledge that Murdoch was a worthy opponent. It was common knowledge that the two enjoyed locking horns with each other. World Channel not only reached millions of people every day in Europe but also America and Asia – it gave Sydney an important world power base.

Before Catherine left to take up her new job, she'd dined alone with her father at Ashburn. Sarah sent her apologies for not joining them – she had a headache and was going to eat in her room. Catherine was relieved when she heard this. Things between her and Sydney had remained tense and her mother's presence probably would have exacerbated the situation. However, when it came to discussing business, father and daughter were different people and although Catherine would never admit it, especially to Sydney, she always felt extraordinarily close to her father when they were talking shop.

'We were one of the first companies to appreciate the potential of global marketing and we took advantage of it long before many of our competitors realised what it had to offer,' Sydney said proudly, as he poured them both a port. 'I want to make sure we stay well ahead of the pack. I'm glad you're going to be in London keeping an eye on things because this is an important time for World Channel. I want you to make our push into China your number one priority – the possibilities that the Chinese market offers us are tremendous.'

London had always been one of Catherine's favourite cities and she was excited at the thought of not only working there but living there as well. She and Tom had spent many a holiday in England with their mother and Catherine always felt right at home the moment she stepped off the plane at Heathrow airport.

Sydney had warned her that running World Channel would test her to the limits, and it didn't take her long to find out what he meant. But in fact Catherine relished the way World Channel stretched her and she quickly learnt to appreciate World Channel's clout as an important force in satellite journalism. She'd been told that many influential opinion-makers watched it but she soon had that confirmed first-hand because they constantly rang Catherine to give her their point of view about the issues of the day before volunteering to make themselves available to World Channel for comment.

'There's nothing like an audience of millions to open the mouths of the world's big players,' she told Sydney, on a late-night conference call hook-up. 'Even Saddam Hussein wants to talk to us! Running World Channel is everything you said it would be. I'm having a ball. I can't wait to get out of bed in the morning!' Catherine didn't tell her father that occasionally she found herself wishing she had more time for herself and also for relationships. She'd been so busy with her studies and then learning the ropes at Walker Corp. that men had taken a secondary role in her life. Of course, she'd had her fair share of love affairs, but few of them had ever been too meaningful and she was never at a loss to find a date if she needed one. Men liked Catherine and were always happy to be seen in her company.

More recently, she'd gone out with a couple of her father's executives – not that he'd known anything about it. Sydney wouldn't have encouraged his daughter to go out with his employees. But where else would she meet men, Catherine reasoned, except at work, seeing she spent so much time there. And now here she was in London with a schedule that seemed to preclude her even meeting someone with whom to share a meal and a little harmless flirtation.

As if to prove her wrong, the following night she met Roger Rowland at the British Television Excellence Awards at the Dorchester Hotel. Catherine was there collecting an award on behalf of World

Channel for excellence in international news communication and Roger picked up an award for the BBC's British-Euro Network News, where he was CEO. The company had been set up by the BBC to enable it to remain an influence in Europe and, from time to time, to present the British Government's point of view to other countries in the European Common Market. It had nothing like the reach of World Channel but was considered a significant player in news broadcasting.

Roger Rowland had enjoyed a distinguished career as a journalist and won six Emmy awards, four Peabody awards and many other honours for his news reporting before he accepted the top job at British-Euro Network. His reputation had allowed him to recruit some first-rate newsmen and women to the network and, like Catherine, he enjoyed what he did for a living.

He was blessed with film star looks – blue eyes, blond hair, and a smile that embraced all who came within distance of it. He had the body of an athlete and worked out every day come rain or shine – 'or even snow', he'd brag. He was also famous for his conquests with the opposite sex.

Roger believed in playing as hard as he worked, much to the delight of the British press, which chronicled his exploits whenever given the opportunity. So even though she hadn't been in London long, Catherine had read a great deal about Roger Rowland, especially in Murdoch's notorious *Sun*, which excelled at infiltrating the most private of inner sanctums. There were times when Catherine felt she almost knew Roger and his retinue of conquests and, like the rest of the newspaper's readers, she was agog when a former lover had tried to run him over after she saw him leaving the famous London nightclub, Annabel's, with a new girlfriend.

When Roger invited Catherine out for dinner within ten minutes of their being introduced she was therefore hesitant, not wanting to become just another scalp on his seduction list.

'Why are you procrastinating?' he asked her.

She told him the truth and he guffawed. 'I'd heard you Australian women were frank – but that's a bit below the belt, my dear. Still, at least I know where I stand. Don't believe everything you read about me in the papers – I'm not as bad as they make out, you know. Why don't you do your own market research?' he suggested cheekily. 'You might even like me.' He was at his persuasive best and Catherine could feel her resolve weakening.

She agreed to have dinner with him the following night and when he picked her up, she was delightfully on edge at the possibility of what might happen between them. He took her to Thames, London's most acclaimed restaurant, with its glorious views of the river and Big Ben. Somehow he'd managed to get the prized window seat even though the place had been booked out for weeks – but then Roger Rowland was powerful. Most people bent over backwards to grant his requests because it was common knowledge that his network could destroy people and businesses if it were in the mood. Few people ever wanted to antagonise Roger, which meant he always got what he wanted.

But not me. I'm not going to be easy to get, big boy, Catherine thought to herself as she looked at the menu.

'The food and service here are excellent,' Roger told her, 'and I thought you'd enjoy the panorama.'

'It is quite splendid.'

'Would you like a glass of Laurent-Perrier before dinner?'

'That's exactly what I feel like.' She couldn't help notice the brown flecks in his deep blue eyes – but why did she feel they were devouring her?

'Are you enjoying London?' he asked.

'Very much – mind you, I've been so busy I haven't had a chance to get around London as I'd like. There are a couple of shows on in the West End that I'd love to see.'

'Maybe we could go together,' Roger suggested.

'Perhaps.'

Roger wasn't fazed by her seeming disinterest in his invitation and continued confidently. 'I really admire the success Walker Corp. has had with World Channel. The rumour mill says you're doing great things there and that you're a clever and capable woman.'

'That's good to hear – and a bit of a relief. I'd been wondering how I was going over with my colleagues. It's hard for the boss to actually ask staff for a report,' she laughed.

Roger laughed with her. 'I'm all for women in decision-making roles,' he said. 'We have a couple of women heading up divisions at BEN and –'

Catherine interrupted him. 'BEN?'

'Oh sorry,' Roger said. 'That's our shorthand for British-Euro Network – it's such a mouthful. In-house we call it BEN . . . and, as I was saying, we have women division heads and they're such hard workers that they make their male counterparts look lazy.'

'My father says much the same thing about women,' Catherine said. 'In fact, he says he'd rather employ women than men because they're prepared to put in the hours when it's necessary without losing their enthusiasm for the task at hand. He also admires their loyalty.'

'He's right about that,' Roger agreed. 'But do you know what I most admire about women?' He looked at her and she shook her head.

'It's the way they think – they're so intuitive. It amazes me how right a woman's intuition usually turns out to be. At BEN we encourage women to aim for the top and we're totally committed to equal opportunity.'

Catherine was impressed with Roger's attitude. She'd imagined that given his notorious reputation, he'd be somewhat chauvinistic in his thinking. Perhaps she shouldn't believe everything she'd read about the man in the press. He was unquestionably good company. She was enjoying herself.

Dinner was as delicious as he'd promised it would be. Thames was renowned for its old-fashioned menu and Roger had insisted on ordering for both of them: baked potatoes heaped with caviar were followed by tender golden roast chicken and for dessert, chocolate soufflés with vanilla ice cream covered with chocolate sauce.

'This is sensational,' Catherine said. 'Sinful puddings are my weakness,' she confessed, as she poured some more sauce over her ice cream.

'I had a feeling you'd have a sweet tooth,' Roger said. On the way out he introduced her to the British Prime Minister, Margaret Thatcher, who was sitting at her usual table.

'I heard you'd arrived to run World Channel, Miss Walker,' Thatcher said. 'I hope you'll have time to come for lunch at Number 10 with my husband and I. We'd like to hear about your plans for World Channel. I'll have someone call your office tomorrow to make a time. Roger, always good to see you. Give me a call in the morning. I have a news item for you and I know you'll like it.'

'Delighted, Prime Minister, thank you.'

As he drove her home Roger told Catherine he wanted to see her again, and at the front door of her house in Eaton Square he kissed her in a way that made her heart flutter. She was astonished at the effect he had on her. 'You're a bewitching creature,' he said, holding her hand. 'I must see you again. How about tomorrow night?' He didn't give her the chance to say no. 'I'll pick you up at eight.'

The following morning, when she arrived at the office, the most delicate arrangement of gardenias in a silver vase from Tiffany's was sitting on her desk. How did he know that she adored gardenias? She read the card: *Enchantress. I can't wait to see you again tonight. Love, Roger.*

She felt a stirring of emotion that was helped by the heavenly scent from his flowers. She read the card again. Enchantress – really! Careful, Catherine, she told herself, you're starting to fall for this man. She pinned one of the gardenias to the lapel of her suit and every time she caught a whiff of the flower's perfume it reminded her of him.

Roger was five minutes early to pick her up for dinner but she was ready, as eager to see him again as he was to see her. This time he took her to The Ritz. Once again he'd snared the best table at short notice – the window table in the right-hand corner, where the richness of the decor of what is probably the prettiest dining room in Europe could be properly admired.

'This room is magnificent,' Catherine said, as she took in her surroundings.

'I've always liked it,' Roger said.

They ordered their meal and made small talk. Once again, Roger impressed Catherine with his attitude to women. 'I had a meeting today with Demos – they're the British futures think tank group,' he explained. 'They've been doing some research and have come to the conclusion that the 21st century is going to be "The Female Age". I hope they're right – I'd like to see more women running corporations,' he said.

'You're very enlightened – for a man,' Catherine laughed.

'I mean it,' he said. 'Look at you: you've a wonderful mind, you're capable and you look sensational. What a concoction of talent! You're one of Walker Corp.'s most precious assets.' He looked at her appreciatively, before adding mischievously, 'I'd hate to cross swords with you in the boardroom, though.'

'Come on,' Catherine protested. 'Now it's my turn to tell you not to believe everything you read about me!'

'I don't, you gorgeous thing – I can see for myself the kind of woman you are.' Roger had slipped off his shoe and was rubbing her foot with his. Before Catherine knew what she was doing she'd slipped off her own shoe and began to stroke his leg with her foot. She couldn't believe she was doing such a thing in a public place but she couldn't help herself. Thank heavens there's a long tablecloth, she thought, hopefully no one can see what we're doing. But it was, she had to admit, an extremely interesting sensation.

'I think we should go,' Roger said quietly.

Catherine stood up at once. They walked quickly to the entrance. 'Put the bill on my account,' he instructed the girl at reception.

They were back at Eaton Square in what seemed like minutes. Sydney Walker had bought the house years earlier, preferring the comforts of a home to staying in a hotel on his frequent visits to London. It was also useful when he entertained his mistresses. A luxurious, elegant house, it had its own gym and indoor swimming pool.

'Come in,' Catherine said to Roger, as she closed the front door.

'Where's your bedroom?' he asked.

'On the top floor.'

'I don't think I can wait that long. Is anyone else here?'

'No, just us. It's the housekeeper's night off and her room is downstairs. She never comes up when she's not on duty.'

There was a fire burning in the drawing room. 'That looks inviting,' Roger said, kissing Catherine and unbuttoning her dress at the same time. Catherine stepped out of it. He took off her bra and kissed her on the lips again before moving to her breasts and tickling her nipples with his tongue.

'Stay there, don't move,' he ordered. She did as she was told. He undressed and tossed his clothes on the floor, then he took a couple of cushions from the lounge and laid them on the rug in front of the fire. 'Why don't we make ourselves comfortable?'

Catherine slipped off her shoes and tights and was about to remove her panties when he stopped her.

'Don't do that, that's my job. Come over here,' he commanded.

Again she did as she was told. Roger pulled her down to lie with him in front of the fire and began to kiss her, at first gently and then more intensely. His tongue was darting everywhere. He moved to her breasts once more. 'God, your breasts are majestic,' he said. 'I love them.' Catherine couldn't believe how excited his tongue on her nipples made her feel.

Unexpectedly, Roger stopped what he was doing and looked at her. 'Do you want me, Catherine?'

'You told me I'd bewitched you, Roger – well, let me tell you, the feeling's mutual.'

'How splendid, my darling,' he said. He resumed kissing her nipples and then began to kiss her navel, his tongue probing, licking, seducing her slowly and pleasurably, while at the same time he began to touch her, ever so lightly, with his fingers. She was so wet that he knew how much she wanted him.

'Shall I take your panties off now, Catherine?'

'I was beginning to think you'd never ask.' Her voice was throaty with longing.

'Let's not be in too much of a hurry, my darling,' he said. 'I want to get to know you a little better first.' Holding her wrists above her head with one hand, he used his other hand to gently massage her clitoris through her panties.

'Roger, you're tormenting me . . .'

Still holding her wrists, he started to suck her nipples.

Catherine was so aroused that she was almost beside herself. Without warning, Roger ripped off her panties. She heard them tear and then she saw his erection. He lunged his penis into her.

She gasped, taken aback by the speed of it all.

His lips were on hers. 'Sorry, my love,' he murmured. 'I couldn't wait to get inside you any longer.' He took her hand and moved it down to her clitoris. 'Make yourself come, Catherine, make yourself come.'

She knew exactly how to make herself come but with Roger inside her and his tongue on her breasts again, she was so excited that she knew it would only take a few seconds before she erupted. As if he could read her mind Roger reassured her: 'Don't worry if you come now, darling Catherine, we have plenty of time to do it all over again . . . and again.'

She began to rub herself faster, then faster. Roger was keeping pace with her rhythm. 'Open your legs to me, my darling, wider,' he demanded, 'as wide as you can, wider.' Catherine felt as if she was going to explode. As she felt herself coming she began to moan; the intensity of her orgasm was overpowering. Roger came at the same time. 'Oh yes, oh yes, oh yes!' he shouted.

With Roger's arms wrapped around her, Catherine felt extraordinarily satisfied. She'd never known such happiness. We're made for each other, she thought. We're wonderfully compatible and we make the most beautiful love.

They napped for half an hour or so before she got up to fetch two blankets, a bottle of her father's finest French courvoisier and two brandy balloons. Wrapped in their blankets, they sipped their brandies and every now and then shared a kiss. Without warning the mood changed. Roger began to kiss her with more urgency. He put his hands on her breasts.

'Just a moment,' Catherine said, placing her hands over his. 'It's my turn now. This time don't you move.'

Roger was lying on his back. Catherine removed the blanket and standing up, looked down at him, enigmatically.

'The fire light makes you look more tempting than ever,' he said. 'You have no idea how enticing your breasts are.'

'Look but do not touch,' Catherine said. She knelt down and took his penis in her mouth. He writhed with pleasure. When she was sure he was well and truly aroused she stopped what she was doing.

'Don't stop.' He was almost pleading.

She began to suck his toes one by one, starting with the small toe first. By the time she got to the big toe, Roger was writhing with anticipation. Using her tongue she kissed her way up his legs, carefully by-passing his penis. She kissed his navel and then she moved to his nipples, kissing them gently and caressing them with her tongue before blowing on them. Then she returned to his toes and began to suck them again.

'Oh my God, what are you doing to me?'

'Aren't you having a good time?'

'Yes, don't stop.'

She didn't.

He was just about begging her to let him come when Catherine announced that she was going to ride him like a horse. She sat astride him like a jockey, and began to move slowly up and down, squeezing his penis inside her with her vaginal muscles.

'Oh yes,' Roger murmured. Keeping her movements exactly the same, she leant back and took his testicles with her right hand and softly caressed them. 'Christ!' he shouted. 'Don't stop, whatever you do, don't stop.'

Later, as they lay together in front of the fire, he told her he'd never forget their first night together. 'You are my goddess of love. I worship you. I'm in awe of your seductive powers.'

'All part of the service,' Catherine laughed. 'Treat me kindly and I'll do it again.'

# Chapter Nine

The next day, Roger sent Catherine a spectacular basket of violets and lily-of-the-valley, the like of which she'd never seen before – but then she had never met anyone quite like Roger before either. She read the card eagerly: *My dearest Catherine – you are the woman of my dreams. Your adoring Roger.*

After a whirlwind courtship, and exactly six months to the day they'd met, Roger asked Catherine to be his wife and presented her with an impressive diamond solitaire ring from Asprey & Garrard's, the Royal Family's jewellers. Catherine declared herself to be in seventh heaven. Roger kissed the top of her nose and told her she looked radiant with happiness.

When she'd phoned her father to tell him the news, Sydney, who was well aware of Roger's reputation, simply asked Catherine if she was sure he was the right man for her. 'Yes, Dad, I am.'

Sarah was cross when Catherine told her she and Roger were planning to marry in London. 'How could you do this to me?' she demanded. 'I'd set my heart on giving you a big wedding extravaganza here at Ashburn some day. I'm very upset with you.' Catherine was sure her mother had been drinking – she was always unreasonably irritable once she had a few drinks on board. She tried to placate her.

'Ma, please don't be angry with me. Roger and I want a small, simple ceremony. We're hoping to get to Sydney in the next few months and if you'd like to give us a big reception at Ashburn, that would mean a lot to us. Will that make you happy?'

'I guess it will have to. I'll start planning now. Let me know when you'll be arriving as soon as you can, and darling . . . I hope Roger knows what a lucky man he is and that he really loves you.'

'He does, Ma.'

Catherine's final call was to her brother. She'd deliberately saved him until last, in case his help had been needed to calm down their parents. She hadn't been sure how they'd react at her decision not to come home to get married. Tom immediately understood her reasoning. Sydney and Sarah's behaviour created such tension and their mother's conduct was so unpredictable that more often than not they spoilt special occasions for everyone else. Tom thought his sister's decision was exactly the right one and he told her so.

And if he was surprised at the swiftness of her romance with Roger, nothing he said revealed any misgivings. Tom was totally supportive, as Catherine had known he would be.

'Sis, if Roger makes you happy then I'm all for him. I hope he's good enough for you.' Tom had always put his sister on a pedestal and Catherine loved him all the more for it. What a lucky woman she was to have two men like Tom and Roger to care about her.

They married the following week at London's Caxton Hall. Somehow the media got wind of it and were there to photograph them getting into their car after the ceremony. Photographs appeared in the British and Australian press. Sally Bellingham, the fashion editor of London's *Daily Mail*, told her readers she thought Catherine the year's most beautiful bride.

She did look breathtakingly lovely in her Giorgio Armani ivory sleeveless silk hand-beaded top, matching layered skirt and silk cape. Roger told her that her halo hat in soft white fox fur made her look like a delicious snow queen. ('And you are,' he'd told her tenderly. 'I knew from the moment we first met.') Catherine carried a spray of gardenias, which Roger had chosen for her.

Jennifer Pickhaver, who was working at the London *Sunday Times*, was Catherine's bridesmaid, and she'd asked Suzanne Stanton, who was holidaying in London with her father, to be a witness. Afterwards

Suzanne hosted a champagne reception at her father's apartment in Mayfair. Roger's brother, Ian, was best man – he was an author with a string of popular gardening books to his name. He and his wife, Caitlin, who illustrated the books, had come from Cardiff to wish them well. Everyone agreed Catherine looked ravishing and that she and Roger made a very handsome couple.

Afterwards they'd flown to France to spend the weekend at the Plaza Athénée on the Avenue Montaigne in Paris. 'The first thing I'm going to do,' said Roger, when they arrived at the hotel, 'is take you to bed and make wild passionate love.'

'How marvellous,' Catherine giggled merrily. 'I bet I'm in bed before you are!' She was but Roger wasn't far behind. At four in the morning they decided they were starving. So Catherine rang room service and ordered pasta with fresh tomatoes and cheese and a bottle of Chateau Margeaux. They ate their dinner in the nude because Roger had insisted Catherine take off her bathrobe.

'Darling, there are no secrets between husband and wife. I worship you and your body and I want to admire your glorious breasts while I eat. This is our honeymoon and my wish should be your command.' After they'd drunk the last drop of wine, Roger put the 'Do Not Disturb' sign on the door and they went back to bed. Catherine had never felt so cherished.

On the Sunday they sailed in a Bateau Mouche on the River Seine and lunched while taking in the sights. 'No one knows who you are, darling, isn't that a relief,' Roger said. It was a strange thing to say, really, but she was so much in love that Catherine didn't think much about it. The only thing on her mind was to enjoy every single moment of their all too brief honeymoon. When it was time to return to London she told Roger she now knew why Paris was known as the city for lovers.

At first she and Roger were ecstatically happy. Roger made himself very much at home at Eaton Square. He took down some of Sydney's paintings and replaced them with paintings of his own. He put his books into the bookcases and placed many of his prized ornaments and knick-knacks in the various rooms.

He and Catherine worked hard during the day and when they got home at night could hardly keep their hands off each other. Catherine thought their sex just got better and better. They flew out to Australia for a week and Sarah gave them a huge reception at Ashburn to which she had asked all of Catherine's friends. Catherine enjoyed introducing them to Roger, who charmed everyone he met.

Her mother had certainly pulled out all the stops for the party. She'd had two giant marquees put in the garden. One had a floor for dancing only and a specially built stage to accommodate the Sydney

Symphony Orchestra, who were providing the music for the evening.

The other marquee, a towering pavilion several storeys high in palest ice blue, its ceiling pleated and draped, was set for dinner, its tables laid with white Irish linen and sapphire blue napkins. Silver candelabras gleamed in the candlelight and silver bowls of cornflowers and gardenias were on each table. Giant white roses tumbled out of silver urns placed in the corners of the marquee.

Sarah had asked Sydney restaurateur and chef Neil Perry to create a meal fit for a king. He more than lived up to his reputation with the dinner to end all dinners. He began by serving 1990 vintage Dom Perignon with freshly shucked Sydney rock oysters and, after an entrée of scrambled egg and spinach tartlets topped with Oscietra caviar, had served slow-roasted saddle of White Rocks veal with truffle sauce.

Coffee and petits fours were served on the verandah and at midnight spectacular fireworks began cascading in gold, silver and red from several points around the waterfront as well as the Harbour Bridge, lighting up the night sky. Sydney had pulled all sorts of strings to get the Bridge for the fireworks display and everyone was suitably impressed. Just as the last cracker exploded, a chocolate wedding cake veiled in white chocolate was wheeled out to the verandah, its arrival announced by two of the Sydney Symphony Orchestra's trumpet players.

One way and another it was quite a night. Sydney and Sarah welcomed everyone to Ashburn as if they were the most happily married couple in the world and Sarah didn't have a drop to drink until after the cake was cut. Before she returned to London, Catherine took her mother out to lunch at Forty One to thank Sarah for giving her and Roger such a tremendous party. She also wanted to find out for herself how her mother was coping. Catherine was anxious about her; she didn't think her mother looked at all well.

'How are you going, Ma?'

Sarah sighed. 'I'm all right, Catherine, but I feel so unwanted. Nobody loves me.'

'I love you.'

'I know, darling, but I miss your father. Some women fall in love with one man and remain in love with him forever, no matter what. That's me – I'm a one-man woman, which means I shall always love your father to bits and pieces. I wish I didn't.' She smiled ruefully at Catherine.

'There are other men. You still look fabulous – you could have some chap eating out of your hand in no time. Instead of turning down all those invitations you get, why don't you accept a couple of them and see what happens,' Catherine urged. 'There's plenty of lonely men around, you know, and you'll never meet anyone if you stay at home by yourself all the time.'

'I really don't think I could,' Sarah demurred.

'Of course you could – ask Susie Blackburn to let people know you're ready to party again.'

'You don't understand, Catherine. Your father's the only man I'll ever want – and one day he'll come back to me. I'm sure of it.'

Catherine thought her mother was mad. How could she love her father after all the hurt he'd caused her? She knew he didn't care about her mother any longer and there was nothing, as far as Catherine could see, that would ever persuade him to resume normal marital relations with Sarah.

'For pity's sake, Ma – how can you still love Dad after the way he's treated you. Your love isn't normal. It's destructive – and you're the one who's being hurt by it.' Catherine spoke crossly – she was so concerned about her mother she couldn't help it. It was so frustrating not to be able to make her see sense.

'Don't get angry with me, Catherine,' Sarah begged. 'I can't help the way I am. We can't all be confident like you – you think you know the answers to all of life's problems, but one day, my darling, you might just find out that you don't. Now that you're in love yourself I think you'll be surprised at how much a woman can forgive the man she adores.'

There was nothing more to say. They finished their lunch. Sarah went home and poured herself a stiff brandy. Catherine went back to her apartment at Bondi, where she and Roger were staying, and wept. Her mother was such a tragedy.

Next day she lunched with Sydney, and was incensed when he didn't mention Sarah once. He did tell her, though, that he was satisfied with the results she was achieving at World Channel and that he thought it would be sensible for her to stay on there for the time being, especially as she now had Roger's career to consider as well as her own.

'Maybe in a couple of years' time Roger might contemplate working in Australia and you could think about returning home then, but it's not something we need concern ourselves about at the moment. You're enjoying yourself in London, aren't you?'

'You know I am, Dad.'

'That's good. However,' he went on, 'I'll still want you to come home every month for the board meeting. Can you manage that now you're married?'

'Of course. Roger travels a great deal and he's as dedicated to his job as I am to mine. He's so busy that he'd probably welcome some time by himself. Anyway, I like being able to get back to Australia every month – I think I'd be incredibly homesick if I didn't.'

'By the way,' Sydney said, 'I've decided to bring Tom home for a while. I want him to go to China to check out a couple of prospects in Hong Kong and Beijing. Murdoch's been over there nosing around and it's essential we put pressure on the Chinese Government to support our expansion plans. I don't want Rupert to edge us out.'

As Catherine took her leave of Sydney he asked her how she was finding married life. 'Are you happy?' he asked.

'Can't you tell, Dad? Married life is sensational!'

But when Catherine and Roger returned to London she noticed a change in him. It was nothing that she could put her finger on, he just seemed different. He'd had a good time in Australia and he raved about Sarah's party but on the flight back he told her he hadn't understood how famous she was in Australia. 'I knew you were well known – I could tell that from the media attention you get in London – but you didn't tell me you were one of your country's favourite celebrities,' he said.

'I never really think about it,' she replied. 'It's something I've lived with most of my life. I've been in the public eye ever since I was a child, because of Dad, and then as I grew up, people just seemed to be interested in me.' She tried to play down her celebrity status but it didn't wash with Roger.

'Come on, Catherine. It's more than that and you know it.'

She did but she could also see that her 'fame', as he persisted in calling it, was something that Roger didn't much like, although Catherine wasn't at all sure why. She hadn't set out to become a public figure – it had all started quite by chance.

While she was studying at university, the editor of the *Sydney Globe* had asked her to write a column about life as a student. It had been well received by the readers and the editor invited her to write for the paper on a regular basis.

After graduation he'd taken her to lunch and suggested that she continue writing for the paper every Saturday, on whatever took her fancy. Her column soon became the talk of the town. She wrote about the arts, architecture, people who ripped off the system, politics, sport, people in need, and sometimes even the weather. She loved the scope the column gave her to bring issues that mattered to the public's attention and it soon became one of the paper's most popular features. It was picked up by its sister paper in Victoria, the *Melbourne Globe*, which meant that something like two million Australians read what she had to say every week. Catherine was often asked on to talk-back radio to debate some of the topics she'd written about.

Then television had beckoned. The ABC asked her to do a daily comment piece for its television network, which reached millions of Australians nationally. She soon became one of the country's most recognised faces. People liked and respected her because it was obvious that she cared about Australia and her opinions were always considered and without bias. The ABC was upset to lose her when she went to run World Channel and had offered to reorganise its programming to allow her to contribute regularly from London but she'd said no, explaining that her new job would take up all her time and energy.

Catherine had been tempted to accept their offer but she knew her father wouldn't approve. He sometimes grumbled that her writing and commentating took her mind off Walker Corp. but she argued that it did nothing of the kind. 'It sharpens my mind, Dad. You've never had reason to complain about my work and I've never let you down.'

Although never quite convinced, Sydney conceded she had a point and privately told his board colleagues that his daughter had a capacity for work that astounded even him.

When Catherine told Roger that she would have to continue going home each month for board commitments he'd reacted badly. 'Obviously separation is the price I have to pay for your success.'

'Don't be childish, Roger,' she said, dismayed by his reaction. 'You knew what I did for a living when you married me. I take my job seriously and you know that. I've been attending regular meetings in Sydney ever since I've been in London. You never said anything about it before we were married. I won't be gone long, only five or six days at the most. Just think how wonderful it will be to make love when I get back. Who was it who said absence makes the heart grow fonder?'

'I couldn't give a damn who said it,' he retorted and left the room. She could hear him making himself a drink. He didn't offer her one.

It was something of a shock to Catherine to discover how possessive Roger was and how much he suddenly seemed to resent her career and her achievements. It hadn't helped at all when the London *Financial Times* published a story on the success of World Channel and declared Catherine Walker to be the 'Wizard of Oz', predicting that she was set to become one of the outstanding women of the new millennium.

If she had to go somewhere on business invariably Roger found a way to be there, too. Like the time she'd gone to Berlin to judge some marketing awards. Roger had arrived without warning; he'd simply turned up at the door of her hotel room. 'Thought I'd surprise you,' he said. She was glad to see him, but in truth, he'd been a bit of a nuisance. This was a working trip and there were things Catherine had agreed to do for the organisers. Roger wasn't pleased when she told him she had obligations to fulfil; he wanted her to spend more time with him. 'I've come all this way,' he said.

'Darling, it's wonderful that you're here but perhaps you should have told me you were coming,' she replied. Somehow she'd managed to keep everyone happy during that trip, but not before she'd developed a fierce tension headache.

In the early days of their marriage Catherine had welcomed his attention but it slowly began to dawn on her that it stemmed from the fact that not only did

Roger resent her success, he also didn't trust her – he didn't like her to be out of his sight for even a second. One night she'd woken up and had to go to the toilet. She'd just sat down when Roger appeared at the bathroom doorway. 'What on earth do you want?' she asked him. 'I wondered where you were,' he said. 'I'm having a pee and if you don't mind I'd prefer to have it without you staring at me.' She couldn't believe he'd got up to find her but when she'd returned to bed, he'd pulled her to him and began to make love to her. She responded immediately, as she always did, and put the incident out of her mind.

However, his attitude away from home often embarrassed her. If they were out somewhere and Catherine spent more than a minute chatting to a man, even someone who worked for World Channel, Roger was immediately at her side being decidedly unfriendly to whoever she was having a conversation with. He seemed to resent anyone who took up her time. Sometimes he seemed to be excessively jealous of her, which puzzled her.

Why couldn't he accept that she loved him so much that no one else could possibly be of interest to her? She couldn't understand how such a seemingly confident man could be so emotionally insecure. He would even ring her at the office several times a day – just to say 'hello', he claimed, but in reality she knew it was to check on her. At times she felt almost smothered by his attention.

He'd put on an awful scene at the British Airways dinner when an old chum from Australia came and sat at her table to have a chat. Roger was somewhere on the other side of the room talking to someone and when he returned to the table, he glared at Catherine's friend before turning to her and saying he wanted to leave. 'Now!' he added angrily as he grabbed her arm and pulled her to her feet. People stared as she tried to look as if it was all meant to happen. 'We have to get to another function, we're running late. See you soon!' she called to a couple of mutual acquaintances as Roger yanked her past them.

When they got outside, Roger turned on her. 'How dare you sit there flirting with that man?' he bellowed.

'I was doing no such thing!' Catherine yelled back at him – she was fed up with his moods.

'I can't leave you alone for a moment, can I? You've always got to have some man grovelling at your feet. You were there with me. How dare you invite some other man to sit in my place at our table! You were giving him "come on" signals. I saw you.'

'You're imagining things, Roger. What has come over you? You left me by myself for at least half an hour – surely you didn't expect me to sit there and not talk to people.' She put her hand on his arm. 'I assure you, he's just an old friend holidaying in London whom I haven't seen in years.'

'Bullshit!' Roger retorted, brushing her hand away as if it were poisonous.

There was no reasoning with him. He'd spoilt the evening for no reason at all. Why? She couldn't work it out. He hadn't always been like this. They'd been so contented in the beginning. She'd even put her friends and other interests on hold so she could spend every possible moment with Roger.

He told her time and time again that he was crazy about her and that he only wanted to make her happy. She usually responded by telling him that she loved him with all her heart. Despite these dramas, their lovemaking was as satisfying as ever, and they always looked forward to Sundays, when their favourite afternoon pleasure was making love. Maybe I've confused lust with love, Catherine wondered. She dismissed the thought at once. Good sex was essential in a relationship. What she and Roger had was definitely love. Maybe whatever has gone wrong is my fault? He keeps telling me I'm too independent – perhaps I am.

Catherine tried to pinpoint exactly when Roger had changed. In the beginning they used to laugh about his 'little black clouds' but lately, not long after they celebrated their first wedding anniversary, his dark moods had become more frequent and unpleasant. She'd had to give a presentation in Birmingham only a week ago and as usual, Roger had insisted on going with her. Afterwards, one of the delegates had come up to congratulate her and to follow through on one of the points she'd made. They'd been talking for about five minutes when she felt Roger's hand on her elbow.

'We have to go.'

'I'm sorry,' said the delegate, 'I'm keeping you.'

'Not at all,' she replied but Roger's voice drowned hers out: 'Yes, you are.' He almost pushed her to the door and out to where his car was parked.

'What's the matter with you now, Roger? I was explaining something to that man. It wouldn't have taken much longer.'

'He was chatting you up and you were enjoying it, too,' he said, his tone nasty.

'Oh, grow up,' she replied angrily. 'We were discussing marketing, nothing more. He was interested in seeing if we could get together on a joint venture.'

'I don't believe you and what's more, you ignored me. Why didn't you introduce me?'

Catherine tried to explain again. 'It was business. You weren't nearby when he came up to talk and then you terminated the discussion before I had a chance to introduce you. We really can't go on like this, Roger. You're making my life – both our lives – a misery.'

Roger braked so suddenly that Catherine's handbag fell off her lap. He'd almost gone through a red light. 'Shit!' he muttered to himself. When the lights turned green he put his foot on the accelerator and the car took off.

'Would you please slow down?' Catherine begged him. He was driving in a way that frightened her.

'Stop giving me instructions!' he shouted. 'You're always telling me what to do. You treat me like a handbag and I'm sick of it! I'm a person in my own right. I don't want to tag along walking two paces behind you as if I was your goddamned consort.'

'Who the hell asked you to?' she snapped furiously. 'I've never asked you to be anyone but the man you are. I wish you wouldn't keep coming with me to everything. I'm sure you are bored, I understand that. You're the one who insists on being wherever I am. I've told you before there is absolutely no need.'

'I knew you'd get to that sooner or later,' he snarled. 'You don't want me around, do you? You don't need me, you don't need any man.'

They didn't speak for the rest of the trip home but once inside the front door Roger took her in his arms and apologised. 'Let's not go to bed angry, Catherine. You know how much I hate it when we do. I'm sorry I reacted like I did. I had a demanding day at the Network and I took it out on you. It was unreasonable of me and it won't happen again.' As he kissed her he slid his hand down the front of her dress. Her nipples were hard. She was furious with herself that he had this power over her.

'Now that's a giveaway,' he laughed. 'Let's do something about it.' He put his arm around her and they walked down the corridor to their bedroom. Roger made love to Catherine with such tenderness that she responded with a passion which astounded her. Once again she put the incident out of her mind. The rest of the week passed happily enough.

On the Sunday, they'd gone for a long walk in Hyde Park and had a late lunch at The Connaught in Mayfair before returning for what they now called their 'Sabbath sex siesta'. It was around four in the afternoon when they got home and as they were undressing Roger asked Catherine if she'd like a liqueur.

'What a good idea – nothing too strong, please.' She got into bed and waited for him to return.

Roger came back with a bottle of Tia Maria. Without saying a word he whipped off the bedclothes and poured Tia Maria over her naked breasts and then began to slowly lick it off.

'Why, darling,' said Catherine, 'you are full of surprises. You're making me feel terribly horny.'

He drizzled more liqueur over her nipples and again sensuously licked it off. 'You're the cream in my Tia Maria, sweetheart,' he said.

He was playing with her clitoris when he told her that he'd like to try something different. 'Do with me as you will,' Catherine replied. (Where had she heard that before? she puzzled.)

'I'd like you to be my slave,' he said, reaching into the bedside drawer and pulling out some silken cords.

'I've always been your devoted slave,' she laughed and held up her arms to him. 'Come here and I'll prove it to you.'

'No, not just yet. I want you completely at my mercy. Just thinking about it excites me. Feel me,' he said, putting her hand on his penis.

'You desire me, darling, I know that,' Catherine said. 'What are you waiting for?'

'I would find it tremendously exciting if I could make love to you while you're completely helpless. May I?'

She nodded, wondering what he had in mind.

Taking the silken cords, he carefully tied her wrists to the bedposts above her head, one to each side. Taking the pillows from under her head he placed them under her bottom and then gently pulling her legs apart, tied her ankles to either side of the bed.

'You look quite delectable,' he said, very softly. 'I could watch you like this all night.' There was a look on his face that she hadn't seen before.

'I'm sure you've never been this powerless before, my dear,' Roger said. 'It must be quite a new experience for you.' His hands were now playing with her nipples. 'You have no idea how erotic it is for me seeing you trussed up like this – I'm going to fuck you until you beg me to stop.'

He stood up and looked at her. 'Are you comfortable? The cords aren't too tight, are they?'

'No,' she said. She didn't tell him how incredibly aroused she was by what he'd done to her. One of her fantasies was about to come true. How had Roger known? She'd fantasised for years about someone ravishing her while she was completely under their control.

She waited for him to put his arms around her and to take her. She implored him with her eyes. Roger knew exactly what she wanted him to do but it turned him on to deny her. He was still playing with her nipples when suddenly he began to pinch them, quite hard.

'Ouch,' Catherine said, 'that hurts.'

He didn't stop and continued to pinch them until he saw tears in her eyes. 'You said I could do with you as I wanted. A slave has no right to complain.'

He turned his attention to her clitoris. She hoped he wasn't going to pinch it too. 'You are so desirable down there,' he whispered. Picking up the bottle of Tia Maria he tipped it over her clitoris. The coldness of the liquid made her jump.

'I am only going to touch you with my tongue,' he told her. Catherine shuddered in anticipation. Bending over her, he began to caress her clitoris with his tongue in the most tantalising way.

'Roger, darling . . .' She lifted her body towards him.

'Patience, my dear. I'm in control, remember?' For a moment Catherine thought his blue eyes looked icy.

He took a large swig of Tia Maria and, holding it in his mouth, lay on top of her – the liqueur trickled down her throat as he kissed her. Then he kissed her eyes and her nose. He tongue-kissed her ears and felt her shake uncontrollably.

'Excited?' He looked at her.

'More than I've ever been in my life.'

'Good, that's exactly what I wanted.'

Catherine trembled again. Every part of her was throbbing and the fact that she couldn't move aroused her beyond belief.

'Do you want me?' Roger asked her softly.

She nodded her head. 'Oh darling, yes I do.'

'I don't think so. Not yet.' He covered her with a blanket. 'Can't have you getting a cold, can we? You might have to miss a day at work and that would never do.'

Then he kissed her. 'You will have to await my pleasure.'

He drew the curtains, turned off the lights and silently went out, closing the door behind him. Then he opened it again.

'I knew you were teasing me,' Catherine laughed. 'Come and get me, for God's sake!'

But there wasn't the slightest hint of jollity in Roger's voice when he replied. 'Didn't anyone ever teach you that patience is a virtue, Catherine? Why don't you think about that while I'm away. In the meantime, I'm going to lock the bedroom door, my dear – I wouldn't want any of the staff to return and find you in such a compromising position. You'd never be able to explain it.' He closed the door again. She heard the key turning in the lock. The room was pitch black.

I hope whatever he's doing doesn't take long, Catherine thought as she lay waiting eagerly for him to return. To her astonishment, she heard the garage doors open and the sound of his car starting up. She couldn't believe it. Surely he isn't going to leave me here like this? The garage door closed with its usual thud and everything was silent. She lay there for some time before she felt the first twinge of panic.

Had Roger lost his mind? He'd been acting strangely lately – his jealous behaviour could hardly be considered normal. Was he having a breakdown? Could that be it? She knew he'd been under a lot of pressure at the Network. Was that the problem? Then she started to get angry. Bloody hell – I don't care what's worrying Roger. Whatever it is doesn't justify him frightening me this way. How long was he going to leave her like this?

She could hear the bedside clock ticking but was unable to see what time it was because Roger had tied her arms and legs in a way that made it difficult for her to move much at all. Making love was the last thing on her mind now. She'd damn well kill him when she got her hands on him.

She had no idea how long she'd been lying there

before she heard him return. He unlocked the door and entered the room. He said nothing. Catherine broke the silence. 'Where the hell have you been?' She almost spat the question at him.

'Slaves are not permitted to ask questions!' He switched on the lights and for a moment their brightness blinded her.

'Are you ready for me?' he asked.

'No, I'm not. Untie me, Roger. I've had enough!'

'You don't mean that, Catherine. I know you better than you know yourself.' As he spoke he undressed. Then, ripping off the blanket, he rubbed her nipples with the palms of his hands.

'Don't touch me.'

He ignored her and began making love to her. Catherine willed herself to resist him but it was no use. She really was Roger's slave when it came to sex, she thought. He could turn her on just by telling Catherine he was visualising fucking her. She felt her resolve melting and at the same time her mother's words came back to haunt Catherine. Now she understood what Sarah had meant when she'd said a woman could forgive the man she loved almost anything.

Roger's kisses were tender at first but then became more ardent – all the time he kept tickling her clitoris ever so lightly with his fingers.

'Aren't you going to untie me?'

'I don't think so. It's so rare having you in such a

submissive situation that I want to enjoy it just a little while longer. You don't mind do you, my dear? I know you want me – what a sexpot you are.' He gave something of a snigger. 'You like everything I do to you, don't you? Go on, admit it.'

'Is that wrong?' she asked. 'You are strange tonight, Roger. Where did you go when you went out? It wasn't pleasant being left here alone while you disappeared for hours.'

'How dare you question me, slave. Now you'll have to be punished.'

Before she knew what was happening, he'd untied her and turned her over his knees. He began to spank her bottom, softly at first and then with more force.

Just when Roger's spanking was becoming intolerable he stopped. He began to kiss her bottom instead and then turned her over to face him and, holding her gently, kissed her lovingly on the mouth.

She began to cry. 'Roger, what do you want from me?'

'Don't talk,' he murmured, kissing her tears. 'Let me love you.' He sucked her breasts ever so softly. Meanwhile, his hands were busy, his fingers pushing into her vagina, touching all the secret parts of her that he knew so well. His tongue explored every part of her until she felt like screaming. He kissed her as if he couldn't get enough of her.

'You are incredibly desirable. As I've told you

many times, nothing is wrong when it comes to sex between a husband and wife. Let me hear you say you want me.' He kissed her passionately, jabbing his tongue into her mouth. 'Say it.'

'I want you.'

'I have a special request for our anniversary.'

'What anniversary?'

'You are so unromantic at times,' Roger said. 'We met on this day eighteen months ago. Don't tell me you've forgotten.'

It was odd, but after all the tension between them recently she had forgotten.

'What's your request?'

'I want to mount you like a dog.'

'No.'

'You are naughty, darling, saying no when you mean yes. Turn over.' When she didn't move his voice changed. 'Do as I say. Turn over, get up on your knees and let me see your cute little backside.'

'No.' He was just like her father. She could see the scene of her childhood vividly. She remembered how shocked she'd been at her father's behaviour, and yet she'd often wondered what it would be like to have sex that way. Roger forced her to turn over and standing, he pulled her up on to her knees.

'Roger,' she said, 'I'm not sure I want to do this.'

He didn't seem to hear her. He was holding her in a way that made it impossible for her to get away from him. He plunged himself into her, intent on only one thing – taking her the way he wanted. He felt himself coming but forced himself not to, determined that Catherine would come with him. He put his hands into her vagina . . . teasing, rubbing, tickling her clitoris. He massaged her nipples. He could feel her responding. She begged him to stop.

'Never, not till you come. No one has ever fucked you like I fuck you. You're a slut in bed, Catherine. I'm going to bang you with my balls in a way you'll never forget.' He was almost out of control. 'Oh yes, oh yes,' he shouted, and he came in a shuddering climax and so did Catherine – Roger's manipulative fingers made sure of that. They massaged her clitoris as softly as a feather until she erupted in a massive, staggering orgasm.

'You were magnificent, darling, as you always are,' Roger told her, pulling the blanket over them. He put his arms around her. 'I think I'm going to sleep for at least a week after that marathon session.'

It was only then that she became aware of Roger's scent. It was a fragrance that she didn't know.

'Have you got a new aftershave on?' she asked. 'I've never smelt it on you before. I'm not sure it's right for you.'

'I'll throw the bottle away in the morning,' he said. 'But now I must sleep. You were wonderful tonight,' he added, with a yawn.

He was asleep in seconds but Catherine remained wide awake. They'd had sex but was it good sex? Roger seemed to take more pleasure in what he perceived as her humiliation rather than in any pleasure she might have had.

But sex aside, she knew he needed professional advice to help him overcome his jealousy. It was out of control. She resolved to talk to him about it in the morning.

However, when they were having their breakfast cup of tea, he informed her that he had to go to Paris and would be staying overnight. 'I'm catching the mid-morning plane so I'll work at home for a couple of hours and then go to Heathrow. I've got so much to do. There are some calls I must make.'

When Catherine left for her early morning meeting he was on the phone. She mouthed a silent goodbye and drove to World Channel. But she never made it to her meeting – on arriving at the office, she was notified about a major satellite breakdown affecting transmission into Asia, which had caused mayhem with programming. It was almost eight in the evening, and she was in desperate need of a gin and tonic, when the problem had been finally fixed and World Channel's operations returned to normal.

'Thank heavens,' she said to Anna Dobkin, her production assistant. 'What a ghastly day it's been. I can't wait to get home and relax. Fortunately my husband has gone to Paris on business so all I have to do when I get home is have a bath and go to bed.'

'Lucky you,' Anna replied. 'My husband's waiting for me at home with our three kids who will demand my attention the moment I walk in the door. Enjoy your peace and quiet, Catherine.'

But when Catherine got home it looked different. At first she couldn't work out why and then she noticed Roger's things weren't there. Where were they? She opened his wardrobes. All his clothes were gone. Had they been burgled? Of course not. Why would a thief take Roger's things and not hers? She sank into a chair. What was going on?

He rang a few hours later and bluntly told her that their marriage was over. 'I won't be coming back. I should have left months ago. Apart from sex – and thank you for last night, it was quite something – we didn't have much else going for us. You don't need me – you don't need anyone. Joanna does.'

*Joanna!* She couldn't believe it. The girl from San Francisco who'd joined the Paris office. Roger was always raving about her. 'She has a great career ahead of her and the makings of another Barbara Walters and we're bloody lucky to have her on our team.'

Now Catherine recollected how often he'd talked about Joanna. She also remembered the fragrance she'd smelt on Roger last night. It was Joanna's – Catherine had remarked on it when they'd met at an industry function at which Roger was speaking. He must have gone to see her while Catherine was tied up in bed. How could he do such a thing to her?

'I'm sorry it didn't work out for us.'

'Don't lie. You're not sorry at all. You couldn't give a

damn and now I know where you were last night when you disappeared – you were with Joanna, weren't you? You bastard, Roger. I hope you used a condom with her before you came home and fucked me!'

'Don't be crude, Catherine. It doesn't suit you.'

'Don't you tell me what I can or can't say.' She was fuming. No doubt everyone else knew he'd been screwing Joanna, too. How humiliating! Why had she allowed herself to be conned by his smooth-talking patter?

'One final thing,' Roger said. 'The only part of me you really ever wanted was my cock. You don't need my name, my money or my position and as for your career, it's a bloody pain in the arse.'

'But you told me you believed in women getting to the top in their careers, having minds of their own, being equal partners.'

'I was lying, sweetheart. Men don't want women to be superior at anything. They want them to be submissive, grateful for whatever crumbs we toss their way.'

She was shattered. This can't be happening. She'd thought she knew Roger – but he was a completely different person. Or was he? Maybe he'd always been this way but she'd been too enamoured to see the real Roger.

'So last night . . .'

'Was a lesson for you and don't ever forget it. You may be the Wizard of Oz, the future whiz kid of the millennium, but when all that's put aside you're just a woman who wants a man to turn you on and fuck you.

'You're a good lay, Catherine, better than most – but then you always have been superior at everything, haven't you? Seeing you last night accepting whatever I dished out and liking it, too, gave me more satisfaction than you'll ever know.' He began to laugh.

Catherine didn't want to hear any more. My God, he hated her that much. She felt sick. How could she ever have loved him? What a bloody fool she was.

She should have realised that he had another woman. How could she have ignored his reputation? She'd been so naive to think that she'd be the woman who would be able to change him. Everything was clear now. She knew why he'd been spending so many nights in Paris instead of coming home. Why hadn't she recognised the signs earlier? He'd gone on a diet, had begun exercising at the gym and had even bought new underpants, a sure-fire giveaway.

And because he was having an affair and knew he couldn't be trusted, he'd decided she couldn't be either – no wonder he'd been so moody and jealous. But his dislike of her was more than that. Her self-sufficiency disconcerted him. He couldn't accept that she was a person in her own right and he'd 'punished' her by making love to her while degrading her for his own entertainment. He hadn't valued her feelings for him at all. She felt utterly mortified.

No sooner was the word out that Roger had left

home than all sorts of people, including those she'd thought of as close pals, confirmed Catherine's suspicions. He'd conducted his affair with Joanna right under her nose. Her friends told her they'd been shocked to see him out with another woman but didn't know how to tell her. She learnt that Roger and Joanna were a regular item at Le Gavroche in Upper Brook Street, a notable lovers' retreat which had the reputation for being the most discreet dining room in London, with a convenient back door for quick exits from jealous spouses.

Catherine felt wretched and embarrassed. How would she be able to face people? Journalists from *The Sun* staked out her house, trying to catch her leaving so they could ask her how she felt. She left undetected by the back door and took up residence at The Connaught. It was known for its unobtrusive service and for the privacy that it afforded its guests, which was just what she needed. Finally *The Sun* gave up trying to speak to her and with the help of so-called 'friends' ran a story about her and Roger, with the heading 'BAD SPELL FOR THE WIZARD OF OZ'.

The news is not good for Australian media boss Catherine Walker. Roger Rowland, her husband of little more than a year, has left her for a younger woman – 25-year-old Joanna Gordon, the up and coming anchor woman of his British-Euro Network News. Walker has the reputation

for being a workaholic and friends say this was a
contributing factor to the marriage breakdown . . .

What rot, Catherine thought. I'm not a workaholic.
Who told the newspaper such rubbish? Roger, of
course! Who else? He never could resist passing on
what he considered a good news story and the fact
that this one was personal wouldn't deter him at all.
Catherine put on a brave face at the office but at
night she returned to The Connaught and wept her
heart out. This went on for a week and then, after a
night of soul-searching, she told herself enough was
enough. She had to pull herself together. From now
on she was going to look after Number One.

She rang Walker Corp. in Australia and asked to
speak to her father. 'Dad, it's Catherine . . .' She
paused to listen to what he was saying. 'How on earth
do you think I feel? Bloody awful! Please, Dad, I don't
want to talk about it. That's not why I'm ringing you.

'This may come as something of a shock and I'm
sorry if it does, but I'm resigning from Walker Corp.
I want to come home to Australia. There's something
else I want to do and I've made up my mind that
now is the time. I don't want to go into too much
detail over the phone, except to say that I want to do
my own thing.

'I'll explain everything when I get back. As soon
as I get off the plane I'll come straight to your office.'

# Chapter Ten

It took Catherine a month to wind up a couple of deals she'd been working on, pack up her belongings at Eaton Square and brief Huxley Edwards, the man who was going to take over her job at World Channel. Huxley was held in high regard by her father and hadn't put a foot wrong since joining the company. A brilliant strategist, he could spot a winning deal long before anyone else, and was blessed with a photographic memory. Huxley Edwards was a man going places and everyone knew it.

He'd started his career as a salesman selling electrical goods at Cooper's Electrics, a fast-growing, statewide discount group in Victoria. His father had deserted his mother and family when Huxley was ten. Fortunately Vivienne Edwards was a qualified accountant and had a good job at Kerry Packer's Channel Nine TV station, in the Melbourne suburb of Richmond, about five minutes away from where the family lived. It was an ideal arrangement. By keeping to a careful budget and without any financial help at all from her husband, Vivienne had educated and raised Huxley and his younger sister, Megan, and even managed to take them to Fiji and Disneyland in Los Angeles during the school holidays. They were well-behaved, thoughtful kids and Vivienne thought the world of them.

She loved her job and at dinnertime would entertain Huxley and Megan with stories of the goings-on of the TV personalities and other happenings at the channel. Huxley always thought she made television sound exciting, as if there were never a dull moment. He made up his mind that one day he'd work in television, too.

After he'd finished school he announced that he was going to university but that he'd pay his own way. 'You've done enough for me, Mum, and I'll always be grateful.' He put his arm around her and gave her a hug. 'You're the best. How do you do it?'

'It just comes naturally, son, you should know that by now!' Vivienne glowed with contentment. There had always been a special rapport between her and Huxley. Megan used to tease them about being so alike. 'You even lose your temper the same way,' she'd laugh.

Huxley had only one complaint and that was his name. 'Where did you get the name Huxley?' he'd demanded of his mother one day. 'Couldn't you have called me something simple like John or Peter?'

'Your father and I had been having one of those "What will we call the new baby?" sessions,' she explained, 'and I looked down at the book I was reading, which just happened to be Aldous Huxley's *Brave New World*, and bingo! If you want to stand out in the crowd you need a name people will remember, and mark my words, Huxley, they *will* remember your name, I just know it. One day you'll thank me for giving you such a distinctive name.'

A natural born salesman with charm and the gift of the gab, Huxley worked at Cooper's Electrics during the day, and put himself through university at night. He completed degrees in Accountancy and Economics and not long before he graduated he joined the sales department of Walker Television Productions, Melbourne, which packaged entertainment, drama, news and current affairs, travel documentaries, lifestyle and quiz shows and sold them to TV networks around the world as well as Australia.

Everything about television gave Huxley a buzz: the immediacy of the daily news programmes, the creation of shows, the tension, the gamble the programmers took in buying new shows that they hoped would satisfy large numbers of viewers – some shows were immediate hits; others, no matter how good their casts, were dismal failures. He admired the creativity of the many talented men and women who came up with story lines and turned them into reality and he even enjoyed the temperaments of the stars. But what appealed to him most of all was the power of the medium to influence viewers and the muscle television gave to the people who controlled it. Years later, when giving an interview to the respected American broadcaster Larry King, Huxley told him that television had been one of the great love affairs of his life.

He spent his time at Walker Television Productions learning everything he could, determined to find out what made the company tick, letting nothing and no one distract him. He had little time for anything but work, not even friends or serious relationships, although he always had a pretty girl on his arm when it was necessary and he talked a lot about women when he had a drink with the other sales staff at the local pub.

Although time was always at a premium he usually managed a beer or two on a Friday night because he liked to catch up on the office gossip, to find out what was what, who was sleeping with whom and whatever else was happening. People were always more relaxed on Fridays in anticipation of the weekend coming up and Huxley usually picked up useful information. He was a good listener – his mother had taught him that.

'Listen, Huxley, always listen,' she'd tell him,

'because that's how you learn. Most people talk too much and don't listen enough.' It didn't take him long to find out that his mother was right as usual.

After three years in the Melbourne office Huxley asked for a transfer to Sydney, knowing that Walker Corp. Television's headquarters were there and that it was the only way for him to get to top management. As it happened, there was an opening for someone to run the sales division of Walker Cable. While government regulations prevented Sydney Walker from owning free-to-air TV stations as well as newspapers, they didn't stop him owning cable TV. However, establishing pay-TV in a country the size of Australia was an expensive exercise.

Huxley's outstanding track record had been noted. The transfer was granted without delay and before long he was bringing in record business. No one else in sales came anywhere near matching his figures. He'd even managed to persuade the upmarket retailer Horton's to advertise with Walker Cable, something the company had never managed to do before. Many attempts and propositions had been put to Horton's but it had maintained that Walker Cable didn't have the right image. Huxley had put together a scheme that allowed Horton's to sample the reach of Walker Cable with a commercial that he assured them could be made for a modest sum. The retailer agreed that if it saw a ten per cent lift in sales within eight weeks of the campaign going to air it would consider spending one million dollars with Walker Cable over a two-year period.

Horton's had stores in every capital city of Australia. In the late '70s and '80s the company had been badly managed. The board was like many in Australia at that time – the directors were all men who'd had a private school education, played golf at the same kind of elite club, and had good-looking, stay-at-home wives who never shopped at Horton's because they preferred to do their shopping overseas. As did the directors themselves, except when they were stocking their cellars, because Horton's gave its directors twenty per cent off all liquor purchases.

No one on the board had retail experience but the directors had never considered such lack of knowledge a problem, arguing that as long as the bottom line was healthy no one could possibly complain. Horton's excellent reputation kept the problem hidden until the early '90s, when changing lifestyles, work patterns and a recession, which the Prime Minister of the day told Australia 'it had to have', changed the shopping habits of many people, especially women. At a board meeting in 1995, shareholders realised that Horton's was being left behind by other, brighter, retailers and that the management skills of the board left much to be desired. For the first time in its history Horton's recorded a loss of several million dollars. Shareholders demanded the resignation of Francis Carroll, the managing director, appointed by the board three years earlier.

Carroll had run department stores in Houston, USA, but had never come to grips with the national branding of Horton's, and the differences between the states of Australia. He failed to appreciate just how large a continent Australia is and how the different states have disparate tastes and needs. Even the weather makes a difference – it snows in New South Wales, Victoria and Tasmania but not in any of the other states and territories. Most Queenslanders don't own an overcoat because it simply never gets cold enough to wear one even in winter, whereas Melburnians consider an overcoat to be an essential item. It was fine points like these that escaped Francis Carroll's notice – small but essential facts that ultimately made the difference between success and failure.

Francis had one other major problem. He didn't like Australians. He thought they were crass and loud and was never at ease in their company. In a way he was quite relieved when the board asked him to step down. He couldn't wait to leave the place and he hoped he'd never hear the expression 'G'day mate' again.

Robert Horton Hopewell was invited to succeed him. His mother, Rosalind, had been a Horton and had worked in Horton's marketing department before marrying Englishman Lord Anthony Hopewell and making her home with him on his estate, Great Pollards, in Wadhurst, Sussex. They cherished Robert, who was their only child, but when he was in his teens and boarding at Eton, the pair had been tragically killed in an aeroplane crash in Africa, on their way to Tanzania where they'd planned to climb Mount Kilimanjaro.

Robert's father had been an only child, too, and both his parents were dead. In their will the Hopewells had appointed Rosalind's brother, Andrew, and his wife, Lizzie, as their son's guardians. Andrew and Lizzie flew to England to bring Robert back to Australia to live with them at their large, comfortable home in the Sydney waterfront suburb of Darling Point with their four sons Matt, Jeremy, George and Simon. They welcomed him into their family as if he were one of their own.

He completed his schooling with his cousins at nearby Cranbrook School and during the long summer school holidays he would serve behind a counter at Horton's Sydney store, where his uncle was national group advertising and marketing director. His aunt and uncle were impressed with his eagerness to get to work, declaring that retailing was in his blood. Robert would have been happy to start working at Horton's the moment he left school but at his uncle's insistence he went to Sydney University and studied Law, graduating with honours.

He then joined Horton's as an executive trainee, starting in men's shoes and working his way up from salesman to buyer, before being transferred to other Horton's stores around Australia, where he worked in a variety of management positions. By the time he was thirty-five there wasn't much he didn't know about retailing.

At thirty-eight he was appointed state manager of Horton's Brisbane, turning it not only into the best performing store in Queensland, but also in Australia. He was there when the board asked Francis Carroll to leave and was quickly summoned back to Sydney to be offered the job of managing director and chief executive officer. Robert didn't hesitate – this was the job he'd dreamt of getting. He intended to turn Horton's into the greatest department store group the world had ever seen. He also changed his surname by deed poll to Horton and hoped his father wouldn't turn in his grave.

Robert had liked Huxley Edwards the moment the man walked in his door, recognising at once that they were both ambitious men. Robert was always prepared to take a gamble if someone presented him with an objective that had potential – and he was very taken with the pitch that Huxley had made on behalf of Walker Cable, which he knew was signing up new subscribers in the thousands every month. Pay-TV's success had taken quite a few people by surprise. Private research had shown Robert that cable viewers were increasingly the kind of people who shopped at Horton's and after looking at Huxley's figures as well as the audience demographics, he was confident that Horton's had nothing to lose, especially as Walker Cable had offered to write, produce and make the commercial. It was an offer too good to refuse.

Of course, he hadn't a clue as to the lengths Huxley was prepared to go to in order to ensure that the Horton's commercial delivered all he had promised. Huxley intended to pull out all the stops. Catherine had been working at Walker Cable at the time, as acting managing director. She and Huxley got on well and had professional admiration for each other's respective talents. Catherine's gut instinct told her Huxley was a man who could be trusted.

Huxley wasn't a great believer in gut instinct but he'd listened to what people at Walker Cable thought about Catherine and the way she carried out her duties and treated 'the workers'. All the evidence reinforced what he'd heard – she was good at what she did and she wasn't afraid to work hard to get results. It was the beginning of a friendship that would grow to mean a great deal to both of them over the years. Huxley also thought Catherine was the most gorgeous-looking woman he'd ever met.

Determined that his campaign for Horton's would be successful, Huxley had asked for half an hour of

Catherine's time to take her through it. 'I think it's brilliant,' she told him afterwards. Buoyed by her enthusiasm he then suggested that Walker Cable give Horton's a hefty parcel of bonus spots at no charge – something Sydney Walker frowned on.

'I know it's not company policy to ever give free spots,' Huxley told her, 'but I believe what I'm proposing should be considered as an investment that will bring us handsome returns in the long run. Giving Horton's extra spots will complement their paid schedule handsomely and it will be like insurance for us. Walker Cable has twenty-two channels. I think we should give Horton's spots on all of them.'

'We'd go broke pretty quickly if you wanted to do something like this for all our clients,' Catherine said. But Huxley had glimpsed the twinkle in her eye and knew she was on side.

'We're not carrying anything like our full quota of advertisements,' he continued, 'and by given Horton's placement on all our channels we'll look like we're doing much better than we really are. I know we might get a few complaints about too much advertising – not that I'd ever consider that a problem,' he chuckled, 'but we can handle that. The fact is, most people like watching advertisements and they'd be lost without them. How else would they know what's coming to a store near them?'

'I couldn't agree with you more.' Catherine sat

back in her chair observing Huxley closely. What a salesman – no wonder he brings us in so much business. He's rather handsome too, she thought – those brown eyes and black hair give him a kind of Cary Grant look. He must be about as tall as Tom, and he doesn't have an ounce of fat on him. She liked the way he was dressed. Catherine always admired a man who cared about his appearance.

Huxley looked particularly good that day – he'd made sure of that – because he was determined to make an impact on Catherine. When he was selling, especially to the boss, he left nothing to chance. His dark navy and maroon pinstriped wool suit was double-breasted and looked as if it had been cut on Huxley's body. The fit was superb and Catherine's expert eye picked it for the Zegna that it was. Just the right amount of the cuff of his white shirt showed below the arms of his jacket. His Hermès tie – Catherine recognised the label at once, her father always wore Hermès ties – was in blues and maroon, cleverly picking up the colours in his suit. He's definitely a class act, Catherine decided. She nodded encouragingly for him to continue.

'Cable TV needs good, upmarket advertising and the Horton's campaign will be exactly that. I promise you, Catherine, it will work its butt off for Horton's and they won't be the only ones who'll reap the rewards. We'll do well, too. It will get people talking about us. We should run a new subscription campaign at the same time. There's a chance for us to put on some significant numbers.'

He leant forward in his chair. 'What do you think?' he asked. Before she could say anything her phone rang. 'Sorry,' she said to Huxley as she took the call, 'it must be something urgent because I said I didn't want any interruptions.' He watched her as she gave instructions to whoever was on the other end of the line. God, her eyes are incredible, he thought, and when she smiles, I can feel myself melting.

As if she could read his mind, Catherine hung up the phone and smiled at him. Huxley's heart flip flopped. 'I'm sure what you're suggesting is exactly the way for us to go and any success we have with Horton's might finally convince Cheng & Farquhar to recommend us to their other clients. I've been trying to talk William Cheng into sampling Walker Cable every month for the last twelve months and getting nowhere. With their reputation and those prestige clients of theirs we would really rake in the dollars if we could get them to put us on a recommended schedule to their clients.'

'It's in the bag,' Huxley said triumphantly, 'especially if you okay those bonus spots. We'll not only get that one million dollars from Horton's but we'll be able to build on the success of what we've done for them to convince the other reluctant so-and-sos to spend money with us also. It's just what we need to get the momentum rolling.'

'If you pull this off you could probably expect a bonus yourself,' Catherine told him.

'I'd never say no to that,' he replied with a grin. 'But seriously, Catherine, it's essential advertisers know Walker Cable offers a real difference and that, with us, their advertisements won't get lost among the clutter as they so often do on free-to-air TV. What's more, we won't just get results for our advertisers but we'll look after them and service their needs in a way that no one else can match. I will love them, even fuck them to death, if that's what they want.'

Catherine laughed. 'I don't think the supreme sacrifice will be required – so rest easy, Huxley.' She laughed again and so did he. They were very relaxed with each other – something both were aware of – as if they'd known each other for years. Catherine's blue eyes flashed with excitement. 'Don't pussyfoot, Huxley – let's do it!'

He could have kissed her. Instead he simply thanked her.


The Horton's promotion was exceptional and sophisticated. By promising to make and show special hour-long documentaries about their favourite charities on Walker Cable – as well as paying them a handsome fee – Huxley had persuaded Sophia Loren and Gwyneth Paltrow to appear in the retailer's commercial with the message 'Horton's is Heavenly'. It had a catchy theme tune and when Sophia and Gwyneth appeared as angels showing the way through Horton's the humour of the situation struck a chord with the viewers.

The campaign was successful beyond Huxley's and Catherine's expectations, not to mention Robert Horton's. It had helped that Huxley had placed stories about what he coined 'an exciting new concept in retail advertising' as well as leaked news about some of the fabulous specials that would be on sale at Horton's to coincide with the advertising campaign. This led to plenty of discussion on talk-back radio around the nation. He'd also arranged an exclusive interview on the top-rating free-to-air TV program *60 Minutes* with Sophia and Gwyneth talking about the trials and tribulations of being beautiful – and naturally, Horton's got a good plug. There was no way in hell, Huxley assured Catherine, that the Horton's campaign wasn't going to work.

'We may be cable but that doesn't mean we can't exploit our free-to-air colleagues,' he told her. 'They're so easy to manipulate. All you have to do is mention a big-name star and you've got them. I wish all my selling were as easy.'

The morning after the commercials went to air, customers were lined up outside Horton's waiting for the stores to open their doors. The retailer did record business, which continued for the entire eight weeks of the campaign. Sales increased by twelve per cent. Robert asked Huxley and Catherine to lunch in the store's boardroom to celebrate and afterwards they went to his office, where he signed the documents committing Horton's to spending one million dollars with Walker Cable as agreed.

'I'm looking forward to further excellent results from our association with Walker Cable,' he said. 'I'm glad you were so persistent.'

'Me too,' Huxley replied.

'If Walker Television continues to work for us as well as it has so far,' Robert continued, 'you can expect an even bigger slice of Horton's advertising budget. We've got some brilliant events planned for the next couple of years, and I believe Walker Cable would be the perfect medium for us to use to tell our customers about what we have planned. We're going to be the most exciting and progressive department store retailer in Australia – in the world, actually,' he added.

There was a knock at the door. It was William Cheng. Robert invited him to join them. 'I've asked William here,' he said, 'because as you know his agency looks after our advertising – except when we're accepting free creative work from you, Huxley. I think it would be helpful to you if he were to out-line some of the things we've got in mind. I'd also appreciate your input.'

William Cheng gave Catherine and Huxley a brief sketch of Horton's future retailing plans before suggesting they come to the agency later in the week for a more thorough briefing with his creative people. He told Catherine he'd call her office to fix a mutually suitable time.

She and Huxley took their leave and on the way down in the lift they couldn't help smiling happily at each other. 'We're grinning like a couple of Cheshire cats,' Catherine laughed.

'Yes, and it feels bloody good,' Huxley said. 'We've got Horton's and it was more than apparent that we've finally won over William Cheng. That agency of his is about to put a lot more business our way, and not before time.'

'I know. Great work, Huxley, and well done.'

His success with the Horton's campaign had brought Huxley to Sydney's attention, although Catherine had already praised his performance to her father several times. But Sydney always wanted to see results and it was the million dollars from Horton's on the projected budget sheets that made him sit up and take notice. Money always had that effect on him.

'I bet that Huxley could sell a pen of pigs to a Jewish commune,' Sydney said. 'Look at his sales figures. Why can't the rest of them get figures like his, that's what I'd like to know.'

He told Catherine he wanted Huxley to come and

have lunch with him. 'Tell him to be here at twelve-thirty tomorrow,' he ordered.

When she'd rung Huxley to let him know her father wanted to see him, he'd asked her if she had any advice for him. 'Yes, I do,' Catherine had replied. 'It might be worthwhile looking over the transaction with Spooners that didn't work out the way you thought it would.'

The next day Huxley was sitting opposite Sydney Walker in his office. His stomach was churning, but he was confident about what he'd done and what he could do for Walker Cable. He knew Sydney would probably spring a couple of tricky questions on him – he'd been warned about the way the old man operated by others who'd been in the same seat as he was sitting in now. His brain was on alert. He remembered something his mother had told him: 'If you want to succeed, always make sure your brain is in control of your mouth.

'Think before you speak, Huxley,' she would tell him. 'Most people just open their mouths and say the first thing that comes into their heads. Don't fall into that trap. When people ask you a tricky question, ask yourself what lies behind that question. What are they really trying to find out about you?'

Sydney pulled out a box of Cohiba Cuban cigars. It was all he smoked. 'Like one?' He offered the box to Huxley.

'No thank you, Mr Walker, I don't smoke.' He

hated the smell of cigars; they always made him cough. As he watched Sydney light up he prayed it wouldn't happen to him this time.

Sydney leant back in his chair, observing Huxley closely, liking the self-assured way he had about him. 'You've done a good job at Walker Cable. Your results are commendable.'

'Thank you, Mr Walker,' Huxley said, hoping he looked suitably modest.

'But what about that deal with Spooners you fucked up? What went wrong there?'

God, he doesn't waste time in going for the jugular, thought Huxley. 'It was my fault completely, Mr Walker. I signed off on that contract and I accept full responsibility. But in my own defence I have to say there were so many unusual factors, the main one being the government, which threw a spanner in the works by changing the rules on what Spooners could and couldn't say about their new telecommunications equipment and services. Gerald Campbell, the Communications Minister, decided that the advertising promotion Spooners had planned would give them an unfair advantage over their competitors.'

'The man's a fucking idiot,' Sydney declared.

'I agree, but he calls the shots – or rather the government does – and there was nothing I could do to alter the decision. I had several discussions with him in an effort to persuade him to change his mind, but he wouldn't consider it. I've learnt a lot trying to make that deal come off and if I knew then what I know now, I probably wouldn't have done it. But I did. I'm sorry it didn't work out.'

Later Sydney told Catherine he'd liked the way Huxley had handled himself. 'He didn't try to blame anyone else. He took the responsibility. It's the mark of a good man if he's able to admit he has made a mistake. I can understand why you've always spoken so highly of him.'

At the time he said to Huxley: 'We all make mistakes, and one day there'll be an opportunity for us to straighten out the government. I'm glad to hear you learnt something out of it all.' He sat back and looked at the young man. 'But, putting that aside, you've had it pretty easy at Walker Cable, don't you think?'

'No, I don't,' said Huxley, immediately on guard. What sort of bloody question was Sydney going to toss at him now? 'Easy? What do you mean?'

'Walker Cable is a good operation, the finest in Australia and I reckon probably the world. We dominate the market. We've superlative entertainment, excellent talk, first-class drama, fun kids' shows that youngsters actually like to watch. Our arrangement with 21st Century Global has given us an outstanding collection of movies, including first releases. Our competitors can't get near us.

'I know we've had something of an image problem – those upmarket advertisers are so up themselves they can't see themselves coming – but we're turning that around. You've played an important part in that and you'll find my appreciation reflected in new remuneration arrangements I'm going to put into place. I think you'll be more than satisfied and,' Sydney paused to take a puff on his cigar, 'if you're not, don't bother coming to see me about it. I won't give you a dollar more – for the time being, that is.'

Huxley began to thank him but Sydney kept talking. 'Not now,' he said. 'You can thank me later.' And he held up his hand to silence him. 'As I was saying, you've had it easy – I want to give you something really hard to sell.'

'What did you have in mind, Mr Walker?'

'Walker Sports Cable. I want to make some money out of it. When I went into cable I knew I'd need deep pockets and I've got them, but that doesn't mean I want to dig into them for ever. We haven't managed to make the kind of profits I want from sport and I know there's plenty of money to be made. We just haven't come up with the right formula – even though we've got the best venue in the country.'

Sydney had supported the Labor government in the last election when it was then in opposition. Nothing had been too much trouble – whenever a Walker Corp. publication or programme could, it pushed the Labor cause.

Even Sydney himself had become publicly involved. He agreed to say a few words at a fundraiser in support of the Labor leader, Jim Griffin, introducing him as a man who was a good friend, honest and caring – rare qualities in a politician, according to Sydney. 'Jim Griffin is also a man who wears his heart on his sleeve for Australia and the only man with the vision to lead our nation confidently and prosperously through the challenges that await us in the next decade,' he told the audience, as well as millions of other Australians by courtesy of Walker Cable and his newspapers.

Jim Griffin and Labor had a landslide victory, recapturing Labor's heartland. Labor paid for some of its advertising but Sydney donated the rest. He authorised hundreds of thousands of dollars' worth of free advertising, which was carefully hidden in Walker Corp.'s account books.

Jim Griffin hadn't been Prime Minister for more than a month when he announced Walker Corp. had been given the okay to build a massive 150 000-seat stadium at the former Australian navy site at Garden Island. It was one of the few prime pieces of real estate left on the Sydney Harbour foreshore and commanded views of the Opera House and the Bridge. The announcement took everyone by surprise – except Sydney. He knew the Labor Party always repaid its debts to people who did them a favour and he'd had the Garden Island development well and truly thought out long before Jim Griffin signed the official documents. It was one of Sydney Walker's greatest moments, although the decision caused enormous controversy. There was an immediate outcry from the National Trust and other conservation groups but their protests were useless. The deal was done.

Ever since the city of Sydney had won the rights to stage the 2000 Olympics, Australia had gone into a kind of sports stupor, the consensus being that sport equalled money. To launch the new Walker Stadium, Sydney planned to stage the Millennium Master Series, an initiative of the long-serving Olympic president Juan Antonio Samaranch, whom he had courted over a number of years. The plan was to run the series somewhat like a mini Olympics – but with only six sports being represented: tennis, swimming, cricket, soccer, athletics and gymnastics.

Bookings for the Master Series were going well but future bookings for the Walker Stadium were lean and Sydney wasn't happy. 'The Walker Stadium and Walker Sports Cable are our two major problem areas,' he said to Huxley. 'I want you to fix them both.

'I'm hungry,' he said abruptly, snuffing out his cigar. 'Let's eat – I can never think properly on an empty stomach.' He stood up. Huxley followed suit. 'I hope you like sausages,' Sydney said, as he opened the door between his office and his dining room.

'I do, Mr Walker,' Huxley assured him.

Once the butler had served them and they were alone again, Sydney resumed their conversation. 'If you can turn Walker Sports Cable and the Walker Stadium into profit-makers, your future with me is guaranteed.'

'That's some challenge you're offering me, Mr Walker,' Huxley replied. 'How long do I have to turn things around?'

'I'll let you know when you've run out of time,' Sydney responded. 'Just get me results – quickly! Everyone thinks that because I've got plenty of money I'll finance the sports channel forever, in spite of its losses. Well, they're wrong. You're supposed to be our resident genius. What ideas do you have?' he demanded.

Huxley was well aware of Sydney's dissatisfaction with the way that the sports channel was operating. In his spare time, he'd been working on a proposal, but he hadn't expected to be asked to produce it quite so soon. He'd heard how difficult the old man was to work with at the moment – Sydney had never been one to hide his frustration when things weren't going the way he wanted. He made sure everyone bore the brunt of his displeasure. Huxley had no desire to be on the receiving end of Sydney's wrath and wished he'd had a couple more weeks to tidy up any loose ends. But there was no chance of that. Sydney was waiting impatiently.

Just as Huxley drew breath and was about to speak, Sydney got up from the table. 'I need a cigar. Let's go back in here.' Without waiting for a reply he strode back to his office. Huxley scrambled after him. 'We'll have coffee here.' Sydney buzzed twice and the butler appeared with the coffee tray. 'Put it down there,' he instructed, pointing to the corner of his desk. 'We'll look after ourselves.' He lit a cigar and puffed on it appreciatively. 'Right,' he said to Huxley, 'continue.'

'We need to introduce super sport to Walker Sports Cable,' Huxley said. He spoke slowly and positively, hoping Sydney's curiosity would be immediately aroused.

It was, but not in the way he'd hoped. 'Super sport! What the fuck do you mean? What's super sport?'

'Mr Walker, if you'd just hear me out I'm sure you'll see the possibilities of what I'm suggesting. It's a question of us buying the best. What I'm recommending will cost you money to begin with, but you'll get it all back. I'm sure there's plenty of money to be milked from sport.'

'Buying the best? Who's left that Packer and Murdoch don't own?'

'Mr Walker, please,' Huxley said, 'just give me a few minutes without interruption.' Sydney waved at him to go on.

'Everyone is in sport today to make money – the

218

players, the promoters, the media, and anyone else who in one way or another is connected with a sport of some kind, and especially a sport that spectators love to watch. The one thing they all have in common is the desire to accumulate as much money as they possibly can.' Huxley took a deep breath, getting into his stride.

'That was one impossible-to-ignore factor that shone through when Packer started World Series Cricket in the '70s and Murdoch came up with Super League in the early '90s. The players were more concerned about money than the sport they played. Sure, they want to play well, but at the end of the day it was apparent they were only interested in how much money they'd make rather than how much they made on the scoreboard. This means every player can be bought – it's just a question of agreeing on the price.

'Now . . .' Huxley paused, to see if Sydney had any questions for him yet.

'Go on, go on,' Sydney ordered.

'Walker Sports Cable will only pay its way when viewers are compelled to turn it on. The way to do that is to create events of such magnitude that people will clamour to watch them.'

'Will you get to the point, man,' Sydney said impatiently. 'Get to the fucking point.'

'I'm going as fast as I can,' Huxley protested. Shit, this is harder than I'd thought it would be. I wish the old man would calm down. Taking another deep breath, he went on: 'We need to create sporting competitions that can be seen *only* on Walker Sports Cable.'

'What about the spectators?'

'We don't need spectators, Mr Walker.' Huxley was silent for just a second. He wanted his words to make an impact. They did. Sydney leant forward as if anxious not to miss a word. 'We're not going to make money from spectators,' Huxley said with a grin. 'Well, not the conventional kind of spectators, sitting in some open-air stadium, many of them drunk as skunks or wishing they were if they have the misfortune to be in a venue with an alcohol ban, and happy to queue for hours for lousy takeaway food. We don't need that kind of spectator.

'We want our bums on seats in people's lounge rooms, where they are paying to watch Walker Sports Cable and events that we have personally organised and which are sponsored by well-heeled advertisers. We want people to subscribe to our service – and when we have a really big sports event, we'll charge them extra, for the privilege of watching. And because they won't be able to see their heroes anywhere else but on Walker Cable, they'll be happy to pay.'

'How do you propose we do that?' Sydney was showing his interest despite himself.

'We buy up the best players in the world in

cricket, tennis, rugby league, union, soccer, athletics, golf, even polo if we think we can make a buck out of it. Walker Sports Cable will own the cream of sports stars from every country in the world.

'Look at the way the cricketers accepted Packer's money to join World Series. They'll join us in a flash because they're fed up wearing themselves out playing cricket almost twelve months of the year. They've got demanding travel schedules that constantly disrupt their family lives. I've heard that their wives are complaining they're never home and several of them are wishing they had more time to be with their children. They're ripe for a takeover.

'We'll offer them a more civilised way of living by having a series that goes only six or eight months, maybe less, and is played at specially built indoor stadiums – such as the Walker Stadium at Garden Island – where they won't be subjected to any weather delays or have to put up with the drunken behaviour of the morons in the crowd.' Huxley was trying not to look too pleased but he was feeling very sure of himself now, and he knew Sydney was eager to hear more.

Sydney had put his feet up on his desk. It just might work, he thought. 'Walker Sports Cable – simply the best!' He puffed on his cigar. 'I like it.' For the first time since Huxley had started outlining his plan he smiled. 'So, how do we make it work?'

Huxley couldn't wait to tell him. 'Our sporting set

221

will always be closed to spectators and the only way our players can be seen will be on Walker Sports Cable. There'll be fewer demands on them, not as many matches, and because our players will be the best in the world, fans everywhere will be glued to Walker Sports Cable to see their heroes perform. I'm convinced it will work.'

'Me too,' Sydney said.

Huxley felt the tension lifting. 'Shall I go on?' he asked. Sydney gave him a nod.

'We could start with the cricket,' he explained, 'and then follow with rugby union, soccer, tennis, swimming, athletics – and just think what we could do with golf. It's one of the most watched games in the world!

'Surprise must be a key element of our approach. Only a select group of people can know what we're planning. Packer and Murdoch and the others have become complacent about sport. They think they've done all that's possible and have taken themselves off to their various empires to plot and plan something else. They won't be expecting Walker Sports Cable to take them on and by the time they cotton on to what we're doing it will be too late for them to do anything about it.'

Sydney was excited. A good idea always made his adrenaline flow and it was on the boil right now. 'Where do you propose we begin?' He was keen to get started.

'We need to put together an exceptional team of sports spokespeople to open doors for us. I'm thinking of champions like Richie Benaud, Mark Taylor, Greg Norman, Steffi Graf, Pete Sampras, Pat Rafter, Kieren Perkins, Dawn Fraser. We should approach Prince Charles for polo. If we offer him a special documentary on the work of his Prince of Wales Charitable Foundation I think it would be a sufficient carrot to entice him, and his endorsement would help us win over the Poms. It won't cost us a lot to make. We can run it on Walker Sports Cable, and also on Walker Cable during an out-of-ratings period, and offer half a dozen repeats, which we can put to air between midnight and dawn. Some insomniac will watch it.'

Huxley was sure he'd thought of everything. He sat back waiting for the old man to praise him but Sydney had a surprise for him.

'What about women's sports?' he barked. 'You've forgotten all about the women. We'll be accused of neglecting their interests and the government will reprimand us. You know what those hairy-armpitted lesbians are like, always wanting more sport on TV. Too bad no one who really follows sport wants to watch women,' he huffed.

'Although,' and Huxley was sure Sydney smirked as he continued, 'now those volleyball girls have stripped down things might change. They're worth looking at without those baggy shorts they used to wear. Putting them into those bikini outfits was an excellent initiative. No one looks at anything but their bottoms.'

'I know what you mean, Mr Walker. I'm sure you're right but think how much more inviting they'll look on the Walker Wide Screen.'

'Walker Wide Screen. What's that?' Huxley had Sydney's total attention once more, his irritation about women's sports temporarily forgotten.

'Something else I've been working on,' Huxley explained. 'Years ago, before I went into television, I worked for Cooper's Electrics. Do you know Colin Cooper?'

'I've heard of him.'

'Colin and I are good mates and we lunch together fairly regularly. The other day he took me back to his factory and showed me a lightweight television and computer screen that he's been developing in conjunction with the CSIRO. It's amazingly flat, and made out of a material not unlike plastic that gives a higher resolution and density of image than anything else on the market. And it has superb stereo-plus sound. I've never heard sound like it, the quality is brilliant. The screen is very thin and fastens easily on to any wall in an average home. Everything needed to operate it is in a compact, hand-held device, similar to your ordinary TV remote control.'

'I'd like to see it,' Sydney said. 'Sounds like a remarkable breakthrough.'

Huxley nodded. 'It certainly is – and the good news is we can get a piece of the action. Colin has done a deal with a company in China to manufacture the screens for a good price – it's based on volume, of course, but it would allow a healthy mark-up and profit. Colin's interested in coming to an arrangement with us based on his company handling the product development and manufacturing while we look after promotion and marketing.

'He's got a world patent and has already received expressions of interest from half a dozen countries in Europe as well as America. He thinks the screen will sell in the millions. If you approve, I think we should package it up exclusively with a subscription offer to our Walker Cable Sports Spectacular Series.'

'Let's not waste any more time,' Sydney ordered. 'Let's do the deal.'

'Right, Mr Walker.' Huxley was jubilant. 'Mr Walker, if I'd known where our conversation was going to lead today I would have prepared a proper proposal. I'll work on it tonight and have it on your desk first thing in the morning.'

'Do that,' Sydney said. 'One final thing . . .'

'Yes?'

'We don't have to worry about women. Let's sign up the sportsmen first – they're the ones that people like to watch. Women may think female sport is a crowd pleaser but ratings have never reflected that. It's the men who will make us money. Once we have them signed up, the women will seek us out, begging us to take them on, too. They won't cost us much at all. Women never understand what they're worth in money, and, my boy,' Sydney chortled, 'they'll be so grateful to us. It's one of women's most endearing features – their gratitude.'

Huxley wasn't sure Sydney was right about that but discretion was the better part of valour. He had enough on his plate to keep him occupied for the time being.

# Chapter Eleven

Everything Huxley had predicted went according to plan. When he and his high-profile helpers approached the key players and suggested there was more money to be made by signing with Walker Sports Cable none of them needed much persuading. They were delighted to find a way to make more money and, at the same time, have a less taxing schedule and more time for themselves and their families. Nothing succeeds like greed, Huxley thought.

Within two months the key players in all major sports were under the control of Walker Sports Cable. By the time word leaked out, the first rounds of the Walker Global Golf Challenge were about to be played in Florida, the Global Series Cricket Cup was due to start at a new Walker Corp. Stadium in Barbados and the Walker Sports Spectacular Soccer Series was about to get underway in London, at the newly built Walker Stadium in Battersea.

With Sydney's approval, Huxley set up Walker Entertainment and when sport wasn't being played at the stadiums they were used for major rock concerts, jazz festivals, large-scale productions of opera and ballet, and major musical recitals and stage shows. Walker Entertainment then sold the shows back to Walker Cable, which packaged them up for lucrative sponsors and put them to air.

It was a clever strategy, but it was in sport that Huxley really made his mark and established his reputation outside Walker Corp. He had worked out contests and challenges for every major sport on Walker Sports Cable. For someone who'd never had the time nor, it must be said, the inclination to play sport it was amazing. Huxley talked about sport as though he ate, slept and breathed it.

The sporting bodies and those players not good enough to join Walker Sports Cable's stable cried foul and said that the sports series would never work. Men past their use-by date, running their tired old clubs and sporting organisations, huffed and puffed, too, but they were wasting their breath.

Walker Cable signed up thousands of new subscribers every day around the world. Sales of Walker Wide Screens were going through the roof, too. It was, everyone agreed, the only way to watch sport. The new flat screen was energy efficient and gave a much clearer picture than the more conventional TV screens. And the sound actually made people feel as if they were there in the stadium watching the game.

Sydney gave an interview on Walker Cable's high-rating news show to talk about the success of the Sports Spectacular Series and Walker Sports Cable. 'We run a business and we approached sport like any other venture in which we've an investment,' he explained. 'The players liked what we offered and agreed to join us. Long term it will be beneficial for the sport, good for the players and even better for viewers.

'By the end of the year we will have developed a Walker Global Sports Channel on the Internet and we'll be showing only sport on it, too. It will be possible to download from the Walker Internet site to the Walker Wide Screen in your own home – for a fee, of course. We are very excited about the future of sport and we'll be putting money back into junior sports organisations around the world to help train champions of the future.'

'Doing the right thing' was a Sydney Walker trademark. 'Always try to look like a good guy,' he'd advised Catherine and Tom. 'Leave people feeling well disposed towards you.' Sure enough, next morning on talk-back radio callers on all stations spoke about Sydney Walker's amazing generosity to young, upcoming sports stars.

Sydney was also generous when he told Huxley how delighted he was with Walker Sports Cable's profits. Huxley received a new Mercedes, a pay rise, shares with options in Walker Cable as well as a substantial bonus, and was made a director of Walker Corp. He rang his mother in Melbourne. She was thrilled for him. 'You've worked hard, darling, and I'm glad to see you properly rewarded. I hope you're going out to celebrate somewhere nice. I'll expect to hear all about it in your weekly e-mail.'

After they'd said their goodbyes Huxley rang Catherine. She had left Walker Cable several months earlier to take up a management role in Walker Corp.'s newspaper division, where she was examining the feasibility of several expansion plans that Sydney was considering.

'I understand congratulations are in order,' she said, when she heard his voice.

'You always know everything,' he protested. 'Trying to keep a secret from you would be downright impossible.'

'My father was so pleased with your results he told us what he had in mind for you at yesterday's board meeting. I've never seen him so happy – and without giving away boardroom secrets, I think I can tell you that the entire board agreed with Dad's decision. You've done a terrific job. Congratulations!'

He could picture the laughter in her blue eyes. 'Your support has been invaluable,' he said, 'and so has your friendship. Thanks for both.' For a split second he hesitated. 'I'm in the mood to celebrate,' he said. 'I don't suppose you're free tonight?'

'I am, and I'd love to toast your success,' she replied.

They went to an intimate little Italian restaurant that Huxley had discovered not far from Walker Corp. It was friendly and comfortable. Huxley was a regular patron and suggested to Catherine they let the owner bring them the specialties of the house – 'And perhaps a fine bottle of Italian red,' he suggested.

'Sounds good to me,' Catherine said.

The meal was lovely and afterwards, over coffees and sambucca, Huxley thanked her again. 'You've given me such good advice,' he told Catherine. 'I'll always be grateful. Maybe one day I'll be able to do you a good turn. I hope you'll never hesitate to ask.' His brown eyes were serious. 'I mean it, Catherine.'

'I won't forget,' she said. 'Perhaps I did open a door or two, but the rest was all your own work.' She raised her liqueur glass to him. 'I'm so pleased for you, my friend.

'Now,' she said, 'let me tell you my new joke.' Exchanging jokes had become something of a ritual with them. She grinned at him. 'What did the elephant say to the naked man?' Huxley shrugged his shoulders.

'It's cute but can you pick up peanuts with it?'

'Catherine Walker, that was one of your worst ones yet.' But he laughed in spite of himself.

'I've got one for you,' Huxley said. 'What do you tell a woman with two black eyes?'

'I don't know.'

'Nothing – she's already been told twice.'

Catherine groaned. 'Oh no! And you dare to complain about my jokes.' The sound of their laughter was pleasing to hear. The other diners looked up and smiled. The restaurant owner was delighted to see his patrons having such a good time and offered the pair another sambucca on the house.

When Tom rang the following day from America to let Sydney know he was having a problem with the actors' union, who objected to Walker Films bringing over Australian actors and actresses for a film it was making in Los Angeles, Sydney said he'd send Huxley over to see if together he and Tom could find a solution.

'Huxley is street-smart,' he told his son, 'and hard-nosed. He's a deal-doer. You'll find him very useful.'

As Sydney had thought, Huxley was able to help bring the warring factions to the conference table. After a couple of weeks the problem with the union had been resolved and he flew back to Australia. A few hours after he'd left, Tom had rung Catherine to sing Huxley's praises. 'The man's a star,' he declared, 'and I like him. Now I know why you and Dad have always spoken about him so highly.'

It was therefore hardly surprising that when Catherine called Sydney with the news that she wanted to resign from World Channel, he sent for Huxley straight away. 'I want you to go to London to run World Channel. We've got that new expansion into Beijing coming up and I don't want anything going wrong. China is important to us. Catherine has done some first-class work there and you won't have any difficulty picking up where she's left off.'

Catherine and Huxley had always kept in touch with e-mails and phone calls, just as Huxley did with Tom. When Huxley arrived in London she'd picked him up at Heathrow. 'Welcome to London,' she said. 'How was your flight?'

'Not bad.' He kissed her on the cheek and took a good look at her. 'Having a bit of a tough time, aren't you?'

'Yes.' She was pale, and thinner than he remembered, but still the most beautiful woman in the world. She was dressed in black and looked so sad that the urge to sweep her in his arms and comfort her was almost irresistible. 'I always survive,' she said.

'I know, but you look as though you could do with the strong shoulder of a good friend.' He put his arms gently around her and gave her a hug. I could love this woman so much, he thought.

'Please don't be too kind, I don't think I can handle it.' Her eyes had filled with tears.

'All right.' What had Rowland done to her? He could see Catherine was struggling to get her emotions under control.

'I thought you might like a light supper before you collapse with jet lag. Are you feeling weary?' she asked.

'Not really. I slept most of the way – I've never had a problem sleeping on planes.'

'Lucky you. I've booked you a suite at Forsythe's on the Thames. I hope you like it. It's fairly new but charming and it has the best service and an excellent dining room. I thought we could have a bite to eat there if that suits you and then, after a good night's sleep, I'll show you what's what tomorrow.'

'Sounds good to me – let's go.'

After dinner and while they were finishing the last of their wine, with the help of some tactful questioning from Huxley, Catherine told him a little about what had gone wrong with her marriage. 'He couldn't cope with me being a successful woman. I thought he was a progressive man.' She laughed bitterly. 'It was all talk. He thinks women should be barefoot and pregnant and kept in the kitchen. That's how liberated he is.'

'But he knew that you were a career woman when he met you, and that you were Sydney Walker's daughter. It's what and who you are that makes you the special woman you are.' Huxley spoke with passion. He couldn't help himself.

Catherine looked at him, somewhat taken aback. 'Why, thank you, Huxley,' she said softly. Her blue eyes showed her surprise.

'I'm sorry, I got a bit carried away,' Huxley spoke quickly. What a fool I am, he chided himself, losing control like that. 'It's just that I don't like to see a good friend like you so upset. You don't deserve it. I'd like to knock Rowland's block off!'

Catherine regarded him pensively before replying. He seems different. Maybe it's me, she thought, imagining things. I haven't been thinking as clearly as usual – thanks to Roger. She could see the concern for her in Huxley's eyes. 'What a good friend you are,' Catherine said. 'I don't think Roger really understood the demands of my job, or how well known I was. Living with a public figure isn't easy – as the daughter of Sydney Walker, I know that only too well. But Roger was also jealous of my success – if I can call it that.'

'Surely not?'

'I know it sounds ridiculous, seeing he's successful himself and highly regarded at British-Euro Network. But he resented my work so much it was unbelievable. And he was so possessive, Huxley. It really shocked me. He disliked anything that took me away from him, anyone who even spoke to me – I couldn't even ask a man the time without him reacting. It was strange.'

She gazed into space, remembering the way Roger had behaved. She looked as if she was about to cry. Huxley watched as she fought to control her feelings. What guts she has, he thought admiringly. She took a sip of her wine and continued with her story.

'Then he started making trips to Paris for business and staying overnight. It never occurred to me that he had another woman.' She shook her head. 'I don't know how I could have been so blind. There were so many signals and I didn't see any of them.'

Catherine looked at Huxley dejectedly. 'I thought I had my life worked out. But now I have to start all over again and it's frightening.'

'Your father once told me that anyone could make a mistake, and that includes personal relationships. I know it will be hard for you to start again emotionally, and it will probably take some time for you to get over what you've been through. There's no hurry. Take your time – eventually you'll be able to put it behind you.' She looks so vulnerable. He tried not to appear worried. 'Roger didn't physically hurt you, did he?'

She blushed. 'No, of course not, but I feel like a bloody fool, Huxley. And such public rejection is embarrassing and hard to handle. The newspapers here had a field day! It seems everyone knew Roger was cheating on me – everyone but me, that is.' There was such pain in her eyes that Huxley felt it, too.

'Are you sure there's nothing I can do for you?' he asked.

She shook her head. 'Please don't worry about me. It's helped being able to – talk with someone I trust.' She smiled at him. It wasn't the usual dazzling smile he knew so well, but at least it was a smile.

'Now,' Catherine said firmly, 'that's enough of my problems. Tell me what you've been doing. How's your love life – better than mine, I trust?'

'Walker Corp. keeps me too busy to have one,' he replied with a grin. 'But I've heard that some of these British girls are worth a look – so who knows? Do you want to leave me your address book?' he laughed.

They ordered coffee and when it arrived, Huxley also asked for the bill. 'Jet lag is beginning to get to me,' he said to Catherine. 'Before we go can I give you some advice?'

'Of course.'

'Don't waste any more sleep over Rowland – he was never good enough for you. I couldn't under-stand what you saw in him.'

'Now you tell me,' she said sardonically.

By the end of the week Catherine was on her way back to Australia. Huxley drove her out to the air-port. They had time for a glass of champagne in one of Heathrow's bars before she boarded her plane.

'Good luck with World Channel,' she said.

'Thanks for leaving the place in such great shape.

It helps! Look after yourself – and good luck to you, too, especially with your empire building. Be sure to send me regular reports on how everything's going.'

During their time together, Catherine had told him a little of what she was going to do. 'You'll hear more about it next week, after I've discussed everything with my father. I'll call you. Oh, by the way, I saw Prince Charles last week. He's going to invite you to tea. He's absolutely thrilled with the growth in popularity of polo, and he says it's all due to Walker Sports Cable. I told him you were the person who'd come up with the Walker Sports Spectacular Series, which has given us the world's leading sports channel. He can't wait to meet you.' She curtsied as she blew him a goodbye kiss.

Catherine's plane touched down at Sydney's Kingsford Smith Airport at seven in the morning. She showered at the airport, reapplied her make-up, and changed her warm London coat, pants and sweater for her favourite travelling outfit, a cool, uncrushable Valentino cotton knit dress, which she'd carried in her cabin luggage on the aeroplane. Dot had arranged for her car to be at valet parking. It's good to be back, Catherine thought as she drove to her father's office.

Sydney was reading the morning papers. 'Welcome home,' he said as he got up to greet her with a kiss. Like Huxley, he examined her closely.

'Are you all right?'

'Yes, Dad.'

'I never trusted Roger.'

'I know, but I'm glad you never said anything.'

'I don't want to know all the details of what went wrong but I'm sure he was jealous of your many accomplishments. He wanted to be as good as you, Catherine, but he never will be.'

She couldn't help herself. 'How did you know?'

'I've met his type before. It always will be difficult for you to meet a man who isn't envious of your success, Catherine. I'm the only man who isn't – if you should ever find another one, hang on to him.'

Catherine was amazed to hear such good advice coming from her father, the man who'd long ago given up on his own marriage. She wondered if she'd ever understand him. Relations between them were the best they'd been in a long time. A lot of the old tensions had vanished as the years had gone by.

'I'll remember your advice,' Dad,' she sighed, 'but it sure doesn't make my future with the opposite sex look too bright.'

'Don't let it get you down, girl. Just look forward to the day when you'll be able to settle your debt with Roger Rowland. If you're patient the opportunity will present itself. It always does. Now, get yourself a cup of coffee and tell me what you're going to do.'

Catherine swallowed a mouthful of coffee,

collected her thoughts and began to speak. She'd had plenty of time to think things through on the plane.

'I'm going to start my own publishing company. And the first thing I want to do is bring out a new monthly magazine for women – one that addresses the modern woman. The 21st century woman has a brain that today's magazines are ignoring.

'My magazine will cater for that woman and I want to make it a world publication. You're always talking about making the most of the global challenge and that's exactly what I intend to do. I put in a call to William Cheng last week and he agrees with me that there's a gap in the world marketplace for a truly international magazine for women. He says that if I can get the mix right he's certain several of Cheng & Farquhar's top clients will want to advertise in my magazine.

'My plan is to bring it out on the same day in Australia, England and America. The language of women is global. It always has been – wherever I've travelled I've never had a problem meeting and talking with other women. I want my magazine to reflect the unique bond women have with one another.

'I'm going to do a series of specials as well on interior design, travel, beauty and fashion. I also want to develop an international fashion range, which we'll promote through the magazine. I'm bursting with ideas!'

Her father's reaction filled her with dismay. 'Not another bloody women's magazine,' Sydney groaned. 'There's too many of them now – the market is saturated with women's interest titles. It'll never work,' he declared.

'Don't you think I've researched this? There's nothing available like the magazine I'm going to produce,' Catherine said defiantly, looking every inch her father's daughter.

'You're out of your mind, Catherine. I tell you there's no room for another women's magazine – the market is crowded and competitive. Women have so many magazines to choose from they can't make up their bloody minds now. All you'll do is add to their confusion. You'll just be wasting your time and your money!' He glowered at her.

Catherine glared right back and folded her arms. 'You're wrong, Dad. I know I'm right.'

'I wish I could be so positive about things,' he retorted. He stood up and held out his hands to her. 'I've got a wonderful future planned for you here at Walker Corp. – much more rewarding than any women's magazine could ever be. I've groomed you to be an important figure here, perhaps one day to succeed me.'

'I know, Dad, and I'm grateful for the opportunities you've given me. But I don't only want to follow in your footsteps, I want to create my own footsteps.'

'You always were stubborn,' Sydney grumbled, as

he sat down again. 'All right,' he sighed. 'Go and do your own thing – but don't say I didn't warn you.' He lit up a cigar. 'What do you intend to call this magazine of yours?'

'*MAUD*, after your grandmother.' She paused, waiting for her father's reaction.

'I know you think you've thought of everything,' he said, 'but has it occurred to you that some people might think the name *MAUD* old-fashioned in this day and age?'

The old fox doesn't miss a trick, Catherine thought, giving her father an approving look that Sydney chose to ignore.

'Of course it crossed my mind, but not for long. Those wonderful women's names of yesteryear like Florence and Grace are coming back into favour because they represent stability and tradition – and any research I've read lately indicates that people are longing for such things. It's only natural, I suppose, given the pace of the changing times we live in.'

'In that case, *MAUD* might turn out to be a very timely choice,' Sydney said grudgingly.

'I hope so, Dad. I've always loved the name and Grandma always talked about Great Grandmother Maud in such glowing terms. She used to tell me amazing stories about her, how she was a woman of the world, with style, wit and presence and a fabulous sense of humour, which is exactly what I want my magazine to have.' Sydney just grunted in response.

'And do you remember Great Grandmother's four-leaf clover diamond brooch that Grandma left me? I'm going to make it the magazine's symbol. It will bring me luck, I know it will!'

'You'll need more than a four-leaf clover to bring you good fortune,' Sydney said cynically. 'You'll need a bloody miracle!'

'Thanks for the vote of confidence.' Catherine scowled at him. How could he be so negative? 'This is something I must do,' she said firmly. 'I know you'd rather I stay with Walker Corp. but I have to do this.'

Sydney was puffing furiously on his cigar, trying to keep his temper under control. 'I give up,' he said with a shrug of his shoulders. 'If you feel you must do this then do it. you're mad.' He was about to start ranting at her again. Catherine held up her hand. 'You've said enough, Dad, don't say anything more.'

'Okay.' He knew when he was beaten. 'I won't pretend I'm happy about your decision but I respect it and I'll support you one hundred per cent. There's one thing I must say,' Sydney conceded. 'You certainly know how to think big.'

She laughed at him. 'Now where do you think I got that from?'

'You'll need money. Publishing isn't cheap.'

'I know that. I've done a cash flow document and I've spoken to Derek Hogg at the bank and he says

243

he doesn't see a problem arranging the finance that I'm going to need.'

'Why the hell would you talk to a bank when you've got me? I'm the best bank you could ever have. I'll finance you on terms better than you'll get from bloody Derek Hogg. I won't be doing you any favours, though – I expect you to pay me back in full.'

'I appreciate your offer, Dad, but I want to do things my way. If you finance me then I'll still be in the nest, safe in the cocoon you provide. It would help if the bank knew you approved of what I'm about to do, but I think it's important that I learn first-hand about all the pressures of running a business. And I'm sure it's a lot more difficult for a person starting up a business to deal with a bank than it is for Walker Corp.'

Sydney was doing his best to be tactful. He understood his daughter wanted to be independent and beholden to no one, especially her father. Sydney Walker's little girl wanted to flex her muscle. He'd known it would happen one day.

'There's no need to make it harder for yourself than it will be. Let me help you, Catherine. It will be better that way. I won't interfere and you'll be treated the same way as everyone else in whose business I invest. I'll get our finance controller, Leonard Kingsley, to draw up the papers.'

He could see she was still hesitating. He held back a grin – she was as obstinate as he was. 'If you're not happy when you talk things over with Leonard then you can go to the bank and do whatever you want. But I understand the publishing business better than any banker ever could, and if you have a cash flow crisis, I won't deny you a loan to tide you over – that's not what you could expect from a bank, you know.'

Catherine sighed, part frustrated, part relieved.

'Okay, Dad, it's a deal. If you get Leonard to draw up the necessary documents I'll sign them. And thanks, especially as I know you'd rather I stay with Walker Corp.'

'I'm happy to help,' Sydney said, 'and you're entitled to try to make your dream come true. I'd never stand in the way of you doing that.'

As she went towards the door, Sydney asked her if she was planning to see her mother.

'I thought I'd go and see her this afternoon.'

He looked down at his lap, suddenly solemn. 'You'll notice a change in her. Try not to look too shocked.'

# Chapter Twelve

When she left her father's office only one thing was on Catherine's mind. Her mother. What did her father's warning mean? At Ashburn, she let herself in and went straight to her mother's bedroom, knowing that Sarah rarely rose before ten. Sure enough, she was having her morning tea in bed and chatting to someone on the phone, as Catherine put her head around the door.

'Darling, welcome home. It's lovely to have you back again. Come in and sit here.' Sarah patted the edge of her bed. 'Susie, I have to go, Catherine's here. I'll call you later.'

Catherine was horrified. Her beautiful mother looked like a caricature of herself. Her mouth didn't seem to be functioning properly and looked strangely lopsided, as if Sarah had some kind of affliction. Her eyes were so taut that Catherine wondered how she managed to close them to sleep. Oh my God, she's had another facelift and something's gone terribly wrong.

Sarah got out of bed, and as she was putting on her dressing gown, Catherine could see how emaciated she'd become. Her head looked far too big for her body. 'Ma, you're so skinny. Have you been sick?'

'No, of course not. I'm wonderfully well. I think I look the best I've looked in ages. Remember what the Duchess of Windsor said: you can never be too thin or too rich.' Sarah smiled at her reflection in the mirror on her dressing table. 'Besides, you know how your father hates fat women.'

Catherine sighed. What kind of magic charm did her father have over women? Its effect was unbelievable.

'Do you know I weigh less now than when I married your father? Isn't that something?'

'If you think so, Ma,' Catherine said, somewhat unconvincingly.

'I'm sorry, darling, prattling on about me. I was devastated when I heard about you and Roger. You poor little thing. I could kill him for treating you so shabbily – if only I could get my hands on him!' Sarah gave her a hug. 'I suppose he resented your career?'

Just like Sydney, even self-obsessed Sarah had got directly to the nub of the problem.

'Resented isn't strong enough,' Catherine said bitterly. 'He loathed it.'

'Most men do, my darling – even though they'd never admit the truth to us. If you ever contemplate marriage again, live with your prospective husband for at least twelve months, to make sure he can accept you the way you are. If he can't, give him the flick! Over the years, I've observed that strong women like you often attract losers.'

Catherine was astonished. Here was her mother giving her excellent advice – just like her father had – but the idea of Sarah giving Sydney his marching orders had never crossed her mind. And never would, Catherine thought wryly. 'You're so lovely and talented, Catherine, and always so sure of yourself – but you need someone to love you and take care of you.'

'Why, Ma,' Catherine replied, close to tears, 'that's the nicest thing you've ever said to me.'

'Nonsense,' Sarah responded hurriedly. 'I've said plenty of nice things to you but you've always been too busy to listen.' She looked at her daughter wistfully. 'On the subject of women needing love, I'm an expert.' For a second, Catherine thought her mother was going to share some intimate secret but her mood changed rapidly, as if she already regretted letting her daughter get so close to her. She switched the subject. 'What are you going to do now that you're home?'

Catherine outlined her plans.

'How wonderful,' Sarah said. 'Your great grand-mother would be overjoyed if she were still alive.

And the brooch is so stylish. You're not my daughter for nothing, are you? Now, what can I do? Assist with the launch party perhaps? I'm good at organising events, as you know.'

'Good? You're a legend,' Catherine declared, 'and I'd love you to help.' Her mother was full of surprises today. She'd never offered to lend a hand before. What is going on?

'It will have to be after I get back from Europe, though. I'm leaving next week for a six-week trip. Susie Blackburn is coming, too. We're going to have such fun – we're booked to see all the new shows on the West End and Susie insists we go to the opera at Covent Garden. She's a complete opera buff.'

Good old Susie, Catherine thought. She's never been one to knock back a free trip or go on a budget, especially when Sarah insists on providing the money. She immediately felt a pang of guilt. What a bitch I am! Ma can't be the easiest person in the world to travel with – she must go on benders when she's travelling, and how Susie manages to cope with them I do not know. Maybe she is a bit of a free-loader but she has a kind heart.

Sarah had put on a navy wool Oscar de la Renta pants suit. 'I do look svelte, don't I?' she asked. Without waiting for Catherine's reply, she draped a large rose pink shawl over one shoulder. 'That's better,' she said. 'It needed some colour. I'm thinking of wearing this on the plane – do you like it?'

'I do,' Catherine said, 'very much.'

'Hmm – I'm not sure. Let me show you something else.' She began to undress. 'Now where was I? Oh yes,' Sarah went on, 'after London we'll be slipping across to Paris to see the autumn collections – Dior has my usual front seats booked for me – then we're going to the Loire Valley for some complete and utter relaxation.' As she talked she'd put on another outfit. 'Now what about this?'

'It's smart too, but I liked you better in the navy.' She stood up. 'The timing's perfect, Ma. I've got stacks of things to do before I even think about the launch party. Let's talk about it when you get back from London.

'And now I really must go. Dad's offered to rent me one of his buildings and I want to go and see what it's like.' Catherine didn't feel up to telling her mother the exact truth about the building. Her father had insisted she take a look at it, brushing aside her protests that she didn't want to be dependent on him.

She walked over to Sarah and kissed her goodbye. 'Take care of yourself, Ma.'

'I will, darling, and don't worry about me. I'm fine.'

But her mother's words failed to set Catherine's mind at rest. She'd seen for herself that Sarah wasn't at all well. I'll call Tom and tell him about it, she decided. He needs to know how ill Ma is. Two heads are always better than one when there are problems to be resolved.

Catherine had been so caught up in her deliberations that it came as something of a surprise to find she'd arrived at her destination in Pyrmont. She stepped out of the car and took a good look at the four-storey building Sydney had bought as an investment a few years ago. It looked as if it would be perfect for her needs – just as her father had known it would be. Damn, she thought, I can see the smug look on his face now.

Sydney had concluded that owning land near the city's casino would be useful in the future and he'd been buying property in the area for several years. The downturn in the Asian economy in 1997 had meant that the casino hadn't prospered as well as had been originally forecast but that didn't faze Sydney. It was only a hiccup – everyone knew that.

He understood the value of patience when it came to real estate and was aware he'd be able to redevelop the various properties he'd acquired and make a good profit. Pyrmont was only a few minutes from the heart of the CBD and had views of the harbour and the city's skyscrapers. One day it would be one of Sydney's most sought-after places to live and work. In the meantime he was more than happy to lease one of his buildings to Catherine for her new venture.

Catherine let herself in and took the lift to the top floor, where the first thing she did was admire the view. She peered through the windows – hey, there's Dad's office. She smiled to herself. He can't help keeping an eye on me. This panorama of the city really appealed to her – Darling Harbour and the mix of office and residential developments blended well together.

Turning around, she leant back against the window and ran a mental check as she took in her surroundings. The place felt so right. The ceilings were high. There were plenty of windows – great light for the art department. She walked down the stairs and checked out the other floors. The building itself was in good condition – she could see that it only needed a coat of paint – but the floors were a bit of a worry. Some of the floorboards had been badly repaired with different coloured timber. Catherine wondered if a combination of polished floorboards and carpet would solve the problem.

She pulled out a small notepad and began to make a list of all the things that needed to be done: get the phones on, put in computer cables, organise security bars for the downstairs windows, check the alarm system. She took a deep breath. This place already smells like a publishing company – I could swear there's a whiff of printer's ink in the air – and how peaceful and quiet it is. Hopefully the ambience will help keep us calm on our frenetic days. She gave a contented sigh.

I wonder how many cars we can fit in the basement area. Catherine took the lift down and, after looking around, decided that there was room for at least thirty-five cars. That should do us – and our visitors.

She locked up the building and drove home, feeling more alive and confident than she had for some time.

'This is the right move for me and the right time for it,' she told Tom on the phone that night. 'I've never felt so sure about anything in my life!'

'That's terrific, Sis. I can hear the excitement in your voice,' he said. 'I wish I was there to give you a hand.'

Tom hadn't believed Catherine at first when she'd told him about Sarah. 'How could her facelift have gone wrong?' he wanted to know. 'Surely she must have had the best plastic surgeon.'

'Naturally,' Catherine said, 'but facelifts don't always turn out the way they should and believe me, this one has gone dreadfully wrong. But there's something else,' Catherine said worriedly. 'I'm positive Ma's anorexic. She's so gaunt that it's quite hideous but she thinks she looks terrific.'

'I can't get back to Australia just now, Sis, but I do have to be in London next week for a meeting and I can see Ma while I'm there.'

'Thank heavens,' Catherine said. 'Try not to look too shocked, Tom. Dad gave me the same warning but I just about passed out when I saw her.'

'I'll do my best and I'll call you afterwards. Good luck with the new venture – keep me posted. You know, I think I envy you a little.'

Catherine laughed. 'You can come and be a part of it any time you like. You have only to ask.'

'You never know, I might just do that. Wouldn't you get a surprise if I did? I'll be in touch.'

The next day, Catherine had organised for her old schoolfriends Samantha James and Jennifer Pickhaver to meet her for lunch at Walker Corp. They arrived together full of curiosity. Catherine came out to greet them at reception, and showed them into her office. There was a plate of smoked salmon and cucumber sandwiches on a small table away from the desk, as well as a pot of coffee and bottles of mineral water.

'Wait till you hear what I have to tell you,' she said cryptically, her eyes shining. 'But before I begin, do help yourselves to the sandwiches.'

'I couldn't possibly eat a thing until you tell us why we're here,' Sam protested.

'I knew that's what you'd say,' Catherine said. 'You always were short on patience.' She grinned at her. 'It's going to come true!'

'What is?' asked Jennifer.

'The dream we talked about when we were at school. I'm going to start my own publishing company and I am hoping you'll both want to come and be a part of it. I can't imagine doing it without you.' She beamed at her friends, who were gazing at her incredulously.

'I can't believe you're finally going to do it!' Jennifer was almost bouncing up and down with enthusiasm. 'It's the best news I've heard in ages. I was sure you were going to remain the most devoted corporate creature of Walker Corp.'

'Oh, ye of little faith,' Catherine admonished her. 'I told you that one day we'd all work together on a magazine and that's exactly what we're going to do, providing you both agree with what I'm proposing. I want to bring out a magazine for women of the 21st century. It will be intelligent, fun, stylish and beautifully laid out – not to mention zippy, mainstream and very contemporary.'

'Zippy?' said Jennifer. 'I like that.'

Catherine laughed at her enthusiasm.

'Mainstream and contemporary – well, we sure need that,' Sam agreed. 'I suppose you've decided what you're going to call it?'

'What do you expect?' Catherine explained how she'd come up with the name *MAUD*. 'There's something else you need to know – this venture is going to be a global one. We'll publish simultaneously in New York, London and Sydney.'

Both Sam and Jennifer looked suitably impressed. 'My word,' Sam said, 'you do have a habit of taking a person's breath away.'

'Nobody's ever done what I have in mind before and, to put it mildly, there's a lot to do. Now, what I want to know is how soon can you both start?'

Jennifer spoke first. 'I'll be available next week. Since I left News Ltd, I've been freelancing, as you know, and I'll have my current assignment finished the day after tomorrow. Then I'm yours!' She clapped her hands with glee. 'I always knew that one day I'd be able to put all that I learnt at the *Sunday Times* to good use – but I never expected this.'

'Calmness, my friend,' Catherine laughed. 'What about you, Sam?'

'I'll have to give the agency at least a month's notice, maybe even six weeks. I'm looking after a couple of major advertising campaigns and I don't want to leave them in the lurch.'

'If you feel more comfortable giving six weeks then by all means do so,' Catherine said. 'It'll be a bloody nuisance having to wait for you but I admire your professionalism and I think it's wise to leave a job with your employers feeling as good about you as is possible. You never know when they'll be useful later on.

'I'm starving – here, have a sandwich.' Catherine pushed the plate towards Jennifer. 'Who wants water?' She poured each of them a glass. As they relaxed the conversation took a more personal turn and the three friends caught up on each other's lives.

'You look terrific, Jennifer,' Catherine said. 'What

have you been doing to yourself – working out at the gym?'

'No – I couldn't think of anything worse – but I have discovered a marvellous new night cream made with honey. I love what it does for my skin.' She looked at them happily, and helped herself to another sandwich. Jennifer made being beautiful seem easy. She wore her long, shining blonde hair in a loose chignon caught at the nape of her neck by an outsize comb. Her alabaster skin was without blemish – she rarely felt the need to wear make-up and was often heard to say: 'The only make-up that interests production editors is page make-up!'

'Good to see you're still wearing your usual uniform,' Catherine teased.

'Now, Catherine, don't start monstering me. I like black and what's more, it suits me!' Jennifer always wore black – it was her trademark – and looked supremely elegant in an expertly tailored pair of pants and jacket worn with a designer T-shirt.

'Shall I pour the coffee?' Sam said. 'I've given up sugar,' she went on, 'and I've lost a couple of kilos.' She looked at the other two for approval. They gazed at her critically.

'You certainly look slim to me,' Jennifer said. Catherine agreed.

Sam had always been the first among them to try a new diet. Jennifer and Catherine used to scold her about her fixation with her size but their arguments fell on deaf ears. Sam simply couldn't see what others saw: a handsome woman, with magnificent shoulder-length red hair, friendly blue eyes and a nicely proportioned figure, which was beautifully shown off by the Louis Vuitton raspberry pink cashmere and silk sweater and pants she was currently wearing. Sam looked every inch the sophisticated woman of the world that she was.

Catherine gave them both a big smile. 'This feels just like old times, and it's exactly what I needed.' The wistful tone in her voice caused Jennifer and Sam to take a closer look at her.

'How *are* you coping?' Sam asked sympathetically. Catherine avoided meeting her gaze. 'You certainly look like you could do with a good feed,' Jennifer observed disapprovingly. 'You've lost far too much weight – are you sure you're eating?'

'You don't look like you're sleeping properly to me,' Sam declared. She'd been scrutinising Catherine while Jennifer spoke. 'Are you really all right? And don't give us that "I'm okay, mate" routine of yours, either – we want the truth.'

'All right, you two – don't get your knickers in a knot!' Catherine tried to sound cheerful as she spoke, but her friends could see the sadness in her eyes. 'The truth is,' she said slowly, 'I'm feeling miserable and lonely. I thought I'd found the man of my dreams but I made a dreadful mistake. Roger used me and then he dumped me, and everyone knows it.' She looked at them wretchedly. 'It's been the worst time of my life.'

She was close to tears. 'My emotions are all over the place,' she said apologetically, and quickly got up and walked around the room.

'You don't have to apologise to us for anything,' Jennifer told her.

'Of course you don't,' Sam said. 'Cry all you like – it'll do you good.'

Sam got up and poured Catherine some coffee. 'Don't waste your time thinking about that swine, he's not worth it. And don't you dare reproach yourself for anything,' she commanded. 'I know you – always shouldering the blame when things go wrong.' She thumped her fist on the table. 'You're well rid of him.'

'Absolutely!' said Jennifer, giving the table a whack as well. 'Roger's the loser, not you. You were far too good for him, Catherine.'

'So everyone keeps telling me,' Catherine replied miserably. 'But I did love Roger very much when I married him – I was so sure he felt the same way about me. I was looking forward to our life together; I had so many plans.'

Poor Catherine, Jennifer thought, so in need of love – why did she have to be the one to fall for such a proper bastard? Sam was thinking much along the same lines. The nicest women always seem to attract the worst jerks. Life was so unjust at times.

'Oh dear!' Catherine said. 'It wasn't my intention to make you both feel gloomy. Just look at us – what a trio of sad sacks.' She walked over to the small refrigerator in the corner of the room and took out a bottle of Moët. 'I have no intention of letting Roger spoil this day for us. Let's have a glass of bubbly to cheer ourselves up – and to celebrate.'

When their glasses were filled and they'd toasted the success of *MAUD*, Catherine told them about the building in Pyrmont.

'Sounds ideal,' Sam said. 'Who else are you going to ask to join us?'

'Brenda Thompson is coming to see me after work tonight. I saw her in London a few months ago and she mentioned to me that she was desperate for a new challenge. Selling advertising for a new magazine should be exactly what she's looking for. You know how bloody difficult it is trying to persuade the advertising industry to support anything new, especially a magazine.' The other two nodded sagely.

'The road to magazine success is littered with corpses of people who have tried and failed,' Sam said.

'But not this time,' Catherine continued enthusiastically, all thoughts of Roger banished. 'We're going to make advertisers sit up and clamour to be in our magazine.'

'That will be a refreshing change,' said Jennifer, helping herself to another sandwich.

'I've put in a phone call to Suzanne Stanton,

who's in New York doing some work on *Vogue* but longing to come back to Australia. I'm pretty confident when she hears about this new project that she'll be home in a flash. And tomorrow morning I'm having breakfast with Fiona Wallace, who's just the person we need to head up marketing and promotions. She's in a class all of her own and she says there's nothing more for her to learn at International Management and that it's time to move on.'

'This is going to be like old times,' Sam said, 'all of us together again. It will be tremendous fun. I can't wait.'

'I was hoping you'd feel like that,' Catherine said happily, 'but it's going to be hard work, too. You know how blasé the media can be and we'll need them to get behind us if we want to attract readers as well as advertisers. We're going to have to make sure they feel positive about what we're going to do, and that's a big ask.

'And don't forget that the Murdoch and Packer groups are bound to make things as tough as they possibly can for us. I can just see them getting up to their usual tricks – spreading rumours about our sales figures, suggesting we're not doing well, ripping our posters down or pasting theirs over ours, moving our magazine to the back of the newsagents' shop and putting their titles over *MAUD* in the supermarkets whenever they get the chance . . .' They all laughed, fired up at the thought of what lay ahead.

'Just as well we have Walker Corp. in our corner,' Sam said. 'Your father will be supportive, won't he?'

'Yes – but I have no intention of rushing to him every time we have a problem. I want to stand on my own two feet.'

'I understand,' Sam replied hastily.

As Catherine had expected, Brenda, Suzanne and Fiona all said yes. It was agreed that each of them would wind up whatever she was doing as soon as possible. 'The sooner you can start, the better,' Catherine told them. 'In the meantime I'll get the painters in and organise the furniture and computers and whatever else we need.'

A couple of days later she rang her mother to wish her bon voyage. 'How's everything going, darling?' Sarah asked her.

'Really well.' Catherine brought her mother up to date.

'I'm so pleased to hear that and I haven't forgotten about the launch,' Sarah said. 'By the way, I spoke to Tom last night. We're going to have dinner together in London. He has a meeting he has to attend while I'm there. I am looking forward to seeing him.'

'That's great, Ma. Be sure to give him my love.'

Catherine put down the phone, feeling as if a tremendous load had been lifted from her shoulders. Once Tom had seen for himself how ill Sarah was maybe they'd be able to come up with some positive way to help her.

In the meantime she had to concentrate her energies on her new business. She'd agreed to give an interview to the *Financial Review* about the direction she intended to pursue with *MAUD* and, as she knew the reporter quite well, she'd suggested to him that they do the interview over lunch at Coast.

The following week Catherine walked to the restaurant in Cockle Bay, which wasn't far from Walker Corp. She couldn't get over how pleasant it was to feel the Sydney sunshine again after her months in London's colder climate.

She had very firm ideas on the way she planned to run CW Publishing and outlined them to Ron Hocking as they ate their lunch. It was such a gorgeous day that the restaurant's large glass doors were open so diners could appreciate the outlook over Darling Harbour. It was a busy area of town and there were scores of people enjoying lunch outdoors in Cockle Bay's enticing line-up of restaurants.

Catherine and Ron had been friends since they were young reporters on the *Sydney Globe* and they quite often had a drink together. Ron's contacts were impeccable and he kept her up to date with industry gossip.

'I want the people who work for me to get up in the morning looking forward to what the day will bring,' she told him over lunch. 'I'm against people working all day and then taking work home at night to prove that they're doing a good job, and I'm not in favour of people staying back night after night in order to demonstrate their dedication to the job either. It shouldn't be necessary. People are entitled to a private life – I think they work better for it.' She took a sip of wine.

'I'm a great believer in eight hours for work, eight hours for leisure and pleasure, and eight hours for sleep.'

'Can I apply for a job with you?' Ron asked, grinning. 'I suppose you don't believe in regular weekend working either, do you?'

'Absolutely not!' That was the way far too many men ran their companies and she didn't think anyone benefited long term. 'Men and women need their weekends – or at least two days off – to recharge their batteries.'

Ron Hocking checked his tape recorder. It was small and unobtrusive – apart from their waiter, no one else in the restaurant could see it. 'How refreshing it is to hear someone like you speak in this way,' he said. 'Everyone seems so fanatical about work these days. It's an issue that I'd like to see my paper take up in a big way.'

'It would be an excellent initiative,' Catherine said. 'Why don't you raise it with your editor?'

'I'm going to.' He refilled their glasses.

'I'm sure you'll find that many women running

businesses today share my views,' Catherine suggested. 'They're simply no longer prepared to put in ridiculously long days at the office and return home totally exhausted, unable to enjoy anything else in their lives – and quite frankly, I don't see why men should either.'

As she explained to Ron, her business plan didn't include employing significant numbers of full-time staff – technology had transformed the workplace, making it possible for people to easily work from home and e-mail their stories to the magazine. 'It's the ideal arrangement,' Catherine said. 'Employees will be happy and it allows me to keep my overheads down.'

'I wouldn't mind working like that,' Ron confided, as he turned off his tape recorder. 'Anything else you'd like to tell me?'

'I think we've covered everything. I'm still putting the finishing touches to the launch and I'd like to have it absolutely right before I reveal what I'm planning.' She looked at him contemplatively. 'Tell you what – why don't you come to my office tomorrow and I'll take you through our presentation, and if you promise not to write about it yet I'll show you the *MAUD* website we're creating. It will enable subscribers to access interactive copy and we'll be able to cross-promote issues from the magazine as well as products.'

Ron pressed the start button on his tape recorder. 'Can't you tell me about it now?'

She shook her head. 'No, I'm not ready to go into much detail yet. I'm only telling you because you're a friend and I trust you.'

As they made their way to the door, Catherine revealed a few more details. 'Once we've got the site up and running we'll be able to offer advertisers exposure, which means we can increase our rates. And we'll have a reference library for ongoing articles and a chat room with the editor – as well as experts and personalities who we plan to feature in the magazine. I'm very excited about it.'

They made their goodbyes. 'I'll see you tomorrow,' Ron said.

She walked slowly back to Walker Corp., feeling that all was well in her world. She hadn't thought of Roger for at least two days! The magazine was keeping her busy and it was exactly the kind of therapy she needed. Everything was going to plan and she was feeling more optimistic about life in general. She spent the rest of the day going over budgets before making a couple of calls to some freelance journalists whose work she admired to see if they'd contribute to *MAUD*.

Before going home she called in to have a drink with her father. 'The renovations at Pyrmont will be completed at the end of the month,' she told him. 'We'll be moving in as soon as they are.'

'I'd like to come over and see what you've done,' Sydney replied.

'Don't you trust me, Dad?'

'Of course I do! Don't be so bloody sensitive,' her father said crossly. 'I'm interested in the building, that's all. I have no intention of checking on you or of prying into your affairs. I realise you know what you're doing.'

He swallowed a couple of mouthfuls of his scotch. 'For God's sake, Catherine, you can be difficult at times!'

Catherine shrugged her shoulders. 'If you say so.' She was too tired to argue with her father. She finished her gin and tonic. 'I must be off.'

'Are you going out somewhere?' Sydney asked her and at once regretted his question; the bloody girl would probably snap his head off again. 'Don't tell me if you don't want to,' he added quickly.

Catherine had the grace to look somewhat ashamed, and answered her father politely. 'No, I'm feeling a little pooped and I thought an early night would do me good.'

She was fast asleep by ten. At midnight the phone awakened her.

'Catherine?' The caller sounded upset.

'Yes. Is that you, Tom? You sound peculiar – why are you ringing so late? Is everything all right?' She'd been in such a deep sleep she was finding it difficult to wake up.

Tom sounded like he was crying. No. It must be her imagination.

But then he said, 'Catherine I've got some very bad news.'

Her stomach sank.

'Is it something to do with Ma?'

'Yes. I don't know how to tell you. Something awful has happened.'

Catherine could feel a chill around her heart.

'She's dead, Catherine. Ma's dead!'

'Oh no!' Catherine yelled down the phone. 'What happened?'

'Ma and Susie were shopping.' Tom was crying openly now and it was hard for her to understand what he was saying. 'They were in a taxi making their way to Harvey Nichols. The traffic was bumper to bumper – you know how congested it gets in London sometimes. Susie said Ma decided that as they weren't getting anywhere in the taxi it would be quicker to take the underground from Covent Garden to Knightsbridge.

'They were standing on the platform when a man came up and asked Ma the time. She told him and had turned back to say something to Susie, when he grabbed her and pushed her off the platform. There was no time to stop him. Susie tried but everything happened so quickly that there was nothing she could do.'

'I don't understand, Tom. What exactly happened?'

'He pushed Ma onto the railway tracks. There was a train coming in. The driver couldn't stop.'

Catherine began to scream. She couldn't help herself. The horror of her mother's last moments enveloped her. She could hear Tom begging her to stop but she was out of control.

'Did she die straight away?' She had to know.

'Yes,' he said. 'But . . . she was . . . Oh God, Catherine, Ma was decapitated.'

Catherine screamed again but this time it was a low, pain-stricken sound that was so fearful it made Tom's blood run cold.

Catherine thought she was going to be sick. She could hear her brother trying to comfort her on the other end of the phone. She began to cry. It was a while before she spoke again.

'Who was the man?' she demanded. 'Why did he do it? Was it someone she knew?'

'No, he was a stranger. The police said he had a history of mental illness and that he was under psychiatric care.'

'Great bloody care, letting him out to kill people. He's a madman. Why would he pick on our mother?' She began to sob again. 'What happens now?'

'There'll be an inquiry. I don't know what will happen to the man. The police have him in custody somewhere. Ma's body will probably be released tomorrow. What happens next depends on Dad.'

Catherine had forgotten all about their father. He needed to be told what had happened.

'You'll have to tell him, Catherine.' Tom sounded anxious. 'Will you be okay?'

'I don't know.' Tom heard his sister exhale deeply. 'I'll go over to Ashburn at once. I wish you were here, Tom – this is the most awful thing I've ever had to do.'

Sydney was horrified. Much later, when Catherine had finally gone, he'd even shed a tear. He had loved Sarah once. She'd become a foolish, vain woman and a drunk, but she was the mother of his children. While he'd often wished she was out of his life, she didn't deserve to die in some dirty London underground station in such appalling circumstances – hell, no one did.

He made arrangements for her body to be flown back to Australia and for a memorial service to be held at St Andrew's Cathedral in the city. He ordered flags to fly at half-mast at all Walker Corp. buildings for a month and he wore a black armband for the same period of time.

Tom came home for the service and he and Catherine did their best to comfort each other. Their mother might have had her shortcomings but they knew that in her own way she'd been proud of her children. Life with their father had never been easy for her – he'd been so demanding and dictatorial that he'd destroyed much of her vitality. Even when she and Sydney led their separate lives he'd still exerted his control.

Catherine and Tom stayed at Ashburn the night of the funeral. Before she went to bed, Catherine knocked on the door of her father's study, to ask if he'd like a cup of tea.

'I'd prefer something stronger,' he said. 'Why don't you have a nightcap with me,' and he invited her to sit with him. He looks old, Catherine thought. Ma's death has knocked him about.

'Port?' she asked him as she walked over to the bar. Sydney nodded. She poured one for them both.

As she settled herself in the opposite chair, Sydney raised his glass. 'To your mother,' he said.

'To Ma,' Catherine responded.

'You're very like your mother sometimes,' Sydney told her. 'Have I ever told you that before?'

Catherine shook her head.

'I couldn't handle her drinking.' His voice was almost inaudible. Catherine waited for him to go on but her father seemed a million miles away.

'Why didn't you try to help her?' Catherine asked, careful not to sound as if she was accusing him of anything.

'I did – many times – especially in the beginning. Even before you were born it was obvious that alcohol didn't agree with her. But she was impossible to help. At first she made a joke of the way she drank – daring me to guess if she'd had a drink before I got home from the office. Later, as she began to drink more heavily, she'd simply deny she had a problem.'

He put down his port. 'It was the same with my mother.'

'Grandma?'

'But in her day people called it "a drinking problem". It was considered shameful and no one spoke about it,' Sydney said. 'My father ignored it completely – it was the only way he could cope. When Mother was going through a sober period we behaved like other families but as time went by there was little respite. When I was a boy my father and I spent many a lonely evening together.'

Catherine recalled the times when her grandmother had come to stay and the evenings she'd had to be helped from the dinner table. There were other times, she recollected, when Grandma didn't even make it to meals. Now she understood why. How strange that she and Tom had never noticed anything amiss. They'd always thought their grandmother eccentric and loved her for it – she was different from all the other adults they knew, and had always seemed so good-humoured.

'I had no idea,' she said. 'Why didn't you say something to me before now?'

'A man doesn't like to speak badly of his mother,' Sydney said huskily. 'She's the first woman he loves.'

Catherine looked at her father as if she was really seeing him for the first time. Sydney was twisting the glass of port around in his hands. How small it seems in his big hands, Catherine thought. She saw a look of disgust come over her father's face. He quickly put the glass down on the table near his chair.

'One night when I was home during school holidays my mother came into my bedroom. It was late and she tripped over something as she came in and woke me. She bent over to kiss me.' He gave an almost imperceptible shudder. 'She smelt of stale booze and as if she'd been vomiting. The smell repulsed me. I turned my head away from her. She stood beside my bed without saying a word. Then she left the room.'

Catherine didn't know quite what to say. It was hard to think of her father as a boy and to imagine how he'd have felt.

He looked at her. 'I've never been able to forget that smell.' He looked pensive. 'When your mother began to drink excessively it wasn't long before the smell of alcohol on her revolted me. I found it difficult to touch her, even to kiss her on the cheek. I tried again to persuade her to seek help. Finally, she agreed she would, but at the last moment she refused to go and see the doctor I'd found.'

Sydney blew his nose, picked up his port and downed it. He got up and refilled his glass. 'I always looked after your mother. Whatever she wanted, she got – you know that.'

Catherine nodded.

'And she gave me you and Tom. I'll always be grateful to her for that. I never expected to feel the way I do about you both.' He spoke gruffly to hide his emotions. 'I'm proud of the pair of you.'

What a night of revelations! Catherine pinched herself to make sure she wasn't dreaming, then she got up and slowly walked over to where her father was sitting. Bending down, she kissed him good-night. 'I love you, Dad.'

# Chapter Thirteen

Tom stayed for a week before returning to New York. He visited Catherine's new offices, still under construction, and pronounced them stunning. He listened as she outlined her goals and told her he knew she was going to make a success of her new venture.

'I don't suppose you could use a column from New York, could you? I know a brilliant writer who'd consider it a privilege to write for you.'

'Tom!' Catherine exclaimed. 'I'd love you to write for us – that would be fantastic. But,' she grimaced, 'do you think you'd have enough time?'

'I'll make time. It's something I want to do.' Tom had discovered he had a flair for writing when he was editing his school newspaper. His cheeky diary, which chronicled the goings-on at Berkdale, had quickly built up a following among the boys. When he was studying at university he'd contributed a couple of provocative pieces on the future of education to the university newspaper. He'd sent them to Catherine to read and she'd quickly recognised her brother's talent.

'You write so well,' she'd told him at the time. 'Why don't you ask Dad for a job as a writer? You could travel the world searching for stories – wouldn't that be stunning?'

But Sydney wouldn't have a bar of it and berated Tom for wasting his time. 'There's no money in writing,' he'd insisted, 'and that's not where your future is. I need you to help me run Walker Corp. It will give you all the challenges you're seeking.'

Tom hadn't bothered to debate the issue with his father. He'd simply determined that one day he would put writing back into his life. Here was his chance: his column in *MAUD* would be the first step.

Catherine missed Tom after he'd gone back to the States but she was grateful that they'd been able to share memories of their mother. Talking about her had helped them come to terms with their grief. When Catherine told Tom of Sydney's revelations about their grandmother he'd been as astonished as his sister. 'It's hard to believe how families keep their secrets, isn't it?' He put his arm around Catherine. 'I wonder if there are any other family skeletons we don't know about.'

After Tom had gone, Catherine threw herself into her work. Her number one priority was to develop a dummy of *MAUD*, on which the magazine would be based. Catherine knew many changes would be made to it before the first issue hit the streets but it was essential that the dummy reflect the voice of the magazine as well as its style and humour. The magazine's character would develop more fully after it had been on sale for a few months. Readers' feedback would play an important role in shaping this.

Catherine was looking forward to their comments. She knew that the mark of a good editor was being able to take on board what readers felt and make subtle changes that would satisfy them but in such a way that they didn't notice the changes were happening.

She'd asked Sam and Jennifer to put aside a week so that they could discuss story lines, photography, columnists, special features, layout and type. Because the Pyrmont offices weren't ready she'd hired an office suite at the Sheraton on the Park, where they could toss ideas around without being interrupted. It was quiet and roomy, and they were able to spread their material over the large boardroom table.

'Isn't this fun?' Sam said.

'Well, I'm enjoying myself,' said Catherine, 'so I'm glad you are.'

'And it's great that we don't have to go out for meals,' Jennifer added. 'I've heard that the room service here is quite something.'

'You and your stomach! I wish I knew how you can eat like a horse and look the way you do,' Catherine said.

'It's not fair,' Sam grumbled.

She and Catherine had always been somewhat green-eyed about their friend's ability to eat anything and everything without ever putting on weight. Jennifer was tall – almost six feet, which helped – but even so, Catherine and Sam were amazed at the huge amounts of food she devoured without it ever showing. She was fond of bragging about her big breakfasts, when it was not uncommon for her to have a bowl of leftover chicken risotto followed by several slices of toast with avocado. And yet mid-morning she'd complain that she was famished and polish off a couple of muffins with her coffee without turning a hair. Incredibly, she'd be starving again by lunchtime.

'I've ordered stacks of food for mid-morning and afternoon tea as well as lunch, so don't fret, Jennifer,' Catherine assured her. 'There's no way you will waste away while we're here. But in between mealtimes and other snacks we have to come up with a stunning dummy. We must get the look of it right because I want to have it researched. We might learn a thing or two that we can put to good use. A dummy will be mighty useful for Brenda, too. She needs to have something to show prospective advertisers.

'The more we know about our potential readers the better,' Catherine continued. 'Although my gut feeling tells me I'm right, it won't hurt to get confirmation that women do have a global language.'

They burnt the midnight oil and were rewarded with positive feedback from research groups that were conducted not only in Sydney, but also in New York and London.

Brenda Thompson had called on four of the top ten agencies in her first week and reported that after showing them the *MAUD* prototype, the consensus was that Catherine's timing was spot on. The market was ripe for something exactly like *MAUD*. Two weeks later, Cheng & Farquhar arranged for Catherine and Brenda to do presentations to their key clients in New York and London. They were equally enthusiastic.

But when it came to getting them to sign on the dotted line, Brenda discovered a major snag – one of their competitors was undermining her sales pitch. 'Whoever it is – and I bet you it's Murdoch – is offering huge discounts on volume business. Book six pages of advertising and get six free. They're offering deals in all their major women's titles – there's no way we can match them,' Brenda said worriedly. 'They're claiming it's impossible for us to deliver the circulation we've promised.'

Catherine had told Brenda to guarantee a circulation of three million for the first six issues. She'd thought the figure conservative and was confident that the magazine would be selling five million copies within eighteen months, perhaps sooner than that if they encountered no glitches.

'Damn.' Catherine ran her hands through her hair. 'We need that money.' She rested her chin on her hands and thought quickly.

'Okay – if the Murdoch mob wants to take us on, we'll fight back,' she said. 'Tell those gutless advertising mates of yours, Brenda, that if they buy the first four issues at the full-page rate, and if we fail to meet our guaranteed circulation or they're disappointed in any way with *MAUD*, I'll refund their money – every last cent of it!'

Brenda asked Catherine if she'd call on some of the bigger advertisers with her. 'I think it would help. You are very persuasive, Catherine – and as editor, you can talk more knowledgeably about the magazine than I can.'

'Just tell me when and where – I'll be there.' Catherine spoke confidently but when Brenda had left her office she rang her brother to tell him what she'd promised. 'I'm worried, Tom,' she said. 'What if they don't take the bait?'

'Some won't, you know that – but I'm sure some of them will give you a run for your money.'

'As long as they don't run away *with* it after the first four issues!' Catherine retorted.

'That's the spirit, Sis,' Tom urged. 'Just don't let the bastards get you down.'

That night Catherine had trouble sleeping. When she did finally doze off it was only to wake at two in the morning. What if Brenda can't persuade those advertisers? What then? Her mind was in overload. Tom had suggested that she ask their father for advice. There was no way she'd do that – she'd never admit to Sydney that she had a problem. He'd only say 'I told you so' and she had no intention of ever giving him that satisfaction.

Next morning Catherine hit the road with Brenda. By the end of the week they'd called on more than thirty agencies. They pleaded their case eloquently enough to persuade several key advertisers to take a gamble on *MAUD*. But there were many – too many, Catherine told Brenda – who were not convinced that the magazine would be all that was promised.

Catherine had poured her heart into her presentation. She rattled off the demographics and target market, assured them about the quality editorial, the expertise of the printer, and she even promised right-hand pages – always the preferred pages for advertisers because of their belief that the reader notices a right-hand page rather than one on the left.

She showed the agency teams printed samples of a couple of the features so they could appreciate the clean look of the art direction; she listed the names of the journalists and authors who'd be writing for *MAUD* – and outlined the launch plans and the marketing and publicity. She answered everyone's questions politely and with enthusiastic conviction.

One agency boss's negativity particularly infuriated her. He was not only dismissive but prophesied that the magazine's future looked bleak and that she was going to come a cropper. He didn't believe there was a market for *MAUD*, no matter what her research said. It was all she could do, Catherine told Brenda later, not to punch him in his smug, know-all face.

'I'm glad you didn't,' Brenda replied. 'His clientele are perfect for us. When he sees the magazine he'll change his mind. You'll see.'

But by Friday night, after a particularly tough session with one of the big-spending cosmetic companies and their agency, who said they'd been prepared to advertise only if they could have a fifty per cent discount on the page rate, Catherine and Brenda slunk out feeling very low. They were disheartened and weary. 'Those bloody cosmetic companies seem to think they're the only ones entitled to make any money in this business,' Catherine said crossly as they made their way back to the office.

'I'm sorry,' Brenda murmured.

'It's not your fault,' Catherine was quick to tell her. 'You're doing a fantastic job – but it's impossible to change the thinking of brain-dead people!' Brenda gave her a grateful look.

Arriving back at Pyrmont, Catherine parked the

car. In the lift, on the way up to the fourth floor, neither of them spoke. When the doors opened, Catherine ordered Brenda to stay where she was. 'We need to forget our troubles for a while. Let's go out to dinner tonight and put those boringly pessimistic advertisers out of our minds. Keep the lift doors open while I go and get the others.' In next to no time the six of them were on their way down.

'Why don't we eat at one of the Chinese restaurants in Sussex Street?' Catherine suggested. 'We're early enough to get a private room – I feel like letting my hair down.'

They all did. They partied on until midnight, with Catherine keeping them amused between courses with her latest jokes. They ate their way through a multi-course Chinese banquet, washed down with several bottles of excellent cabernet sauvignon. When Jennifer stated she couldn't possibly eat another thing, the others greeted her announcement with disbelief, before breaking into applause and cheers. 'This is a red letter day,' Sam declared. 'Jennifer had enough to eat.'

'I never thought I'd live to see it happen,' Brenda said. 'Hallelujah!'

'Catherine's jokes are as bad as ever,' Fiona said to Suzanne, as they went to powder their noses.

'Aren't they, though – but they do make me laugh and we could do with a bit more of that. We've all become very serious lately, especially Catherine.'

'Well, that's only to be expected – don't you

think? I wouldn't be in her shoes for quids.' Fiona looked solemn. '*MAUD*'s the biggest gamble of her career and I'm sure it doesn't help her to know that her father thinks she's going to fall flat on her face.'

'It'll take more than her father's misgivings to make Catherine think she might fail,' Suzanne said. 'I don't think failure comes into her vocabulary – except when she thinks about that bloody ex-husband of hers. She's still in a state of shock over his treatment of her, even though she's putting on that brave face of hers. What a prize shit he turned out to be!'

'Suzanne, your language – really!'

'Come off it, Fiona. I've heard you say a lot worse.'

'Just kidding,' Fiona giggled. 'I couldn't agree with you more about Catherine. Brenda was saying much the same thing to me earlier. We both think she shouldn't spend too much time on her own – particularly after work. One of us should ask her out to dinner – or take her out for a few drinks, or perhaps a movie. We can take it in turns.'

'Good idea! Count me in,' Suzanne said with alacrity. 'We'd better go back or they'll be wondering what's happened to us.'

Next morning, the six of them arrived at the office refreshed and ready to do battle once more.

The countdown to the launch gathered momentum. With less than six weeks to go, Catherine told the others she was satisfied with the way the first issue was shaping up. The editorial content was coming together well. She admitted she was disappointed with the advertising content – she'd hoped to have forty per cent of the magazine's pages filled with advertisements, but in the end she had to content herself with only twenty-eight per cent.

'We can live with that,' she reassured Brenda, who was depressed that she'd been unable to meet Catherine's quota. 'Just wait until those procrastinators see *MAUD*. They'll be sorry they weren't in the first issue. It will sell like hot cakes and they'll never forgive themselves for missing all the publicity we're going to get.' She looked so sure of herself that Brenda had to smile.

'That's better,' Catherine said. 'Why don't you put some new packages together for issues two, three and four – we don't want anyone to think we've got our tail between our legs. That would never do!'

She didn't tell Brenda that she'd been to see Leonard Kingsley to inform him that she would need an increase in her loan from Walker Corp.

'I don't think your father will like this, Catherine,' he'd told her.

'Nonsense,' Catherine had replied. 'As long as you're charging me interest he won't mind at all. Business is business – even when it's all in the family.' The look on her face was one Leonard had often seen on Sydney. He knew better than to argue the point with her – after all, he reasoned, she is the boss's daughter and Sydney had told him he wanted to support her in every way he possibly could.

But when Leonard had reported their meeting to Sydney he'd reacted badly. 'I'm not a fucking money tree,' he barked at the hapless finance controller. 'Next time my daughter comes asking for more funds, send her to me!'

Neither of the two men mentioned their conversation to Catherine.


Fiona Wallace had come up with a spectacular launch idea but at their first meeting to discuss it, Catherine had remembered how keyed up her mother had been at the prospect of helping her and had excused herself to go to the Ladies. When she'd composed herself she returned.

'You okay, Catherine?' Fiona asked.

'Yes – keep going.'

Fiona had placed a large chart on the table and slid it across in front of Catherine. 'Would you look through this schedule and see if there's anyone you don't want to talk to – I'd like to finalise the interview requests as soon as possible,' she explained. '*60 Minutes* rang this morning to ask if they could do a profile on you – that's not on the list yet. They'd do it here in Sydney and it would be shown in the US and the UK as well as Australia, of course. Larry King wants you for his CNN interview, too.'

'That's terrific – this all looks okay to me,' Catherine replied as she ran her eye down the list. 'Now, tell me about Oprah.'

Fiona consulted another file. 'I've made a special folder for her,' she said and handed it to Catherine, who sat back and studied it. 'They want you on the show the day after you arrive in America – you'll have to fly from New York to Chicago because that's where it's recorded.'

'How many viewers does she have?'

'Millions and millions – at least something like thirteen million in the US alone. It's hard to get a complete estimate of viewers because not all countries do ratings like we do, but the show goes out to 140 countries and there's nothing else like it in the world.'

Fiona considered getting Catherine on the top-rating show her tour de force. She'd badgered Oprah's producers by phone, fax and e-mail, bombarding them with promotional material. As she told Catherine, 'If Oprah likes the magazine and endorses it, *MAUD* will take off.'

Confirmation of Catherine's appearance had caused great jubilation at Pyrmont. It had been followed up with a request from Catherine for Oprah to be interviewed by Australia's top-selling author, Bryce Courtenay.

'That profile piece Bryce has done on her is the best thing he's written in a long time,' Fiona said. 'It was such a clever idea of yours to ask him to do it.'

Catherine nodded. 'I wasn't sure if he'd agree – in fact, I thought as a best-selling author he might be a bit precious and consider it beneath him – but because he'd never done anything like it before he loved the idea. He and Oprah hit it off straight away and he's got her talking about herself in a way that I didn't think was possible.'

Fiona leant across the table. 'I've put a selection of Sally Grahame's photographs together for promotional uses – I think they're stunning.'

'Me too. Oprah looks fabulous, doesn't she?' Catherine said, as she scrutinised them. 'Perry's clothes look sensational on her.'

'Oprah is mad about Perry, Catherine. This could be his biggest break yet.'

Probably Catherine's most complex task was working out the printing and distribution of the magazine. Given the logistics of publishing in three countries it was extraordinarily difficult and time-consuming but she'd been very thorough in her preparations before contracting Universal Press, one of Australia's leading printers, with the necessary infrastructure required for a job the size of *MAUD*.

The company had gone global in the early '90s and acquired factories in London and New York, as well as Sydney. Catherine was confident the magazine would be in good hands.

Because she was breaking new ground Catherine

decided to go for broke as far as distribution was concerned. The magazine would be sold on news-stands, in supermarkets and also by subscription. To tie in with the Oprah interview, a series of TV spots had been booked on the star's show encouraging viewers to subscribe to *MAUD* by phoning a toll-free number and using their credit card.

It wasn't the way magazines were usually sold, Catherine conceded to Fiona, but then nothing about *MAUD* was like other magazines.

'Everything including the kitchen sink is sold by direct marketing these days. I want to try it,' she said.

'I'm with you, Catherine. I've a hunch it will work well for us.'

A month before printing was due to start Universal Press's British printing factory at Wapping was destroyed by fire. Finding a new printer at short notice, to produce the 1.3 million copies for the UK market, was just about impossible but Universal Press had found one prepared to do it. It would mean using two machines so as to complete the printing in three weeks, instead of the six weeks that had been originally allowed by Universal, and other work would have to be set aside to accommodate such a late order.

But the new printer had thrown a spanner in the works by demanding more money than the price previously agreed upon between Catherine and Universal Press – seventy-five thousand pounds more. There was no way Catherine would even consider such a figure. Her budget couldn't stretch to it.

'It's blackmail,' she told Huxley, when she'd rung to ask for his help. 'I'm sorry to ring you at such short notice – I know Dad has you working flat out on the China project – but I'm desperate. I can't afford to pay any extra for the printing. World Channel is not without influence in publishing circles – I'm sure that by combining its might with that of Universal Press, we could find a printer with some free time on their presses for a job of this size, without trying to financially ruin me. We're up against the clock – that's the problem.'

'Leave it with me,' Huxley said. 'I'll call you back as soon as I can.'

'Thanks. There is one more thing . . .'

'Yes?'

'I'd appreciate it if you didn't tell my father about this.'

'You're placing me in an awkward situation, Catherine.'

'I know, I'm sorry.'

'Tell you what – if your father doesn't ask me, I won't mention it. After all, I do owe you a favour or two.'

'Bless you, Huxley.' She hung up. Fiona and Brenda put their heads around her door. 'Any progress?' Fiona asked.

'Huxley said he'd ring me back as soon as he

could. If we don't find a printer soon we're going to be in serious trouble in the UK. I never imagined anything like this happening to us.'

'Let me get you a coffee,' Brenda suggested and rushed off.

'Can I sit down?' Fiona asked.

'Go ahead.'

'I've been thinking.'

'Yes?' Catherine was more than interested – disasters often produced some of Fiona's best ideas.

'If we do have to go on sale late in the UK, why don't we announce it with a couple of sizzling press releases. What about "Aussie Girl's Big Dream Goes Up In Smoke" followed by "Aussie Girl Blazes Back" – no, no,' Fiona corrected herself, '"Aussie Girl Fights Fire with Fire!" Then I'll write something pithy about how you've set the publishing world aflame with your vision.'

Catherine's laughter rang out. 'I'll say one thing for you, Fiona – you don't let anything ever stop you. You'd probably have found a way to turn the sinking of the *Titanic* into a positive experience.' She was still chortling when Brenda returned with her coffee.

'What, good news already?' she exclaimed.

'No – well, yes. Madam's fertile brain has been hard at work turning this mess of ours into a marketing strategy. Go on,' she urged Fiona, 'tell Brenda your new plan.'

Later in the day, Huxley rang as promised to

advise an increasingly anxious Catherine that he had no good news to report – yet. She had another one of her sleepless nights. By mid-afternoon the following day she was sitting in Fiona's office, considering the ramifications of changing the launch date.

Fiona wasn't at all happy at the prospect of that. 'I don't know that I'll be able to get Oprah's people to agree to that – I doubt they'd be able to give us another opening on her show this year. She's booked out for months.' She groaned. 'This is terrible, Catherine. All this worry will give me a migraine.'

'I think I'm getting one, too,' Catherine said. They looked at each other in despair.

Some hours later, when everyone had gone home, Catherine was sitting in her office having a quiet gin and tonic. She was worried. The UK situation would cost her money and not only for the printing. The media for *MAUD* had already been booked and to reschedule it for another date at this late stage would be expensive, as she would also have to pay cancellation fees.

She'd have to reorganise her timetable, too – Fiona had worked out a detailed schedule of appearances for Catherine but all her launch preparations would be wasted in the UK if the magazine wasn't even on sale yet. God knows when it would be. Damn, damn, damn – why did this have to happen?

She was tidying up her desk, getting ready to leave, when her phone rang. It gave her a fright and she jumped. She prayed it was Huxley with good news.

It was. 'You'll have to split the print run,' he said, without wasting time on pleasantries. 'We've found two printers who are prepared to print 650,000 copies each. Universal Press will work out a collection process and dispatch the magazines to the necessary outlets. It's more complicated than you'd planned but it will work – and the magazine will get out on time.'

'Fan-bloody-tastic!' Catherine was ecstatic. 'I knew I could count on you. I know you've busted a gut – thank you so much, Huxley, and please thank the guys at Universal Press for me. I'll give their boss a call as soon as I hang up. You've no idea what it's been like – I'd just about given up hope. I've been working on alternative plans all day.

'If you were here I'd buy you a drink or maybe two,' she laughed. 'There's no one here to celebrate with me – the others have all gone home.'

'That's their bad luck,' Huxley said. 'But I'll take a rain check, thanks. Now why don't you go home, too, and have a good night's rest? I bet you didn't sleep a wink last night.'

September was a good time to launch a magazine, whichever part of the world you called home. It was spring in Australia and autumn in the northern hemisphere. Christmas wasn't far away and usually people were in the mood to buy in the lead-up to the festive season. It was also the most appropriate time to suggest that a gift subscription to *MAUD* was the perfect Christmas present.

In the middle of everything Richard Sterling rang Catherine. They'd commissioned him to be the magazine's astrologer and he and Catherine had become quite close in the last few months. 'I've just had a look at your horoscope and I noticed that Mercury in Aquarius is forming the best possible star pattern with Jupiter in Gemini. You're on a winner, Catherine!'

'I think so too, Richard, but I'm glad the Zodiac agrees.'

The six months that Catherine had allowed to get the magazine out had passed all too quickly, and suddenly there was only a week to go before the official launch. Catherine was due to see the first copy before the day was out. She was on tenterhooks. Everyone was – even Sydney, who'd rung several times to ask if any issues had arrived.

Catherine assured him she'd be over with a copy as soon as she had one in her hand. 'Put the champagne on ice, Dad, and we'll wet the new baby's head together!'

While she was waiting, a splendid arrangement of spring flowers arrived. She read the card: *You are on your way to fame and fortune! I know MAUD will break all sales records. Looking forward to seeing you soon so you can buy me that drink you owe me. As ever, Huxley.*

Dear Huxley, Catherine thought, remembering how helpful he'd been.

There was a knock at her door and she called out for whoever it was to come in. George Panos, Universal Press's managing director, walked in carrying a bundle of magazines and smiling broadly at her. 'You're going to like this,' he said, as he flourished a copy of *MAUD* in the air, before putting the magazines down on her desk. 'As you'd expect, the printing is excellent,' he said proudly.

She picked one up and sniffed it. 'Gorgeous – it's almost better than Chanel No 5! I love the smell of a magazine not long off the presses.' She appraised the cover critically. 'It's effective and it will grab people's attention. They won't be able to resist picking up the magazine.'

Catherine had laid down some strict guidelines for the cover with Sam, who as creative director had the responsibility for coming up with a design that would ensure *MAUD* stood out from the busy magazine racks in newsagents and supermarkets. Other than that, though, the cover was Catherine's responsibility. It was the unwritten rule of magazine publishing – the editor, and no one else, was responsible for the cover. Every element had to work; nothing could be left to chance.

'The cover has to immediately let our readers know who we are and what we're about,' Catherine had said. 'And let's not overdo the cover lines – most of the other magazines look far too cluttered, which is why their covers don't grab attention.'

Sam had gone for what she described as 'a luscious rich look with a touch of fantasy about it'. She'd had the four-leaf clover diamond brooch photographed so that the diamonds kept their glitter, and then enlarged the shot to almost fill the width and depth of the cover. The brooch gleamed enticingly on a background of deep, rose pink velvet. The cover lines and masthead were in a white type outlined in silver. It was a cover that held the eye, an essential prerequisite of a successful magazine, as Catherine was well aware.

'You're right about the printing, George.' She leafed through the pages slowly. The layout was crisp, the editorial pages didn't fight the advertising – the invitation to keep turning the pages was irresistible.

She'd commissioned a piece on Camilla Parker Bowles from Sarah Ferguson, the Duchess of York, who'd forged a name for herself as a talented writer after the breakdown of her marriage to Prince Andrew. Camilla had agreed to talk to *MAUD* about the issues she thought women would have to confront in the 21st century. She wouldn't discuss any aspect of her relationship with Prince Charles, but she and the Prince had been happy to pose for one official photograph.

It was the first interview she'd ever given and

Sarah Ferguson had done a sensitive job, giving the reader a much better understanding of why Camilla had captured Prince Charles's heart. The story showed the caring and compassionate side of Camilla, which had always been overshadowed by the reputation of the much-loved Princess Diana.

Catherine had also persuaded Brad Pitt, Richard Gere, Leonardo DiCaprio, Nicholas Cage and Sean Connery to take part in a think piece, 'Across the generations: the fears and hopes of men'. She'd done the interview herself and had thoroughly enjoyed encouraging the men to talk openly. Somehow, Catherine had managed to get them all together in Los Angeles just after the Oscars. She'd organised a slap-up dinner in the Presidential Suite at the Regent Beverly Wilshire and had paid for it by giving the hotel contra advertising in *MAUD*.

It had been some night. While the men had their ports and coffee she'd switched on her tape recorder and started asking them questions.

Afterwards, when she was listening to the tape, she couldn't believe how frank they'd all been. The following morning she'd rung Suzanne in Sydney and gloated, 'You'll never guess what Richard Gere told me.'

'You are a pain, Catherine,' Suzanne said. 'Are you going to tantalise us with tales of your liaison with those hunks forever?'

'You bet!'

'You would. All right – what did Richard Gere say?'

'That I had the most amazing eyes.'

'Oh go away, will you.'

The memory of their conversation still amused Catherine. She looked up at George Panos. 'I couldn't be happier. The printing is everything you promised and then some – thank you so much. I just hope the London and New York print runs will be of similar quality.'

'They will be,' George assured her, 'and don't worry about the UK. I've got half a dozen of my best blokes watching over those two printers we ended up with.'

'Stay and have a glass of champagne with us,' she invited, stepping outside her office. She shouted to the others: 'Hey everyone, it's here – and it looks bloody beaut! Come and see for yourselves.' There was a rush and a buzz of excitement and then silence, as everyone appraised the magazine.

Fiona was the first to speak. 'You've done it, Catherine. It's terrific!'

'*We've* done it,' Catherine corrected her.

'The fashion looks superb,' Suzanne said.

'And look at the advertisements,' Brenda said happily. 'We couldn't possibly get any complaints about the printing. It's terrific, George!'

'Can we open the champagne now?' asked Sam.

After they'd all had a glass, Catherine made a

speech of thanks telling the thirty-five men and women, who made up the editorial and sales staff, how grateful she was for their commitment and hard work. 'When you look through this,' she said, waving a copy of MAUD in the air, 'it's obvious this magazine is going places.' Amid cheers and clapping, Catherine proposed a toast to MAUD and its glorious future.

'Brenda,' she whispered, 'keep the champagne coming. I'll be back as soon as I can. I've got to go and see my father. What if he doesn't like MAUD?'

'Don't be ridiculous,' Brenda said. 'He'll love it.'

Sydney was waiting for her when she arrived. 'Let me see,' he said brusquely, and held out his hand.

Catherine handed him the magazine and sat down, nervously awaiting his verdict. The silence as he looked through it was excruciating. She desperately wanted her father to say 'well done'. What he thought was important to her. She hadn't realised just how much his opinion mattered to her until this very minute.

'The printing's some of the best I've ever seen,' he declared. 'I like the fashion spreads, too. Good colour,' he said approvingly. He began to laugh at one of the cartoons, turned the page and found another one that tickled his fancy.

He stopped when he came to Tom's column, a whimsical piece about the characters he'd met one afternoon in New York's Central Park. Sydney read it without comment to the end. 'Your brother's column is excellent,' he pronounced. 'He does have a flair for the written word.' Catherine beamed. 'Now don't go telling him I said so – I want him to concentrate on the company, not on writing.'

He started thumbing through the magazine again. 'I like the food pages. This "How to turn Takeaway into Gourmet" is a smart idea – not that I approve of takeaway,' he added.

'I know, Dad, but it's the way lots of people eat these days.'

'Yes,' he said, as he kept turning the pages. 'I think you've done it, Catherine. This magazine is a credit to you.' He smiled at her approvingly and suggested she open the champagne.

'Now what's this here?' Sydney was still reading avidly. 'What possessed you to do a makeover on Shane Warne? He'll never live it down, but who cares? It's a good story.'

There was a pleased expression on Catherine's face as she watched her father's reaction. Warne had agreed to follow a low-fat diet she'd asked a nutritionist to create for him, and have his hair and look restyled. The whole thing had been a huge success – the money they'd paid him went as a donation to charity and even Shane couldn't believe how well he had scrubbed up.

When he'd said to Catherine that his team mates would knock him for it, she had assured him: 'Just send them to me, Shane. I'll take care of them.'

'I hope Warne thanked you for his transformation,' Sydney said.

'He did indeed, Dad – especially when I told him he looked like a young Robert Redford.'

'You definitely have a success on your hands. I like it.' He started turning the pages once more, chuckling again at the cartoons.

Catherine had poured the champagne. Sydney stood up and raised his glass. 'Congratulations.'

Catherine was so relieved she sank into one of the chairs in front of Sydney's desk. There was no way her father would praise *MAUD* unless he really thought it was up to scratch.

'Have some of this – looks like you need it.' Sydney handed her a glass of champagne. She took a long sip.

'You're right,' Catherine said appreciatively. 'I did need that.'

The magazine sold out in Australia in just two days. By the end of the first week it was hard to find copies in America and England.

Oprah was very happy with her interview with Bryce Courtenay and personally rang Catherine to tell her. She was thrilled with the photographs, too. As Fiona had anticipated, she'd talked about the magazine on her TV show – and held up a copy showing the cover – giving *MAUD* publicity that

Catherine could never have paid for and guaranteeing its success. Oprah's audience was so loyal that when she said 'buy' they did as they were told.

It helped, too, that the official launch went off without a hitch. Fiona had found a large, empty warehouse, not far from Darling Harbour. She'd had the inside draped in deep rose pink net – to match the colour that Sam had used on the cover – and with the use of skilful lighting cleverly hid the old building's defects.

With Catherine's approval, she'd had the cover and selected pages from the magazine blown up into giant posters and placed in silver-edged frames. 'Not real silver,' she'd assured Catherine, 'it's only paint – but the effect is the same, for a fraction of the cost.' The pages, hanging in clusters around the room, looked spectacular.

Catherine made the only speech of the night, and charmed everyone. Her passion about the magazine was so convincing and heartfelt that people came up afterwards and sincerely wished her well. The champagne flowed. 'Only Moët,' Fiona had informed Catherine. 'Moët and MAUD have to be the ultimate, sparkling combination!' As guests literally floated out into the night they each received a copy of the magazine.

Catherine left the next day for a whirlwind of appearances overseas, keeping in touch with her office by e-mail and mobile phone. At night Sam would transmit pages of the second issue to her and she'd okay them, making a few changes and sometimes rewriting the occasional heading or whatever else she thought needed adjusting. A few days before the second issue was due to go to the printer she was back in Sydney to choose the cover.

She was glad to be home. Travelling and talking about *MAUD* had been fun but tiring and she was looking forward to relaxing at Bondi Beach. Catherine felt as if her whole life had changed. Even though she'd been well known before *MAUD*, she'd now become a household name. She couldn't go anywhere without being asked for her autograph. But she found that she actually enjoyed the experience and what touched Catherine most was people's genuine pleasure about her success. Complete strangers would come up and tell her how much they liked her magazine and how delighted they were that everything was going so well for her.

*MAUD* was a runaway success. Catherine's timing and judgement had been proven to be spot on – women were looking for something different in their magazines and *MAUD* gave it to them in one fabulous read.

The extraordinary thing was that the magazine kept selling out. Catherine increased the print run but it still wasn't enough to meet demand. It was several months before she managed to do that. No one could remember such an outstanding magazine launch – although Kerry Packer, when he sent Catherine a congratulatory note, said that *MAUD's* sales triumph reminded him of the success of *Cleo*, the magazine his company had created in the 1970s for the newly liberated woman of those times.

Tom rang from America and told her that wherever he went everyone was talking about it. 'It's head and shoulders above anything else that's available on the news-stands,' he assured her. 'It has a real character all of its own. You know what I think people like best? That Australian confidence we all have – it's like a breath of fresh air over here.'

She'd no sooner put the phone down when it rang again. She picked it up.

'Hello, Catherine, my dear. What a star you've become.'

She recognised the voice at once. 'Roger, what do you want?' Her tone was frosty.

'I've made a terrible mistake.' His voice was apologetic but friendly. 'I know I hurt you dreadfully and I can't explain why I behaved the way I did. Can you ever forgive me?'

When she responded with stony silence he simply continued. 'Darling Catherine,' he said, 'I'm still in love with you.'

She couldn't believe her ears. 'You've taken your time to decide that! Why are you telling me this now, Roger? After all, I'm probably better known these days than when we were together. I seem to remember you didn't like my "bloody fame" – you were always carrying on about it.'

'I was a fool. You're unique – I understand that now. Being separated from you has made me appreciate just what an extraordinary individual you are. I truly understand that now, darling,' he said, turning on all his charm.

'It's not too late to sort things out between us. Can't we just talk? That's not too much to ask, is it?' He was pleading with her now. 'Why don't I get on a plane tomorrow,' he suggested. 'I'd be with you in no time.'

He sounded nothing like the Roger who'd so cruelly told her he no longer wanted her. Had he really changed? Was there a chance things could work out for them after all? But then she remembered all the angst and pain he'd caused her. He'd hurt Catherine far too much for her ever to consider taking him back. There was no way she was going to let him con his way into her affections again. She hardened her heart.

'Don't waste your time, Roger – there's nothing for us to discuss.' Catherine slammed the phone down with a thud. Then she put her head down on her desk and burst into tears.

# Chapter Fourteen

Jack Clement was halfway across the world to London relaxing on board his Hawker 800XP jet. It was as comfortable as it was luxurious. He'd had the interior redesigned so that it was like a mini apartment, very sleek and stylish in soft brown suede and leather. Part of the seating area had been converted into a bedroom with an ensuite that included a shower. His plane was an indulgence, he knew that, but what was the point of money if a man couldn't splash out every once in a while?

He was stretched out on his bed and just starting to nod off when the pilot's voice came through on the intercom system. 'Mr Clement, sorry to disturb you but Mr Murdoch is on the line. He says it's urgent.' Jack frowned at the satellite phone in the plane's office. Some sixth sense told him that Rupert Murdoch was going to be the bearer of bad news. Anticipating that the call would be a lengthy one he made himself comfortable in his favourite armchair before picking up the receiver.

'Rupert, this is Jack. What's up?'

'Charles Webster is no longer sure that he wants to sell.'

He knew it. 'Shit! Why not? What's gone wrong?'

'I wish I knew.' Rupert sounded annoyed. 'We had lunch together at the Savoy Grill last week and he seemed happy enough with everything. He was pleased that the name of the company wasn't going to be changed, excited at the thought of Lucian Freud painting a portrait of his father for the National Gallery of Australia, and looking forward to launching the Oscar Webster Scholarship at Murdoch University. He said his father would have been delighted at the thought of some bright young man or woman studying to become a journalist on a scholarship named after him.' Jack could hear the frustration in his voice.

'I was sure I had everything stitched up,' he went on. 'Then this morning Webster rang without warning to say he wanted to call off the deal. I couldn't believe it.'

'He's not renowned for his business ethics – we should have expected him to behave erratically like this,' Jack said morosely. Charles Webster was better known for his outrageous ways and total lack of interest in his father's company.

'What a disappointment he must have been to

Oscar. Thank God my boys didn't turn out like that.'

'They're a credit to you,' Jack concurred. 'When I have a son I'll make sure it's drummed into him that the company comes first.'

'My sentiments exactly.' Rupert Murdoch was like a father figure to Jack, who always enjoyed the older man's company and had been looking forward to seeing him face to face in London, when he'd expected they were going to have something to celebrate. It didn't seem likely now – not unless they could find a way to make Webster change his mind.

'There's nothing for it, Jack. We'll have to go and see him again and find out what's gone wrong. He probably wants more money – but everyone has a price. He won't be any different.'

'Where's he now?' Jack inquired, as he fiddled absent-mindedly with the knob on the drawer of his custom-made mahogany desk, which was a superb piece of craftsmanship. He'd spared no expense having it made to his requirements.

'Somewhere in London. I hear his mother's in town – he's most likely been seeing her. As soon as you get here come straight to my office so we can figure out a new game plan. In the meantime, I'll make a few phone calls and see what I can uncover.'

'Right, you do that. I'm going back to bed.'

But sleep eluded Jack – he had more important things to occupy him. What had gone amiss with

Charles Webster? He and Rupert thought they had a done deal. What had happened to make the bloody fool turn them down?

Webster Media was a successful and wealthy independent newspaper chain with quality newspapers in cities that were important players on the world stage. Rupert and Jack each owned a fifteen per cent stake in the company and had long been eyeing it like a couple of predators, searching for a way to get greater control. Discovering their mutual interest, they'd quickly realised there was a better chance of them achieving their objective if they joined forces.

While government regulations and his adversaries could make it difficult for Rupert to own or control any more newspapers in England, America and Australia, Jack was unencumbered. There was no reason why he couldn't command the massive Webster Media empire with its influential metropolitan dailies in Sydney, London, Berlin, New York, Paris, Beijing, Brazil and Tokyo. Even though the rules on media ownership changed constantly and plenty of examples existed of governments bending rules to suit their needs, both men were of the view that there was no time to waste if Webster Media was to change hands the way they intended. Neither of them could see any merit in drawing attention to what they had in mind, nor did they have any desire to get bogged down in arguments and red tape.

Rupert was skilled at taking over newspapers and prepared to share his expertise with Jack. Also it would suit him to have a friend, almost a de facto son – he knew perfectly well how Jack regarded him – in a position of power there. They'd come up with a plot that necessitated Jack buying Charles Webster's twenty-five per cent interest.

This would give him forty per cent of the company. Rupert would keep his fifteen per cent holding, giving him the right to nominate a representative to the board. This way he and Jack would control Webster Media. They knew that on those occasions when it suited them to do so that by combining the might of Rupert's News Limited with that of Webster Media they'd be able to lobby governments and big business to their mutual benefit. It was an arrangement that would serve their needs admirably.

But before they'd even had time to approach Charles Webster the man had called Rupert – whom he'd known since he was a small boy – to ask for his advice. Without explaining his reasons Charles had informed Rupert that he wanted to dispose of his shares in Webster Media with a minimum of fuss, and preferably to someone who would have Webster Media's best interests at heart. Rupert had counselled the younger man to sell to Jack and helpfully offered to set up a meeting.

Charles had been so excited at the prospect of the

riches coming his way that as soon as he'd left Rupert's office he had popped into the nearest pub, only to run into an old chum, a financial journalist from the BBC. Over a pint of bitter, he had confided to his friend that The Clement Group was about to buy him out. 'I'll be loaded! Let me shout you another drink,' he said expansively.

They whiled away a genial couple of hours at the bar. A few days later the first speculative comments began appearing in the media about the likelihood of The Clement Group making a bid for Webster Media.

When Oscar Webster had died unexpectedly from a heart attack at fifty-nine, Charles was thirty. Oscar had hoped that eventually his son would grow to love Webster Media as much as he did, and that, even if Charles didn't want to play as hands-on a role as his father had, he would at least keep the company going in the way he'd wished. Oscar had put together an experienced board and his trusted, long-time friend Walter McNeil succeeded him as chairman after his death. He'd been with Oscar from the early days when he'd owned only one newspaper, the *Sydney Argus*. Walter had been his right-hand man, heavily involved in the company's growth. He knew all there was to know about Webster Media and Oscar had felt confident that with Walter's guidance, his company and his son would be in good hands.

Charles Webster had a talent for selling and there

were times when he admitted to himself that he quite enjoyed the demands of Webster Media, but they were few and far between. After all, he'd say to his friends, why work your guts out when you've got money. He could never comprehend why his father put in such long days, was on the phone doing business at all hours of the day and night, and made numerous trips overseas but never took a day off just to relax and sightsee. It was something they often argued about.

'Dad, when you were starting out it might have been necessary to work day and night but you've made it. You're rich and you're not getting any younger either. How much does one man need? You're addicted to making money, Dad, and I don't want to be like that. Why don't you just enjoy life for a while? Why don't you sleep in, go to the movies, stay in bed all day and read a book? Don't you ever dream of doing nothing?'

Oscar would rather have dropped dead than do that. Sometimes he couldn't believe Charles was his son.

'It's not only a question of money. Work keeps you young, Charles,' he used to reply. 'Besides, I enjoy what I do.'

Charles would just shake his head. 'Sure, Dad, but if you ask me you're like all the other wealthy men who call the shots these days. All of you suffer from the greed syndrome.'

He couldn't understand the satisfaction Oscar experienced from breaking a major news story or exposing a corrupt politician. He never felt the surge of joy after an unexpected increase in a newspaper's circulation or the heady rush of power and the responsibility that came with owning such a significant media chain.

'Who wants responsibility?' he would say to whichever girlfriend he was seeing at the time. 'All I want is fun. Webster Media was my father's dream, not mine.'

And when she'd ask what his dream was, he'd respond: 'I don't have one. Never had. Some of us have to be different. That's me.'

Without Oscar's firm hand and with more money at first than he knew what to do with, Charles went wild. His escapades with girls and his wins, and losses, at the gaming tables and the racetrack often landed him in the media, which didn't perturb him at all. By anyone's standard Charles Webster led a flamboyant, somewhat decadent life. The truth was that like many sons of self-made men, he just wasn't up to following in his father's footsteps.

But everyone liked him – it was impossible not to because he had so much charm. Charles was handsome, fun, and rampantly heterosexual. He was a familiar face at all the social events that mattered; he rarely missed a first night at the theatre and opera and dined regularly at only the finest restaurants. He skied at Aspen, went to the races at Ascot, had the best seats for the centre-court matches at Wimbledon, never missed the Grand Prix in Monaco, and often disappeared for a week or two to Fiji, where he owned an island off the coast of Nandi. And, although he always told everyone he was going to Fiji to rest, he partied on there as he did everywhere else.

What no one knew was that Charles was ill with cancer. Unbeknown to him, he'd had the disease when his father died. It wasn't uncommon for him to feel off-colour occasionally. His 'bad days', as he called them, had become more frequent in the year before his father died but he'd just put it down to too many cigarettes and too much alcohol, never thinking for one moment that it could be anything more serious.

It was his mother, Claudia, who'd insisted that he see a doctor. Charles had come to have lunch with her on one of his visits to London and was a terrible colour. When he told her he didn't feel well enough to eat, she became very worried.

'Don't fret, Mother,' Charles told her, 'it's only a virus. I've had it for a while – the rotten thing refuses to go away.'

But Claudia wasn't convinced. She told him she'd hassle him until he gave in and went to see a doctor. Finally to have some peace Charles did, but he'd left it too late to seek help. Cancer was diagnosed, along with the news that there was little medicine could do for him as the tumour had spread to his liver.

Claudia was shattered. Charles had disappointed her with his attitude to business and, like her husband, she regretted that he'd never wanted to run Webster Media, but he was her son and she loved him dearly. They shared common interests and when he came to London they'd do the rounds of theatres and art galleries, enjoying each other's companionship very much.

She had moved to London after Oscar died. Claudia liked England and the British, especially their sense of humour. She'd bought a substantial period terraced house in Belgravia with six reception rooms, five bedrooms (all with ensuites), a swimming pool complex and sauna. She was never short of company. Her friends, especially those from Australia, loved to visit.

They all agreed her home was stunning but most of them couldn't understand why she'd ever want to live in a place renowned for its lack of sunshine. Surely she missed Australia's brilliant blue skies? they'd ask. She did, but she didn't miss the happy-go-lucky Australian way of life. When Charles had told her about the cancer, Claudia had offered to return to Australia to look after him – a sacrifice of which he was well aware.

'It's very sweet of you, Mother, but you will do no such thing. I may be ill but I'm not dead yet. I intend to go on living like I always have and that means I'll be spending my usual time with you in London this summer. Start booking the tickets for the opera and let's take in Wimbledon as well.

'There's only one major change that I intend to make,' he told her, after a long pause.

'What's that?'

'I'm going to sell my shares in Webster Media, pay all my debts, and then I plan to enjoy to the hilt whatever time I have left.' He didn't tell Claudia about his meeting a few days' ago with Rupert. Why upset her further? Quite frankly, Charles didn't care who bought his bloody stock, he just wanted the money. He didn't mention that to his mother either.

Claudia was dismayed. She'd never considered the possibility of Charles selling his shares in Webster Media, not while she was still alive at least, and told him so.

'But Mother, circumstances have changed everything, you must understand that. I am going to die, hopefully not as soon as the doctors say, and there are places that I want to see, and a million things that I still want to do. I need money now – it's no use to me when I'm gone!'

'I do understand, Charles. I guess I just don't want to accept it.' Claudia was a strong woman and a fighter, but she was also pragmatic. 'Please don't do anything with the shares yet. Let me consult my advisers and see what they suggest – twenty-four hours is not too much to ask, is it?'

It was agreed that she'd phone Charles the following evening. 'Before you go there's something I want to tell you,' she said. 'I love you very much. You've been a good son and given me a great deal of joy. I want you to know that.'

'I love you too. I'm well aware I've been a big disappointment to you and I'm sorry about that. Life is so unfair sometimes, isn't it?'

'Don't be so bloody silly, Charles. I wouldn't have wanted any other son but you.'

'I believe you, but thousands wouldn't.' He kissed Claudia on her forehead before embracing her tenderly. 'Bless you, Mother – don't you dare cry,' he said disapprovingly, as Claudia's eyes began to water.

But after he'd gone she'd bawled her eyes out. It was bad enough that Oscar had died as young as he had but she'd never envisioned such a terrible thing happening to her darling Charles. Why my son? Claudia wept. It's so unjust. When she had no tears left to shed, she'd poured herself a hefty scotch and soda, drunk it quickly, then picked up the phone and rang Sydney Walker.

Some years before their respective marriages, Sydney and Claudia had gone out together, something that very few people remembered. Both good-looking, strong-willed, up-front people, they'd discovered an attraction for each other, which might have led to marriage if Claudia's parents hadn't been so against it. As Jews, they wanted their daughter to marry a boy of her faith. They'd gone to great lengths to make sure Claudia only went out with Jewish boys but somehow Sydney had slipped under their guard and, when they'd learnt he was a Catholic, they were distraught.

Sydney didn't care what faith Claudia was – all he knew was that she was unlike any other woman he'd met.

It wasn't the first time she'd had that effect on a member of the opposite sex. With her vitality and joy for life, Claudia left an indelible impression on everyone she met, but it was her poise and control that most appealed to Sydney.

They'd been introduced at a party held after one of Horton's gala fashion parades, which Claudia was covering for *The Australian Women's Weekly*, where she was employed as fashion editor. As Sydney chatted her up while at the same time admiring her neat, petite figure she'd listened politely and laughed when he said something amusing but her expressive dark brown eyes indicated no interest in him otherwise. Sydney felt as if he'd been hit by lightning. He wanted Claudia like he'd never wanted anyone before in his life.

He'd rung her the following day and asked her to have dinner with him. It was the beginning of a tumultuous romance. In the first month of their knowing each other Sydney sent Claudia a red rose every day. He wined and dined her at intimate hideaway restaurants; they went sailing on the harbour and drank champagne on secluded beaches; they danced the nights away at his favourite nightclub; and finally, one evening, he took her back to his apartment and made love to her – and discovered she was a virgin.

'Are you sure you're all right?' he'd asked her, surprised at his reaction. He'd bedded virgins before without a second thought. Claudia assured him she was. It was the first of many nights of lovemaking. They were both deliriously happy. The only sour note in their relationship was her parents. Of course they liked Sydney, they said, but he wasn't Jewish. 'How can you do this to your mother?' Claudia's father had pleaded with her. 'You'll break her heart.'

It was Claudia who made the decision to end their relationship. 'I can't upset my parents any longer. I'm making their lives a misery. Last night my mother told me that my grandparents would be turning in their graves,' she informed Sydney miserably. She was so heart-broken that Claudia's parents took her overseas in the hope that the trip would help her forget Sydney, who was as desolate as she was.

But when she got to Paris Claudia sent Sydney a postcard telling him about the places she'd seen. It was warm and friendly, nothing more. She sent another one from her next stop and the one after that. Soon, Sydney had quite a collection. When Claudia returned home after six months of travelling he'd asked her out to lunch. It turned out to be the first of many. They'd always got on well and a lasting friendship, which they managed to keep a secret, developed between them.

After they had both married, and on the rare occasions when the opportunity arose, they would meet for dinner. Occasionally, if they were in the mood, they'd go to bed together – although they hadn't done that for quite a few years now. But it hadn't harmed their relationship at all. Even if months went by, they picked up the bonds of their friendship as if only a day or two had passed since their last meeting. They trusted each other completely. Sydney often confided in Claudia and found her practical mind useful in helping him make decisions on some of his many business ventures.

'I wish I were with you, Claudia,' Sydney said when she'd told him about Charles. 'It's not good to be by yourself at a time like this.'

'I'm coping, you know me. And it's doing me the world of good just to talk to you and to know that you're there for me.'

'I'll always be here for you, and speaking as a friend, let me say that it would be most unwise if

Charles sold his shares to just anybody. It could be dangerous for you and the future of Webster Media. Twenty-five per cent is a big parcel of shares.'

Claudia could hear him lighting up a cigar. He took a long puff before continuing. 'Why don't I buy his stock? I'm cashed up and can afford it. The shares will be safe with me and they'll yield me a good return.' He puffed on his cigar again. 'I give you my word that whatever happens I won't sell them without your permission.'

'But what about any government regulations?' Claudia asked.

'I'm not worried about bloody rules and regulations – and besides, I'm only adding to the newspapers I already have. The deal might be subjected to an investigation but I doubt it. Media guidelines are now very flexible. There are so many grey areas because those bloody moronic politicians are anxious to come up with laws that suit their needs, and that includes keeping me on side at all times.' Sydney spoke with the confidence of a man used to getting his own way.

Claudia was relieved and surprised. 'Would you really do that? I thought of buying them and adding them to my own stock but I really can't afford them right now. Well, that's not true, I could find the money but I'd have to sell some of my property and then organise some refinancing and I don't really want to do that.'

'Don't sell any property. I know how much you like your villa in Monaco and your penthouse in New York. You could consider getting rid of that chateau you have in the Loire Valley – but then why do that? You like going there too, don't you? You can't sell your penthouse here, of course, because you need a place of your own when you come home, even though that's not very often. But property values are skyrocketing here and look like going higher – you should hang on to that penthouse for the time being.'

'You've taken such a load off my mind,' Claudia managed to get out, before Sydney carried on enthusiastically.

'Tell Charles to call me tomorrow morning at ten sharp. I'll take care of the rest. Don't you worry about a thing, Claudia. Webster Media will be in safe hands. My purchase will take everyone by surprise. They'll want to know what I'm up to and will imagine all sorts of things. It's a situation that appeals to me!'

Claudia couldn't help laughing. 'You're going to love it, I know. Thank you so much. I don't know what I'd do without you, Sydney. It would be lovely to see you again – why don't you come and spend a few days with me in Monaco next time you're over this way?'

'I'd like that.' Sydney hung up the phone. It would be nice to see Claudia again, he decided.

Charles rang on time the following morning. Their conversation was short but convivial and when they'd concluded their business, Sydney told him that he was sorry to hear about his ill health.

'Is there anything I can do?'

'No, thanks,' Charles replied. 'But there is one thing I'd like to ask you about.'

'What's that?'

'My mother – I didn't realise you and she even knew each other.'

'We've known each other for years. We're old friends.'

'I'm worried about her being alone when I've gone. She's very self-reliant but I don't like to think of her without someone to turn to if she has a problem. We've always been very close.'

'Don't worry about your mother,' Sydney said. 'I'll always look after her.'

'You don't know what a relief it is to hear you say that.' It was one of the rare occasions that Charles spoke from the heart.


Jack had worked himself into quite a rage. Something – or someone – had come between him and his ambition and he wasn't amused. His well thought-out plan was slipping through his fingers and that wasn't on his agenda. He was determined to acquire Webster Media – ever since he'd sold his own newspapers he'd missed the fulfilment and power they'd given him and he wanted this back. He kicked the corner of his chair. There must be a way to persuade Charles Webster to sell, he thought. There has to be.

As a rule, Jack enjoyed flying because there were so few interruptions and he usually managed to get through a great deal of work. But this trip is a nightmare, he thought angrily. All I've done so far is worry. Maybe food would help me calm down. He pressed the intercom button and called for his driver, Martin, who worked as a flight attendant when Jack was airborne.

'Orange juice, eggs, lots of toast and coffee,' he ordered. 'I'm going to take a shower and I want it ready in twenty minutes.'

Martin and breakfast were waiting when Jack reappeared. 'Excellent, thank you.' He was hungry and ordered some more toast. Pouring himself another cup of coffee and feeling more at peace, he opened his briefcase packed with papers and documents and settled down to work his way through them, relieved to have something to take his mind off Charles Webster. In eight hours he'd be in London – Webster would keep until then.

# Chapter Fifteen

Back in Sydney Catherine, unaware of the drama happening with Webster Media, was counting the hours, too. By the end of the day Jack will be in London, she thought. God help him if he lets his work prevent him from calling me as he'd promised. She longed to hear the sound of his voice once more.

She wasn't, however, the only one at CW Publishing with romance on her mind. Brenda had just announced that she was going to marry William Cheng and had asked Catherine to be one of her bridal attendants. Catherine was delighted, although not surprised. She knew Brenda and William were crazy about each other, and there'd been some added intimacy between them of late.

'And you'll never guess what else has happened,' Brenda said breathlessly.

'What?' Catherine looked at her, enjoying her

friend's excitement. I *am* better these days, she thought. I'm happy for Brenda without feeling sad about my own marriage disaster.

'I'm going to have a baby. Isn't it marvellous?'

Catherine shrieked. 'Brenda, I'm thrilled for you – and William! That's great news. When is it due?'

'I'm almost two months pregnant. That's why William and I are getting married. Now the baby's coming we want to do the right thing. I want our child to have a proper upbringing with a mother and father who care enough to make a commitment.'

'I'm sure the baby will thank you profusely when he – or she – is old enough to understand what you've done,' Catherine said mock-seriously.

'Do you mind, Catherine? You're going to be its godmother. Have some respect for the institution of marriage!'

'Sorry,' Catherine laughed, 'I couldn't help myself. I'd love to be the godmother, thank you! But first things first. Where and when is the wedding?'

'As soon as possible. We thought we'd marry in the Hunter Valley; you know how much we love the place. We haven't time to go away afterwards – William is so busy – but if you can spare me for a week, we'll stay at our vineyard and honeymoon there.

'We're going to have the ceremony in the chapel at The Convent Pepper Tree and the reception in the grounds, which are so lovely, nestled in the vineyards the way they are. I'm planning a sumptuous feast but

I want it to be relaxed and Italian with long tables, umbrellas and plenty of music and wine, including our very special Cheng Chardonnay. It's a nice drop, even if I do say so myself. We've been saving it for a special occasion and this definitely is it.'

Catherine nodded. 'It sounds heavenly.'

'I'm going to ask Perry Wolf to design me a clever gown, something long and concealing, in a heavy silk so that my little bump won't show. William's taken to calling it Bumper,' she laughed, patting her stomach lovingly.

'Whatever you wear you'll look fantastic, you always do. As a matter of fact, Perry's coming in again to see me this afternoon about the *MAUD* Collection. Shall I ask him to call on you when we've finished our meeting?'

'Brilliant! Oh Catherine, I'm just so happy. William is, too. We had dinner with his parents last night and they're as thrilled as we are.'

William's parents had come to Australia from Hong Kong not long before their son was born in Sydney, where they lived in the North Shore suburb of Wahroonga.

'Have you told anyone else yet?'

'No,' Brenda replied. 'I wanted to tell you first.'

Catherine was frowning and tapping her desk with her pen. 'Why are you looking so worried?' Brenda stared at her friend anxiously.

'It's just occurred to me,' Catherine replied slowly,

'that perhaps you're thinking of giving up work when you have the baby.'

Brenda laughed with relief. 'You worry too much! Of course I'm not going to do that. I'd like a couple of months off when Bumper is born – but then I'll hire a nanny.'

'I've just had a brainwave!' Catherine exclaimed, jumping up excitedly and walking over to the windows. She thought for a moment, before turning around. 'We'll put in a creche for you – so you can bring the baby to work, and you'll be able to breastfeed as long as you want.'

Brenda's face lit up. 'That would be fabulous.' She rushed over and gave Catherine a hug. 'You think of everything.'

'What I'm really thinking,' Catherine went on, 'is that I'm willing to bet that it will only be a matter of time before some of the others feel the yearning for the patter of little feet. And you know me, I like to be prepared. I'll get someone to start looking at how we can do it today.'

Brenda also asked Fiona to be a bridesmaid. 'Although strictly speaking as you've been married, I guess you should be a matron of honour.'

'Brenda.' Fiona ran her hand through her curly chestnut hair. Her hazel eyes flashed dangerously. 'Do me a favour, please, and forget about my marriage. I don't want to be reminded of it!'

When she was in her early twenties Fiona had married Paul Warner, the boy next door. He was an accountant specialising in taxation and he was so good at what he did – his client list included all of Australia's major corporations – that a bright future seemed certain. He and Fiona had started dating in their last year at school.

They'd been married for eight years when Fiona was stricken with a mysterious illness. At first it was thought to be flu but then bacterial meningitis was diagnosed. She was whisked to hospital with a very high fever and put on intravenous antibiotics, so ill that doubts were expressed about her recovery. Paul was grief-stricken and refused to leave her side. Most of the time she seemed to be sleeping but she later told her friends that she had been conscious of what was going on around her.

One night, Paul was sitting beside her bed when he confessed that he'd had an affair for two years with the wife of one of his office colleagues. Afterwards he wondered why he'd owned up but at the time he was so overcome with self-reproach that all he could think of was making a clean breast of it. He didn't want Fiona to die leaving him to cope on his own with his guilty conscience.

'I'm sorry I cheated on you, Fiona darling,' he whispered. 'But I thought I loved Penny,' he said somewhat defensively. He kissed his wife's hand. 'I feel awful about deceiving you and betraying your trust.'

Fiona subsequently told Catherine that it was exactly the kind of shock she needed to make herself well again. 'I was so damned angry when he confessed that I just had to get better so I could tell him what I thought of him!'

However, it wasn't her husband's confession of adultery that triggered her recovery. 'Severe bacterial illness often responds quickly to antibiotics,' her doctor had explained.

When she was completely recovered, Fiona told Paul that it was all over between them. 'I never want to see or speak to you again.'

'But Fiona, it's ended between Penny and me.'

'I couldn't care less. But I can assure you that it has definitely ended between you and me. You broke your marriage vows. How could I believe anything you said to me ever again?'

After twelve months' separation Fiona filed for divorce and never talked about Paul, or her marriage, again. It was almost as if it had never happened. She threw herself into her work. Publicly she announced she was available; privately she didn't think she'd ever be able to trust a man again. Fiona had plenty of male friends but kept them all at arm's length.

Catherine used to argue with Fiona about her attitude. 'You were unlucky to have married such a loser,' she'd said, 'but I'm sure there's someone, somewhere just waiting to whisk you off your feet.

Don't close the door on your heart,' she'd urged her friend. 'I know I'm not the one who's been hurt and I respect your right to feel the way you do. But one day you'll feel differently – you have to believe that.'

Fiona had shrugged. 'Maybe, but I wouldn't bet on it.'

When the news had reached Catherine's friends that Roger had left her, Fiona had been one of the first to ring to offer commiserations, knowing from her own experience how Catherine would have been feeling. They agreed to meet as soon as she got back to Sydney. 'We'll have a girls' night out,' Fiona suggested, 'and really let our hair down – it's just what you need.'

In the end Fiona had cooked dinner for them both at her apartment because it gave them more privacy. Catherine needed to talk – and possibly even to cry. Fiona had a large box of tissues ready just in case.

They were on their second glass of red, when Catherine broke down. 'I trusted Roger,' she sobbed. 'I shared things with him that I've never told anyone else.'

'You feel completely used, don't you?' Fiona said knowingly. She tossed the box of tissues over to Catherine. 'Help yourself.'

'Thanks.' Catherine pulled out a tissue and blew her nose. 'Yes, I do. It's an awful feeling, to know that he made love to me while he hated me!' Gulping back her tears, she said, 'That's what I can't forget. How could he have done that to me?'

'What woman could ever hope to understand the peculiar workings of the male mind?' Fiona said harshly. She refilled her glass.

'I'll have some more.' Catherine held out her glass and took a generous slurp of her wine. 'Roger told me he loathed my kind of woman – all ambitious women give him the shits, he said.' She heaved a big sigh. 'What if all men feel that way about us?'

'Don't be silly, Catherine,' Fiona called out from the kitchen, where she'd gone to open another bottle of red. 'Women are entitled to use their brains and have ambition – there's nothing wrong with that.' She put the wine and a plate of cheese and biscuits on the table. 'You wouldn't have wanted to be a bimbo?'

Catherine looked horror-struck at the suggestion. 'But I once read that men wouldn't have heart attacks if women didn't go to work but stayed home and looked after them.' She helped herself to the cheese. 'Seems bloody unfair to me, to suggest women take total responsibility for men's health. When do men start looking after themselves?'

Fiona giggled. 'Never! But that's their problem not ours.' She proffered the wine bottle to Catherine, who took it, and topped up her glass and unburdened her heart. They talked until quite late and Fiona insisted Catherine sleep in the spare room.

When she left the following morning Catherine felt more at peace with herself than she had for some time. She also had a fearful hangover.

In spite of the general excitement about Brenda's forthcoming nuptials, Catherine refused to let herself be distracted from the task at hand. She called Fiona on the intercom and asked her to come to the meeting with Perry Wolf. 'We haven't all that much time to get everything done. I want to draw up our final countdown lists. I'm sure the *MAUD* 21st Century Collection will have a major impact on fashion trends around the world. After this meeting I want to lock up every detail so that nothing can go wrong.'

Perry was on time, as always. 'Hello, darling, you look happy,' he said, as he kissed her on the cheek. 'What's the big smile for?'

She told him about Brenda's wedding and her quest for a fabulously clever gown. 'Would you have time to pop in and see her after we've finished our meeting?'

'Consider it done. What a challenge – I can't wait to dress her.' He looked around Catherine's office appreciatively. 'I always like coming to your office, it's so relaxing.'

'I spend more time here than anywhere else, that's why,' Catherine laughed. One end of the room was a long wooden bench, on which she kept files, books, reference magazines, and her computer. Above it were rows of bookcases filled with more books and magazines. Her glass-topped desk was round and could sit six easily for meetings. Her tan leather high-backed chair was ergonomically approved. She'd insisted on that, knowing how much time editors spend sitting in their chairs, working.

There were no curtains – Catherine liked plenty of light and being able to admire the view whenever she had the time. Sometimes she read submissions on the sofa by the window. It was in rattan with cream cushions, and two matching armchairs sat opposite.

'Have you heard from Nicole yet?' Perry asked, as he bounced into one of them.

'Yes – and her answer is yes. She's coming to Sydney with Tom and the kids next week. He's doing a movie here and she and I are going to have lunch together so I can tell her everything and she can ask questions. You know how thorough she is about facts and figures.'

Perry gave a groan. 'I've heard. I hope she isn't going to make my life difficult.'

'Of course not,' Catherine replied briskly. 'But she did ask if she could come and see your sketches and whatever you've got made up from the collection. I told her it was fine by me if it was okay by you.'

'That's fabo! Nicole, Elle and Kylie – I never thought you'd pull it off.'

'I don't mind telling you now that I wasn't sure myself. But I was determined to get them if I could.'

Catherine was trying hard not to look pleased with herself and failing completely.

'We're going to knock people's socks off!' Perry spoke excitedly. 'Wait until they see my clothes – this collection is the best I've done!' While he and Catherine had been chatting, his house model, Annie, and his assistant, Rory, had commandeered Catherine's well-appointed bathroom as a change room.

'I'm dying to see it.' Catherine settled herself on the sofa. Fiona came in and sat beside her. She was carrying a copy of the British magazine *Hello*.

'Have you seen this?' she asked Catherine.

'No. Why?'

'There's a fantastic shot of Huxley in it with that French star Genevieve Dupont at the opening of her new film.' She flipped through the pages. 'Here, isn't she gorgeous?'

The photograph showed Huxley, resplendent in a dinner suit, holding hands with the star, who was wearing a figure-hugging flame red gown that left little to the imagination.

'That dress makes her look like a tart,' Catherine said snappishly.

'Huxley doesn't seem to share your opinion,' Fiona laughed. 'He's positively drooling over her.'

Catherine turned to Perry. 'How long before you're ready to show me what you've got made up?' she asked impatiently.

'Well, excuse me – I was waiting until you'd finished ogling that magazine.' Perry looked seriously close to throwing one of his famous tantrums.

Catherine was immediately contrite. 'I'm sorry.' She smiled at him. 'May we begin now?'

'Okay, Annie,' Perry shouted. 'We're ready to go.'

The model came out in the most wondrous Empire-line chiffon evening gown in varying shades of aquamarine, an enchanting mixture of luxury and simplicity.

'Perry, it's just divine,' Catherine exclaimed.

'I want it!' Fiona said.

He was elated by their reaction. 'You haven't seen anything yet,' he said from the bathroom door, where he was standing so that he could make any last-minute adjustment to the garments. He looked thinner than Annie in his black skivvy and trousers and was longing for a smoke, but knew better than to admit to such a thing in front of Catherine, who always lectured him on the perils of cigarettes whenever she saw him with one.

Perry was doing a running commentary and Fiona was taking notes – she wanted to get down his descriptions so that she could put together a press release closer to the launch. 'You can see I've used lots of luxurious rich fabrics . . . and beautiful knits are essential – a woman can wear them anywhere. I've combined heavy fabrics with light, and used fur trims and beading for day and night . . . but everything in the collection is ultra feminine and glamorous, yet practical, when it needs to be.'

His pants were soft and wide and worn with delicate cashmere sweaters. His coats came in all styles: there were magnificent fur-trimmed princess-line styles, brilliantly coloured quilted parkas, one of which he teamed with a sheath gown of burnished orange chiffon; and a classic coat in the palest of pink tissue wool which Annie wore over a straight, sleeveless dress in even paler pink beaded silk.

His skirts were long, some pleated, some straight, and combined with all kinds of sweaters – turtle-necks, body-skimming and ultra sleek, big and slouchy – which he beaded for day as well as night.

When the preview came to an end Catherine and Fiona broke into spontaneous applause. 'Perry, if the rest of the collection is as good as this the world will snaffle you up and we'll never see you in Australia again,' Catherine declared.

'Sounds good to me, darling, but whatever happens I'll always call Australia home.' They laughed.

'How many pieces will be in the collection altogether?' Fiona asked.

'There'll be seventy garments, and as well as Kylie, Elle and Nicole, we'll need to have six other models, maybe eight.'

He was sitting in one of the armchairs again. 'I'm going to run through the logistics of the parade tonight with Beril Jents – she's my guru. There's nothing she doesn't know about fashion and she's coming in later this afternoon to give me her opinion of the collection. I'm going to ask her to join my company as a special consultant.'

'That's a good idea. But how did you meet her?' Catherine asked, intrigued.

'My mother used to work for her and she'd let me watch her parades when Beril ran her own haute couture salon in Sydney – they were amazing. She not only made the most beautiful evening gowns in Australia, she also showed clothes on a catwalk better than anyone else.' He spoke with conviction.

'Isn't it a small world!' Catherine exclaimed. 'My mother had a wardrobe full of Beril Jents evening gowns. She adored them and so did I,' she laughed. 'Once when she was out I tried them all on. I never told her, of course. She would have had a fit. She thought of those gowns as treasures.'

Catherine rarely shared memories of her childhood. Fiona and Perry were all ears, hoping she'd continue. 'Goodness, why am I prattling on like this? Sorry, you two.' She had remembered where she was. 'Has Beril given you any ideas about the parade?'

Perry nodded. 'She says I've got to grab the audience's attention and give them a bit of fun before I get into the essence of the parade.'

Catherine was listening thoughtfully. 'I can see the sense in that. What else does she suggest?'

'Beril favours a long room, with a central catwalk, and rows of chairs on three sides like they do at the Valentino, Ungaro and Yves Saint Laurent haute couture parades.'

'Minimum of fuss?' Catherine asked.

'Precisely! It allows for the clothes to be the focal point. It also gives the TV cameras plenty of scope, which is essential.'

Catherine went over to her desk and made a few notes. 'Can you please jot down anything else Beril comes up with so that we can talk about it when next we meet.'

'Will do, Catherine, darling. And come round for coffee on the weekend,' Perry said. 'I want to have some "girl talk" time with you.' He kissed her goodbye. Rory and Annie had packed up the clothes and were quietly waiting for Perry to finish his discussions. 'Come along you two,' he said with a dramatic wave of his hand. 'We've got oodles of things to do before Beril arrives.'

'Don't forget to see Brenda, will you?' Catherine said, as she blew him a kiss.

A week later the three of them met again. They sat around Catherine's desk, and meticulously worked their way through detail after detail, ticking each item off their respective lists when they were satisfied nothing had been overlooked.

'Is everything on track with the collection?' Catherine asked Perry.

'One little bolt of fabric from France has gone walkabout but I've had my tantrum and the importer has assured me I will have it in time!'

'What if you don't?' Catherine persisted.

'I'll have another tantrum and think of something else!' Perry tittered.

Catherine had a number of files in front of her. She opened one of them and glanced at it for a moment before speaking.

'Kylie, Elle and Nicole have all promised they'll be here about a week before we start photography – that will give them time to get over their jet lag and do fittings. They'll do the same thing for the actual parade as well.'

'Good,' Fiona said. 'That means I can have them for some publicity shots.'

'Exactly.' Catherine was searching for another file. 'But don't wear them out! I want them looking their very best for the special presentation of the collection in *MAUD* – and the cover, of course.' She'd found what she was looking for. 'These are the rough layouts for the pages I've allocated in the magazine for the clothes. Suzanne and I worked on this yesterday with Sam,' she explained.

'Twenty pages,' Perry shrieked. 'Wow!'

Catherine gave him an amused glance. 'Each guest will receive a copy of the magazine as a souvenir of the inaugural collection. We'll also show the magazine on camera at the end of the presentation. I'm not going to waste an opportunity to show the new issue to such a massive audience. I want people to rush to buy the magazine as well as your fabulous clothes.'

Catherine chose her next words carefully. 'Perry,' she said, while making an apologetic face, 'I hope you won't be offended but there's one thing that's bothering me about the collection.'

Perry was instantly uptight.

Oh dear, Catherine thought, but continued nonetheless.

'Most of the skirt lengths in the collection are long but I can't see Kylie looking as good as she can in a long skirt. She's such a tiny thing, the longer length skirts won't do much for her at all.'

'Is that all?' Perry gave a sigh of relief. 'Don't worry your head about it,' he said. 'I've always agreed with Christian Dior about skirt lengths. He insisted it's a matter of individual proportions. He only ever put ultra-short skirts on petite models. I know that not every woman wants to wear long, even though I think it's the right look. Today's woman makes her own choices – all I can do is suggest. We'll be manufacturing our skirts in the shorter lengths as well and Kylie will be the model. I'll have some of the short skirts to show you next time we meet.'

After he'd gone, Catherine and Fiona settled down to some serious discussion about the venues. 'How are things going at the Opera House?' Catherine asked.

'Terrific! After Perry mentioned a central catwalk, I went over and got permission for us to have one without any trouble. I've also arranged to have a giant marquee erected on the forecourt of the Opera House. I like the thought of being able not only to see the harbour but to hear it as well. Splashing sea sounds are always comforting, aren't they? Anyone feeling stressed will relax almost straight away. I've found a company who will put down a floor of specially treated timber – to absorb the sound, you know – and they're happy to build us a catwalk as well.'

She handed Catherine a selection of photographs. 'These are some of the things they've done in the past.'

Catherine laid them out on her desk. 'Outstanding. I really like this,' she said, pointing to one of the designs. 'Who is this company?'

'They're a European outfit who've recently set up here, and they are keen to do something out of the ordinary for us because they know they'll benefit from the publicity we'll get for them. So they're prepared to give us a special price,' Fiona said triumphantly.

'Fabo, as Perry would say!'

Fiona continued animatedly. 'They'll create a domed ceiling of mirrors in the tent and from it will flow pale pearl grey silk walls – I thought they'd be a good background for the clothes and also an excellent colour for the cameras.'

She looked at Catherine for her approval – and got it. 'I love the sound of all that. It will be breathtaking.'

They turned their attention to New York and London. Again Catherine had files on both places. Her attention to detail was well known. It was something her father had drummed into her. 'Many a person has failed because of inattention to detail,' he'd cautioned her, time and time again.

'We've got the Grand Ballroom at The Waldorf Astoria, in New York. It's the most amazingly opulent, two-tiered ballroom, recreated in the image of the Court Theatre in Versailles. It has an incredibly high ceiling and a huge chandelier decked out with Art Deco medallions and ornaments. I've never seen anything like it anywhere else in the world.'

The time difference between Australia and America meant that the collection would be shown in the early morning over there, and Catherine had chosen the Walker family's favourite breakfast dish – Eggs Benedict – for the presentation. 'Guests will also be offered Bloody Marys, with and without vodka,' she guaranteed Fiona.

'You've always preferred the Waldorf to the Plaza, haven't you?'

'Definitely, it's one of the crown jewels of Art Deco New York and not as impersonal as the Plaza. Plus it's only a short walk to the shops on Fifth Avenue.' Her eyes twinkled. 'Of course the Plaza's lovely because it's near Central Park, but the Waldorf is on Park Avenue and in the heart of Manhattan. It always gives me a buzz.

'More importantly, as far as we're concerned for our presentation, the staff is so helpful. Nothing is too much trouble and they're used to putting on prestigious events. And you know how crazy I am about clocks. I could stand in the lobby and gaze at that wondrous ornate bronze and mahogany clock of theirs all day.'

'It's probably the clock that won you over.'

'I wouldn't be at all surprised,' Catherine laughed, closing her US file and opening her UK one.

For that presentation she'd managed to book the spectacular restaurant at the legendary Ritz Hotel. 'We can also use the terrace that looks out over Green Park,' Catherine said, as she showed Fiona a brochure highlighting The Ritz's amenities.

'Huxley's sending technicians from World Channel around there some time this week to work out where the screens need to be placed for maximum impact – Tom's doing the same in New York. Neither of them sees any problems. We're thinking of a semi-circle of screens, which should result in a visual knockout. It's lucky for us that Walker Corp.'s technical people are the best in the business. Huxley is always raving about them.'

'How is Huxley?' Fiona inquired, with a wicked gleam in her eye.

'I can't begin to tell you how helpful he's been,' Catherine replied. 'Really fantastic – he's even gone over to The Ritz several times to sort out a couple of glitches. We're lucky he's there.'

'Really?' Fiona said playfully. 'You know he's crazy about you.'

'Garbage!' Catherine protested. 'You're imagining things. We've always been good friends. Don't talk nonsense.'

But Fiona's remarks had thrown Catherine off balance. Flustered, she'd gone to pull out another file, but instead knocked it onto the ground. She scrambled around the floor, picking up her papers, and bumped her head on her desk. 'Damn!' Fiona watched her performance with interest.

'Don't you dare say another word,' Catherine said, as she composed herself. 'Now, let me tell you something you don't know! I received an e-mail last night from Barneys in New York to say they're sending their chief buyer down here to sample the collection because they're considering stocking it. Bergdorf Goodman and Saks Fifth Avenue want it, too.'

Catherine was jubilant. 'And just this morning Leonard Lauder rang me to ask if we'd let Estée Lauder do the make-up for the models.'

'Fantastic!'

'He wants to come to Sydney with his wife, Eve-lyn, for our presentation here and he's been talking with Robert Horton about running special Estée Lauder promotions at Horton's afterwards.'

'This is so exciting.'

'Isn't it!' Catherine's adrenaline was working overtime. 'I lunched with Robert yesterday and he's going to give us display windows in every Horton's store throughout Australia and all the mannequins will be holding a copy of *MAUD*! They've never done anything like it before. It's going to blow everyone's mind away.'

Catherine paused, and looked sideways at her friend. 'You know, Fiona, Robert Horton is one of the nicest men in Sydney.'

'Yes, he is,' Fiona agreed.

'He'd be perfect for you.'

Fiona shook her head in exasperation. 'I keep telling you, Catherine, I'm not interested in men.'

'I don't believe you. One day you'll change your mind.'

'Well, for the moment, can we please talk about something else. What about the London retailers – have any of them expressed any interest?'

'Absolutely! Both Harvey Nichols and Harrods want to send buyers to talk to us, and Perry's also had a call from Galeries Lafayette in Paris.'

'This is going to be bigger than *Ben Hur*.'

'I bloody well hope so,' Catherine replied happily. 'Who would ever have thought that one day we'd be doing something of this magnitude.'

Determined to leave nothing to chance, the two women spent the next hour going through Catherine's travel arrangements and the timing of the show, which would begin in Sydney at 9.30 p.m. and simultaneously in London at 12.30 p.m. the same day, and New York at 7.30 a.m. the previous day. Catherine would be in Australia to host the telecast from Sydney and then leave the following day for New York for media appearances. She'd agreed to speak at a breakfast at The Waldorf Astoria Starlight Roof room as well as make public appearances at Barneys if a deal was stitched up between them for the collection. A similar programme of events was planned for London.

'Then,' she told Fiona resolutely, 'I'm going to take a couple of weeks off.'

'You've earnt a break. Where will you go?'

'Haven't decided yet, but somewhere relaxing.' As she spoke she glanced down at her watch. 'Oh my!' she yelped. 'Look at the time – I've got to make some phone calls to a couple of writers and then I told Brenda I'd help her with her wedding plans. How we're going to fit her wedding in with everything else we have on the drawing board I do not know.'

'We'll manage, Catherine. We always do. Brenda asked me to come along this evening, too.'

'I'll see you later, then.' Fiona left and Catherine went over to her desk and began to make a call but before she could finish dialling, Clare put her head around the door.

'Boss, there's a call for you from London. It's Jack Clement.'

'I miss you,' she said after picking up the phone.

'The feeling's mutual, I assure you.'

Having satisfied themselves about their emotions, their conversation took a more mundane turn. They chatted about the weather, Jack's hotel, Catherine's day at the office – she told him about Brenda and William's forthcoming wedding. She had to exercise all her self-control not to ask him whether his 'big deal' with Rupert was connected with The Clement Group's attempt to take over Webster Media.

She'd have been flabbergasted to know Jack was fighting the urge to quiz her about Webster Media. By now he knew, like everyone else did, that Sydney Walker had picked up Charles's parcel of shares but there was great speculation as to what was behind his purchase.

Jack and Rupert were as curious as anyone else, especially as the acquisition could affect their plans. They still had one more card to play. When Rupert had learnt that Jack knew Catherine he'd suggested he pump her for information. 'Surely she'd have some idea as to why her father had bought the shares,' he said. But Jack was wary about mixing business with pleasure.

Catherine had no idea why her father had become

involved. Sydney had rung not long after Jack had left for London to inform her about his new acquisition but hadn't shared any of the details with her. He'd prefer to do that, he'd insisted, face to face.

Fortunately Jack didn't raise the subject with Catherine or she'd have given him short shrift. There was no way she'd divulge any of her father's business secrets to anyone, including him – that wasn't the Walker way. Instead Jack filled her in on an unexpected change in his travel plans but he did it so nonchalantly that Catherine was upset. 'But you were only going to London for a short while,' she said, her dismay obvious in the tone of her voice. 'Now you're telling me you won't be back for three months. That's unbearable.'

'My business associates often throw my plans into disarray. I'm sorry, darling,' he said contritely, before adding quickly, 'I do miss you.'

Almost as a bloody afterthought, Catherine told herself crossly.

'It's essential that I go to the States and Germany,' Jack went on. 'Then I have to come back to London to tidy up a few loose ends and –'

'Is this the way it's always going to be?' Catherine interrupted him. 'You disappearing for months on end?'

'Of course not!' Now Jack was annoyed but she didn't care. A long-distance love affair was not on her agenda, not now, not ever.

'Darling Catherine, work doesn't go away just because a man is in love, you know.'

'That's for sure,' she retorted.

'When you lose your temper you certainly are a chip off the old block,' Jack teased. 'Come on, darling, forgive me. I'll mend my ways, turn over a new leaf – anything you like – but don't stay mad at me. I'm just a mere male who's never professed to be perfect.'

In spite of herself, Catherine gave a tiny laugh.

'That's better,' Jack said. 'I have an idea.'

'Yes?'

'I expect to be back in London around about the time you'll be here for the *MAUD* collection promotion.'

'That would be a fluke.'

'Now, now,' Jack gently rebuked her. 'Why don't we spend some time together then?'

Catherine told him she intended to take a holiday after the promotion was over.

'Where are you thinking of going?'

'I haven't made up my mind yet, but Italy does have appeal.'

'I wouldn't mind spending some time relaxing in Italy. Perhaps we could go there together?'

'I would like that very much indeed,' Catherine said.

'Leave everything to me. I'll get my office to have a look at what's on offer and get back to you.'

'Fine. Will you call me?'

'Most certainly.'

'Until then . . .'

'Until then, darling.'

She sat back in her chair and closed her eyes. What a complex man he was and what a challenge. How was she going to get through the next three months without him? Clare, coming in to say good-night, interrupted her musings.

'I'm off, Boss. Have a good night.'

'I'm leaving also.' Catherine stood up. 'I've a date with the bride-to-be. See you in the morning.'

Later Catherine, Fiona and Brenda acknowledged that the weeks before the wedding, coupled with their workload, had been one of the most hectic periods they'd ever experienced. Still, it kept Catherine's mind off Jack and she'd even managed to find the time to get to Honolulu to spend Christmas with Tom and was pleased that she had. The break had revitalised her.

They'd swum and soaked up a little sun, eaten far too much, done a spot of shopping, and had more than one Mai Tai in the lush gardens of the Royal Hawaiian. It was during one of these cocktail hours that Tom told Catherine about Belinda Appleby, his current girlfriend.

'You don't mean Greg Appleby's sister?' Catherine asked, remembering Tom's former schoolmate who'd stayed at Ashburn occasionally during the school holidays. 'You and he drove me mad with those awful war games you used to play.'

'But that's a brother's main role in life.'

'What is?'

'To annoy his sister.' Tom grinned at her cheekily.

'You are a pain!' She laughed fondly, genuinely pleased to see her brother so happy. 'Tell me, how did you meet Belinda?'

'At a drinks party at the Australian Consulate where she works. I couldn't believe it was her when she said hello to me – she'd changed so much from the days when I knew her as Greg's kid sister.'

'Really, what's she like?'

'Very pretty, and there's not a trace of the brat that she once was! Actually, she's the nicest girl I've ever met,' he confided. 'I've never heard anyone say a bad word about her. She loves sport. You should see her on the tennis court, she plays like a champion.'

'Maybe we could all have a game one day.'

'Come to New York – if you can stop working long enough – and we'll play you any day. David can make up the four.'

'Who's David?'

'Just a guy I know.'

'Well, is he a good sort? Would I like him?'

'How would I know?' Tom shook his head. 'You're so fussy about your men.'

'Garbage!' Catherine folded her arms. 'You always

were prone to exaggeration. Anyway – *that's* a brother's real role in life.'

'What is?'

'To keep his sister supplied with men!'

They were in good form and continued teasing each other when they went to eat at the nearby beachside dining room.

'Are you eating tonight, sister dear,' Tom said, 'or are you going to eat only salad because you're on a diet?'

'Get stuffed!'

At that precise moment the waiter arrived to take their order. Catherine almost choked with embarrassment.

'Could you come back in a moment,' Tom gasped at the waiter, before he broke into loud guffaws, which caused Catherine to laugh uncontrollably, too. It was several minutes before they'd collected themselves enough to tell the waiter what they'd like to eat.

Tom sighed contentedly, as he looked out over Waikiki Beach. 'This is so peaceful compared to New York.'

'Do you like living there?'

He nodded enthusiastically. 'New York is such a stimulating place – my mind is never idle. There are ideas everywhere. That's what I really like. And the place never stops. It's a city that's on the go twenty-four hours a day. When you come over for the

*MAUD* Collection presentation I'll take you to some of my favourite haunts.'

'Don't remind me of work,' Catherine almost hissed the words at him. 'I'm in veg-out mode! I'll be back on the job soon enough.'

Brenda and William's wedding day went off without a hitch. Weather-wise, it was a perfect summer's day. It was hot but not as warm as some February days can be in the Hunter Valley.

Brenda shone with happiness, the glow of expectant motherhood making her look breathtakingly lovely. Her grey eyes and high cheekbones were framed by her auburn hair, newly cut in a short Joan of Arc-style bob. Perry's gown in heavy white silk hid her pregnancy completely. It was long and narrow, its hem encrusted with crystals, and over the top she wore a sleeveless tunic top, cut on an A-line with long side slits and a square-shaped neckline, also edged in crystals.

Perry had designed a wreath of delicate crystal leaves for her hair and had personally supervised the making of her bouquet of white rambling roses tied in white silk. Somehow he'd also found the time to unearth a brilliant bootmaker who'd covered Brenda's shoes in the same material as her gown and then adorned them with crystals.

'These are your Cinderella slippers,' Perry told Brenda. 'May you and your prince live happily ever after.'

Thoughts of her own wedding day came back to Catherine. She blocked them out, not wanting any unhappy memories to spoil the day. 'Be happy, dear Brenda,' she whispered, bending forward to kiss her friend on her cheek and then, in a louder voice, said, 'you look beautiful.'

'Simply stunning,' Fiona chimed in.

Brenda's wedding dress was much admired, as were Catherine's and Fiona's outfits. Perry had dressed them in long gowns of deep golden silk, with draped bodices and skirts that fell softly. He'd edged their necklines with matching crystals, and made wreaths of tinted crystal leaves like Brenda's, but smaller, for their hair.

'As usual you've excelled yourself,' Catherine told him, while they shared a quick glass of champagne to steady their nerves and toast the bride. As an aside she added: 'May the *MAUD* Collection be equally as successful.'

'My darling, I promise you it will be. I have a feeling in my bones that this is going to be my year! Okay, madam, are you ready to make your grand entrance?' he asked Brenda. 'Let me take one last look at you.' He nodded approvingly as he appraised her.

'Everything is in order so why don't we get on with the show – you don't want poor William to think you've changed your mind,' and he flung open the door so that Brenda could lead the way to the chapel. Her father was waiting for her at the entrance.

Inside the little chapel, Brenda had placed urns of white tulips and tuberoses, their scent filling the air. The altar was covered with a white linen cloth, and a white candle stood at either end. Brenda and William wanted a small, intimate wedding and had invited only thirty people, including their parents. The guests sat on simple wooden benches and watched as the pair took their vows.

Everyone was in a cheerful mood as they made their way through the charming landscaped gardens to the reception, where a long farmhouse table had been set up looking out over the Pepper Tree vineyard. It was the perfect setting. The table was shaded with ochre-coloured canvas umbrellas with masses of green ivy and talisman roses woven around the umbrella stands. The chairs were covered in the same colour canvas, the exact shade of soft yellow so typical of buildings in Tuscany.

That ochre colour was cleverly picked up in the linen cloth that covered the table, which was also laid with crisp white overcloths. An array of white Italian plates was at each guest's place at the table and topped with a white linen napkin, on which had been put a small red satin pouch containing a Chinese fortune cookie made in silver and engraved with William's and Brenda's names and the date. The centre of the table from one end to the other had been covered with small terracotta pots of red geraniums.

As everyone sat down the first of the many Hunter Valley wines that were to be consumed that day was poured. Brenda had asked Stephanie Alexander and Maggie Beer, two of Australia's leading foodies, to prepare a Tuscan banquet. The two women were over the moon to have been asked and conveniently used recipes from their latest bestselling cookbook, which *MAUD* had described as the 'Number One Cookbook of the Year'.

Waiters came and offered many courses – chicken liver crostini and tomato bruschetta; marinated mussels; pasta with pine nuts, currants and zucchini flowers; and, to follow, grilled leg of lamb with rosemary and garlic served with carrots, potatoes and fennel that had been roasted together. The Cheng Chardonnay had been praised and drunk with enjoyment. A couple of the guests who considered themselves wine buffs debated whether the Cheng red was better than the white.

Just when they thought they couldn't eat another mouthful everyone somehow found room for mouthwatering caramel chocolate puddings served with a puree of plums.

'It was the feast to end them all,' Catherine told Jack, when she rang him later. 'I've never enjoyed a wedding so much. If only you could have been here, too, that would have been wonderful.'

Lunch was a long and leisurely affair and after the coffee had been served William and Brenda both spoke and thanked everyone for coming and making the day so special for them. 'Whenever we think of this, the most important day of our lives,' William said, as he held his new wife's hand, 'we will also think of you, our dearest friends and family. We are honoured that you've been able to be with us.'

Then the dancing began. Brenda had found a group of Italian musicians who played the most romantic Italian music. The urge to dance was irresistible. The guests, as well as William and Brenda, danced the night away, the mother-to-be showing no signs of tiredness. Finally the band pleaded exhaustion and bade everyone goodnight.

It was, Catherine assured Brenda when she made her farewells, the nicest wedding she'd ever been to. 'I had a marvellous time and so did everyone else.'

'It was the best day of my life,' Brenda said blissfully. 'Oh Catherine,' she went on, 'I'm happier than I ever thought it was possible to be. I adore William. He is just perfect. I wish you could find someone like William. You deserve a nice man.'

'I might just surprise you,' Catherine said.

'Excuse me? What are you up to, Catherine Walker?'

'Nothing – well, it's nothing I'm going to tell you about yet. So don't even waste your time trying to bully it out of me. Anyway, it's your wedding night.

Look at William waiting for you patiently over there. Away with you.'

As she got ready for bed Catherine thought over their conversation. Watching all the love between William and Brenda had put her in the mood for a little loving, too. If only Jack was here, she thought, for the millionth time that day.

Brenda had arranged for everyone to stay at The Convent, which originally had been built in another part of New South Wales for an order of Brigidine nuns, before being relocated to the Pepper Tree vineyard and transformed into luxury accommodation. The serenity that Catherine always associated with nuns seemed to pervade the place.

If only I could be as certain that my own love story will end as happily as William and Brenda's, she thought, curling up under the bedclothes. She drifted off to sleep wishing she knew what fate had up its romantic sleeve for her.

# Chapter Sixteen

Arriving bright and early at CW Publishing after her weekend in the Hunter Valley, Catherine was in the mood to tackle the world. 'It's just as well,' she said to Clare, 'because I want to do a phone link-up today with London and New York. Find out when the entire team is available and then mark off a couple of hours in my diary so that if there are any problems we have enough time to sort them out.

'And I also want to talk to Huxley Edwards. I want to make sure that there haven't been any glitches with the sound checks World Channel has been doing. But first, try to find Tom for me, would you?'

Catherine placed her *MAUD* 21st Century Fashion Collection file on her desk. This thing's getting bigger by the minute, she thought. Extracting the 'Sydney Gala' folder, she began checking the catering details. Then she did the same for New York and London.

Perry Wolf had dropped off a huge envelope containing drawings of the entire collection, with an outline of the way he saw them being paraded, for her to approve. As well as Kylie, Elle and Nicole he'd booked another seven models to show the clothes – the cream of the crop, Catherine concluded, as she skimmed through the list: Sarah O'Hare, Linda Evangelista, Naomi Campbell, Kate Moss, Amber Valetta, Claudia Schiffer, and Christy Turlington. Catherine could visualise exactly what Perry had in mind. *Our parade is going to be a razzle dazzler!*

Because of the time differences between Sydney, London and New York, Catherine knew that coordinating the different kind of hospitality she'd planned for each venue would be the most challenging part of the simultaneous showing.

The Sydney part of the presentation was to begin at 7.30 p.m., when arriving guests would be greeted and offered champagne, which they would take with them to the domed marquee where the parade would begin at 9.30 p.m. sharp. Catherine didn't want the evening to be bogged down by speeches, which was so often the case at gala events. She'd promised the sponsors that they would each get a mention and they were satisfied with that. She would speak before the collection was shown so as not to spoil the effect of Perry's grand finale, after which he would come out and take his bows.

The entire parade plus Catherine's speech would

take just over an hour, perhaps a little longer depending on the applause.

Perry had reminded her several times to be sure to leave time for the applause. 'I love the sound of clapping,' he'd told her.

She was so involved in what she was doing that when her phone rang she jumped. 'I've got your brother on the line, Boss,' Clare said, as she put through the call.

'Sis, good to hear from you – I guess you're ringing to find out how things are going.'

'Of course.'

Tom confirmed that everything was proceeding smoothly and that he'd be at The Waldorf Astoria on the day wearing his new suit, bought especially for the occasion. 'I'm confident that it will be the year's most talked about event.'

'What – your suit or my collection?' Catherine laughed at him.

'Droll, Sis . . . very droll. But seriously,' he went on, 'I can't wait to see it all unfold – I'm getting begging calls from New Yorkers wanting to know where their invitations are – and the media interest is mind-blowing.'

Not for the first time Catherine thanked her lucky stars that her brother had been able to persuade their father into letting him stay on in America for a few more years. Originally, Sydney had wanted Tom to come home when Huxley was posted to England, which would have made it far harder for her to organise the presentation in New York. Having Tom there took a big weight off her shoulders.

Sydney had grumbled in the beginning but later conceded that it'd been a wise move. His son had achieved remarkable sales for Walker Wide Screens in the United States and Canada and, by working closely with Huxley, he'd been able to sign up some notable sportsmen and women for Walker Cable Sports. Sydney had appointed him to the International Board of Walker Corp. and Tom attended regular board meetings in Australia, followed by general discussions about company matters with his father.

'Any problems your end?' Tom inquired.

'Not . . . really,' Catherine faltered.

'Not really? What do you mean?' Tom demanded. 'What's wrong? Tell me the truth.'

'It's the bloody sponsors – you know how they always like to keep us in suspense.'

'Only too well. What can I do to help?'

'Nothing at the moment – I'm trying to keep my cool – but thanks for the offer and also for keeping such an expert eye on everything for me over there. I'm so glad you're in New York, Tom.'

'Me too, but I'm not sure that I'll be here much longer. Dad muttered something about it being opportune for me to return to headquarters because he wants to spend less time in the office. I couldn't believe what I was hearing when he said it.'

'I had the same reaction when he told me,' Catherine said. 'I'm sure it was Bill Donaldson's death that triggered it.' Bill and Sydney had been friends since their school days and regularly played golf together as well as the occasional game of tennis. Bill's passing had shocked everyone. He was such a fit and healthy-looking man who'd always watched what he ate and drank. He'd been out sailing his yacht, *Best Mate*, on the harbour about a month ago, when he'd collapsed at the helm. 'It was the way he'd have wanted to go,' Sydney said when he comforted Bill's wife, Louise, at the funeral, 'but I'll miss him.'

Catherine wasn't the only person who'd noticed the change in her father. Even faithful Dot, a soul of discretion at all times, had commented on it. 'He's just not his old self,' she said to Catherine. 'He seems to have lost some of his zest for living.' Catherine had passed on her remarks to Tom.

'And now this mystery trip,' Tom added. 'It's so unlike the old man to just pack up and disappear. I think it has suddenly dawned on Dad that he's not getting any younger and that the clock is ticking on. Do you know he actually told me that he no longer gets excited about the thought of going to the office? I never thought I'd live to see the day when Dad would say something like that.'

'Let me tell you something else you'll find hard to believe,' Catherine said. 'The other night he told me there were things he wanted to do and when I asked him like what, he said he'd always wanted to paint. And then he said that he was going to put some time aside when he got home, to find out whether he's any good or not.'

'You're joking! Old age must be mellowing him.'

'He's not that old, Tom! He's only sixty-five.'

'I know. I didn't mean he was past it, Sis, but perhaps Dad is finally realising that life is meant to be lived, not just worked. And not a moment too soon!'

It would be nice having Tom back in Sydney, Catherine thought, as they chatted. We're such kindred spirits.

'How does Belinda feel about you coming home?' she asked.

'I haven't told her anything about it,' he murmured.

'Why on earth not?' Sometimes her brother's behaviour amazed her. How could he be so secretive with the woman he loved? Catherine had been pleased when Tom had begun taking Belinda out, and delighted when it became apparent that the relationship was a serious one. Although girls had often chased Tom, he'd never shown much interest in anyone in particular. Catherine had often worried if he'd ever meet the right girl. It had even crossed her mind that perhaps he might be gay. Obviously that wasn't the case.

'I couldn't see the point of upsetting her,' Tom

said, almost impatiently. 'After all, I don't have a definite departure date yet.'

Catherine ignored the tone in his voice. 'But wouldn't she want to know about something as life-changing as that?'

'Listen, Sis, I may be your little brother but I am grown up, in case you hadn't noticed. Would you mind letting me handle my relationships my way?'

Well aware that her mild-mannered brother could put on a tremendous display of temper if pushed too far, Catherine backed off. 'I've got the message – keep my nose out of things that don't concern me,' she laughed apologetically. 'I'll go quietly.'

'Hang on,' Tom said. 'You're not going to get away that easily. You're the one who brought up the topic of relationships, so tell me, what's this about you and Jack Clement?'

'Dad told you, did he?'

'Yes, and he says that you're pretty smitten with Clement. Are you?'

'As a matter of fact, yes, I am. So what?' she said boldly. But her brother's approval meant a great deal to her and Catherine was amazed at how tense she felt as she waited for his reaction.

'I hope you know what you're doing. It's my observation that married men are good at making promises but useless when it comes to keeping them. When push comes to shove most married men – who invariably claim to be unhappily married – give their girlfriends the heave and keep their wives.'

'That won't happen to me!' Catherine was adamant. 'Jack's a man of his word.'

They'd no sooner hung up than Clare announced she had Huxley on the line.

'Good morning, Catherine, how's everything going in your part of the world?'

'Reasonably well, thanks. Gosh, it's great to hear your voice, Huxley, but what's happened to your Aussie accent?' she kidded him. 'You're beginning to sound frightfully British, old chap.'

'Cut it out, will you,' he laughed. 'I'm the same as I ever was. What can I do for you?'

'I'm on countdown to the big day, which is the purpose of this call.'

'Your timing's just right. I went through a final sound check late yesterday afternoon and you don't have to worry about anything here. It's all under control. We've done several run throughs with the Walker Wide Screen, too, and the results have been excellent. I'm sure you'll be pleased.'

She could hear him rustling some papers. 'Ah, yes – your booking on the World Channel's satellite for the simultaneous presentation is confirmed, but they want to know when you'll be sending them the draft rundown so they can start working on lighting and camera angles.'

Catherine was taking notes as he talked. 'Probably tomorrow but I'll send you an e-mail later in the day to confirm it one way or the other.'

'Fine, I'll let them know. I've also spoken with the people at Global Access and they've confirmed that all is in order with your Internet link-up.

'And now,' Huxley said, pausing for a moment, 'prepare yourself for a surprise! Because Global Access is as excited as we are about the project and understands its tremendous marketing potential, they're going to show the collection on their Internet Fashion Channel the following day – not twice, as we'd originally discussed, but six times in twenty-four hours, at four-hourly intervals.'

'Six times in twenty-four hours! Huxley, I can't believe it. You're a marvel!'

'I know that,' he chortled, 'but it's your genius that's wowed Global Access, not mine. If you were available I think they'd offer you a job, they're that impressed. And they really like that illustrious assortment of first-class sponsors you've lined up.'

'Some of them still have to sign,' she said hastily.

'Really? I thought they were all in the bag.'

'If only,' she replied, somewhat wistfully.

'You're not worried about any of them, are you?'

'Not really but I won't relax until the contracts have been signed.' She spoke confidently enough but Huxley could tell that something was niggling her. 'There's nothing better than closing a sale – you know that as well as I do.'

In fact, selling always gave Catherine a kick. She'd thoroughly enjoyed calling on her prospects.

'I wish you could have seen the pack at BMW when I told them what I was planning. They were twitching with excitement. It was wonderful just watching them, Huxley. They were giving me signals that told me they were mine before they knew it themselves. I loved every moment of it.' She gave a little chuckle. 'Brenda reckoned a couple of them were frothing at the mouth!'

He was reassured to hear her laugh. 'I'm glad you've still got your sense of humour. But you're certainly working extremely hard – are you sure you're leaving enough time for yourself? You know what they say about all work and no play.'

'That's impossible! There aren't enough hours in the day at the moment but I've just had a fantastic weekend in the country, and there's always time to play later. It won't stay as busy as this forever.' She forced herself to sound cheerful.

'Don't kid with me, Catherine,' he said sternly. 'You're overdoing it. You need more than the occasional weekend off. You've got a work schedule that would kill most people.'

'I can't help that, there's a lot of pressure on me. Surely you understand that?' she insisted. 'I have no intention of bombing – imagine what my father would say. I'm prepared to work twenty-four hours a day if I have to.'

I might have known her father was mixed up in this somewhere, Huxley thought. No wonder she's so stressed. Her father's opinion always made her push herself to the limit. Walkers had to win – whatever the cost. But something else is bothering her. If only she'd confide in me. He shook his head in exasperation. She can be so pigheaded at times but she's not as tough as she makes out. She needs someone to look after her. How on earth do I say that to her?

But he had no chance to tell her anything because Catherine cut short his ruminations. 'I'm not going to argue with you, Huxley.' There was a determined edge to her voice. 'Let's change the subject.'

'Fine.' His tone was abrupt.

'I'm sorry. I didn't mean to bite your head off, but I've got a lot on my mind.' She stifled a sigh.

For an instant Huxley thought she was going to share whatever it was that was bothering her, but the moment was gone in a flash as she adroitly switched the topic. 'It's your turn to buy dinner when I'm in London, you know! I trust you'll be taking me to the newest, glitziest restaurant in town.'

'Just make sure you leave time for a meal in your crazy schedule. I'll find the restaurant.'

It will be good to have dinner with Huxley, she thought as she hung up, and to forget my cares and woes for a while. Perhaps I should have levelled with him – it was one of her worst faults, she knew, the way she kept things to herself. But she'd been sorting out her problems on her own since she was a child and it was hard to change her ways now, even for an old friend like Huxley.

Catherine's list of big-spending sponsors was impressive but Qantas, American Express and Telstra had gone lukewarm and were giving her the runaround. If she didn't get them on board soon she'd have to go out selling again, in search of new ones, and that was easier said than done. Advertisers with the kind of money she required weren't in plentiful supply and at this late stage, they probably would have allocated their money elsewhere. It was industry practice to assign funds well in advance so that promotions could be coordinated with the release of advertised products. Even if she were fortunate enough to find someone who did express interest in the *MAUD* package they'd almost certainly have to dip into their contingency funds, something no one did lightly. In other words, Catherine thought morosely, they'd take their time before making a decision and she was up against the clock.

The two-million-dollar package she was offering each sponsor was a great deal of money, but – Catherine had argued this point many times – it was generous. It included naming rights at all the collection venues; advertisements throughout the televised presentation and also Global Access's Fashion

Channel; and full-page ads in the programmes as well as in *MAUD* itself. There would be numerous fringe benefits, too. Obviously the event would generate tremendous publicity, which was bound to flow on to the sponsors, all of whom would be invited to the live presentation in the city of their choice as Catherine's guests.

She'd determined that she needed to stitch up eleven sponsors to meet the budget she'd set herself. Eight of them had signed off on the deal and things were still looking good when her father had rung to find out how her selling was progressing.

'Just three to go,' she said brightly.

'Are you anticipating any problems?'

She crossed her fingers. 'Not at all.'

'To have sold as many packages as you have is a bloody good result,' Sydney said. 'You should be feeling quite buoyed up about it all.'

'I am, Dad, although I know I still have to watch costs,' she said, reminding him that her bottom line had benefited by Walker Wide Screen and Global Access, who had both decided to give their involvement as a sponsorship-in-kind arrangement.

'What I'm going to stage is certainly not cheap, but I want to put on something quite out of the ordinary to introduce the collection to the world. If I get it right, we'll not only sell millions of dollars' worth of clothes but also hundreds of thousands more copies of *MAUD*, and that should result in more advertising for the magazine. If it doesn't, I'll want to know why!' She gave a hearty laugh. 'Gosh, that sounded very like you, didn't it?'

Sydney laughed good-humouredly with her. 'There's nothing wrong with that.'

Only an hour later, Brenda had asked to see her urgently. She looked agitated as she rushed into Catherine's office. 'We've a major catastrophe looming.' The words came tumbling out. 'Qantas, Telstra, and Amex are having serious second thoughts! They rang and told me within ten minutes of each other.'

'What!' Catherine frowned. 'But why?'

'They didn't say – each of them gave me some nonsense about needing more time to consider our package before making the final decision.' She flung herself into the chair in front of Catherine's desk and thumped the arms. 'I smell a rat!'

Catherine was utterly dismayed and for once didn't bother to hide her feelings. 'I need this like I need a hole in the head.' She was staring at Brenda, but her mind was a million miles away, trying to fathom what had gone wrong. 'If we can't persuade them to stay with us I'll have a financial disaster on my hands. We'll have to go and call on them again, as quickly as possible. Get on the phone and see what you can organise.'

Appointments were made and confirmed. Before the day was out Brenda rushed into Catherine's office once again. 'I've found out what's going on,' she

373

announced. 'The Seven Network is wooing them with one of their Melbourne Colonial Stadium deals coupled with their "Super Sports Sponsorship" packages.'

'Bloody sport! Wouldn't you know it,' Catherine said. 'I wonder if Perry plays footy,' she giggled.

Brenda looked at her, puzzled.

'We could have him and the models stage a scrum on the catwalk.' In spite of the seriousness of the situation both women laughed.

'Thank heavens you're able to find something amusing about it, Catherine. Laughter's the only thing that keeps me sane at times like this.'

By the end of the week Catherine and Brenda had talked with the CEOs of the three companies. Each of them had said they needed time to consider Seven's sports offer. Yes, the *MAUD* package was exciting, they agreed, but so was Seven's, and sport was a major drawcard for so many of their customers. When Catherine asked if they'd be able to make up their minds within seven days they were non-committal.

Later, back at CW Publishing, Catherine sat at her desk, elbows on the table, head in her hands. Looking up, she said gloomily to Brenda: 'I'm going to ask my father for his advice.'

'You'd do that?' Brenda gaped at her.

Catherine nodded. 'There's too much at stake. I'd be a bloody idiot to let pride stop me from doing what I know is the only sensible thing to do.'

Sydney Walker had heard on his well-connected grapevine that his daughter was having problems but prudently said nothing when she called him on his mobile in Monaco. The stress she was under was evident in her voice and when she told him what had happened he was furious. 'The bastards,' he thundered, 'treating you this way.'

Catherine said nothing, knowing from past experience that it was wise to let her father rant and rave without interruption. When he was done, his mood changed unexpectedly. 'I have an idea,' he said slowly, a triumphant grin spreading over his face. 'Why don't you offer them our integrated multimedia scheme.'

'Our what?'

'Our solution to their advertising needs! It will allow them to combine the original *MAUD* deal with Walker Stadium packages, including advertising and naming rights, plus advertising schedules on Walker Cable and in all – or any – of my newspapers. There's more than enough sport in that lot, if that's what it'll take to make them sign with you.'

The notion of cross-selling multiple mediums had occupied Sydney's attention for some time. He'd been waiting for the right opportunity to raise the concept with his daughter and had only hesitated because of her insistence that she run her business without his help. Maybe now she'd be able to see that there were benefits in working together, he thought.

Catherine felt the aching tension pain in her

shoulders beginning to subside. Calling her father had been the right decision.

'This kind of multimedia advertising is the way of the future.' Sydney was so positive only a brave person would have dared to argue otherwise. 'And that's exactly what you're going to tell Qantas, Telstra and American Express, when you go back to see them,' he instructed her.

'Dad, it's inspired.' Catherine's enthusiasm bubbled over; she couldn't wait to revisit those damn recalcitrant sponsors of hers. 'We'll get a much bigger slice of their budget, maybe even all of it.'

'Precisely! There's no longer any need for them to have endless discussions with numerous media groups – they can one-stop shop with us.'

Catherine and Brenda spent the next day working out the financial structure of the new arrangement with the sales and marketing team at Walker Corp. When they were satisfied that they could justify their figures, as well as the handsome profits each company could expect to make, Catherine called Sydney and took him through the proposal.

'It's good,' he said approvingly. 'I don't think you'll have any problem convincing them to sign with us.' He gave a satisfied laugh. 'This alliance between Walker Corp. and CW Publishing will take the wind out of one or two people's sails and, mark my words, it won't be long before they're all following our example.'

'Dad.' Catherine cleared her throat. She was so

tired that it had gone croaky. 'Dad,' she began again, 'thanks for your help.'

'That's all right,' he grunted, trying to hide his emotions. His daughter was the apple of his eye and he would move heaven and earth if necessary, to make sure that she succeeded, not that he'd ever tell her that, of course. He simply said: 'Let me know how you go.'

Qantas and American Express eagerly took up the integrated packages and pronounced them to be precisely what they'd been looking for, but Telstra still wanted more time to deliberate. Catherine waited twenty-four hours before she rang to inform them that another advertiser had expressed interest – did Telstra want the package or not? They took it.

In high spirits, Catherine and Brenda took themselves off to lunch at Forty One to celebrate. 'We've earnt this,' Catherine said. 'Besides, I haven't eaten properly for days.'

'Me neither,' Brenda confided. They both ordered three courses and ate the lot.

When, later, Catherine brought her father up to date with her success he was more than satisfied. He'd received an earlier call from Huxley who'd told him he expected sales of Walker Wide Screens to go through the roof after the fashion presentation, and Tom had predicted the same thing. Sydney would make a great deal of money, something that always put him in high spirits.

# Chapter Seventeen

The big day was on them before they knew it.
Catherine had chosen 5 April, the beginning of
autumn in Sydney, and spring in London and New
York. The last-minute details had been taken care of
and it was all systems go. Perry had thrown a couple
of tantrums, which hadn't fussed Catherine one little
bit. In fact, she told Clare later, Perry and his fits of
passion always amused her. 'Creative people are supposed to throw tantrums,' she said. 'Could you
imagine life without them? It would be utterly
boring.'

The truth was that Perry was so nervous before a
parade that the slightest thing could set him off – as
one of the models discovered, much to her chagrin.
She turned up five minutes late and copped a blast
the like of which she couldn't believe.

But when a hapless dresser, giving the clothes a
last-minute iron, accidentally scorched one of his

beloved designs, he screamed at her to get out of his sight. 'Now!' he ordered. However, when the gown appeared on the catwalk no one would have guessed its earlier fate – Perry had cleverly improvised a new look, and sewn a cluster of flowers over the offending burn mark.

For the night, he'd made Catherine a long slip of a gown in emerald green chiffon, beautifully cut and clinging but not enough to stop the material from floating when she walked. It was simple but superbly elegant.

'You do like your chiffon, darling,' Perry teased, as he checked her out.

'I know what suits me,' Catherine retorted, 'and chiffon and I were made for each other!'

She wore the most magnificent necklace, which had belonged to her mother, of lustrous Broome pearls from which hung an impossible-to-ignore, pear-shaped emerald. 'Your eyes have turned the colour of emeralds, Catherine,' Perry told her. 'You look stunning.'

She wished Jack was in Sydney to share this with her. When he had rung to wish her good luck, Jack had expressed his disappointment, too, but assured her that he'd be with her in spirit as he was attending the showing at The Ritz. She'd arranged that with Huxley.

'I'll put him next to Camilla,' he'd said. 'They'll be perfect for each other.'

'Yes, they'll get on famously. I do hope Prince Charles won't mind!'

As the guests took their places in the marquee the atmosphere was electric. Everyone could feel it, especially Catherine. She gave her welcoming speech, telling the audience that they were making communications history. 'Nothing as ambitious as this simultaneous fashion showing has ever been attempted before.

'Fashion will take a major step forward as we break through the geographic barriers to make it truly global. What's more, the *MAUD* 21st Century Collection reflects the changing tastes and needs of women in a way that no other collection ever has. What we will show you in our presentation are the kind of clothes that, from today, modern women will want to wear.'

As Catherine left the catwalk the applause was deafening and as she made her way to her place at the top table the melody of Dvorak's *New World Symphony* rang out, immediately capturing the audience's attention. It was the same special arrangement that her mother had used for her gala Italian fashion parade years earlier and Catherine had chosen it both as a tribute to her mother and to tie in with the global ambitions that she and Perry had for the collection. Played by Harry Connick Jnr, and the exceptional orchestra he'd hand-picked for the night, it sounded sensational.

The music smoothly dissolved into a medley of well-known romantic love songs, to which the models swayed down the catwalk. When Perry's 'Dress Yourself Up and Let Yourself Go' evening creations came down the catwalk there was spontaneous applause, and when Harry began to sing 'What is Love?', a song he'd written especially for the grand finale to accompany Perry's exquisite parade of bridal gowns – in which all the models took part, led by Kylie in a dainty froth of white tulle and lace – the words of his song touched many a heart. Catherine let herself think of Jack and wondered if his thoughts were with her, too.

*What is Love?*
*It's the happiness our heart most desires.*
*Sometimes we think we've found Love only to discover*
     *that it's an illusion,*
*And so we keep on searching.*
*What is Love?*
*Love is when our dreams come true.*
*But every now and then fate likes to make Love elusive.*
*It's all part of the game called romance that all of us*
     *like to play.*
*What is Love?*
*Love is needing, wanting, being.*
*What is Love?*
*Love is trust.*
*It's there for all who seek it.*
*Let your heart roam freely. Go wherever it takes you.*
*What is Love?*
*It's the happy ever after ending we all yearn for.*
*I love you my darling – that's why Love is you.*

The consensus afterwards was unanimous: the parade was Perry Wolf's finest hour. The applause had begun with the appearance of the first garment and continued as one by one his designs came and conquered all who saw them. Kylie appeared in the prettiest of pastels, Elle was brighter than bright in vibrant orange, Nicole in dramatic red – her husband's favourite colour, she confided to Perry. The audience adored the collection's femininity and the uncluttered line of Perry's designs.

'You could have shown a brown paper sack and they would have applauded it,' Catherine told him as they made their way to join the guests for dinner. 'You're a star, Perry.'

'I would never have made the galaxy without you,' he said, putting his arm around her. 'I will owe you forever. I am your most devoted supporter and servant from this day forward.' And he planted a big kiss on her forehead.

The guests were utterly rapt when they entered the dinner marquee. 'This is marvellous, Catherine,' Leonard Lauder said. He and his wife had been so impressed with Perry's clothes that Evelyn had already ordered two of his designs. 'I'm so glad we were able to be here and I'm looking forward to returning your hospitality.' He told Catherine of his plans to host a dinner for her the following week at the prestigious Le Cirque restaurant, the much-favoured haunt of celebrities and the elite of New York.

Everyone was seated at a giant E-shaped table covered with a crimson damask tablecloth – it took up most of the marquee. Catherine had read about a similar concept in the 'Suzy' column of the American *W* magazine and loved it. 'There's no copyright on ideas,' she often told her team. 'Good ideas are meant to be used.'

Clare had found some glorious silver candelabra at the Sydney Antique Dealers' Fair and Catherine had persuaded the owner to let her borrow six of them for the night. They stood, tall and grand, filled with high tapered candles and surrounded by thousands of crimson roses that spilt from the candelabra and ran down the centre of the table. In the soft candlelight it was a scene of beauty. Catherine's aim, she told her guests, was to create the effect of a Renaissance banquet. 'Because,' she'd explained, 'the whole evening is to do with renaissance – after all, it will mark the revival of fashion in a way that is long overdue.'

In the same spirit, she'd asked the much-admired Japanese-born chef Tetsuya Wakuda to create a memorable banquet, believing that the combination of East and West in his cuisine signalled its own renaissance in terms of the way people thought about food in Australia. Tetsuya created a dinner of fourteen luscious courses, cleverly combining French and Japanese cuisine with the freshest and best Australian produce. Each course was outstanding in its presentation and served with some of Australia's finest wines from the Hunter and Barossa valleys.

Catherine had the menus printed in black on gold parchment paper so that guests could keep them as a memento of the evening.

### TETSUYA'S 21ST CENTURY BANQUET

Cold Soup of Potato and Leek with Sea Urchin
and Oscietra Caviar

Julienne of Marinated Squid with Quail Egg
and Ocean Trout Roe

Marinated Trevally with Preserved Lemon
Marinated Tuna with Black Truffle and Olives

Scallop with Yuzu and Green Chilli
Snapper with Salt and Lime Zest

Cocotte of Truffled Egg

Warm Salad of Yabbie Tail with Pigs Trotters
and Black Truffle Vinaigrette

Roasted Lobster with Chestnut Mushrooms,
Rosemary and Tarragon

Tataki of Venison with Honey and Rosemary Vinaigrette

Slow-Roasted Abalone with Braised Oxtail and Sansho

Roasted Breast of Squab with Pine Mushrooms
and Chrysanthemum Cress

Boudin of Foie Gras, Pigs Trotters and Truffles
with Port, Mustard and Red Wine Vinegar Sauce

Fig Sorbet

Marinated Japanese White Peach with Banyuls
and Black Pepper

Fresh Nashi Pear with Sea Salt

∽

When Jack rang to tell her how well the collection had
been received in London Catherine was thrilled by his
reaction. 'Everything worked – the venue, the presentation, the clarity of the transmission, and the sound
was superb. Lunch was marvellous, too,' he added.

Catherine was ecstatic. 'Darling Jack, you've
made my day. That's exactly the kind of reaction I
wanted.'

She'd spent a great deal of time e-mailing the
chief chef at The Ritz organising the traditional

British menu with a touch of something Australian. When the final choice had been made she'd insisted Huxley go one lunchtime and sample each course, to make sure everything was as perfect as possible. As a man who always enjoyed his food, Huxley had been more than happy to do the taste test and gave the meal ten out of ten. 'You've chosen well,' he'd told Catherine.

And the guests agreed as they tucked into terrine of foie gras with truffles, baby leeks and toasted brioche, roast Devon scallops in a citrus and saffron chowder, followed by Aberdeen Angus beef, York-shire pudding and creamed horseradish with fresh steamed string beans, glazed carrots and roast pota-toes. The Australian element was provided with Mango Melba, a variation of the famous dessert, Peach Melba – created in honour of the great Aus-tralian soprano Dame Nellie Melba, when she was at the height of her career. Catherine had arranged for the mangoes to be flown to London from Queensland.

In New York, Tom had hosted breakfast at The Waldorf Astoria and reported that the reactions of the guests there had been as enthusiastic as those of audiences in Sydney and London, and that the diet-conscious American women had enjoyed themselves so much that they'd actually eaten the food. 'The waiters couldn't believe their eyes,' he said. 'They were sure they'd have to throw out plates and plates of Eggs Benedict. But everyone was on such a high after the presentation that they didn't want to leave. It was party time!

'And wait until you see the press cuttings, Sis. The *New York Times* fashion writer has told readers that Perry's clothes are "to die for" *and* she's nominated him as the season's in designer. As for you, they reckon you're woman of the year. Wait until you get here, Catherine – you'll be mobbed.'

By late afternoon the following day Catherine was on her way to New York. After a glass of champagne and a light snack, she fell asleep, exhausted, and didn't stir until the plane was about two hours out of Los Angeles. After ten hours' rest she felt wonderfully refreshed.

It was just as well, because New York was a frantic rush of interviews and appearances. Barneys had chosen the *MAUD* Collection for its Fifth Avenue new season's launch and Saks Fifth Avenue had featured six styles from the collection in its advertisements in the *New York Times* the morning after the presentation.

Catherine did in-store appearances at both retailers, gave an interview to the *New York Sunday Times* fashion magazine, and also conducted a 'Dressing for Now' session on *Oprah*. Since the launch of her magazine, Catherine and Oprah had become firm friends and regularly spoke to each other on the phone, sharing business problems – and successes – as well as aspects of their personal lives.

Oprah declared the *MAUD* Collection the best range ever produced anywhere in the world, claiming it was of more significance to fashion than Dior's celebrated New Look, which he created after the end of the Second World War. She raved about the way the collection had been shown to a worldwide audience. Anna Wintour, the very stylish and powerful editor-in-chief of *Vogue*, gave a lunch in Catherine's honour at the famed Four Seasons, and Catherine spent her only US weekend at Martha's Vineyard in Massachusetts, talking to well-known author and writer Dominick Dunne, whom *Vanity Fair* had commissioned to do a special profile on her.

Catherine knew these last events were highly unusual for the very competitive publishing world, where publications rarely go out of their way to help potential rivals. But *Vogue* and *Vanity Fair* had decided to overlook this because they considered Catherine such an outstanding woman that her achievements were worthy of recognition by as wide an audience as possible, including their own readers.

Then it was on to London for another round of media interviews, including one with David Frost, who had been contracted by the BBC to do a TV series on women of the new century and had asked Catherine to be his first interview. Harvey Nichols had given the *MAUD* Collection its Knightsbridge windows and, as she had in New York, Catherine did several in-store appearances promoting the range and signing autographs.

'It's the most beautiful sight I've ever seen,' she told Perry on her mobile phone while she stood in busy Knightsbridge, describing the windows to him. 'The clothes look *brilliant*, as they love to say over here. One window even has a caption 'The Style Wizard of Oz'. The British overdo that Wizard of Oz thing, but right here, right now, it looks absolutely fantastic, Perry.' She made an odd sight, standing in the middle of the pavement, occasionally gesturing with her arm, as she talked excitedly on the phone. Several passers-by stopped to look at her – a couple of them recognised her from the interview she'd given David Frost and waved hello.

Catherine waved back at them. 'Oh heavens, Perry, I'm causing a scene.' She continued the conversation as she began walking briskly in the direction of The Ritz, where she was staying. 'I've asked Harvey Nichols's marketing people to e-mail some photographs to you. They're really looking forward to your visit and want to put on a special dinner for you. Do you think you'll be able to get here next month?'

Perry groaned in mock frustration. 'I'm pretty sure I will but, Catherine darling, you have no idea what a madhouse it is here. The phone has been ringing non-stop since the showing. Canada, Japan,

Germany – they all want the clothes. New York wants to reorder some of the garments, which is unheard of. I said no at first, but they begged me to reconsider, would you believe? The factory is going crazy with overtime. We can't even meet the demand here in Australia. Horton's have been fabo, though.

'That lovely Robert Horton certainly delivered as he said he would and the *MAUD* Collection has window displays in all of their stores. Everyone is talking about us and I'm doing so many radio and TV chat shows that I think I might lose my voice. It's just amazing. Long may it last!'

The reaction was positive wherever Catherine went, too. She was often stopped in the street in London by enthusiastic women who not only expressed their approval about *MAUD* but who were also in seventh heaven about the collection. She talked to her circulation department every day and they told her to expect a record sale, as there wasn't a copy of *MAUD* left in any of the distribution centres. The magazines were all out in the market-place waiting to be snapped up.

On Catherine's one weekend in London, Huxley had arranged for her to go to a polo match in the grounds of Windsor Castle. Prince Charles was there to cheer his team on and, over tea, he told Catherine that he'd heard the collection was simply marvellous. 'You must be pleased with the way things are going.'

'I certainly am, Sir. It is most encouraging.' She found the Prince easy to talk to and the afternoon passed quickly and pleasantly. Catherine was glad she'd had the opportunity to get to know Prince Charles a bit better, but the only thing on her mind now was some well-earned R & R.

She had been so flat out since arriving in London that she'd only had time for a couple of quick phone conversations with Jack. She'd hoped they might have found time for dinner or at least a drink together before now, but without warning Jack had announced he had to go to New York again for a few days, to see Rupert Murdoch.

Catherine hit the roof when she heard. 'Not again!' Bloody Rupert, she thought, he's always coming between us. 'I can't believe how much we both travel yet manage to keep missing each other.'

'Don't go off the handle – you terrify me when you get angry with me,' Jack said. 'I'm sorry, darling, but this can't be helped.'

She felt herself thawing. 'All right, but goodness, when are you going to make time for us?' Although Jack had assured her things would get better she was still uneasy – work seemed to have a habit of coming between them. It was something they would have to resolve. Before she'd had the chance to ask if the trip had something to do with Webster Media, Jack had hung up.

ᗞ

But Catherine's worries disappeared as Jack's trip drew to an end, and soon she was bubbling over with happiness at the prospect of seeing him again. There was a gleam in her eyes and a spring in her step as she walked. She was longing to hear what he'd been doing and to tell him the latest happenings in her life – and looking forward to having him all to herself for what she knew would be two blissful weeks. She'd been keeping an eye on the time all day. Jack was due back in London in a few hours and they'd agreed to meet at The Ritz Bar.

Not long after she'd got to the hotel, Perry had rung in a state of high excitement to tell her that he'd received a call from the director Peter Weir asking him to design the clothes for his new film, a remake of Baroness Orczy's classic, *The Scarlet Pimpernel*.

'Cate Blanchett is going to play Marguerite, wife of Sir Percy Blakeney, alias the Scarlet Pimpernel. Can you imagine, Catherine – all that passion, romance and intrigue set in France during the revolution? It's a designer's dream! I'll be able to really let my head go.'

Catherine was genuinely pleased at the animation in Perry's voice. 'I couldn't be happier for you, Perry, but don't forget to leave yourself time to design next season's collection.'

'As if I wouldn't! I know which side my bread's buttered on – but, darling, designing clothes for Peter Weir's film will be the icing on the cake for me.

And I'm going to enjoy every moment of it because I know it will be fun. I'm aiming for an Oscar, and you will be my guest when I go to Hollywood to collect it.'

'It's a date,' she promised. After she'd finally managed to stop Perry talking and said goodbye, she rang Clare to make sure there were no problems or crises looming, before speaking to Brenda and getting an update on advertising revenue for the next couple of issues of *MAUD*, and after that to Suzanne to run through several of the editorial pages. 'You can e-mail me the pages for checking as soon as you're finished with them and I'll turn them around without delay,' Catherine said.

'Otherwise, unless there's a real emergency I don't want to be disturbed, as they say. I'm going to take two very well-deserved weeks off. I'll touch base every day so don't worry, I won't disappear altogether, but I desperately need to opt out for a little while – I'm exhausted! Now I must go and get ready . . . I'm meeting a friend for a drink.'

# Chapter Eighteen

Jack was waiting for her at the bar. 'My plane arrived early; some romantically minded tail wind blew us along in record time.' Their eyes told each other what they wanted to know. 'It's good to see you again,' he said, kissing Catherine on the cheek.

'It's been too long! I didn't know it was possible to miss someone as much as I've missed you.' She hugged him before sitting down.

'That's reassuring to know, seeing we're going to spend the next two weeks together. Would you like a champagne cocktail?' An attentive waiter was hovering, keen to get their order.

Catherine nodded appreciatively. 'I'll have a Champagne César Ritz.'

'What's in that?' Jack asked.

'Champagne, with Armagnac, peach liqueur and grenadine, sir,' the waiter informed him.

'Make that two,' Jack said. When their drinks

arrived he made a toast: 'To your dazzling eyes: may they always look at me the way they are tonight.'

Jack had booked dinner in the hotel's main dining room – the same one Catherine had used for her presentation lunch – and when they finally made their way to their table the cocktails had given their appetites a nice edge, as well as heightening their desire for one another. A state of delightful suspense existed between them. The ambience of the dining room pacified them momentarily, as they decided what they'd eat. They settled for poached wild salmon with dill watercress sauce. This was Catherine's idea. 'Then', she said with a wicked smile, 'we can have hot raspberry soufflé with rich Jersey cream as our sinful pudding.'

Catherine's sweet tooth was legendary. Whenever she gave a media interview journalists asked her about it. They couldn't believe she could eat desserts and keep her figure. She often joked that one day she'd bring out *The Catherine Walker Book of Sinful Puddings*.

Jack was amused at her evident pleasure at the thought of dessert. 'It's my only weakness,' she confessed. It was a well-known fact that Catherine always read the dessert list before looking at anything else on a menu.

'The only sinful thing I want you to do is something that includes me, and I'm not sure I'd classify it as sinful, but rather as essential,' Jack said, taking her hand.

In spite of their longing for each other, they both enjoyed the meal and the chance to relax and exchange their respective news. They were so immersed in each other that they were unaware of much else going on around them, even the occasional sticky-beak glances of the other diners who'd identified Catherine, and were only too aware that love was in the air.

'Let's have coffee and cognac at the bar,' Jack suggested, 'and while we do I'll arrange for the door between our suites to be unlocked.' He stood up and held out his hand. She took it and he escorted her out of the room. As they passed the maître d, Jack told him to add a fifteen per cent tip to the bill and charge it to his room account.

They lingered over their cognacs and coffee, enjoying the feeling that they had the whole night ahead of them, before Jack once again took Catherine by the hand and led her to the lift. Once inside, he kissed her. 'I've been wanting to do that all night.'

'More please!'

He held her close and kissed her again, this time with more passion.

'I love second helpings,' Catherine whispered, gently nibbling his ear.

'Keep that up and I'll make love to you right here.' The lift doors opened on their floor. 'Your suite or mine?'

'Who cares?'

He drew Catherine into his room, took her in his arms and kissed her lovingly.

'Jack, I feel as though I'm home.'

'You are, my darling,' he murmured, as he took off his jacket and tie, throwing them on a chair in the corner. Still kissing her, he undid the top buttons of his shirt. Catherine slipped her hand in and ran it across his nipples.

She felt him react – and playfully tapped the bulge on the front of his trousers with her other hand. 'What have we here?' she asked softly, as she unzipped his fly. She put her hand down the front of his underpants and fondled his penis. 'Very impressive,' she said impishly.

Jack manoeuvred her towards the bed, where he lay down. 'Are you going to get undressed or am I going to have to rip those clothes off you?'

She undressed in seconds, tossing her clothes on top of his jacket and tie. The coolness of her skin as they embraced excited him. 'Your body feels incredible,' he said almost inaudibly, enjoying the sensation. 'You have no idea how much I've longed for this moment.'

'Darling Jack,' she murmured. She bent over him, swaying her breasts over his chest and letting them gently touch his nipples while she kissed him amorously. Then she did the same to his penis, which quivered excitedly. She kissed him again and began to massage him all over, leaving no part of him untouched.

'If you don't stop what you're doing to me I'll come, and I don't want to – not yet anyway. Come up here and lie beside me and let me calm down.'

They lay facing each other. Looking into Jack's eyes, Catherine was overwhelmed by a sudden rush of emotion and kissed him impulsively. She couldn't imagine her future without him.

'I love you so much.' She had no doubts now. Jack was her destiny.

Jack held her face in his hands. 'You're so very precious to me – never forget that.'

He began to smother her with kisses – her lips, her breasts, her navel, even the tips of her fingers. Then he began to fondle every part of her body. Catherine felt as if she were on fire.

Suddenly Jack stopped what he was doing and kissed her on the mouth. 'Having a good time?' he teased.

Catherine's eyes were lustrous with desire.

He embraced her and they forgot everything except the joy of making love.

They were still in each other's arms when they fell asleep. Much later, the next morning, when Catherine opened her eyes, Jack was lying very still, looking at her. 'How long have you been staring at me? Have you been willing me to wake up?' she laughed.

'Not at all. I was thinking how lovely you look

when you're sleeping and how very precious you are to me.' He kissed her tenderly. 'I love everything about you: your beauty – and your brain.'

He traced the outline of her face with his finger. 'I once asked you to grow old with me and I meant it.' He kissed her again, long and lingeringly. 'Will you marry me?'

'Yes,' she said, and threw her arms around his neck. 'It's what I want more than anything else in the world.'

Then she began to cry.

Jack was dismayed. 'What's the matter?'

'I'm so happy,' she sniffed.

'You're a silly little thing sometimes,' he said, as he wiped her tears away. Her brow puckered again.

'What now, woman?'

'Have you forgotten you already have a wife?'

Jack put his arms around her and gave her a cuddle. 'Fleur won't be a problem – I told you before, we haven't lived as man and wife for four years and everything's been amicable between us since we went our separate ways. I'll go and see her and tell her it's time we finalised things. God knows, we should have done it ages ago,' he said grimly.

'Nothing will change for Fleur. She'll still have the income I give her. She can stay in Paris and travel and spend in the manner to which she's become only too accustomed. All I want from her is the right to see the girls. She probably thinks we should have done something about a divorce before now, too. Anyway, it's quite likely that one day she'll meet someone else she wants to marry.' Jack spoke with all the self-assurance of a man used to people doing whatever he wanted.

But Catherine was filled with misgivings. Jack made it sound all too easy; what if something went wrong – what then? She tried to tell Jack about her doubts but he brushed them aside. 'Stop worrying. Fleur will do as I ask – she'll be pleased to get rid of me.'

'You seem so sure.'

'I am, darling. Trust me.' He held her to him. 'Nothing will go wrong. We will be husband and wife before you know it.' He kissed her. 'You are so desirable,' he said. 'Shall we?'

'Are you reading my mind?'

And they made love again. Afterwards, all Catherine's misgivings had vanished and, feeling at peace with the world, she gave a huge sigh of contentment.

'Happy, darling?'

'Blissfully.'

Over brunch in the suite, Jack told her what he'd planned for their holiday. He had booked a cruise on the *Seabourn Spirit*, one of the most luxurious ships in the Cunard Group. They would pick it up in Rome, he explained, and then sail down the Italian and Greek coasts, stopping at Sorrento, Capri, Taormina and Corfu before getting off in Venice.

'I thought we'd spend a couple of days in Rome before we sail – I've booked us into Le Grand – and then have a few days at the Cipriani in Venice at the end of our cruise, before we fly back to London,' he said.

'You've thought of everything.' Catherine leant over and kissed the top of his head. 'And it's such a refreshing change for me not to have to bother about any of the travel details. I adore being spoilt like this.'

Jack was delighted by her reaction. 'The ship's like a floating hotel; I'm sure you'll love it. There's no rush, no fuss. We can do what we like, when we like.'

'It sounds perfect, darling, and just the kind of holiday we both need.' Catherine stretched lazily. 'How did you know cruising is my favourite kind of travelling?'

Jack smiled knowingly.


Their time away went all too quickly, as Catherine knew it would. In Rome she and Jack were like any other tourists. They went to the Colosseum, the Pantheon, the Vatican and the Sistine Chapel, where they stood for some time admiring the work of Michelangelo, before climbing the Spanish Steps to lunch in the rooftop restaurant of the Hotel Hassler Villa Medici, with its panoramic view of Rome. Catherine declared the curried onions that were served as part of its renowned antipasto to be the best she'd ever eaten.

'I hope you like them too, Jack,' she said. 'I'm going to recreate them when I get back to Sydney. Expect these on the menu when you come to dinner!'

Later on they wandered along the Via Condotti, where Catherine popped in and out of the many fashionable boutiques and bought a couple of beautiful Italian silk shirts and matching sweaters. Jack didn't mind at all. 'I like shopping,' he told her. 'Any time you want to stop to try something on it's okay by me.'

'Where have you been all my life?' Catherine asked, kissing him. 'A man who actually enjoys shopping! I didn't think it was possible. You are a rare species.'

'I'd be the first to agree with you, sweetheart.'

Before they sailed Jack took her out to dinner at an intimate trattoria and asked her about Roger. 'What went wrong between you two?'

'I doubt I'll ever really know,' she said. 'Roger is such a complicated kind of man. He comes across so confident but he has a huge inferiority complex. I think he saw me as some kind of competition – anything I could do, he could do better, that kind of thing.

'We did have some good times together and I was prepared to try and sort things out, but Roger refused to even think for one moment that he might have a problem. In fact, when I suggested we seek professional help he went ballistic.'

She heaved a sigh. 'I was a fool, Jack – I confused lust with love.'

Jack's eyes were full of understanding. 'You

haven't made that mistake this time. What we have between us is love. I've never felt the way I feel about you before.' He picked up her hand and kissed it, looking at her so lovingly as he did so that Catherine wished the moment would last forever.

'I love you so much it hurts,' she replied.

'You darling,' he murmured, and raised her hand to his lips once more. 'Have you told your father about us?'

'I told him I liked you very much, but I didn't go into great detail. However, he understands me well enough to know that you're more than just a casual relationship. When I get home I'll tell him that we're going to be married.'

The *Seabourn Spirit* was all that Jack had promised. Their suite had its own lounge area and deck, as well as a huge window. They would sit there in the evening before dinner, having a glass of champagne and admiring the view. 'This is just divine,' said Catherine. 'I know we're going to have a wonderful time.'

When they were at sea they spent much of the time in bed. 'Our lovemaking just gets better and better,' Catherine told Jack.

'But practice makes perfect!' He threw himself on the bed. 'Come and do your homework – at once.' There were times when Catherine wished she didn't have to go ashore.

They meandered hand in hand through the streets of Taormina in Sicily, charmed by its ancient splendour and medieval charm. They made their way to the city's amphitheatre, originally built in the third century BC by the Greeks – and still used for performances today – and imagined Taormina's glorious past when it flourished during the rule of Julius Caesar. They sat together holding hands, admiring the breathtaking view across to Mount Etna and hoping Europe's most active volcano wouldn't play up while they were in the area.

In Corfu Jack insisted on buying her a souvenir. He found what he was looking for in a small jewellery store whose proprietor practically dragged them inside when they stopped to look in the window, and proceeded to bombard them with suggestions.

'We want that,' Jack said, pointing to a ring in the display case. It was in gold, and set with the face of an owl with emerald eyes. 'Owls are supposed to bring luck,' he told Catherine, as she put it on her finger. Then he took her to a nearby cafe where they snacked on octopus, cheese and salad, and toasted their future with a glass of ouzo.

'I will treasure the memory of our holiday and the places we visited as long as I live,' Catherine told him, as they flew back to London. 'Especially Venice,' she added.

She'd giggled when Jack had suggested they take

a gondola ride on the Grand Canal, not knowing he'd already tipped the gondolier to sing a love song. Even though he'd sung it in Italian there was no mistaking its meaning.

'Venice is made for lovers and it was exactly as I'd imagined it would be. It must be the most beautiful city in the world.' She leant back in her seat and gazed at him fondly.

They'd agreed that as soon as they reached London Jack would make arrangements to go to Paris to talk to Fleur before returning to Australia. Catherine had to leave for Sydney almost immediately. There were the early sketches of Perry's second *MAUD* Collection to be looked at, not to mention the next issue's cover to be chosen.

'I hate to leave you, darling.' Inexplicably she felt uneasy again and was immediately irritated with herself. Jack loved her – nothing would go wrong. She was behaving foolishly.

'I don't want to say goodbye either but it's not for long.' Jack kissed her with such passion that she felt unsteady on her feet. Looking deep into her eyes, he said, 'I'll be back in Sydney before you know it. Stop worrying about Fleur. Our divorce will be through in no time, and then,' he kissed her again, 'you and I will get married.'

In her fashionable apartment on the rue de Rivoli, impeccably furnished with French antiques and overlooking the Tuileries Garden, Fleur Clement looked as Parisian as any native-born Frenchwoman as she waited for her husband to arrive.

She'd just returned from lunch with a girlfriend and was dressed in an elegantly styled Christian Dior dark navy silk suit and a soft pink silk crepe blouse with a high neckline of tiny pleats and similarly pleated cuffs, which peeped out from under the sleeves of her jacket. With her long blonde hair swept up in a simple chignon and diamond and gold stud earrings sparkling in her ears, Fleur was a vision to behold and she knew it. After all, she went to a great deal of effort to be that way. She walked for at least an hour every day before working out in her private gym and never missed her massage and fortnightly facials. Nothing was ever allowed to come between Fleur and her beauty routine.

She enjoyed her life as Mrs Jack Clement. People respected Jack and as a result were always eager to please Fleur, which is why it had suited her not to get divorced. That, plus the fact that Jack was a wealthy man. Men with the kind of money he had didn't come along every day. She went out with other men, naturally – 'Heavens, cherie,' she'd explained to her best friend, Dominique, 'I'm not a nun. And besides, sex is essential for any woman who wants to keep her good looks.' If any man became too serious Fleur easily dispensed with him by saying she and Jack had an arrangement which suited them both, and that as far as she was concerned he was the only permanent man in her life and always would be.

It never crossed Jack's mind that Fleur used him as an excuse not to get seriously involved with anyone else. He was sure she'd marry again and he genuinely wished her well. They'd had some good times together and were united in wanting only the best for their daughters, having long ago agreed to do their best to raise them without acrimony.

He wasn't sure why the marriage had gone wrong. He had loved Fleur when he married her and he was pretty sure she'd felt the same way about him, but they had grown apart. He knew his work took him away from home a great deal and he worked long hours as well, but Fleur had always accepted this, something which set her apart from other wives who constantly complained about the excessive hours their husbands worked. Fleur didn't seem to mind at all and she'd never made him feel guilty for it.

When Jack was away she'd gone to the theatre with a gay escort and had been able to choose from half a dozen 'walkers' who enjoyed being seen in her company. She entertained whether Jack was home or not and was an excellent hostess with an enviable reputation of which she was proud.

Their home had been one of the showplaces in Sydney's northern suburb of Hunters Hill – an elegant 1870s waterfront sandstone mansion with sweeping views across the Lane Cove River. Invitations to dine there were treasured and always accepted.

They'd been married for two years before the girls had been born and things seemed to change after that. Fleur was content to have only two children and didn't want any more. She made that quite clear to Jack, maintaining that in this overpopulated world two children were enough in any family. 'I think we were so lucky to have had twins,' she'd declared once, much to his amazement, 'and got the business of making babies behind us.' She still allowed Jack to make love to her but there was no longer much excitement in their lovemaking. Jack felt tolerated but not wanted.

It was as if Fleur had fallen out of love with him. She was the perfect wife otherwise, caring for the children beautifully, running the household efficiently, entertaining Jack's business associates whenever he asked. Jack couldn't fault her performance and because he was busy, the marriage was comfortable enough. In a way it suited his needs. Their relationship was uncomplicated and not at all demanding, which – although he felt bad for thinking this way – was something of a relief given the many work pressures he had. When he felt like sex, he'd ring Georgia Jones, an old girlfriend with whom he'd had an affair long before he met Fleur. Lonely in her own loveless marriage, Georgia was always eager to go to bed with Jack. He was, as she often told him, the best lover she'd ever had. She offered Jack an additional benefit – he felt safe with her. Married mistresses rarely caused scandals. Life went on and Jack had seen no reason to change the status quo.

He and Fleur never argued. In fact, they'd only ever had one serious disagreement in their entire marriage, and that was over the girls' names. Jack had wanted to call his daughters Anne and Barbara, after his mother and her sister, but Fleur would have none of it. 'You couldn't possibly saddle your children with such boring names,' she'd scolded him. 'In years ahead when the girls go out into the world to make their fame and,' she laughed, 'increase their fortunes, no one will ever forget their names. Violetta and Camille suit them perfectly.' In the end he gave in, just to keep the peace.

But when the children were two years old Fleur had told Jack she wanted to spend the summer in France without him. 'I thought I'd take a cottage in the countryside, somewhere in the Loire Valley. I always feel so at home when I'm in France. I wouldn't be at all surprised if in an earlier life I'd been a Frenchwoman.'

Fleur's parents had died in a car accident when she was only six and she'd been raised by her well-to-do spinster Aunt Tess, who had loved the little girl as though she was her own and had taken Fleur to France with her during school holidays.

Then Tess died when Fleur was eighteen, and

she never got over it. Her trips to France represented some of the happiest times of her life and her decision to live in France was prompted by a need to be closer to those memories. Unbeknown to Jack, Fleur had also made a vow to herself never to return to Australia, a place she considered to be a backwoods, with no style and no ideas at all.

Fleur had been in France for only three months – she'd found a charming farmhouse in the Dordogne area, not far from the picturesque town of La Roque-Gageac – when she rang Jack to tell him she wanted to live apart from him. 'Jack, you're a good man and an excellent provider, and I've enjoyed being married to you, but our marriage has run its course. There's no one else and I don't especially want a divorce but I want to stay in France. I feel I belong here.

'I want to live in Paris and I'd like you to buy me an apartment so that I can live here with the girls. I promise never to let them forget their Australian heritage, and you can come and visit whenever you like, but I also plan to give them some French know-how and class.'

Jack had always prided himself on being a reasonable man but Fleur's request was too much. 'You're bloody mad,' he told her. 'I don't want Violetta and Camille to grow up in France. They're my daughters, too, you know, and you're my wife. Your place, and theirs, is with me.'

But Fleur wouldn't budge. 'Jack, you're rarely at home. Think of how much you travel. Your aeroplane is your home. You'd probably see more of Violetta and Camille if they lived in France!'

When he'd calmed down Jack had to admit she had a point. He was frequently in Europe and it would be just as easy for him to spend time with the girls in Paris as in Sydney. He could see the sense of them having a contented mother and if that meant setting up a home for them all in Paris then perhaps, he conceded grudgingly, it wasn't such a bad idea after all. Jack made sure his business trips included frequent stopovers in Paris and Fleur had never objected to the girls spending as much time with him as possible.

He arrived at the rue de Rivoli just as Fleur had ordered some refreshments. 'Jack, how nice to see you – do come in and tell me your news.' She led the way to the drawing room and asked if he'd like some tea. 'Or perhaps coffee? I've a new cook who makes the best coffee in Paris.'

'No, nothing thanks, Fleur.' He sat down and candidly explained why he'd come to see her. 'I've met someone I want to marry. It's time we finalised things between us and got a divorce.' Fleur was silent as he told her how he'd met Catherine and they'd fallen in love.

When she did finally speak her reaction shocked him. 'How sweet, Jack, finding true love at last at your age.' Her voice was quiet and reserved, but there was no mistaking its cold-hearted tone. 'But let me tell you, if you want to get rid of me as your wife then I want half your fortune, half your company, half of everything you own.' There was nothing demure about Fleur now – the gloves were off and she'd delivered Jack a knockout blow.

'What the fuck do you mean?' He jumped up, outraged. 'Our marriage has been over for years. Why would you want to hang on to something that means nothing to both of us and why are you talking about money? Your allowance is more than adequate and you know it.'

Fleur sat before him and primly examined her nails. 'I didn't mind our marriage being over because you were still mine – in name only, I admit, but it's such a good name and I'm rather fond of it. It wasn't on our agenda that you'd fall in love with someone else. I don't want a divorce and if you persist then I'll go for your money and I'll get it, too. You should know that my lawyer is Richard Crosswaite. I'm sure you're familiar with his reputation,' she gloated. 'Did you know *Le Monde* described him as the best divorce lawyer in the world just the other day? He comes and dines with me whenever he's in Paris and I've made it a habit to keep him up to date with our so-called marriage and my situation.'

Jack was fuming. 'Why would you want half my company, for Christ's sake? You couldn't give a damn about The Clement Group. I've made sure you lead a pampered, luxurious life. You've never wanted for anything.'

'No, I haven't, but if you really love the remarkable Ms Walker then you'll be wanting to have children, I expect. I remember how much you wanted children, Jack, and your desire to have a son.' She gave an icy laugh. 'My, how you badgered me for one! Well, I happen to know that children have a habit of diverting money and I have no intention of that happening to me, or to Violetta and Camille. You decide what you want to do, Jack, but my mind is made up. I'll be ringing Richard the moment you leave to give him my instructions.'

'I can't believe you mean it – you really are a prize bitch.' Jack had never felt violent towards any woman but if he stayed a moment longer he knew he'd completely lose control. He stormed out of Fleur's apartment and strode down the rue de Rivoli. How had he lived with such a vile creature? How had he been so blind to the kind of woman she really was? He hadn't counted on Fleur's reaction at all.

Half his company? No fucking way, not under any circumstance, not for anything or anyone.

He loved Catherine, but he couldn't give in to Fleur's conditions. Catherine was a wonderful woman and he wanted to spend the rest of his life with her. But no matter how much he loved her he couldn't give up half of his fortune and definitely not

half of his company. Catherine would surely understand that. He hadn't built up The Clement Group to
give it away to a bloody fool of a woman like Fleur,
whom he'd once foolishly loved. Love is madness,
thought Jack, utter madness if you don't control it,
instead of letting it control you. Love makes people
forget the important things in life.

He and Catherine didn't have to get married to
enjoy their love, he knew that. What difference
would a piece of paper make to them? He'd married
Fleur for love and look what had happened to them.
Marriage was not essential between a man and a
woman who loved each other in the way he and
Catherine did.

I'll stay married to Fleur, which will allow me to
keep my money and company where they belong,
and Catherine and I can live together. Other people
do it successfully. So can we. Marriage is so old-
fashioned.

His mobile phone rang. 'Jack darling, how did
everything go with Fleur? I know you said you'd call
me but I couldn't stand the suspense.'

Catherine's call took him by surprise. 'Fine,' he
said, automatically, then he paused. 'No, that's not
true. Fleur doesn't want a divorce and if I try to get
one, she's going to fight me.'

Catherine's silence was more telling than anything she might have said to him. Jack started to talk
again.

'I don't want to talk about it over the phone. I'll be back with you in no time and we'll work everything out then. And darling, whatever you do, don't worry. Everything is going to be all right – I know exactly what we'll do.'

'Jack, you are going ahead with the divorce, aren't you?' she asked quietly.

'No, Catherine, I'm not,' he said. 'It's not possible.'

# Chapter Nineteen

Over in the United States Tom Walker would have been appalled at the turn that his sister's love life had taken, but Catherine was the last thing on his mind at this time. Other matters were preoccupying him. Profits for Walker Corp. United States were well above budget and looked like staying that way. He'd spent the afternoon going through figures which confirmed that the Walker Cable Sports Channel was now valued in the United States at five billion dollars. It had been an outstanding success, far bigger than even Tom had anticipated – after all, it had only been operating less than four years – and now it had reached more than seventy-five million American homes. If his takeover bid for Capricorn Media Corporation were successful he'd have another thirty-five million homes to add to the sports cable, giving it even greater penetration.

The *New York Times* had written about the success

of Walker Corp., describing it as one of the best managed and positioned global media groups in the world. Not only that, but in the same article Tom was described as one of the most successful strategists in the industry, and his handling of the positioning of the company in America as 'inspired'. The general feeling was that shareholders would be very relaxed about the prospect of Tom succeeding Sydney as Chairman of Walker Corp., when the old man decided to call it a day. The *Times* commented that:

> Tom Walker is not just a chip off the old block. He is a man of intellect and impressive entrepreneurial flair, which he combines with a business acumen not seen often enough in this country. He has the aggression and decision-making power of Kerry Packer and Rupert Murdoch. Some investment bankers have called him a smart-arse, however, he has put together some of the cleverest corporate deals ever seen in this country. His handling of Walker Cable in America has been impressive and, at the same time, he has made thousands of investors seriously rich.

Even Huxley, who'd come up with the concept of Walker Cable Sports, had been bowled over by the company's success in America. It had taken off well in Australia and Britain but Americans had overwhelmingly embraced it. 'I think the growth in America's aged population has something to do with it,' Tom had told his fellow directors when they'd met in Sydney for Walker Corp.'s annual general meeting. 'After all, more than twenty-five million Americans are now over the age of sixty. They still love their sport but they don't have as much energy as they once had to actually take themselves off to watch their favourite game. Watching sport in the comfort of their own homes makes it extremely easy to do something that gives them a great deal of pleasure. And the Walker Wide Screen gives such an excellent picture, combined with extraordinary sound, that they feel very much a part of the excitement of whatever sport they're watching.

'Our advertising campaign summed it up perfectly: "Walker Cable Sports and Walker Wide Screen are like love and marriage. You can't have one without the other."' The board had moved a vote of thanks for what they described as Tom's 'exceptional marketing campaign'.

He had been flattered by their praise but reminded them that the campaign had been helped considerably when President Clinton had ordered the Walker Wide Screen for the White House and subscribed to Walker Cable Sports the same day. Tom had looked after the President's order personally and on his return to Washington he'd e-mailed his father with the news. *Clinton's endorsement is like money in the bank*, he'd written. *Mark my words, it's going to be superb for business. I wish we could get the President to approve everything our company does.*

Immediately after Tom discreetly leaked news of the President's purchase to the media, sales took off and never looked back. Americans reasoned that if the Walker Wide Screen was good enough for the President then it was also good enough for every man, woman and child in the country.

One of Tom's favourite pastimes was to visualise a Walker Wide Screen in every home in America. What a beautiful sight! At the rate we're going it could just happen, he thought. Tom sat at his desk grinning. If Dad could see me now he'd tell me to get that smug look off my face. What the hell – the old man couldn't have done better himself. If he's not pleased with these results he'll never be satisfied with anything. Tom had worked his guts out to get the kind of results that would not only satisfy his father, but also his own determination to succeed. He wasn't Sydney Walker's son for nothing.

He remembered everything his father had ever told him, especially his advice on marketing: 'Successful marketing doesn't just happen, son. First of all you need a bloody good idea, *then* you need to use all your energy in making sure it works. Nobody buys your product just because you tell them they should. You have to make them want to buy it. You have to convince them that they need your product.'

Tom had followed that advice when he'd first come up with the concept of securing an order from the President. To get to the President, he'd cultivated the Vice President, Al Gore, inviting him to his special viewing room for the Sports Spectacular finals of baseball and tennis, which he knew Gore followed. These were very grand affairs with a sumptuous dinner served beforehand and first-class Australian entertainment. When Al Gore told Tom he'd always been a fan of Olivia Newton John ever since he saw her in *Grease* with John Travolta, Tom had arranged for Olivia to sing a medley of the Vice President's favourite songs at one of his dinners. The President's order came through not long after.

As time went on a friendship grew between Tom and Al Gore. Tom was passionate about the environment and admired Gore's strong stand on the need for the world to not only spend more money on environmental protection but to change its destructive ways. He shared Gore's concern about the decimation of so many of the earth's precious resources. They spent many an hour debating the best ways to raise world awareness.

'You could do a great deal through the media that Walker Corp. controls, Tom,' Gore said. 'In fact, I believe you have a responsibility to do so.'

'I don't control Walker Corp., Mr Vice President,

my father does, and as long as he's in charge there's not much I can do. Dad has many good points but unfortunately saving the environment is not one of his priorities.'

Gore arranged for Tom to be invited to White House dinners, which he enjoyed not just for the excellent cuisine but also because such invitations led to him meeting other influential men and women with whom he could do business. It helped, too, when the President would raise the subject of Walker Sports, because it usually allowed Tom the opportunity to talk about some venture Walker Corp. was pursuing. People were impressed that Walker Corp. was discussed at Presidential dinners and Tom had no trouble getting doors to open when he called later to make appointments.

He liked his life in America, particularly the chance it gave him to step out of his father's shadow. Sydney had such a strong personality and was such a dominant figure, especially in Australia, that few people had given Tom much credit for his ability, which he knew he had. He was as ambitious as his father had ever been, and perhaps even more so because he felt he had more to prove.

And yet, despite being the extraordinarily busy man that he was, the feeling that something was missing from his life often troubled Tom. What it was or why he felt this way baffled him. After all, he had Belinda, and she was a great girl, whose company he enjoyed. She was such a good listener, a trait he particularly admired, that he was able to talk to her about anything and everything. He'd never met another girl quite like her.

They also got on well, probably because they had so much in common. They liked the same books, films, and music – both were passionate jazz enthusiasts – and not only played tennis together but also golf. They'd managed to go skiing at Aspen the previous winter, too. In fact, they did most things together and people thought of them as the ideal couple.

Belinda was drop-dead gorgeous, too – a blonde version of Audrey Hepburn, complete with her charm and style. It didn't do Tom's reputation any harm to have such a glamorous girl on his arm and neither did her connections at the Consulate. She'd joined the Department of Foreign Affairs after completing a degree in Political Science at the Australian National University, and had worked for the department in Canberra and Sydney before getting a posting to Kenya, and then New York.

Like Tom, Belinda enjoyed New York and all that it offered. *It truly is a city that never sleeps*, she wrote home to her mother, Sheila. *There's always an impatient car horn to be heard somewhere in the city, even in the early hours of the morning, and I can never get over the fact that there are always people around. There's such vitality in this city. I've never felt so mentally stimulated in my life.* Sheila was glad her daughter was happy but told her husband she was worried Belinda might never come home.

'Don't worry about that, dear,' he'd said. 'She'll come home when Tom does, as he will one day. Sydney will make sure of that. He'll want his son back here and not before long, if I read the signs correctly. You wait and see.'

Sheila and Barrington ('call me Barry') Appleby lived in Charlesville, a magnificent Victorian mansion in the posh Melbourne suburb of Toorak. Their son, Greg, had been a boarder with Tom at Berkdale College and during the holidays they'd often invited him to stay with them at Charlesville and also at their lodge at Mount Buller on the Victorian snowfields. It was here that Tom and Belinda first started skiing together.

The Applebys had never discussed with Belinda the possibility of her marrying Tom but it was something they often talked about to each other. They thought it would be a splendid match – not only was Tom rich but they liked him.

'I wouldn't want Belinda to marry a poor man,' Sheila told her husband. 'Money is important; it keeps marriages together long after love has gone.'

'Don't be so cynical, Sheila,' Barry protested. 'Surely it wasn't only my money that attracted you to me. I thought you loved me for myself, not my wealth!'

'I do, I do, darling.' She walked around the dining table where she and Barry were having breakfast and kissed him on the top of his head. 'But you're special, Barry – a one only! You're a man in a million and I've always considered myself the luckiest woman in the world. I know Belinda loves Tom, mothers can always tell about such things. I just wish I knew how he felt about her.'

Sheila was right, of course. Belinda was head over heels in love with Tom. From the moment Greg had introduced them she'd known that Tom was the man for her. She had no idea he was in New York when she'd accepted the position at the Consulate and was at first surprised – and then delighted – when they'd bumped into each other at a drinks party there. When Tom had asked her out she'd quickly said yes, and it hadn't taken long before they'd become a constant twosome.

Their likes and dislikes were so similar that sometimes Belinda was able to convince herself that Tom loved her, too. At other times, although he was always excellent company, there seemed to be a barrier between them. It mystified her. But as he'd never mentioned how he felt about her she was careful not to reveal her true feelings either.

But whenever she lunched with Abby, an old friend from Australia who worked at the United Nations, Abby would always bring up the subject of marriage. 'When is that perfect man of yours going to ask you to marry him?' she'd demand to know. 'Your vagina will wither up from lack of use if you're not careful.'

'Abby, do you mind?' Belinda pretended to look shocked but she was used to her friend's outrageous ways and laughed in spite of herself. 'Anyway, you know the rules – some things never change, even in these liberated times. Well, they don't as far as I'm concerned. I believe a woman has to wait for the man to ask and I don't intend to do or say anything that might frighten Tom away. I don't think he's even thought of marriage yet.'

'Well, it's time he did! How long a courtship does he want?' her bossy friend continued. 'I don't under-stand how a girl as modern as you are can be so old-fashioned! You don't have to wait for him to say he loves you. Sweep him off his feet. Tell him you're wildly in love with him.'

But Belinda reasoned that if she didn't pressure Tom then surely his feelings for her would develop into love and a proposal of marriage would follow. They'd never slept together because she wanted to be a virgin when she married. She'd confessed this after a party where they'd both had a little too much to drink and Tom had told her he simply respected her all the more. The topic never came up again.

Her friends thought she was nuts, especially Abby, who enjoyed an active sex life. 'Sweetie, when you work at the UN the whole world is available to you and believe me, travel not only broadens the mind, it does wonderful things for the body! I made love to an Ethiopian once who was unbelievably hot; I simply couldn't get enough of him. And there was a gorgeous Spaniard who was so bullish that I couldn't help yelling out "ole" when I came. When I think about the orgasms I had with that man!' She fanned herself jokingly.

'But seriously, you're missing marvellous opportunities, Belinda. Why on earth do you want to remain a virgin? You'll be sorry when you're older.'

'No, I won't.' Belinda was adamant. 'This is my body and I'm very proud of it. I don't intend to share it with just any old Tom, Dick or Harry. Well,' she laughed, 'perhaps a certain Tom, when the time is right.' She took a deep breath. 'Abby, I'm sure sex is everything you say it is but I'm prepared to wait until I marry to find out. Now, if you don't mind, let's talk about something else.'

Alone in his office, Tom was thinking about the conversation he'd had with his father a couple of hours earlier. Sydney had rung from Monaco to compliment him on the company's excellent US results. 'You've run a good operation there but now it's time for you to come home. I've been mulling things over while I've been in the South of France – I intend to stand down as chairman.'

His father's bombshell had rendered Tom momentarily speechless.

Sydney could picture the shocked look on his son's face and muffled a laugh. He was enjoying himself enormously – he knew Tom was taken aback, but keeping his children on their toes always amused him. 'I've spoken to the other members of the board and we've unanimously agreed that you should take over as chairman. Now that we've made the decision, we want to announce it. We don't want the market to think there's no one controlling the company, it will only make our shareholders edgy.'

Tom simply hadn't anticipated leaving New York quite so soon, or that his father standing down as chairman would trigger his return to Australia. He spoke sharply: 'You can't be serious about retiring, Dad, you're too young. Surely you're not planning to sit in a rocking chair and watch the passing parade. You'd be bored. How on earth do you intend to occupy yourself?'

He was astounded to hear his father chuckle. 'I'll manage, don't you worry about that. But don't imagine that I won't be taking an active interest in the affairs of Walker Corp. – nothing could be further from my mind. I'm remaining on the board and when decisions are taken that I believe are not in the best interests of the company, I'll be asking questions – and you'd better have the right answers,' he warned.

His voice mellowed. 'I've always believed old dogs

should know when to bow out and let the young hounds have their heads. You've shown what you're capable of with your successes in America and now it's your turn to stamp your mark on Walker Corp. If you ever want my opinion on anything, you have only to ask – but you know that.' He stopped to clear his throat. 'However, son, there is one thing . . .'

'Yes?' Tom replied diffidently, wondering what else the old man had up his sleeve.

'You need a wife. You're in your thirties. It's time you settled down with a good woman and had a family. How are things between you and Belinda?'

'She's a wonderful girl,' Tom said stiffly. 'I like her very much – well, I suppose I love her, but I'm not sure I love her the right way to marry her.'

'What the fuck are you talking about? What's love got to do with it? That's romantic twaddle. You like each other, she comes from a good family. She's got money of her own and she's beautiful. She's a fine asset for a man like you. She'll give you handsome children, she'll run your home well and charm your business acquaintances and friends. You must know she's crazy about you – everybody else certainly does. It stands out a mile.' Sydney had dined with them both on one of his visits to New York and had at once approved of Belinda, but had said nothing until now, knowing full well that children preferred not to have their parents' approval for their relationships, especially in the beginning.

Tom could hear his father pacing around the room. It was what he always did when he had a lot on his mind. For an unpredictable man Dad sometimes could be very predictable. He heard his father's chair creak as he sat down, and the familiar sounds of him lighting up his cigar. 'You don't have to love a woman to marry her you know, son. Treat her decently and give her good sex – and I know you know how to do that,' he said meaningfully.

'If a woman isn't sexually satisfied she'll look for it somewhere else. Too many men make the mistake of thinking women don't care about fucking but they do and believe me, son, I know what I'm talking about. Women like good sex just as much as men do.'

Tom was tempted to hang up the phone. He could sense the conversation was going to bring back memories that he'd rather remain forgotten but few people, and that included him, were brave enough to cut off Sydney Walker when he was in full flight.

'Why do you think I made sure you knew how to fuck properly?' Sydney demanded. 'It was worth every penny it cost me to arrange those excellent teachers for you. I hope you've been practising!' He gave a filthy gurgle.

Tom went to say something and stopped. Why should he dignify his father's suggestive remarks with a reply? Bugger him! But Sydney, completely unfazed by his lack of response, was still laughing at his own humour.

'Get cracking, son. Propose and then start packing up. I want you home by the end of the month.' There was a clunk as he hung up. Tom sat with the phone in his hand, deep in thought. Marriage! Belinda would make a good wife, sure – but he'd never thought about marrying her. He hadn't contemplated marriage with anyone.

He went over to the bar and poured himself a vodka on ice. He was elated at the prospect of becoming chairman but getting married – that was something else. Having seen his parents' version of wedded bliss he'd vowed not to let a similar fate happen to him.

As for his father's 'coaching lessons', he tried never to think of them. When Tom was sixteen, his father had taken him along to a brothel run very discreetly, from a good address, in the exclusive suburb of Double Bay. Sydney was on reciprocal first-name terms with Susan, the brothel manager, a handsome woman and, as Tom had gratefully discovered, kind-hearted.

Handing Susan a wad of notes, Sydney had told her not to mollycoddle the boy. 'Make sure he isn't a premature ejaculator – teach him control as well as technique. When he has a woman I want her to plead for more.' Turning to Tom, who was wishing he was anywhere but where he was, Sydney ordered him to relax and enjoy himself. 'You'll learn why fucking is one of man's greatest pleasures. Susan will teach you everything you need to know.' As he walked out the door he'd called out that he'd send the car back in a few hours' time.

Left alone with Susan, Tom didn't know what to do. 'Don't look so frightened, I won't hurt you,' she said, as she smiled at him. 'Come over here and let me undress you. Then you can help me take my clothes off . . .' When the driver called for him later Tom couldn't look him in the eyes. He was so embarrassed that he sat in the back instead of the front passenger seat, as he usually did, and didn't say a word the entire trip home.

The lessons continued for several months and constituted one of the most miserable periods of Tom's life. He'd thought of telling Catherine about his father's 'educational programme' but decided against it. There were some things men couldn't talk about with their sisters nor, he discovered, with their mothers. Sarah firmly believed it was a father's duty to instruct his son about sex. But Sydney had hired Susan instead. Tom's feelings of revulsion when his father left him at the brothel often came back to irk him.

One evening, when both Sarah and Catherine were away in the country, Sydney rang Susan and asked her to send a girl over to Ashburn. He'd invited a couple of business acquaintances for dinner and had asked Tom to join them, too. They were having coffee in the lounge room when the girl was shown in and introduced. It was the night before Tom's eighteenth birthday.

She was pretty enough but Tom could see she was nervous in the presence of Sydney and his high-powered friends. 'Will I sit here?' she said, gesturing to a chair near one of his father's colleagues.

'No, you won't,' Sydney said curtly. His father's next instruction horrified Tom. 'You're here to suck my son's cock – not to enjoy yourself with my guests. You won't be doing much sitting down tonight.' He looked suggestively at the older men and winked. 'What's your name?'

'Julia.'

'Wait outside, Julia. My son will be with you in a moment.' Then turning to Tom he said, 'Happy Birthday, son. Enjoy yourself with my present and make sure she gives you a good blow-job.' As he closed the door, Tom heard him say: 'Fuck, wouldn't it be great to be that young again? I wouldn't mind a little after-dinner pussy myself.'

'Is your father always like that?' Julia asked Tom.

'Yes.'

'I'm glad he's yours and not mine. You might be stinking rich but I think your father's a proper bastard.'

'Let's not talk about him,' Tom said, showing her to his room, which, like Catherine's, had its own lounge room and ensuite. 'Have a seat.' He pointed

432

to one of the chairs. Julia looked apprehensive. 'Don't worry about me,' Tom said. 'Unlike my father, I'm more than happy for you to sit down and by the way, I don't feel like sex tonight, so don't think you have to perform.'

'But your father has already paid.'

'That's his problem. I won't tell him if you don't. Buy yourself something nice, not to remember tonight, but to forget all about it. Now, would you like a drink?'

She nodded. He poured them both a Bacardi and Coke and sat down beside her. 'How old are you?' She told him she was twenty and taking acting classes during the day with the intention of becoming a TV actress and starring in a long-running soap.

'And how old are you?' she ventured.

'Eighteen tomorrow, and I'm going to be a writer.'

'Is that what your father wants?'

'No.'

'I knew it. I bet you have to do whatever your father tells you and that he wants you to go into the family business.'

'You're right on both counts. But one day I'll be a writer. I know it – because it's what I really want to do. There's something about the written word that really turns me on. If my father knew that he'd probably have bought me a dictionary and told me to fuck it!'

He broke into laughter and took a swig of his

drink. 'As I was saying,' he said grandly, 'it might take time for me to achieve my goal but I'm a persistent kind of a bloke. In the meantime, I'm going to fine-tune my writer's eye by observing and absorbing all the things I see and hear, as well as the people I meet, and believe me, I've met some real oddballs. My father has more uses than he realises.'

Julia was impressed. 'I'm sure you'll become a famous writer,' she said confidently, 'just like I know I'm going to be a famous actress. We'll have to get together and celebrate – and remember the night we first met – won't we?'

'Let's drink to that,' Tom said gleefully. He gulped down the rest of his drink. 'Want another one?'

Julia shook her head. 'One's my limit, thanks.' She looked at him hesitantly before plucking up the courage to ask if he'd mind if she went home. 'It would be nice to have an early night for a change,' she explained.

'No worries. But can I show you out the back way? We don't want to run into my father.'

She kissed him gently on the cheek and murmured, 'One day I hope there'll be a chance for me to do you a good deed.'

She slipped away into the darkness, towards Ashburn's front gate. Tom heard a car starting up and the sound of its motor slowly disappear into the distance. He stood in the shadows of Ashburn's majestic magnolia trees, letting the silence of the night envelop him, all thoughts of his father and the embarrassment he'd caused him temporarily forgotten.

It was such a long time ago, Tom reflected, draining the last of his vodka. No point dwelling on it any further. Besides, if he didn't get a move on he'd be late for tennis. He liked a game after a busy day. He played once a week and on Sunday mornings with Belinda and a group of friends. But two or three nights during the week, he also had a game at the Central Park Racquet Club with David Nelson, the Club pro. David was a strong player with a powerful serve, and Tom enjoyed playing with him. They were evenly matched – sometimes Tom won, other times David trounced him comfortably.

'I'll be with you in a sec,' he called out to David, as he rushed to change.

'Don't stress out,' the other man called back. 'Take your time. I'm practising my serve with the ball machine and I'm winning!'

Tom stopped to watch. David was a natural athlete, well toned and muscular. Tom had once told David what a great body he had. 'You can have one, too,' the other man had replied. 'All you have to do is work out at the gym five days a week. You know what they say – no pain, no gain.'

I never seem to have time for much else but work, Tom thought to himself. I've become a victim of the rat race.

David looked up. 'I know I said take your time, but I didn't mean all day.'

'Sorry, I don't know what came over me. I was daydreaming.' Tom changed hurriedly and before long was on court belting balls at David. 'Let's play,' he shouted, and served an ace and then another.

'You've been practising!' David protested. Tom won both sets and as they collected their gear David congratulated him. 'You were in fine form tonight but I'll get my revenge next time.'

'We'll see about that. I could do with a drink.'

'Have you got time?'

'As a matter of fact I do.'

'Great, why don't we go to Harry's?' They showered and dressed and headed for the popular local bar, which was just around the corner from the tennis club. It was an unpretentious place with comfortable lounge seats, excellent service and great music. It had a regular jazz trio that had entertained Harry's guests for something like twenty years and no one could ever get enough of them. Like Tom, David was a jazz aficionado, one of the reasons why Harry's had become their favourite watering hole. They both ordered vodka on the rocks.

Over the couple of years they'd been playing tennis the two men had become good friends. Sometimes David helped make up the numbers at a Walker Corp. dinner. Other times he and Tom would have dinner before taking in one of the latest movies. Every Saturday morning they went jogging in Central Park.

'I've had an amazing day,' Tom announced. 'My father's resigned as chairman and he wants me to go home and take over from him.'

'Hey, that's great – he probably should have done it years ago. Why don't we go out and get drunk? You can buy!'

'Mate, I would if I could but I have to pick up Belinda at nine.'

'Have you got time for another quick one then?'

Tom shook his head. 'No, I must go or I'll be late. Are you right for tennis tomorrow night?'

David nodded.

'Good, I'll see you then.'

Tom had arranged to meet Belinda at the home of the Australian Consul General, Michael Baume, who was entertaining visiting Australian politicians, most of whom he considered fairly heavy-going, and he'd asked Belinda if she and Tom would help him get through the evening. A former journalist himself, Baume was always interested in the goings-on at Walker Corp. and relied on Tom to keep him up to date with the latest media happenings.

Baume was a convivial host and good company. In spite of his misgivings about his guests it turned out to be a pleasant evening and the politicians were full of the latest gossip about Canberra. Later, when

Tom drove Belinda home to her apartment on Second Avenue, he told her his news.

'Why, Tom, how wonderful. You'll make an excellent chairman. I'm so proud of you.' She gave him a warm hug.

'You're biased, Belinda, but thank you.' He hugged her back. 'Why don't we have dinner at Le Perigord tomorrow night to celebrate?'

'I can't tomorrow. I'm going to see a new play with Abby but I am free the night after.'

'It's a date.'

Belinda watched Tom walk down the corridor. He waved goodbye and stepped into the elevator. Why did I have to fall in love with the strong, silent type? She gave a rueful shrug. Surely he won't go home without saying something to me. But what if he does? What would she do then?

Nervous tension gave way to excitement. He'll need a wife now that he's becoming chairman. Yes! She raised her fist triumphantly. Of course he will. She began to hum the first few bars of 'Here Comes the Bride'. Tom was going to ask her to marry him – she was sure of it. Dinner really would be a celebration!

The following night Tom had his usual game of tennis with David and this time, much to David's satisfaction, he won. 'You seem preoccupied tonight, something on your mind?' he asked Tom, as they showered.

'One or two things.'

'Can I help?'

'Doubt it.'

'Thanks for the vote of confidence. I'm not a bad listener, you know. Have you got time for dinner?'

Tom had missed lunch because of a meeting and he suddenly realised he was hungry. 'I haven't eaten all day. Food is just what I need. Where shall we go?'

'What about coming back to my place? I don't feel like a restaurant tonight. I could whip up a mushroom risotto and I've got some good French red to wash it down.'

David lived in Manhattan's trendy SoHo. Tom had warmed to the harmony of his apartment from the first moment he'd stepped through the front door. 'There's something very welcoming about this place and this might sound strange, but it feels happy.'

'I like to think that my home has that effect on people,' David said, pleased.

Tom also liked the way he'd furnished the place with its creamy walls and tasteful mixture of contemporary and antique furnishings in beige, cream and the occasional caramel shade.

He dropped into one of the armchairs. 'This chair is so comfy I don't think I'll ever be able to get up.'

'Don't. Just sit there and relax, it's what you need. I won't be long.' Tom could hear him getting things ready in the kitchen. He leant back in the chair and closed his eyes.

David interrupted his reverie. 'Don't fall asleep on

me! Here, I've poured you a glass of wine,' and he handed it to Tom. 'If you'd like to make yourself useful why don't you set the table. By the way,' he asked, as he went back to the kitchen, 'where's Belinda tonight?'

'At some play with a girlfriend.'

It didn't take David long to get dinner on the table. He'd made a rocket, tomato and Parmesan salad to have with the risotto. As he poured more wine for them both, he told Tom to help himself.

'This is delicious,' Tom said, eating hungrily. 'And exactly what I felt like.' Both men devoured their meals in companionable silence. As Tom scraped the last morsel of risotto from his plate David opened another bottle of wine. 'I hope you've got room for dessert,' he said, going out to the kitchen and returning with two plates of fresh peaches with mascarpone. 'Desserts are my specialty.'

'You'd like my sister then,' Tom said. 'When we were kids, if I wasn't quick when sweets were served she'd lean over with her spoon and swipe the lot off my plate!'

David was pleased to see his friend relaxing. Sometimes Tom seemed so tense. 'You must be looking forward to seeing more of her when you get home.'

'I am. She'd love these,' he said, indicating the peaches with his spoon.

David refilled their glasses. 'Have you enjoyed being in New York?'

'Yes I have, but it's strange. I'm always busy, surrounded by people, I go to lots of parties, play sport – some days it seems I've hardly time to sleep – but the fact is, every now and again I feel incredibly alone.'

They'd moved to the lounge room to have coffee. As Tom made himself comfortable, David opened a new bottle of wine. 'Another glass?' he asked.

'I know I'll regret this in the morning,' Tom said, 'but you were right, this wine is excellent.' He held out his glass.

'How do you feel about becoming chairman now that you've had twenty-four hours to think about it?' David asked, looking at him closely. 'It's what you want, isn't it?'

'Yes, of course, and I've got big plans for Walker Corp.' Tom idly twirled his wine around in his glass before continuing. He gave his friend a look extraordinarily reminiscent of his father.

David hadn't met Sydney Walker, but he recognised naked ambition when he saw it. 'I'm sure you'll take the company to new heights but I'll miss our tennis and our friendship.'

Tom was taken aback. 'My going home doesn't mean the end of that. Maybe we won't play tennis on such a regular basis but I'll be making regular visits here. I want to stay in touch with you.'

'Maybe I'll finally stop making excuses for not going to Australia.' David had the grace to look shamefaced – it was something of a contentious issue between them, albeit a light-hearted one. Tom had often ribbed him for using the long flying time to Australia as a reason for not going there.

'I'll get Catherine to make you a sinful pudding if you do finally make it!' he said. They laughed and quaffed their wine. David refilled their glasses once more.

Tom was very relaxed now. 'Your friendship has meant a great deal to me, David. I'm glad we met.'

'It's been important to me, too.' Something in the tone of David's voice made Tom look up at him. David held his gaze. Tom felt his face redden and, embarrassed, jumped to his feet. 'Mate, what have you done to me? We've knocked off almost three bottles of wine. I'll never be able to drive home.'

'Stay the night.' David leant forward and put his hand on Tom's shoulder. 'There's no need for you to rush off. There's plenty of room. Here, let me show you.' Tom followed David into the bedroom.

# Chapter Twenty

He never could remember at what stage he got into bed, but when Tom awoke the next morning, he was lying in it naked and David was asleep beside him.

Shit! What am I doing in bed with him? Christ! Tom sat up, horrified. They'd had sex, that much he did remember. Then he recollected something else. It had seemed so right. He could recall that clearly. He'd actually enjoyed sex for the first time in his life. He'd felt complete. Shit, what does it mean? What have I done? I must have been mad. David seduced me, got me drunk and took advantage of me. What a fool I've been. He fell out of bed, pulling on his clothes frantically.

'Good morning.' David was awake and watching him. 'You were wonderful last night. You're a great lover.'

'Don't be crazy, David. It was a mistake. I was drunk. So were you! Neither of us knew what we were doing. I must go.' Tom couldn't bring himself to look David in the eye. He rushed madly out of the apartment, down the fire stairs, and into the street. But once there he didn't know what to do. He felt confused. He found a cafe and went in and ordered a coffee and sat thinking about what had happened.

What made me do it? Here I am about to ask Belinda to marry me and I've just been to bed with David. He put his head in his hands. I was drunk, that was it. I didn't know what I was doing. He ordered another coffee. What am I going to do? Forget it! That's what I'm going to do. David won't say anything and I certainly won't. It was just one of those things. It was that third bottle of wine – I knew I'd regret it.

He got up and paid the bill. I'd better get to the office, or they'll have a search party out looking for me. Although Tom threw himself into his work and his day was packed with calls and meetings, his mind refused to let go of one important fact. He had *enjoyed* sex with David and had felt an indescribable sense of relief but wasn't sure why. It's not normal, he thought. There must be something wrong with me. He determined to put the whole affair out of his mind. It was a bachelor's last stand, a drunken fling, that's all.

At lunchtime, he went to Tiffany's as if he hadn't a care in the world, and selected the most dazzling, and expensive, diamond solitaire engagement ring.

He was certain Belinda would be crazy about it. But before he'd reached his office he was hit by a massive attack of guilt. He was a creep for cheating on Belinda. His behaviour had been reprehensible. He would never forgive himself for putting their relationship at such risk. He would never do so again.

They'd only just sat down at Le Perigord when he put the distinctive blue Tiffany's box in front of her and asked her to marry him. Belinda stared at the box, overjoyed, but a little perturbed at the same time. Tom had never told her he loved her. She had to be certain of his feelings before she committed herself to him.

'You really do love me, Tom, don't you?' she asked purposefully.

'Why, yes.' Her question took him by surprise. 'Of course I do, Belinda. Don't you know that?'

She gave a nervous laugh of relief. 'Well, I'd hoped – but a girl likes to hear the magic words every now and again, you know.' Her obvious happiness made her lovelier than usual. Tom found it very touching and looked at her fondly.

'I'll never forget tonight as long as I live,' Belinda said, as she opened the little blue box. 'Oh Tom,' she enthused, 'it's the most glorious diamond I've ever seen. What excellent taste you have.' She slid the ring on her finger and held it up to the light admiringly. 'And it fits perfectly!'

This time Tom beamed at her. He couldn't help himself.

Over dinner, Belinda enthusiastically began to make plans. 'We should have an engagement party, don't you think?' Tom nodded. 'Darling,' she said, 'Mum and Dad are going to be so pleased. They've always liked you. Where do you want to marry – in New York or will we go home?'

'You'd like to be with your family and friends, wouldn't you?'

'Yes, of course, but I don't mind where we get married. Now that I have you, nothing else is important.'

She's so nice, Tom thought as he returned her smile. Perhaps his father was right. Belinda's love would make up for any deficiency in his feelings but oddly enough he now found he rather liked the idea of marriage to her. He was so lonely for love and affection it seemed the right thing to do. It killed him to think what a heel he'd been. Bloody David should never have taken advantage of him the way he had.

'Why don't we have the wedding at home and invite our friends from New York to join us? I'm sure Dad wouldn't mind if I got the Walker jet to fly them all to Australia.'

Sydney was elated to hear his son had taken his advice and naturally took full credit for the decision. Sheila and Barry Appleby were equally delighted and not long after Belinda had called her, Sheila was on the phone to her dressmaker, discussing what would be the most appropriate outfit for her to wear as mother of the bride.

Catherine was also overjoyed for her brother. She liked Belinda and could see the girl was head over heels in love with Tom when he'd introduced them on her last visit to New York. 'As long as you're sure this is what you want and not something that Dad would like,' she said.

'What a strange thing for you to say. Of course I am, Sis.'

'Are you absolutely sure, Tom?'

There was the slightest pause. 'Positively. Don't be silly.'

'You told me once that you thought you'd never marry,' Catherine persisted.

'I was young and stupid when I said that,' Tom replied defensively. 'Life isn't meant to be lived alone, I know that now. I need to love and be loved, just like anyone else.'

She understood that desire better than most people did. 'I hope your path to true love doesn't turn out to be as rocky as mine.' As the words slipped out she'd wished she could have bitten off her tongue.

Seizing the chance to get out of the limelight, Tom demanded to know how her love life was. 'Something's not right between you and Jack, is it? I can tell by your voice. What's gone wrong?'

'Nothing,' she said. 'We're just working our way through a few problems. We're going to be fine.' She wished she could be as certain as she hoped she sounded.

It was decided that the wedding would be held in Melbourne at St Patrick's Cathedral and the reception at Charlesville. Belinda asked Catherine to be one of her attendants. 'I want this to be a real family affair,' she said.

Tom stopped going to the Racquet Club, explaining his change in routine to Belinda by saying he had too much to do – what with getting married, putting the office in order for his replacement, as well as preparing himself for his new company responsibilities. Belinda gave notice at the Consulate because she was going to return to Australia ahead of Tom to organise the wedding with her mother.

Their many New York friends gave parties in their honour, overjoyed that two of the nicest people they knew were going to marry. Tom dreaded running into David at one of them but he knew it would happen sooner or later. When he did, David acted as if nothing had happened between them. He'd just held out his hand and offered his congratulations. 'I hope you and Belinda will both be very happy.'

'Thanks.' Tom's response was muffled. 'I don't know what to say,' he muttered.

'What's done is done.'

How could he be so nonchalant? Tom was incredulous.

'The club's not the same without you – maybe we can have a game before you go home.' The invitation sounded harmless enough and anyone listening would never have suspected that the pair had been lovers for one night.

'I'd like that, it would be like old times. I'll call you,' Tom said, as he walked over to stand at Belinda's side. He had no intention of ever calling David again, he thought, as he put a protective arm around his fiancée.

When Sydney had brought up the subject of his replacement in New York Tom had immediately suggested Huxley. He was Sydney's choice, too. They both knew Huxley was looking for new challenges and that America would provide them. Huxley arrived in the States a few weeks before Tom was due to leave, giving them ample time to run through things. Tom also gave a dinner for Huxley at his apartment and introduced him to some of the city's key players.

As soon as he was back in Australia, Tom was caught up in an endless round of meetings and briefing sessions with his father. Belinda was in Melbourne, where her mother was in seventh heaven organising what she was determined would be the wedding of the year. Belinda spoke to Tom every day on the phone, happily telling him about the arrangements.

Four days before the wedding the overseas guests, including Huxley, arrived in the Walker Corp. jet.

David was among them – Belinda liked him and Tom knew she'd have thought it odd if he hadn't been invited. Sheila Appleby had organised dinners and lunches as well as sightseeing tours for them all, but Huxley had been summoned to headquarters for meetings with Sydney and Tom. They required his input for a big deal they were putting together – Walker Corp.'s takeover of 21st Century Global, the massive entertainment group. After one particularly intense session, he'd phoned Catherine and asked her out to dinner.

Huxley was staying at the Park Hyatt so they met at the hotel's main restaurant overlooking Sydney Harbour, and caught up with their respective business activities. They were very relaxed in each other's company, in the way that only old friends can be.

'I must tell you my latest joke,' Catherine insisted. 'What can a squirrel do that a man can't?'

'Haven't a clue,' Huxley replied. 'What?'

'Climb a tree with his nuts in his mouth!' The other diners turned to see what all the merriment was about.

'It's been too long since we did this,' he said.

'I agree,' she replied fondly. 'You always take my mind off my troubles.'

'I'd never have said anything if you hadn't brought up the subject but you do look a little peaky.' He smiled at her disarmingly. 'What's bothering you? I thought everything was in great shape at *MAUD*.'

'It is.'

'Ah.' He nodded wisely. 'Have you and Jack had a row?'

'No, not at all. All relationships have their teething problems – we're sorting them out.' She gave him the same kind of vague answer she'd given Tom. There was no way her dilemma with Jack would overshadow her brother's wedding. The only love affair that mattered now was his and Belinda's.

Two days before the wedding Tom, Catherine, Huxley and Sydney left for Melbourne. Sheila had insisted that they stay at Charlesville. 'We've plenty of room,' she told them. 'I've also taken several rooms at the Sheraton at Southbank. Tom can sleep there the night before the wedding. So can Greg and the other groomsmen.'

Everything was going smoothly. Tom was enjoying having some time off and being made a fuss of and Belinda was so deliriously happy that it was infectious. The day before the wedding, fairly late in the afternoon, Tom was having a cup of tea and reading the newspapers in the Applebys' library before leaving for the Sheraton when the phone rang. When no one answered it after a few rings, he picked up the receiver.

'Hello, Tom Walker speaking.'

'What a surprise – how are you?'

His voice took Tom completely unawares. 'Why, David,' he stammered, 'how are you? I hope you're enjoying Australia.'

'I am! Everything you told me about the place is true. It's a fantastic country. No wonder you love it here. I'd hoped that we might have a meal together or at least a game of tennis while I was here. I rang you a couple of times at your office – did you get my messages?'

'Yes, I did. I'm sorry, but I've been busy.'

'I think you've been avoiding me,' David said firmly.

'Not at all.'

'Have it your own way, but you must listen to me. I'm in love with you, Tom. I have been for some time. Maybe I'm not the one for you but you really haven't given our relationship a chance because you're not prepared to admit that you're gay. From the moment we met I knew you were unlike any other man I've ever known, and whether you want to admit it or not, our lovemaking was special.' He paused to take a breath before continuing. 'You're making a dreadful mistake and you won't only hurt yourself. There's also Belinda to consider.'

'Please, David, don't say anything else. I'm so confused. Our night together was a dreadful mistake. I was drunk. What happened was an accident. I'm not like that.'

'Like what, for God's sake? What the hell are you ashamed of? I'm a gay man and I'm proud of it. Has your father bullied you so much that you can't admit the truth, not even to yourself? Are you going to live a lie for the rest of your life? It won't work, Tom.'

'I don't know what to do. I've missed you more than I thought I would but . . .'

'But you don't think you love me.' David finished his sentence for him. 'I can accept that. But Tom, you know as well as I do that there is *more* to our friendship. What we have between us is unfinished business and it's because I care for you that I'm begging you to think again before you go through with your marriage. You don't love Belinda in the way she deserves to be loved.'

'Please, don't go on – I can't take any more.' Tom hung up. He felt guilty enough as it was and the sound of David's voice only made him feel worse. His father would never let him hear the last of it if he called off the wedding. How could he ever explain things to Belinda? I've made a bloody mess of everything, he thought, his head in his hands.

He was still sitting like that when he heard someone enter the room. It was Belinda. She was crying.

'I heard you talking to David,' she sobbed. 'I picked up the phone, about the same time as you did. I was going to say something but when I heard what you were saying to each other I couldn't.' He went over and attempted to hold her.

'Don't touch me!' She pushed him away. 'You bastard,' she said bitterly. 'How could you string me along the way you have?' Belinda looked like a wild woman.

453

'I'm sorry,' he said.

'You're sorry!' She almost spat the words at him. 'Is that all you can say? I loved you with all my heart. Doesn't that mean anything to you?'

She was walking angrily up and down the room. 'Of course not,' she answered the question herself. 'Why would it? Someone like you wouldn't even know the meaning of the word.' She began to cry; long, heartfelt sobs of despair.

'How will I ever hold my face up in public after this? What will our friends say? You never loved me, did you?' She glared at him accusingly. 'What a fraud you are, Tom, pretending to be one thing but really the other! You make me sick.'

'It was never my intention to hurt you, Belinda, and whatever you care to believe, I am truly sorry.'

'Well, you have hurt me, more than I can say.' She wrenched the engagement ring off her finger. 'Here, take this,' she said.

Tom gazed unseeingly at the diamond gleaming in his hand. What have I done? he thought. The media would have a field day, and then the gossip would start. People would be shocked. His father would demand an explanation.

He looked at Belinda blankly. 'But what will we tell people?'

For a fleeting moment, Belinda felt sorry for him, then she remembered how he'd used her. Damn him, she thought. She squared her shoulders. 'We don't owe anyone an explanation. This is our affair. We'll say we mistook friendship for love.'

How strong she was – he had to admire her courage. 'If that's what you want to do . . .'

'We can hardly tell people the truth,' she said sadly. 'I've always loved you, Tom. I knew you were different – that's probably what attracted me to you in the first place – but it never occurred to me that you might be gay.' She brushed away her tears with her hand. 'When you were talking to David there was an expression in your voice that I've never heard before. Perhaps you are in love with him like he says.'

'I don't know,' he said glumly. 'But I'll never forgive myself for causing you so much unhappiness.'

'I always knew that what we had was too good to be true.' She gave a sour laugh. 'Don't worry, though, I won't tell anyone that you're gay. They'd find it as hard to believe as I do.' The tone in her voice made Tom wince.

She stalked out of the room without a backward glance, almost knocking over her mother who was carefully placing a vase of November lilies on a nearby table. One look at her daughter's face and Sheila knew that something dreadful had occurred, but she still had the presence of mind to close the library door before putting her arms around Belinda and hugging her tightly.

'Darling, what's wrong? Tell me at once!'

'Oh Mum,' Belinda said, breaking down completely. 'I wish I was dead.'

Left by himself, Tom collapsed into one of Sheila's treasured Chippendale chairs. What a dreadful mess I've made of everything, he thought with a groan. But he couldn't refute, even to himself, that he was relieved the wedding wasn't going ahead. He was still in a state of denial about his sexuality, though. I mightn't be getting married, but that doesn't mean I'm gay, he thought angrily. Then the old feelings of confusion swept over him. David's nothing more than a good friend, that's all. But why does he make me feel this way? Tom recalled again the pleasure and sense of satisfaction he'd felt the night they'd had sex. He'd never experienced anything like it. He remembered the touch of David's lips on his and their warmth.

He had no idea how much time had passed before he let himself out of the Applebys' mansion. No one would miss him – certainly not now, he thought – and he needed to clear his head. He walked in the general direction of the city, his mind in turmoil. Is it possible that I could be gay? What will people think? What will Dad and Catherine say? He didn't look gay. He was sure of that. He'd been to the recovery party after Sydney's Gay Mardi Gras and he didn't think he was anything like the extraordinary collection of men that had been there – the leather set, drag queens, the boys in T-shirts and jeans, bikies, men in cotton frocks and wearing so much make-up that it was impossible not to stare. He'd chatted up a girl and bought her a drink only to discover that she was a he.

No, he wasn't like them at all. And what about David? He dressed as conservatively as Tom did and he didn't look gay either. Tom hadn't even suspected that David was homosexual. He passed a hotel and went in and ordered a beer, hoping it might relax him. It didn't. He went outside and hailed a passing taxi that took him to the Sheraton. He figured Sheila Appleby would have been too upset to think of cancelling the room she'd reserved for him.

He was right. The Sheraton welcomed him warmly. Sheila – determined to make a splash – had booked him into the Presidential Suite. It was huge, far too big for someone who felt as alone as Tom did.

He poured himself a scotch and sat down. He'd never felt so confused. What if he was gay? He had to face it. But he was Tom Walker, Sydney Walker's son and heir, Chairman of Walker Corp. He was familiar with the rules of corporate life. Homosexuals weren't welcomed. Corporate men were expected to be heterosexual, especially in Australia. If his father ever found out about his one-night stand with David he'd disown him. Sydney would never be able to understand how his son could fuck, let alone be fucked by, 'a poofter'.

Tom could hear his father as clearly as if he were in the same room. 'If a faggot ever comes near you, son, kick him in the balls. What those queens do is bloody wrong, dirty and disgusting.'

The phone rang. Who was ringing him at four in the morning? He hoped it wasn't his father. 'Yes?'

'It's me,' said David. 'I heard about the wedding being called off. It was on the news. You've done the right thing. I know what you're going through. I've been through it, too, you know. You're not the only man in the world who has had to come to grips with being gay. You might think you're alone but you're not. I know all about hiding gay feelings from others. It takes its toll on you, Tom. Believe me, I do know. Would you like me to come over?'

'I'm not sure,' he said. 'It mightn't be wise and . . .' Tom stopped in mid-sentence. What am I saying? What kind of bloody fool am I? David is the one person I would like to see.

'Yes, I would. If I don't talk to someone soon I'll go out of my mind. I'm in the Presidential Suite.'

'And I'm in the lobby downstairs.' David was outside Tom's suite in what seemed like seconds. 'You look terrible,' he said, as he walked in and sat on the lounge. 'Whatever you may think, it's not the end of the world.'

'I know that, but I've spent my life trying to be someone I'm not and it's not an easy thing to accept after so much denial. I'm not normal, I'm gay.'

458

He heaved a big sigh. 'But at least I now understand why I've always felt the way that I have, as if there was no one else quite like me.'

David could see his pain. 'You're not the only one,' he said.

Tom scarcely heard him. 'I've craved the kind of love people share with the special person in their lives.' He shivered and looked away before continuing. He spoke slowly. 'I honestly did think the love I had for Belinda was enough to see us through, even though I knew her feelings for me were much deeper. But I was still convinced we could be happy together.'

Tom looked shamefaced as he remembered what Belinda had said to him. 'My behaviour's been unforgivable. She told me I was a bastard and she was right.'

'Stop being so hard on yourself,' David said.

'I can't help it.' His face was a picture of despair. 'Now I feel more alone then ever.'

'Not any longer. You have me.' David patted his hand gently. Tom jumped. 'Don't worry,' David laughed, 'I'm not making a pass at you!' He gave his friend an amused look. 'And if you'll excuse my choice of words, let me set you straight about something – you are normal. Being gay doesn't mean you're not! You've been subjected to too much propaganda.'

Tom nodded. 'You're probably right.' He felt a sudden surge of hope. 'Where do we go from here?'

'Nowhere unless you want to, and there's no rush. Let's just take it one step at a time. You know what they say – one step at a time is not so very difficult.'

He walked over to the bar and poured a nip of scotch into a glass. 'Drink this, it'll do you good and then you should try to get some sleep. You've had one hell of a day.'

'That's the understatement of the year,' Tom said before he downed the stiff drink David had poured him.

He walked David to the door. 'I may not be ready to tell all and sundry that I'm gay but I won't deny it to myself any longer.'

He held out his hand. David turned it over and held it. 'That's the best news I've heard in ages,' he said, giving Tom a friendly hug.

'Thank you for everything,' Tom said. 'Whatever happens, I'll always be grateful to you for making me face the truth about myself.'

# Chapter Twenty-One

When Tom woke several hours later the message light on his bedside phone was flashing. He groaned. Everyone's going to be looking for me. Hell! He didn't feel like talking to anyone. Thank God he'd had the foresight to tell the operator to hold all his calls. But now, someone was knocking at his door. *Maybe if I just lie here quietly whoever it is will go away.* He put the pillow over his head. The knocking persisted. Pulling on the hotel's white towelling bathrobe, he went to the door of his suite.

'Who is it?' he called out.

'It's me, Catherine. Let me in.' He undid the safety lock and opened the door. 'Oh, Tom.' She hugged him. 'Are you all right? What on earth went wrong between you and Belinda? Everyone's got their version of what happened.' She shook him lightly by the shoulders. 'I'm on your side, my dear brother!'

'It's rather a long story, Sis,' he said. 'Come in and sit down.' Catherine followed him to the lounge.

The windows of the Presidential Suite looked out over the Yarra River across to Melbourne's elegant cityscape. It was a beautiful day, the sun was shining and all kinds of activities were underway on the Yarra – canoeists were taking part in training practice, casually dressed tourists were admiring the vista from their pleasure craft, joggers were running along the river foreshore and scores of people were simply taking it easy, basking in the warmth of the sun, enjoying the spectacle.

It would have been a perfect day for our wedding, Tom thought, as he looked out at the view. Belinda would have said she'd ordered the sun personally. Belinda! He'd been so wrapped up in himself that he'd forgotten all about her. What a bastard I am. Poor, sweet Belinda – how could I be so indifferent after all the grief I've caused her? He gave an involuntary shudder, imagining the scene Sheila Appleby would have staged.

'Tom, I'm still here. Would you rather be alone?' Catherine said.

'No, of course not. Sorry, I was a million miles away. How's Dad taking it?'

'How do you think? He's swearing and cursing as only he can. He's told Sheila and Barry you must be off your head because only a madman would have called off his marriage to a girl as wonderful as

Belinda.' She put her hand over Tom's and gave it a comforting squeeze.

'Sheila's distraught, Belinda is as calm as a cucumber and won't hear a bad word about you. She says the real reason you called off the wedding is a private matter between you and her and as far as she's concerned that's the way it's going to remain. She even told Dad that there was nothing to be gained by him losing his block and that he should be comforting, not berating, you.

'I thought he was going to have a heart attack! No one has ever told Dad to pull his head in so politely before. He couldn't believe what he was hearing. I wished you could've seen his face – it was a sight to behold.'

She couldn't help laughing as she recalled her father's amazement. Even Tom managed to smile.

'That's better,' Catherine said. 'But that's enough about Dad, it's you I'm worried about. What happened between you and Belinda – and don't give me that nonsense about mistaking friendship for love. I won't buy it!'

'Well . . . well . . .' Tom stuttered, suddenly tongue-tied.

'Well, what?' she demanded. 'For God's sake, Tom, tell me!'

'I'm homosexual.'

He sat back and waited miserably for her reaction, for the look of disgust, the physical recoil.

Catherine just looked shrewdly at him. 'I've often wondered if you might be.'

He stared at her in amazement. 'You have? Why didn't you say something?'

'But why should I? It's your business, and if you weren't going to talk about it I certainly wasn't. Anyway, so what if you're homosexual? What's wrong with that? Does it worry you? It sure as hell doesn't bother me.'

'You're not shocked?' he said. 'You don't hate me? You know what Dad thinks about "bloody queers". He probably won't want to have anything to do with me.'

'Stop that, Tom. You are who you are and as far as I'm concerned, you're my brother and I love you – and I always will. I couldn't give a damn whether you're gay or straight. All that matters is that you are a fine, decent human being.

'Quite frankly,' she said resolutely, 'it doesn't matter what Dad thinks either. If his reaction concerns you then don't tell him until you feel the time is right. He doesn't have to know.'

'I'll have to face him about it some time. I can't stay in the closet forever.'

He looked so wretched Catherine put her arm around his shoulders and gave him a reassuring hug. 'You must do whatever you think is right but there's no hurry, is there? Tell Dad when it suits you. Put yourself first in this. Why don't you give yourself more time to adjust before you tell him?'

'I guess you're right,' he said. 'But I'll never be able to forgive myself for what I've done to Belinda.' He closed his eyes for a moment. 'Why does everything have to be so hard?'

'Stop torturing yourself, it won't help. What happened to make you realise the truth about yourself?' Tom looked down at his hands and began to fiddle with his watch. The silence seemed interminable.

'Don't you think it might help if you talked about it?' she ventured.

Tom took a deep breath and let it out slowly. He told his sister everything. It had never been his intention, he told Catherine, to cause Belinda so much pain.

'It's funny, isn't it? She would have made the ideal wife, just like Dad told me she would. She doesn't deserve any of this,' he said abjectly.

'You mustn't blame yourself for everything. Of course Belinda's upset – why wouldn't she be? It's only natural. When time passes and she's able to think more rationally, she'll understand that this was something beyond your control. In her heart she knows you're not the kind of man who'd deliberately set out to deceive or hurt her.'

Tom shook his head. 'I wouldn't be so sure of that.'

'Well, I would! David's phone call took you completely unawares. You might never have admitted that you were gay had you and he not spoken. And it's not your fault that before you could tell Belinda the truth, she beat you to the punch by confronting you after overhearing your conversation with David.

'As Dad likes to say, timing is everything in life, isn't it?' Catherine said ruefully. 'You know perfectly well that you'd have told her everything as soon as you had the opportunity. I'm positive you would have called the wedding off.'

'I don't know about that, Sis. No one likes to be humiliated. Maybe I wouldn't have gone ahead but I'll never know because the matter was taken out of my hands. Perhaps it was just as well.'

'Whatever you might both be thinking now, it's a bloody good thing your marriage didn't take place.' Catherine spoke with conviction, almost daring her brother to disagree with her. When he said nothing she went over to the dining-room table, where there was a large bowl of fruit, and helped herself to a couple of strawberries. 'I'm hungry – have you had anything to eat?' He shook his head.

'Me neither. Why don't you have a shower and get dressed and I'll order something from room service. I need food. I'm feeling somewhat emotionally drained and you, dear brother, certainly must be.

'I know,' she said triumphantly. 'Let's have Eggs Benedict.' This seemed just the time for the comfort of their childhood treat.

'Suits me,' Tom said, 'but instead of hot chocolate can I please have coffee?'

Catherine laughed. 'Well, I don't know, child-hood pleasures can be very reassuring, you know. Are you sure you don't want hot chocolate?'

'Positive!' Tom grimaced. 'Coffee with milk, please.'

He went off to the bathroom while Catherine rang room service and gave their order. She sat down and switched on the TV, more out of habit than from a desire to watch anything, and although she looked at the screen her mind was elsewhere. Poor Tom, life can be so tough at times. But what a disaster it would have been if he and Belinda had married and then a few months into the marriage Tom had told her he was gay. That would have been far worse. She sighed. I wonder if Ma knew.

'What are you watching?' Tom asked as he returned to the lounge room.

'I haven't the faintest idea.' She switched off the set. 'Our Eggs Benedict should be here any minute.'

'Great.' He came up behind her and gave her a big hug. 'You're the best sister a man could have. Thanks for everything.'

'My pleasure,' she said. 'I was just wondering, do you think Ma knew you were gay?'

'I think she may have. Do you remember when I was about seven, and I wanted to learn tap dancing instead of going to football? Ma said it showed I had a creative streak but Dad wouldn't have a bar of it, of course. Last night when I was sitting here thinking about everything, I remembered her once telling me never to fear being myself. At the time I didn't really understand what she meant but now I think it was her way of telling me that she knew I was gay.'

A knock on the door announced the arrival of the room service waiter with their breakfast. 'Mmm, it smells wonderful,' Tom said, as he signed the bill. As soon as the waiter had gone, they attacked the food with gusto.

'This was just what I needed.'

Catherine beamed at him. 'Me too – aren't these eggs scrumptious?' Tom's mouth was too full to speak so he gave her the thumbs-up sign instead. They wolfed down their meals in silence and then over coffee Catherine asked him what he planned to do next.

'When I've finished my coffee I think I'll ring Sheila Appleby and see what I can do to help. Presents will need to be returned, letters written, that kind of thing. Now that I've calmed down I'd also like to talk to Belinda.'

'That's a good idea,' Catherine said encouragingly. 'Then I think you should get back to work.'

Tom was very still. 'It's all I have left.'

'Now don't start feeling sorry for yourself,' Catherine said in her best big sister voice. 'As chairman you have certain responsibilities, you know . . .'

'Give me a break! Of course I know.'

Catherine slammed down her coffee cup. 'Sometimes you can be so infuriating.'

'Just kidding, Sis.' He grinned at her. 'You always did have a short fuse.'

'Go to hell.'

'Charming! Seriously, I have a couple of grand schemes in mind for Walker Corp. I want to expand the entertainment side of the business. Huxley's been working with me – and the old man – on our bid for 21st Century Global. I'm confident we'll be successful. The deal will give us access to its incredible library of movies, including first runs, which will be a huge boost to our sales.' Tom was so animated and enthusiastic about all this that Catherine was glad she'd changed the subject.

'Dad started the push into China and I'm going to consolidate it by increasing our investment in telecommunications and setting up Walker Telephone Communications. It will make a significant difference to the company's future.'

Catherine's eyebrows lifted. 'That's putting it mildly! Communications companies will be the power players in the 21st century. You'll have Walker Corp. nicely positioned to make the most of everything technology offers. It's exactly the right approach, Tom.'

'Naturally – what else would you expect?'

She rolled her eyes and laughed. 'That's the last praise you'll get from me! By the way, Huxley told me over dinner the other night that he was enjoying working so closely with you on the Global deal.'

'The man's a genius.'

'Isn't he though?' She flashed him a grin. 'I recollect telling Dad that very same thing.'

'Huxley thinks you're a bloody marvel, too. He's always singing your praises. I reckon he's got a crush on you, Sis.'

'Rubbish!' But Catherine could have kicked herself for blushing.

He got to his feet and patted her on the cheek. 'My, my, what have we here,' he scoffed. 'Are you sure you don't fancy him?'

'Would you stop?' She spoke crossly.

'I'm only joking,' he protested. 'Don't lose your block!'

Tom got himself some more coffee. 'I'm going to bring your mate Huxley back to Australia because I need someone like him here. He has such a sharp mind. He can see all the problems in any deal long before anyone else, plus he's got a better eye for a major share play than Dad ever had, and he's not afraid to make decisions. I'm going to make him CEO.'

'Good idea,' Catherine said. 'How does he feel about that?'

'He's really happy because he has been missing Australia. Of course, he enjoyed his time in the UK – he did an excellent job there picking up where you'd left off and he really settled into the British lifestyle quite well but he still had bouts of homesickness. You know what they say: "You can take the man out of Oz . . ."'

'That's true enough. I yearned for Australia's blue skies when I was working in London. Those never-ending winter grey skies were so depressing.'

Tom gave her a smile. 'Yes, I remember those mournful letters of yours. "How I wish I could go surfing at Bondi instead of gazing at the rain-sodden River Thames."' He tried unsuccessfully to duck as Catherine gave him a thump.

Tom just laughed at her and went on. 'Huxley also got the occasional bout of winter blues but his yearning was for an icy beer at the pub on a stinking hot summer's day.'

'That sounds just like him,' Catherine said, smiling.

'He's disappointed not to have more time running the American operation because New York seems to have cast its magic on him, as it did you – but in his heart, he's excited about coming home on a more permanent basis.'

In fact, Huxley had been somewhat taken aback when Tom had told him of the change in plans. Sure, he had a touch of homesickness every now and again, but he'd been looking forward to living in New York and getting to know Americans, whose enthusiasm for life was something he admired. Catherine, who'd loved New York, had told Huxley so much about the place that he'd been curious to see it for himself.

The first day he'd walked down Fifth Avenue he'd begun to understand why her love affair with the Big Apple was so fervent. The city had an exciting vitality and a beauty that stopped you in your tracks. It had been a late winter morning and as he'd walked he could see the spires of St Patrick's Cathedral reaching into the mist. It was a breathtaking sight and he had to stop so that he could take it all in. As far as he could see there was a succession of mighty buildings. He passed shops dressed in lavish, festive Christmas decorations. Santa Claus seemed to be on every street corner wishing passers-by the compliments of the season.

That day Huxley had made his way to the Rockefeller Center to buy some chocolates at Catherine's favourite chocolate shop. It was close to the Center's skating rink, which was packed with skaters having such a good time that he stopped once more to enjoy the spectacle. Their obvious pleasure made him feel happy, too, although as he ate a couple of caramels (which Catherine had told him to be sure to buy) he'd wished she were there to share them. The thought took him unawares but he put it out of his mind, as he had to get to a meeting and was now running late.

Walker Corp. had a strong reputation in the States and he'd been eager to earn kudos for expanding the company's American operations and increasing profit levels. But when Tom had explained to Huxley the reason behind his decision and his intention to create Walker Telephone Communications, he'd known that what Tom was offering him was a glittering prize. It was what Huxley had been working for, ever since he joined the company. As CEO, America would still be part of his responsibilities, and he'd have to travel there several times a year.

Catherine could hear the cleaners vacuuming the hallway outside the Presidential Suite. This was usually a signal that it was time to pack and vacate the room. She was pleased that Tom seemed more like his old self. He'd been forced to make some important decisions about his life, and the enormity of his relief showed. Now he was in the mood to chat.

'I'm giving a dinner for Huxley in a few weeks' time at Ashburn,' he was saying. 'He needs to be welcomed home in style and I want to formally announce his appointment as CEO. I'd like you to come, too, Sis – it's going to be a typical Walker bash, the kind of party Ma would have given in her heyday.'

'I wouldn't dream of missing it.'

'I'll ask Huxley to escort you.'

'Now don't start that again.'

'Cool it, would you,' Tom protested. 'All I'm suggesting is strictly a business arrangement. Huxley's girlfriend hasn't arrived from the States yet.'

'What girlfriend?' Catherine regarded him suspiciously.

'Rosemary someone or other. He met her the day after he arrived in the Big Apple and they hit it off. I think they've missed each other. She's never been to Australia before and he's invited her to come and stay for a few months.'

'He didn't mention anything about a girlfriend to me,' Catherine said.

'Why should he?' Tom couldn't help himself. 'You're asking a lot of questions, Sis,' he said provocatively. 'Are you sure you couldn't possibly be interested in Huxley? He'd be a better bet than Jack Clement – to begin with, he's not married.'

To his horror Catherine looked as if she were about to break down. Turning away from him abruptly, she got up and walked quickly to the guest bathroom near the front door of the suite. 'I've got something in my eye.' She closed the door and turned on the tap in the hand basin, letting the water run. When she was sure she'd be able to speak without howling, she reappeared. 'It was an eyelash,' she lied, as she resumed her seat.

But Tom knew his sister too well. He'd been bewildered by her reaction to his teasing. It was obvious she'd been crying and he didn't like seeing her so upset.

'What's wrong?' He bent over and gently wiped a tear away from her cheek.

Catherine lifted her shoulders and said nothing.

'Is there anything I can do to help?'

'I'll manage. Like I always do.'

Tom could have shaken her. 'It's got something to do with Clement, hasn't it?' he persisted. 'You've been so busy worrying about me that, as usual, you've kept your own problems bottled up.'

'Apparently there's a problem with his wife, Fleur,' she finally admitted, pointing a finger at him warningly. 'Don't you say "I told you so"!'

'I wouldn't dare.'

'Jack keeps telling me not to worry – that he'll fix everything and we'll get married as he promised. But I don't know . . .' She looked pensive.

Tom stroked her hand reassuringly and then began to laugh. 'I'm sorry,' he said. 'I know it's not funny but what a prize pair of duffers we are when it comes to affairs of the heart.'

Catherine gave a wan half smile.

On the flight back to Sydney they were both so wrapped up in their own thoughts that neither of them talked much. Tom was astonished at how quickly his life had changed. The sense of liberation he felt was indescribable. I'm now in control of my life. The prospect exhilarated him. He'd no idea if his relationship with David would develop into something more meaningful but he wasn't worried about it either. If it was meant to be then so be it!

Whatever lay ahead, he would be able to handle

it. He was excited at the prospect of running Walker Corp. and looking forward to showing everyone, especially his father, what he could do. His time had come and he was going to make the most of it.

Oddly enough, Sydney Walker was sitting in his office – his former office, he reminded himself; it was Tom's now – thinking much the same thing. Walker Corp. had taken up most of his waking hours for so long that the idea of his daily routine without it was hard to imagine. Not that he regretted any aspect of his life – he didn't believe in looking back. He did have the occasional pang of guilt about Sarah but not for long. After all, he reasoned, a man has only one chance at life. If you don't find happiness with one woman then it's time to find another. Life is so short; there's not a moment to waste.

Building up Walker Corp. had been challenging and immensely satisfying. By anyone's standards it was a remarkable achievement. He'd revelled in the power it gave him and also the fear he was able to put into people. Just thinking about it now made him feel good. Power was heady stuff. Sometimes it wasn't necessary to say even a word – he had only to walk into a room and he could see anxiety written all over their faces. He'd certainly miss that.

But the cut and thrust of business no longer had the same appeal. He'd got a jolt when he first realised this. It was a bolt from the blue. He'd woken up one morning and thought, I don't want to go into the office today. Nothing challenged him any more. Bill Donaldson's sudden death had brought home to him how little time he had left.

Sydney had decided then and there that it was time for Tom to take over. The boy had a flair that impressed him. He'd always wanted Catherine to run Walker Corp. but she'd been so determined to go out on her own that nothing he could have said or done would have stopped her. Sydney had known she'd never return to Walker Corp. the day she started CW Publishing. The girl had done well, too, but again he knew this was only the beginning for her. She had no barriers on her ambition. He smiled to himself. Aiming for the stars was never enough. Walkers always wanted the moon as well.

There was no doubt that Tom also had the moon in his sights. He had big plans for Walker Corp. all right – pity the boy couldn't sort out his own life, Sydney thought, fuming again at the memory of the wedding botch-up. Still, in spite of the mess with Belinda, Sydney had to admit that there was nothing wrong with his son's business brain. When Tom had explained his future strategy for Walker Corp. Sydney had been impressed by the direction in which his son intended to take the company. If Tom hadn't been so caught up in outlining his blueprint for Walker Corp. he might have noticed that his father was listening to him almost enviously.

'I can see I'm leaving the place in capable hands, son,' he said, but he'd still felt a twinge of regret. Maybe he was wrong to be stepping down. This new chapter that Tom had outlined was going to be exciting and he'd like to have a part in it. Yet the notion was gone almost as quickly as it had come. He knew it was time for him to let go. So many tycoons hung around, overstaying their welcome, wrongly believing that their companies couldn't successfully go on without them. Such thinking actually did their companies more harm than good, he'd seen that happen often enough.

Besides, there were other things that he wanted to do. He was not only going to paint, he wanted to travel. He'd been all around the world on business but had rarely had the time to see much of any of the places he'd visited, having always been too busy with Walker Corp. matters.

Sydney also intended to marry again. Claudia Webster was still an attractive woman, intelligent and charming. When he'd been with her in Monaco and the Loire Valley recently he'd enjoyed her company. Their old relationship had rekindled after she'd rung and asked his advice about her son's shares.

He'd always liked her but it was some years since they'd spent much time together and it had come as an agreeable surprise to him that Claudia was still such a delightful companion. He was glad he'd been able to help her through this difficult time in her life.

He knew she needed to talk to someone about Charles and his illness. She'd wanted to see her son marry and have children – her grandchildren – and Sydney knew she felt she'd been robbed of her future. Claudia was sad and more than a little frightened about facing it on her own.

'Children aren't meant to die before their parents,' she told Sydney one night when they were having dinner at the Savoy in London.

'No, they're not,' he replied, 'and I wish I could change things for you.'

'If only you could, dear Sydney, but I know the rules. We have to accept what we're given in life. We mightn't always like it, but there's not much we can do about it.'

Sydney found that he was looking forward to seeing Claudia whenever possible. She made him feel special and it was a pleasant feeling. There was so much about her that appealed to him. He liked her style. She was trim and dressed with an elegance that seemed second nature to her. She had an earthy sense of humour, too, which he appreciated because it matched his. Nothing shocked her. She was remarkably even-tempered and, perhaps best of all, she knew how to look after a man. And what a superb cook she was. When she'd learnt that Sydney's favourite meal was tripe and onions she'd insisted on making it for dinner when he was staying at her villa in Monaco.

'I don't think many – if any – people in this rich little principality eat tripe and onions, my dear, and I'm sure Prince Rainier never serves it at the palace,' Claudia had said as a delighted Sydney heartily ate the meal she'd prepared. 'I do hope I've done it the way you like it. I don't cook much when I'm here on my own. I can't be bothered, really. I always think food tastes better when you have someone to eat it with.'

She'd been thrilled when Sydney pronounced the dish a culinary masterpiece and asked for a second helping.

Afterwards when they'd gone to bed together Sydney couldn't believe his good fortune. Claudia was still the warm, sexy woman he'd remembered. When he'd thought about it later he had to concede that it was the most enjoyable sexual encounter he'd had in years, although initially she'd been nervous about going to bed with him. 'It's been a while since you and I did this, Sydney,' she said shyly. 'I'm not the woman I used to be.'

'I'm not the man I once was either, my dear. I assure you, though, that I find you very desirable.'

The young Sydney who used to think nothing of bedding two women in the one night would have been astonished at the older Sydney, who confessed to Claudia that he sometimes worried whether or not he would have an erection. 'There are times when the old fella lets me down,' he'd admitted that night.

As it turned out neither of them need have

worried. Their lovemaking was pleasurable for them both and, much to their delight, they felt a passion that they'd thought was forever gone with their youth. 'I read once,' Claudia told him, a few days later when they were enjoying a cocktail at sunset on the balcony of her villa, 'that every now and then, love likes to spring a surprise. I never thought I'd feel like this again. You are a remarkable man, Sydney Walker.'

Sydney hadn't felt so alive since he'd had his little flutter with Luxi Chen – 'your Asian affair', Claudia had chided him. Luxi had enthralled him with her looks and sexual expertise and, he had to admit, her youth. But he should have known better. Luxi turned out to be an ambitious young woman trying to get ahead. She not only wanted Sydney but also a job at Walker Corp. and even then, not just any old job. She had wanted a position that would give her some clout and she'd seen Sydney Walker as her stepping stone to success. He thanked his lucky stars that he'd come to his senses in time.

He'd told Claudia the whole sorry saga. 'There's no fool like an old fool,' he said, looking a little sheepish. She had been completely sympathetic and her understanding had touched him. He liked being able to talk to Claudia safe in the knowledge that whatever he said would remain between them. Claudia wasn't the kind of woman who betrayed confidences. It occurred to him that he'd missed having someone like her with whom he could discuss the little things in life as well as the bigger issues.

He'd asked Claudia to marry him before he left Monaco. She'd said yes without hesitation. 'We make a good pair, Sydney. I also think you need some spoiling and I'm the perfect person to do that. I've always thought it was a woman's duty to make life as easy as possible for her man.'

'Not many women think like that these days.'

'Well, I do. A woman can care for and look after her man without sacrificing any of her independence,' Claudia said, giving him a kiss. 'Modern women have lost their way and so, for that matter, have men. Neither sex seems to know what they want from each other any more. Love is about putting the person you love first. Men and women seem to have forgotten that altogether, which is why, in my opinion, so many relationships don't last the distance. People don't work hard enough at love – they take it for granted and that's a mistake. I'm going to tell you I love you every day for the rest of our lives together.'

'Sounds good to me,' Sydney said. 'You can spoil me as much as you like. I won't complain.'

When he'd phoned Catherine to tell her his news she was stunned. 'Why, Dad,' she'd exclaimed, 'what a sneaky Romeo you are. Tom and I never suspected for one moment that you were having a romance in Monaco – we thought you were masterminding some big corporate deal. Getting married! I can't believe it.'

Sydney gave a satisfied laugh, pleased at his daughter's reaction to his news. 'You and your brother aren't the only ones who can fall in love,' he said. 'It happens even when you're my age, you know.'

He cleared his throat. 'While I think of it, how are you and Jack getting along?'

'Splendidly.' Even over the phone the happiness in her voice had been evident. 'He's asked me to marry him, Dad, and I've accepted.'

This time it was Sydney's turn to be taken aback. 'Aren't you both rushing things a little? What's he done about that wife of his?'

'There's no need to worry, Dad.' She'd hastily explained how Jack was on his way to see Fleur to work out the divorce settlement.

'The sooner, the better. I don't approve of a future son-in-law with messy baggage,' Sydney griped. 'Have you told your brother?'

'Yes.'

'What was his reaction?'

'If you must know, Dad, he gave me a lecture on the dangers of keeping company with married men.'

Before Sydney could say anything else, Catherine had changed the subject. 'Tell me more about Claudia. I've met her, of course, but only at parties. What's she really like?'

'She's a woman in a million and when you get to know her properly, you'll think so, too.'

Sydney and Claudia had decided on an intimate ceremony in London with a celebration dinner afterwards at the Savoy for just the two of them. Claudia would fly to London ahead of Sydney to make the arrangements for the wedding, which would be held at her home. They'd discussed whether or not Charles, Tom and Catherine should come over for the ceremony but decided against it.

'Let's just get married without making a song and dance about it,' Claudia had suggested. 'And we'll celebrate with the children later.' A quiet wedding suited Sydney, too – he didn't want the media turning it into a circus.

They also agreed to make Monaco their principal place of residence. Claudia loved living there and Sydney had found that he enjoyed the lifestyle. He was also aware of the considerable taxation benefits the principality offered its residents.

They were going to honeymoon in France for a month or so. 'When we've had enough we'll go home,' Claudia said. 'Your timetable days are over. We'll do things as the mood takes us!'

Sydney had only ever been to Paris on business and Claudia had declared that it was high time he saw the rest of the country. 'If you want to paint watercolours and landscapes, the French countryside will inspire you. We'll buy all the supplies you need before we leave.'

He was looking forward to sharing his life with

Claudia and to enjoying the freedom from responsibility that would come with his retirement. Sydney could feel all his old zest for living returning. He had something new and exciting to look forward to and he was exhilarated at the thought of what lay ahead.

# Chapter Twenty-Two

Only one member of the Walker family was uncertain about the future. All Catherine's dreams and plans were in tatters. Sitting in her office back in Pyrmont she was utterly miserable. She couldn't sleep or eat and she felt unwell. It seemed she'd only just found Jack and already she was losing him.

On his return from his ill-fated trip to Paris a few days after Tom's wedding fiasco – his return having been delayed by yet another business deal – Jack had rung Catherine to let her know he was at his apartment and that he'd wait there for her. She had left the office at once, eager to see him, but as she neared his place all her old uncertainties returned. She knew how she felt about Jack but she was no longer sure that he reciprocated her feelings in the way she'd once thought he had.

When Catherine arrived he went to kiss her but she drew away.

'Darling, don't be like that,' he said. 'I've missed you so much. You look so beautiful.' He held out his arms to her and tried to kiss her on the cheek. But again, she avoided him.

'If you won't let me kiss you, you will at least sit down, I hope,' he said. 'Can I get you a drink?'

She smiled for the first time. 'I think I need one.'

'I know I do,' Jack replied. He poured them both a gin and tonic. 'I can see you're upset.'

'Is that so surprising?' Her voice was pinched. 'How would you expect me to be? When we said goodbye in London we were going to get married and enjoy a glorious life together. A few days later you tell me it's not going to happen but you refuse to tell me why.'

'Don't be angry, Catherine, we'll work this out. But first let me tell you the whole story.'

And she sat there, unshed tears in her eyes, while he told her about the reception Fleur had given him.

'I was staggered by her attitude,' he said. 'She was so unreasonable, nothing I could say or do would budge her. She's had expert advice from that snake Richard Crosswaite and, as she reminded me several times, as my wife she can go for any percentage she chooses of any assets I own and that includes the company. She doesn't have to restrict herself to half, although that's what she said she wanted – half of everything I own.' He shook his head. Catherine stared at him, numb with pain.

'I've talked to my lawyers and they say she has an excellent case, and with Crosswaite representing her, an even better one. The man's never lost a case. He'll be able to show that Fleur has been an outstanding wife and partner. In the early days I simply couldn't have made it without her. She knows that as well as I do. Crosswaite will argue that I wouldn't have prospered without her support and that it was my success during the first years of our marriage that's enabled me to get to where I am today.'

'But you always had money, surely, Jack?' Catherine thought her voice sounded odd and far away. She looked down at her glass, her eyes stinging. The last time they'd seen each other everything had been wonderful and so full of promise.

'Yes, but when I was building up the newspapers, and later when I sold them for that incredible profit, Fleur was vital to the scheme of things. She has a great personality and she observed and listened, reporting back to me useful information that she'd picked up. Both the wife and the lover of my main competitor were often outrageously indiscreet and Fleur would listen when she met them on social occasions, take notes and give them to me. To say that she was immensely helpful would be an understatement.'

He moved closer towards Catherine, locking his eyes with hers, imploring her to understand what he was going through. 'She's been the perfect corporate spouse. And, until I met you – even though she's been living in Paris – if I needed Fleur to appear at any important business function she'd always come along and play her part well. I've always known she was clever but I didn't comprehend just how shrewd she was until all this blew up. I've completely under-estimated her,' he said caustically.

'I love you more than I thought it possible to love any woman, Catherine, but I cannot give up half of everything I own, and I won't give up half of The Clement Group. I can't! It's mine and I've worked bloody hard getting the company to where it is today. I'm going to build one of the biggest global media empires the world has ever seen and I need my com-pany to be intact to bring that off. What I have in mind will be costly and I'll need every asset I possess to raise the necessary capital.'

He looked at her pleadingly. 'Tell me you under-stand. You of all people must know what a person's company means to them. After all, you wouldn't give up half of CW Publishing, half of *MAUD*, half of all your dreams, would you? Tell the truth!'

Catherine put down her glass and walked over to the windows, glad to feel the sun warming her body, which felt unexpectedly cold.

She turned round and faced him. 'I would give up half of my company for you, Jack, because I love you more than anything else in the world. You are all that I want – I know that without you my life would have no meaning.'

As she continued, her voice cracked with anguish. 'Of course my company and *MAUD* matter to me and I'm damn proud of what I've done, but they're just material things – my life wouldn't be empty without them. I could always find other things to take their place. Perhaps they mightn't give me as much pleasure or satisfaction, I don't know – but if it were a question of having you or not having you, the company wouldn't stand a chance, as far as I'm concerned.'

A tear trickled slowly down her cheek. 'There's obviously a big difference in the way you love me and the way I love you, isn't there?' she said forlornly.

'Don't talk such bloody nonsense. You know how I feel about you.' He came towards her, refusing to be denied what he wanted any longer. Holding her so that she couldn't get away from him, he kissed her. He could feel her responding and was relieved. Smiling down at her, he brushed the hair from her eyes and said, 'I had no idea what love was until I met you. I was living in a vacuum. You have shown me a world I didn't know existed.' He kissed her again, more passionately this time.

'Now that I've found you I have no intention of losing you. You mean everything to me – but you must be reasonable, darling. I can't give Fleur what she's demanding. My company means too much to me.'

'More than I do, that's patently clear,' Catherine said bitterly.

'That's not true.'

She began to cry as though her heart would break. The tears were cascading down. 'I feel as though you've died,' she said. Jack was horrified by the look of utter misery on her face.

'Here,' he said, 'sit down.' She didn't move. 'Please sit down, Catherine.' He gently steered her into the armchair. She put her head down on the armrest and cried as though she would never stop. Jack waited quietly, resisting the urge to hold her. Whatever he said or did would be of little comfort at the moment. Once she's cried herself out I'll tell her what we'll do, he thought.

As if she could read his mind, Catherine looked up at him, her eyes full of tears. 'What are we going to do now?'

He held her hand. 'What thousands of other people do. We're going to set up home together. We don't need a marriage certificate to make what we have any better than it already is. No piece of paper can do that. We're committed to each other – you know that as well as I do.

'Catherine, we will love each other until the day we die. Nothing will ever change the way I care about you, I swear it.'

'But what if we have children, Jack? What then?' Her eyes narrowed.

Jack sensed the change in her mood and it per-plexed him. What did it mean? A couple of seconds passed before he answered.

'We will love them and cherish them.' His voice was solemn but there was no doubting its sincerity. 'My darling girl, I want you to have my son. How many times do I have to tell you?' He made as if to move closer but Catherine held up her hand.

'Please don't.' Her eyes hadn't left his face. 'I long to have your son but,' her voice faltered, 'I don't want our son to have parents who weren't prepared to invest in their relationship. What would we say to him when he was old enough to understand?'

'Don't be so quaint,' he said, irritated. 'People do it all the time – no one cares less these days. It just doesn't matter any more.'

'It does to me. I'm the marrying kind of woman. I thought you understood that but it seems you don't really understand me at all.' She got up. 'We're not getting anywhere. I want to be your wife, Jack. I'm not some rich man's plaything, some possession for a man to own under terms that are unacceptable to me. I'm definitely not the mistress type. I'd never be happy just living with you and bringing up our child without marriage.' She gulped back the tears. 'And I don't want a relationship with you that doesn't include children.'

Jack was on his feet now. 'Don't be so bloody stupid, Catherine. I've never considered you a plaything.'

'But others might see it that way.'

'It doesn't matter what people think.'

'It does to me, Jack. I wanted to marry you and grow old with you, but I can see you're married not only to Fleur but also to The Clement Group. What a fascinating love triangle,' she said bitterly. 'There's really never been room for anything else in your life, has there? Have you ever considered that maybe it was The Clement Group that drove Fleur to Paris in the first place? It wouldn't surprise me either if some of your business acquaintances had warned you off me, telling you that marriage to me wouldn't be good for your business.'

'Stop being ridiculous. You don't know what you're saying.' But in fact a couple of his colleagues had done exactly that, telling him that Catherine was too smart and knowledgeable about the media for Jack's own good. They'd warned him that the day would come when she'd want to play a major role in his company and had advised him to stay with Fleur, who'd never interfered in his business affairs.

'I'm not being ridiculous at all,' Catherine countered, beginning to feel a little stronger. 'I know all about the corporate male mind. I've grown up with one of the best, you know. You and the other blokes like to keep the jungle to yourselves. Women are seen as predators, aren't they? At the end of the day, I might distract you from running your beloved company and even worse, I might make a suggestion about something to do with The Clement Group.

Heaven forbid.' Catherine shook off his hand and got out of the chair.

'Keep your precious company, Jack. I wouldn't dream of asking you to give it up for me, but you can't have your cake and eat it too. I'm not prepared to be the crumbs in this relationship, which is already very crowded, don't you think? Fleur, The Clement Group and me – goodness, Jack, how have you been able to find time for us all? It must have been quite a strain for you!'

She blew her nose, picked up her handbag and rifled inside it until she found her sunglasses. Putting them on, she walked towards the door. Then she stopped, and took off the glasses before turning to look at him. 'Just being in love isn't enough, Jack. Don't you understand that? Love can't flourish without a future. Our love doesn't have one.'

Jack took a step towards her and held out his hands. 'Catherine, darling, we can sort this out. Trust me.'

'Don't talk to me about trust!' She was upset enough to lash out at him. 'Trust you? What a joke! Never again.' Her eyes were cold and disdainful now. 'How could you compromise our love for the sake of your bloody company?' She looked at him contemptuously, then turned on her heel and closed the front door with a bang. It made her feel better but not for long.

The ache in her heart was excruciating. It hurt

even to breathe. Life without Jack would be awful. No, worse than that, she despaired. It would be bleak and desolate. She would never forgive herself for misjudging him the way she had. What had possessed her to trust him so completely? Catherine gave a choking laugh at her own stupidity.

Of all people, she should have known better. Men could never be trusted, she thought scornfully. Her father had let her down – sure, he'd helped her financially when she was starting off CW Publishing and she was grateful for that, but his ego had always come between them. That had been driven home to her the night she heard him telling someone, 'She'll never be as good as me.'

She could forgive her father's sense of self-importance, however cruel it sometimes was, but not the fact that he'd let her down emotionally. He had been a flawed parent. No wonder she'd always felt emotionally alone. And it hadn't helped that her mother had been flawed as well. Thanks to Sydney and Sarah, Catherine had learnt early to keep her deepest, most intimate thoughts to herself.

Until Roger had entered her life. Then her heart had begun to sing. She'd been so sure about him – just like she'd stupidly been about Jack. Catherine sighed. Would she never learn? But when a person has been starved of love the heart does foolish things. She knew that now.

Why on earth had she ever thought Jack would

be different? But on the other hand, how could I have known that his company would be my rival for his affections. What a fool he is! He's simply replacing a vacuum with a vacuum.

'One day, Jack Clement,' she said, 'you will regret the decision you made today.' Especially when the baby is born, she thought. She'd been delirious with joy when she'd discovered just a few days ago that she was pregnant. 'Little Jack' – she was sure her baby was a boy – was already beginning to make his presence felt by giving her recurrent bouts of morning sickness.

Catherine had automatically driven back to work. Probably a good thing, she decided as she parked the car. At least it might keep my mind off Jack and the appalling muddle my life is in. As she made her way to her office she passed Clare, who took a good look at her and frowned.

'Are you all right? You look awful. What's up?'

'Nothing. I'm fine thanks, really I am,' Catherine said, but her assistant's face showed she wasn't convinced.

'Please don't fuss about me, Clare. I don't think I could stand it. I would appreciate it, though, if you could get me a cup of black tea and hold all my calls.'

Clare nodded. 'Right, but there are a couple you need to know about. Roger Rowland has rung three times.'

'Oh no. Not now. That's all I bloody need!' Catherine's voice shook. 'What the hell does he want? You'd think he'd have got the message by now that I never want to talk to him again.'

'He's arrived early for the Government's New Millennium Communications Conference, and he wants to call in and say hello – "for old times' sake", he said. He thought you might like to have dinner with him. He wants to tell you about his new literary venture.'

'Why he thinks I'd be interested in anything he's doing is beyond me. As for dinner – I'd rather eat poison.'

'Huxley Edwards also called. He's seeing someone else at this end of town later and said he'll drop in on the off-chance that you've got five minutes for him. He promises not to stay any longer and said that if you're too busy to see him he understands.'

'Of course I'll see him, but if Roger calls tell him I'm out.'

Catherine sat at her desk, unable to do anything. For once in her life she found it impossible to put her personal problems aside and concentrate on work. All she wanted to do was wallow in her grief. She felt dejected – and rejected.

Why does love always go wrong for me, she thought angrily. Surely I have the right to be loved just like everyone else.

What the hell is love anyway? Nothing but heartache and pain, she thought. There's so much crap written about love but none of it is true. Love is a big con.

There was a knock at her door and Fiona appeared. 'Is everything all right? Clare's worried about you.'

Another tap announced Brenda's arrival. 'Clare's right – you do look awful. What's the matter?'

They both stood before her desk, looking anxious.

'You are pale, Catherine,' Fiona said.

'You are,' Brenda agreed. 'And you haven't been your usual cheerful self lately.'

'I'm sorry,' Catherine said. 'I think I must be coming down with a virus.' She couldn't tell them the truth – not yet.

'Why don't you go home early and go to bed,' Brenda suggested. 'A good night's sleep is what you need.'

'I think I will,' Catherine said, touched by their concern.

Clare returned with her tea and the news that Huxley had arrived.

'We'll leave you,' Fiona said, 'but make sure you go home soon.' She and Brenda greeted Huxley warmly as he walked through the door. So did Catherine. 'It *is* good to see you,' she said. 'I could do with some light relief.'

'I don't think I've ever been described as that before,' he said, kissing her on the cheek. He put his hands on her shoulders. 'You look as if something terrible has happened. Is everything okay?'

'Yes, of course,' she said crisply.

'I don't think I believe you. You look so bereft – I've never seen you this way before.'

Catherine gave a listless smile. 'You know me too well. I'm feeling so miserable I don't know what to do,' she said sadly.

'Do you want to tell me what's worrying you?'

But before she could answer him her phone buzzed. It was Clare. 'Boss, sorry to interrupt you. I know you said to tell Roger you were out but he insists on talking to you and says he'll keep ringing until you speak to him.'

'Oh no, I don't think I can.' She sighed and looked at Huxley.

'Tell me,' he said.

'It's bloody Roger. He keeps calling me. We've both been invited to speak at the communications conference next week and I've been dreading even having to see him again. But it doesn't seem to worry him at all. He's rung several times this afternoon, saying he must speak to me.' She looked at Huxley with tear-filled eyes. 'He wants us to have dinner together, for old times' sake. Can you believe it? Why would he think I want to see him, let alone eat with him?'

'He's weak, that's why. He also thinks he's God's gift to women, and having once possessed you he can't stand the thought that you've now become unobtainable. Would you like me to talk to him?'

'I'd be eternally grateful.'

Huxley took the phone and instructed Clare to put Roger through. 'This is Huxley Edwards. Listen, Rowland, Catherine doesn't want to talk to you, not now, not ever, and she doesn't want to have dinner with you either. Stop pestering her – you had your chance with her years ago and you blew it. If you don't stop ringing her I'll send my personal messenger around to make sure you understand. Do I make myself clear?

'You don't think so. You always were a moron, weren't you, Rowland? Well, let me make it clearer for you. Fuck off!' He went to put the phone down but stopped. Unabashed, Roger was still talking.

Huxley scowled. 'What do you mean you're writing your autobiography? It's all about what?' he demanded. 'Your life with Australia's goddess of love. You don't mean it.' He looked aghast at Catherine, whose face was ashen. 'What kind of man are you?'

He put his hand over the mouthpiece. 'Let me deal with this, Catherine. Okay with you?' he asked.

She nodded mutely, wondering what else could possibly go wrong for her. The thought of people being able to read intimate details of her marriage with Roger turned her stomach. No wonder she felt like throwing up. How could he do such a thing to her, let alone himself? Didn't the man have any pride at all? She felt cold and frightened.

'What's your price, Rowland?' Huxley's voice was hostile. 'You're out of your mind!' he snarled. 'I'll call you back in a couple of hours. Give me your number.' He wrote it down.

Sitting on the edge of her desk he stared at Catherine with such an unfathomable look in his eyes that she felt strangely awkward. 'You're not to worry – there's no way that book of Rowland's will ever see the light of day. He says *The Sun* has offered him one and a quarter million dollars for it.'

'Wouldn't you know Roger would do a deal with them!' The words hissed from her lips. 'The bastard!'

'I'm sure he's lying – they've probably made him a handsome offer, but I doubt it's as much as that. Rowland is setting the stakes high because he wants to milk us for as much as he can,' he said, punching his fist in his hand. 'It's going to cost you to get rid of him.'

'Offer him one million dollars but before he sees one cent of it, he has to sign over the rights and agree in writing never to reveal any aspect of our married life. And don't forget to remind him that this way he'll keep his reputation of being a good bloke. He prides himself on that,' she added scathingly.

'I'll take care of everything,' Huxley said. 'And if he makes any attempt to contact you, let me know immediately. I'll make sure Rowland doesn't come anywhere near you, even if I have to break his legs to see that he doesn't.'

Huxley was pacing the room. 'As for that conference,' he said over his shoulder, 'I'll take you to it and stay by your side the entire time.'

'Thank you.' Catherine watched him as he walked up and down the room. Not for the first time, she thanked her lucky stars that they were such good friends. What would I do without him, she thought. He's always coming to my rescue.

He swung around to face her. 'I've just remembered,' he said. 'Before I took that call from your former husband you were about to tell me what else was bothering you – do you still want to enlighten me?'

'I don't want to burden you with all my worries,' Catherine said apologetically. Huxley sat down, leant back in the chair and folded his arms. 'I've got big shoulders,' he said, shrugging them at her.

She rubbed the edge of her desk with her fingers. 'It's Jack.' Her voice wavered.

'Jack?' The astonishment showed on Huxley's face. 'I thought everything was coming up roses for you two. Tom told me you were going to marry Clement.'

'I thought I was,' she replied sorrowfully, 'but he doesn't want to marry me.'

'Why not?'

'How much time do you have?'

'When you have a problem I have all the time in the world.' He looked at her expectantly. She related the whole unhappy story.

He listened without comment, knowing it would do her good to talk. He thought that she'd never looked so lovely or so vulnerable.

'You poor girl,' he said, when she finally stopped talking. 'You sure know how to pick them, don't you? I never imagined Jack Clement would treat you this way. You two seemed made for each other.'

'That's what I thought, but as usual I'm bloody hopeless when it comes to men,' Catherine said.

'Does your father know?'

'Not yet. Dad was in such a state about Tom calling off his wedding I thought it best to give him time to calm down. And as for Tom – well, he has enough on his plate for the moment.'

She sighed, looking down at her hands. 'But there's something else . . .'

'What else could there possibly be?'

'I'm expecting Jack's baby.'

'Shit!' He was stunned. 'Have you told him?'

'No.' She folded her arms defiantly. 'And I'm not going to either.'

# Chapter Twenty-Three

As Huxley sat listening to Catherine all kinds of emotions swept over him. He prayed his face wouldn't betray him but Catherine, lost in some painful world of her own, was too preoccupied to notice. Outside, CW Publishing was unusually quiet, its customary hustle and bustle subdued, as if its staff knew all was not well with their boss.

A baby – what a complication! She'd floored him completely with that information. Given Clement's usual good fortune it was probably a boy, too, he thought briefly. But perhaps Jack might never know about this new addition to his family. From what she was saying, Catherine seemed determined that he would never have anything to do with the child.

Huxley couldn't work it out. How could someone as supposedly canny as Jack Clement have handled the situation so badly, not just with Catherine but also with Fleur. He never should have told his wife the real reason for his decision to finally get a divorce. That was a serious error. No matter how bad the relationship, no woman likes to think she's replaceable.

He could understand why Clement didn't want to lose half his company – what man would? But if The Clement Group meant so much to him, he should have put it safely out of Fleur's reach long before this.

He'll never be able to find another woman capable of giving him as much joy and pleasure as Catherine. She's the most fascinating woman in the world, Huxley thought, a tantalising mix of beauty and brains. Knowing the kind of woman Catherine was, how could Clement have humiliated her by offering her a de facto *ménage-à-trois* arrangement? Catherine was a woman who would only ever settle for marriage with the man she loved. It was written all over her.

Huxley had fallen for her from the first moment he'd laid his eyes on Catherine back in the days when he was a brash, hustling salesman at Walker Television Productions. Even now, all these years later, he could still picture her the day they'd met. She'd come to give the staff a pep talk because her father wasn't happy with the profits.

'I'm here to tell you that Walker Corp. has begun a process of restructuring to help control costs,' she'd told the assembled men and women. 'Maintaining the company's relevance in as competitive an industry as the one in which we work is becoming increasingly difficult.' She'd outlined the initiatives the company intended to take and spoken so confidently that before long she had everyone eating out of her hand. It was quite a performance. Huxley had been impressed.

Afterwards she'd introduced herself to him, telling him that based on his reputation, the company was expecting big things from him. As she shook his hand, he'd felt desire in the pit of his stomach. As he got to know her better he fell in love with her mind. She thought so quickly and was always miles ahead of everyone else. Huxley admired the way she could always see the potential of a good idea and how she never said something couldn't be done until she'd explored every avenue to see if it were possible.

There was never a dull moment when Catherine was around. Much to his astonishment Huxley found that he enjoyed working with her in a way he'd never imagined possible with a woman.

Of course, he'd had all the usual male prejudices about women bosses – he remembered with guilt a conversation he'd had about her with a male colleague in his early days at Walker Television Productions. 'She writes such excellent reports,' he'd said, 'that you'd think a man had written them.' Catherine would have been furious if she'd known he had even thought such a thing, let alone uttered it.

On the other hand, after ticking him off for being so bloody sexist, she'd probably have taken his comment as a compliment. That was another thing he liked about her. She was the first to admit that she was a feminist and although she didn't suffer incompetent men – or women either – lightly, she wasn't a man-hater like so many of her more militant sisters seemed to be.

He liked to think he understood her pretty well. He loved her sense of humour and the fact that her word was her bond. Everyone knew when Catherine Walker said she'd do something she never failed to deliver the goods. And her loyalty to people was renowned.

Huxley often warned her that she was too trusting. 'You always give everyone the benefit of the doubt. You shouldn't trust anyone. I don't.'

'You're wrong,' she'd retort. 'I always have faith in people until they give me a reason not to do so.'

Catherine was Huxley's only exemption. He would have trusted her with his life. She had a special place in his heart. He'd taken other women out, naturally, and gone to bed with them – he didn't believe in celibacy. In fact, he thoroughly enjoyed the company of women. He was very fond of Rosemary, his current flame, and knew she cared for him, but he hadn't made any promises to her, nor had she asked for any. She was a sweet, uncomplicated woman and he relished her company.

Catherine had never given any indication that she was aware of his feelings for her, but then why should she? He'd never said anything and she wasn't a mind reader. Initially he'd just been one of the many ambitious young men who had found their way to her father's company and by the time he'd reached executive status, Catherine had met Roger and then, before Huxley could make a move, Jack had come along. There'd been no room in her life for anyone else.

He'd always appreciated her support and the way she'd encouraged him when he was starting out. It had been a plus, too, when she'd praised him to her father – no matter how talented a person was, it never hurt if someone in authority helped you get your foot in the door. Huxley had learnt that early in his career. It hadn't harmed his progress, either, that he and Tom had got on well. Huxley didn't care what the man's sexual preference was as long as it wasn't him. He'd always suspected Tom was gay – there was just something about him. Huxley couldn't put his finger on exactly what it was, but he knew he was right. He liked Tom and admired his business acumen but when his wedding had been cancelled so dramatically Huxley was sure Tom's sexuality must have been the reason.

He became aware that Catherine was watching him. 'Sorry if I'm boring you,' she said pointedly.

'Don't be silly, you could never do that. I've just been racking my brains trying to work out your best plan of action.' His brow furrowed. 'Can I ask you something?'

She gave a nod.

'Why didn't you tell Jack about the baby?'

'I was going to tell him but when he told me our wedding was off because he wanted to stay married to his precious company there didn't seem to be much point.'

'He might have rethought his decision.'

'I doubt it. Anyway, I'm not interested in using the baby as some kind of bullet to Jack's head. He either wants to marry me or he doesn't. It's as simple as that – or at least I thought it was. I'm such a dim-wit. When will I ever stop trusting men?'

'Don't tar us all with the same brush, Catherine.' Huxley's reply was sharp. 'Most men aren't as indifferent to their women as Jack. You've just been unlucky.'

'Unlucky? That's something of an understatement, don't you think?'

'There is one thing.' He hesitated.

'What?' she prompted.

'Have you considered an abortion?'

She sighed. 'Yes, I have. After all, Jack is very well known – people have seen us out together, and I know I won't be able to keep my pregnancy a secret forever. Poor baby,' she said covering her stomach protectively with her hands, 'what have I done to you? You're not even out in the big wide world yet and already I've presented you with an enormous hurdle to overcome.'

She stared resolutely up at Huxley. 'I couldn't have an abortion, I just couldn't. Terminating this baby would be repugnant to me. I don't think I could live my life in the way that I wanted if I knew that I'd been responsible for destroying a life that had begun with so much love.' She put her hands on her stomach again as if to set the baby's mind at rest.

'But you'll have to tell Jack some time, you know,' Huxley said gently. 'A child has a right to know who his or her father is. Have you thought about that?'

'The way I feel at the moment it's unlikely to ever happen. I'll face that dilemma when I feel a little stronger. Right now I'm an emotional wreck and totally shattered.'

'Are you sure you shouldn't have your feet up?' he asked earnestly. 'I read somewhere that pregnant women should do that.'

She couldn't help laughing. 'Now Huxley, please stay calm. I don't think I need to put my feet up just yet.'

Huxley could have kissed her on the spot. She reminded him of a wounded sparrow and looked so fragile that it took all his resolve to resist the overwhelming urge he felt to take her in his arms and comfort her properly. He knew she was strong and capable but at times she was so determinedly independent that it infuriated him. Everyone, no matter how self-reliant they were, needed someone to take care of them and comfort them when things went wrong. He knew that life without love was not just lonely but incomplete. When it was apparent she'd lost her heart to Jack, he'd resigned himself to loving Catherine from afar, and never telling her how he felt.

But now, after all the years he'd known her, he felt a glimmer of hope. Maybe there was a chance for him after all. Fate had dealt him an unexpected card but the sixty-four-thousand-dollar question was, had he been handed the winning card or the joker? For the moment he'd have to tread carefully.

'Would you like me to drive you home?' he asked.

'Thanks, but no. I can't tell you how much it has helped talking to you – you're my Rock of Gibraltar. And thanks for taking Roger off my hands. I hope he won't give you too much trouble. You've gone above and beyond the bonds of friendship. I'm forever in your debt.' Her blue eyes were full of gratitude.

'I think I might try to concentrate on all of this for a while.' She lifted a pile of papers out of her in-tray and laid them out on her desk. 'I've been that distracted, poor Clare's probably thinking she won't get any work out of me today. But it will take my mind off everything, which is what I need. I don't want to have to think about anything to do with

511

me.' She smiled at him and added, 'For at least an hour.'

'What about having dinner with me – or can I get you some takeaway?'

She gave him a thankful look. 'You are kind but I'm having dinner with Dad tonight. I really don't feel like it but he was so insistent when he rang and asked me. He and Claudia have something important to tell me before they leave for London to get married next week. I hope nothing's happened to make them change their minds. We Walkers seem to have a jinx on us when it comes to love and marriage.'

'Aren't you going to their wedding?' He raised his brows inquiringly.

'No, they don't want any fuss – just the two of them and a marriage celebrant. Claudia's house-keeper and her husband are going to be the witnesses. It's rather romantic, don't you think? We're going to have a big celebration at Ashburn when they come back here in a couple of months' time.'

She shifted in her chair and drew in a sharp breath. 'And I suppose I'd better tell them tonight that Jack and I have called it a day. I'll tell Tom tomorrow.'

Huxley smiled back at her. 'I think you should – you need some support.' He got up from his chair. 'Perhaps you should also tell your father about Rowland tonight,' he suggested.

'It never rains but it pours,' she said, screwing up her face.

'I'll leave you to your work. I'll let you know the outcome of my meeting with Rowland – don't hesitate to call me if there's anything else I can do or even if you just feel the need to talk to someone.' As he opened her office door, Huxley turned back and said, 'Take care of yourself.'

'I will, and thanks again for everything. There are times when I don't know what I'd do without you,' Catherine said gratefully. 'Our friendship is very precious to me.'

Her words stopped him in his tracks. He walked back towards her. 'All you ever have to do is whistle and I'll come running.'

'Why, Huxley,' she said, looking up to find his eyes fixed firmly on hers. Catherine couldn't fathom the expression she saw in them and forced herself to look away. 'How gallant of you. I'll remember that – but I hope I won't have to whistle for you too much!' She gave a little laugh.

They said goodbye again and, turning to some *MAUD* proofs, Catherine picked up her pen and circled something that she didn't like on one of them. As she worked her way through the pages, she became so engrossed in what she was doing that she temporarily forgot about her problems. When she finally put down her pen, almost two hours had gone by. She took the corrected proofs outside and laid them on Clare's desk. 'See they get to the printer first thing tomorrow,' she instructed, feeling more herself than she had in days.

Catherine had arranged to meet her father and Claudia at Beppi's but as she drove to the restaurant she wished she hadn't because it would only bring back memories of Jack and their wonderful first lunch there. She wasn't sure she'd be able to endure it. You will, Catherine, she told herself firmly, you always cope. People expect it of you. Pull yourself together. She took several deep breaths.

Sydney and Claudia had arrived ahead of her and were sitting at the VIP table, where they looked relaxed and happy chatting together, very content with each other's company.

'At last,' Sydney said when he saw her. 'I was beginning to think you'd never get here. Let's order, I want to eat.' They made small talk throughout dinner, and when coffee had been served Sydney told her of their decision to make Monaco their permanent base.

'I'll still be coming back to Australia for board meetings,' he explained, 'and we'll be visiting London and New York fairly frequently.'

'I never thought you'd like a place like Monaco, Dad,' Catherine said.

'Why not?'

'I went there once and that was enough for me. I

couldn't believe the amount of gold everyone wore. Gold bracelets, necklaces, earrings, rings, even buttons! It made me wish for an immediate drop in the price of gold.'

'How mean of you, Catherine,' Claudia said, laughing. 'But that's just one side of Monaco – there is another, you know. My Monaco is exceptional. It's essential to have a good circle of friends and I do.'

Sydney was scrutinising Catherine closely, trying to figure out why she looked different. She looks pale and washed-out, he concluded, not like herself at all. 'Are you all right?' he asked unexpectedly.

'Yes. Why wouldn't I be?'

'I don't know, but you don't look it. Has someone been giving you a hard time?'

'I've one or two things on my mind, nothing for you to worry about,' she said, making an instant decision not to tell him about Roger and his book threat. Huxley is more than a match for Roger, she thought. There's no way I'm going to let that bastard spoil this dinner or Dad and Claudia's wedding next week.

She smiled brightly at them. 'We're not here to talk about me. You two asked me for dinner to tell me something important. I'm bursting with curiosity to know what it is.' Catherine put on her most cheerful voice and hoped her performance was convincing. 'It's more than deciding to live in Monaco, surely? You could have told me that on the phone.'

They exchanged an intimate look. 'It's something we wanted to tell you together,' Sydney said, 'because it's to do with Webster Media. As you know, The Clement Group has been trying to buy up shares in the company. My old sparring partner Rupert Murdoch has been working closely with Jack as an adviser and ally. They even took Claudia to dinner and made her an outrageous offer for her shares.'

'You're kidding!' Catherine's face was disbelieving. 'But why? Did you give some kind of indication that you were interested in selling?' she asked Claudia.

'No I didn't,' the older woman replied. 'Well, perhaps for the merest second.' Claudia looked a little sheepish. As Sydney put his hand on hers and held it, she gave him an appreciative smile.

Catherine's expression was even more incredulous.

'Rupert painted an impressive picture of the kind of life I could have with the money Jack was prepared to pay me for my stock. He is a salesman extraordinaire, you know. I've never encountered anything like his sales pitch in my life. No wonder he's had the kind of success he has.'

A wry expression flitted across her face. 'He kept reminding me again and again of the millions I would receive and tempted me further by telling me that I would be richer than Janet Holmes à Court. I wouldn't have minded replacing her as Australia's richest woman! Vanity is a terrible thing, isn't it?' She looked at them remorsefully.

'And then I remembered how much Oscar had loved his company, how hard he'd worked to build it up and, more importantly, how he had entrusted its care to me, and I knew I couldn't part with any of it – not yet, anyway, and not to someone who I didn't really know. I didn't need the money, Oscar left me well provided for.'

As an afterthought she added, 'I thought Jack was going to explode – his temper was a bit frightening.'

Sydney gave Claudia's hand a comforting squeeze and asked, 'Would you like me to continue?'

'Please, darling . . .'

'As I'd foiled the raiders when they tried to buy Charles's twenty-five per cent, Claudia was their last hope but what they didn't know was that I'd only done that as a favour to her. I had no ulterior motive of my own.' He gave a malevolent grin. 'If Jack – and indirectly, Rupert – had got Charles's stock, the two of them would have been able to do whatever they wanted with Webster Media, which was precisely what Claudia didn't want to happen.'

'Dear Oscar was the eternal optimist,' Claudia confessed, leaning forward. 'Ultimately my stock would have gone to Charles because his father was convinced that one day he'd turn into a good company man. We talked about it so often.' She smiled nostalgically.

Sydney pushed his chair back and beckoned to the waiter to bring them another pot of coffee and some more wine, before he continued once more. 'Jack and Rupert would have carved up the company between them. They'd probably have merged a couple of Oscar's much-loved newspapers with Rupert's, people would have been made redundant and they'd have changed the feel and look of the papers, too. Claudia was determined that Webster Media would remain intact in the way Oscar had intended.'

Catherine was fascinated by what she was hearing but she was equally intrigued by the way her father and Claudia related to each other. It's as if they've been together for years, she thought, before turning her attention back to Claudia.

'Webster Media employs several thousand people around the world,' she was saying, 'men and women who have given the company their very best talent and expertise and still do. Oscar always said there was no way his company would have thrived without the dedication, skills and hard work of the people he employed. The significance of their contribution was something he felt very strongly about.'

Catherine nodded her head sympathetically.

'I don't approve of the current way of running business – of downsizing and redundancies, of throwing people on the scrapheap and not giving a hoot what happens to them. If the people who work for your company can't trust you, why should they make a commitment to that company? How can a boss expect employees to give of their best if they know they're not valued?' Claudia waved her arms around as she spoke. Sydney was bemused. He'd no idea she could get so hot under the collar about such things. The woman was full of surprises, he thought happily. Life with her was going to be very interesting.

'I believe in profit – handsome profits, for that matter,' Claudia continued, 'but I don't believe in greed and in my view, far too many companies today are obsessed with it and with the belief that people are expendable.' She spoke with such enthusiasm that a passing waiter turned to listen.

Catherine went to say something but Claudia stopped her. 'Please hear me out. You probably consider my thinking somewhat antiquated.'

'Not at all!' Catherine protested.

'Well, some people would, I know that, but I don't care,' Claudia declared spiritedly. 'People define their worth by their work. Employment is essential for the good of the human race and people like us, you and me – and you, too, Sydney – who control the kind of companies we do, have a responsibility to make sure people have jobs. Between us we have considerable power and we also have the means to influence decisions through our respective media outlets. We should use them to bring about a rethink, or at least a moratorium, about the present corporate disregard for the rights of people to jobs and a secure future.'

Sydney gazed in admiration as Claudia expounded her views even more forcibly.

'There's no doubt in my mind that civilisation, as we know and understand it, will crumble if we don't take a stand against increasing global unemployment and lack the guts to argue that for the good of the world, it is imperative that people be employed. A world where people are regarded as non-essential will be a dangerous place in which to live.

'If Webster Media fell into the wrong hands I know that huge numbers of people would be laid off and many of them would probably never get a proper job again. I couldn't bear to have that on my conscience.'

She sat back and looked at them both fondly. 'I'll step down from my soapbox now but as you can see, it is something I feel very strongly about.'

'Don't you ever get off your soapbox,' Catherine said. 'I agree with everything you said.'

'I was sure you would,' Claudia said approvingly, and nodded in agreement as Catherine went on.

'Women always take the commonsense approach to major issues – if only the world would pay more heed to what we have to say. Our voice has been muffled for too long. That bloody glass ceiling has a lot to answer for!' Catherine winked at Claudia.

Sydney groaned. 'Now don't you two start that – next thing I know you'll be telling me you both have hairy armpits! Let's keep focused. We're talking about Webster Media, not women's rights.'

Claudia patted his hand and grinned at Catherine. 'All right, darling.'

'As I've often told you, timing is everything in life.' Sydney's gloating laughter boomed out, drowning the conversation of the neighbouring diners. 'I can't wait to see the look on Jack's face when he hears what we're going to do with Webster Media now.' Catherine tried not to let the mention of Jack's name distress her.

'What are you two up to?' she demanded. 'And what on earth has Jack got to do with it?' She poured herself a glass of water, thankful that her father hadn't seemed to notice she wasn't drinking her wine.

'Are you sure you don't want to tell her?' Sydney asked Claudia.

'No, darling. You can do the talking for both of us.'

'Right.' He stroked his chin slowly, savouring the tension of the moment.

'Dad, the suspense is killing me.'

'Don't be so bossy.' He popped one of the chocolates that had come with his coffee into his mouth and slowly and deliberately began to eat it before he deigned to speak.

'Claudia and I are going to merge our shares in Webster Media and we're going to give you twenty-five per cent as a wedding gift.'

'What?' She looked at them both sceptically. 'You don't mean it? It's too much.'

'No, it's not – and yes, we most certainly do,' Claudia replied. 'This way Webster Media gets new blood at the top, which is what it must have if it is to thrive and prosper in the new century, and it also means the company stays in the family where it belongs. After all, when your father and I marry next week I'll become part of your family, as well as your stepmother.'

'I'll never think of you as the wicked stepmother!' Catherine managed to quip, even though she was still shell-shocked.

'I should hope not.'

'But you are being so incredibly generous. Are you sure you want to do this?'

'Yes we are,' Sydney said. 'Claudia and I will jointly look after her forty-five per cent, and with you holding twenty-five per cent Webster Media is safe from outsiders. We'd like you to become Chief Executive Officer. You've always said you wanted to run a global media group – well, here's your chance. You'll be able to keep CW Publishing operating – in fact, we'd like to suggest you consider making it a subsidiary of Webster Media.' He paused. It wasn't often he had the pleasure of being the bearer of such good tidings and he was enjoying himself.

'We understand that you'll probably want Jack to be involved in some way. I suggest the two of you sit down and come up with a scheme that will allow you to work together. He told me once how much he missed newspapers and that his ambition was to get back into media in a big way. You'd make a formidable team.' He looked at Claudia, who beamed in agreement.

'You would,' she added emphatically. 'Webster Media couldn't fail to profit substantially from your combined skills.'

Then quietly but firmly Claudia delivered an ultimatum. 'I know I can trust you to keep Jack under control and not do anything untoward with the newspapers. If you have any doubts about this, I'd prefer him not to have a role in the company. Sometimes it's best to keep your business and personal lives separate.'

Catherine stared unseeingly into her coffee cup, trying to compose the turmoil in her head. Conscious that her father and Claudia were waiting for her to say something, she looked up and slowly began to speak. 'I'm bowled over by this . . .' She shrugged her shoulders. Uncharacteristically, she was at a loss for words.

Sydney and Claudia were more than satisfied with her reaction. 'I would have expected nothing less,' Sydney muttered in Claudia's ear.

Meanwhile, Catherine's mind had already begun coming up with ideas for growing the company. I'll expand into electronic media and concentrate on increasing the influence of my newspapers. She smiled inwardly. 'My' newspapers – that didn't take long. Webster Media was a dream come true. How she and Jack would enjoy running it . . .

The colour drained from her face. In all the excitement she'd forgotten that Jack was no longer a part of her life. Her aspirations collapsed in a heap. When, after a few minutes, she'd said nothing further, they exchanged a puzzled look.

Finally, Sydney couldn't stand her silence any longer. 'Have you lost your tongue, Catherine? Aren't you pleased?'

She sat up straight in her chair. 'More than you'll ever know. I'll never be able to thank you both enough. It's the most wonderful thing . . . a fantastic opportunity.' Her voice wavered. 'But . . .'

'But what?' Sydney demanded. 'What is wrong with you? You're behaving very peculiarly tonight.'

'I can't help it.' She looked at them abjectly. 'You see, Jack doesn't want to marry me.'

'Oh Christ, not you too!' Sydney exploded. 'What the hell is wrong with you and your brother? You tell us you're getting married and now, just like Tom, you tell us you're not. Are you both raving mad? For God's sake, Claudia, pass the wine.' He filled his glass and drank it without stopping.

'Sydney don't,' Claudia protested. 'That's Grange.'

'I couldn't care less what it is. Both my children are crazy.' He poured himself another glass.

Catherine was on the verge of tears.

'Sydney, darling, you didn't listen properly to

what Catherine told us. She said Jack didn't want to marry her, not that she didn't want to marry Jack.' Catherine managed a weak smile of gratitude.

'Obviously something has gone dreadfully wrong. What is it?' Claudia said to her kindly. 'Maybe we can help in some way.'

Catherine told them about Jack's disastrous trip to Paris and the events that had followed. When she got to the bit where he'd suggested they live together without marriage – and without him getting a divorce – Sydney couldn't restrain himself any longer.

'What does he think you are? Some kind of cheap tart?'

'Please, Dad, don't say anything you might regret. I don't want you to bad-mouth him.'

'He isn't worth talking about,' Sydney declared contemptuously. 'You deserve better. What are you going to do now?'

'Get on with my life – what else can I do?' Catherine said. 'Thank you both for such a fabulous wedding gift. I'd have loved to run Webster Media.' She bit her lower lip. 'You've paid me a great compliment but given the way things have turned out I won't be able to accept your proposal.'

Claudia kicked Sydney under the table and gave him a sidelong glance. 'Nothing has changed as far as Webster Media is concerned, has it, dear?' she said. 'Why should it? You don't need a wedding ring or a man, for that matter, to run Webster Media. The fact that you're not getting married doesn't alter our decision to make you CEO in any way at all. You agree with me, Sydney, don't you?'

'I do,' he said, feeling less fraught. 'Your appointment is in the best interests of the company, Catherine. Webster Media is in need of strong leadership and you're the perfect person to deliver it. The big loser in all this is Jack. He not only loses you but also the chance to play a role in one of the world's most important media groups.'

Catherine's face brightened as she leant across the table. 'You really still want to go ahead with everything?'

They nodded in unison. 'Instead of a wedding gift, consider it a family business arrangement,' Claudia said. 'As we keep saying, Webster Media needs someone young and vigorous like you at its helm.'

'Quite right,' Sydney assented, 'and hard work is the best way to forget an unhappy love affair. Your brother is fully occupied at Walker Corp., which should help him get over whatever damn nonsense went on between him and Belinda, and running Webster Media will take your mind off that' – the look on Catherine's face warned Sydney to be careful with his choice of words – 'ah, Jack.'

'This is the most amazing night,' she said. 'One part of me is sad; the other is in such a high state of excitement that I'm sure I won't be able to sleep a wink!' There was an excited gleam in her eye. 'I want to stand on the table and shout out the news for everyone to hear.' She hugged herself with glee.

Claudia and Sydney smiled with satisfaction, thankful to see the re-emergence of the Catherine they knew so well. 'I don't think I'll be able to wipe this grin off my face for some time.'

But then her mood changed. 'I must get serious for a minute.' She put one hand on Claudia's arm, and the other on her father's. 'Thank you both for having such confidence in me. I'll do my utmost to manage Webster Media in a way that will not only satisfy you both, but also Oscar, wherever he may be. I'm sure he's up there listening to all this,' she said to Claudia, pointing upwards. 'I won't let him or you down.'

Sitting back in her chair Catherine felt bushed. It had been such a mixed day of emotional ups and downs, it was little wonder, she supposed. Stifling a yawn, she stood up. 'I must go.' She kissed them both goodnight. 'Will I see you before you leave?' she asked her father.

'We're flying out late tomorrow afternoon, so I doubt it,' Sydney replied, 'but I'll call you in a day or two. There's still some paperwork to be done with the share transfer but everything's under control – a couple of documents require your signature and I'll have them sent across to you.' He grabbed hold of her hand. 'Don't sit up all night thinking, try to get some sleep.'

'Yes,' Claudia said, 'do that, because you look tired. Are you sure you feel well? You look sort of peaked.'

'I've had a trying few days, that's all. I'm emotionally bruised but otherwise I'm fine.' She hoped she sounded convincing. There was no way she was going to tell them about the baby, not yet anyway. They'd only worry. Worse still, they might postpone their wedding or change their minds about her new role at Webster Media and that would never do. My baby is not going to make any difference to the way I work, she thought determinedly.

Within seconds of walking in her front door, she was in bed. She'd read that early in pregnancy it was customary for a woman to feel more tired than usual, which probably explained why she was so pooped. She couldn't keep her eyes open a moment longer.

Catherine probably would have slept well into the morning if the phone hadn't rung. It can't be time to get up yet, she thought, yawning sleepily. She looked at the clock on her bedside table. Eight o'clock. Good grief, she'd slept in, something she never did. Now she'd be late for work. Thank heaven for whoever this is on the phone. 'Hello?' she said drowsily.

'Catherine, it's me, Jack. Please don't hang up. I have to see you.' He spoke hurriedly.

'Why?' she asked coldly.

'Because I miss you. You mean everything to me and I don't want to lose you. I love you – you know I do – and you feel the same way about me.'

'What is love, Jack?' She flung the words at him. 'You don't know the meaning of the word!'

'I love you like I've never loved anyone before. How many times do I have to tell you that? My life would be incomplete without you.'

'Well, I can't picture mine the way you envisage it. You'll have to manage without me, Jack.' There was hardness in her voice. 'What else is there to talk about? We both know where we stand. Our relationship has no future and I'm finding it hard to cope with the pain of that. Please leave me alone.' She put the receiver down and pulled out the phone connection so that he couldn't call her back.

I will not cry, I won't, she told herself. But she'd never felt so miserable. All this agony can't be good for the baby, she fretted. She got up and walked slowly towards the bathroom. She felt ghastly. Bloody morning sickness, she cursed. Why doesn't anyone tell you what it's really like? She sat on the corner of the bath, willing herself to feel better.

She remembered Brenda telling her that in the early weeks of her pregnancy she'd found a dry biscuit with a cup of black tea helpful for nausea. Catherine made her way to the kitchen and made herself a pot of tea. She found some plain crackers in the pantry and nibbled at them while she drank her tea. Gradually her stomach settled down. When she was dressed and ready to leave for the office, she plugged the phone back in and was almost out the door, when it rang again. She answered tentatively. It was Huxley.

'Good morning,' he said. 'This is just a quick call to see how you are and to let you know that Rowland has accepted your offer and signed on the dotted line. I've also suggested that he find some crisis in London that will make him miss the conference.' He laughed. 'It took some talking but I finally persuaded him to see things my way.'

'That's the best news I've had in a while.' She gave a thankful sigh.

'You've agreed to pay him a large sum of money, Catherine,' Huxley said. 'Can you afford it?'

'I managed to get hold of my bank manager after you'd left yesterday and all is under control. I'm going to have to sell some shares and an apartment I own in the city.'

Huxley was disturbed at hearing this. 'It's never a good move to sell assets – can't your father help you with a loan?'

'I'd never ask my father to help pay for my marriage stuff-ups.' There was no mistaking the resolve in her voice. Huxley knew it would be pointless continuing the discussion.

In spite of everything, he thought Catherine sounded far more cheerful. 'How do you feel?'

'I'm fine and you'll never believe what happened to me last night.'

'Knowing you, I'm frightened to ask,' he joked.

'I can't possibly tell you on the phone. Are you free for lunch?'

He was. She invited him to share a sandwich with her in the boardroom. When he arrived he discovered she'd asked Tom as well.

'A pair of Walkers – I am honoured! You must have something major to tell us!' He looked at Catherine inquiringly. 'What's up?'

'Patience, Huxley. First you should know that I've just told Tom all about Jack and the baby. He agrees with me that for the time being no one else needs to know but us. After all, this baby is nobody's business but mine.' She looked at them both, daring them to disagree. Both men sensibly said nothing.

'And now, talking about business, I do have an announcement to make.' Her eyes sparkled as she told them about her dinner with Claudia and Sydney. When she'd finished, Tom was the first to speak.

'How marvellous,' he said, giving her a brotherly bear hug. 'You're exactly what Webster Media needs.'

'I couldn't agree more,' Huxley said, administering a hearty peck on the cheek. 'It's inspired thinking on their part. Just imagine what you'll be able to do with that company. I'm more than a little envious.' He held up his coffee cup and made a toast. 'Congratulations, Catherine, and every success.' He waved his cup in her brother's direction. 'And to you too, Tom. May good health and fortune always be with you both!'

'Hey, and you, Huxley. You're a part of it, too,' Tom said. 'And if you thought you were busy before, you ain't seen nothing yet. I've got all sorts of plans for you.'

The three of them smiled at each other. 'The three Aussie musketeers,' Catherine laughed. Tom and Huxley joined in.

'So when will the appointment be announced?' Tom wanted to know.

'As soon as all the documents have been signed,' she explained. 'I'll be going to London probably in a week or so to have a two-day conference with all the Webster Media editors. I want to hear from them first-hand what problems they think we face in their respective countries. I'm going to reassure them that we consider the people who work for us essential to the profitability and future of the company and we recognise that it's their expertise that gives Webster Media its edge.' She was in an ebullient mood, high on the adrenaline at the thought of being boss of such a prestigious group.

'I also intend to tell them that our newspapers are going to make a commitment to pressuring governments to do something positive to combat the growth in world unemployment. We will argue that a planet that is apathetic about the global destiny of the human race is indifferent to its future.'

'Hello, hello, a CEO with a heart and a passion for a good cause. Watch out world, here comes Catherine Walker!' Tom teased.

'Unemployment is no laughing matter, Tom,' Catherine said. 'I intend to make a difference – just you wait and see. I'm sure I've given people some idea of the kind of woman I am through *MAUD* but Webster Media gives me a much bigger power base and I'm going to make the most of it. I can't wait to get started!'

'What about the baby? Won't it make a difference to your plans?' he queried.

'Cut that out, Tom. You're not going to suggest that being pregnant will affect the way I work, are you? This is the 21st century, not the dark ages. I'm pregnant, not ill. The baby isn't going to make a scrap of difference to my work performance.'

'Okay, okay, just asking, don't get militant.'

'Shut up, little brother, would you? I refuse to let you needle me. I'm so excited about everything.' She was glowing with anticipation.

Huxley was pleased to see her in this mood. It suits her so well, he thought. That ability of hers to enthuse everyone around her was remarkable. He again found himself wishing he could be part of her grand plan.

'I don't know what you two have on your agendas for the rest of the afternoon but I have to get back to work,' Catherine said.

The rest of the day passed quickly. Catherine had been asked to join the official party at the opening night of the opera but didn't feel up to it. 'Make an excuse for me would you please, Clare, I don't feel all that well.'

She'd felt off-colour all afternoon and had presumed it was just morning sickness again. But as she was driving home she felt as if she were going to faint. She turned up the air-conditioning full blast and drove carefully to Bondi. The smell of the sea will make me feel better, she thought. She went outside on to the deck and found the fresh air did help at first, but suddenly the mild pain she'd felt earlier turned into a severe cramp. She doubled over as if she was winded.

Something awful is happening, I know it. She was frightened and went into the bedroom to call her doctor.

'Lie down at once, Catherine, and try not to move. I'll be there straightaway.' Her advice was of no use. Catherine knew she was having a miscarriage. By the time the doctor had arrived she'd lost her baby.

# Chapter Twenty-Four

When Catherine woke up in the morning the events of the previous day hit home forcibly. She thought of her lost baby; she'd wanted it so much. She covered her face with her hands as the tears flooded down her cheeks. When she'd cried herself out she lay silently, staring bleakly at the ceiling. Her head throbbed. Her heart was filled with pain.

'You'll feel depressed and tired but I don't think there'll be any complications,' the doctor had said last night, after examining her. 'It's important that you rest. Don't think of going back to work until I say you can. I'm going to give you something to make you sleep and I want you to ring me tomorrow to let me know how you're feeling.'

It took all her willpower to make herself get up. Wallowing in misery won't get you anywhere, she told herself.

After speaking to her doctor, Catherine rang

Huxley and told him what had happened.

'Are you going to be all right?' he asked anxiously.

'Yes. I'm just very tired, that's all, and dreadfully sad. I don't think I've ever felt as unhappy as I do right at this moment. It's awful, Huxley.'

'I don't think it's right for you to be alone.'

'I really don't feel like seeing anyone. I know it's probably not good for me to be by myself,' she spoke swiftly before he could lecture her, 'but it's what I want.'

'If you must.'

'I must.'

While Catherine was ringing Clare to inform her that she wouldn't be in for a few days because her virus had worsened, Huxley called Tom. 'You mustn't let her know I've phoned you – you know how bolshie she can be. She thinks she can handle this all by herself but I don't think she should have to, Tom. Can't you take her home to your place for a few days and have those terrific people who work for you there make a fuss of her?'

'Consider it done and don't worry, I won't let her know we've talked.'

Tom had only just hung up from Huxley when Catherine's call came through. He tried to comfort her as best he could but secretly he was relieved. Under the circumstances he felt that what had happened was for the best, but of course he mentioned none of that to his sister. Instead he said: 'I've a great idea – why don't you come and stay at Ashburn for a few days? You'll be spoilt rotten by the staff and it will do you good. It would be like old times to have you here.'

He had moved into Ashburn at his father's suggestion. 'It needs to be lived in,' Sydney had told him. 'It's going to be yours one day and I don't see why you should wait until I die before you move in. Claudia and I will stay at her penthouse in Point Piper when we're in Sydney – it's more than big enough for the two of us.' It was an excellent arrangement and everyone was happy, most of all Tom, who'd always loved Ashburn and could now enjoy the place properly as it was free of the friction that he'd always associated with home when his parents had lived there.

'The thought of being pampered at Ashburn does sound appealing,' Catherine said. 'I'd love to come for a few days.'

Tom rang his father to tell him Catherine had been unwell and suggested that the announcement of the changes at Webster Media be postponed until she was fit again. 'It's nothing serious, Dad, just a virus, but it made her pretty ill and she's going to take a few days' break from work and come home to Ashburn. I'm going to take some time off too so I can keep an eye on her. We'll both be back in our respective offices next week.'

A stunning arrangement of flowers from Huxley

was waiting for her at Ashburn when she arrived. 'How thoughtful,' Catherine said to Tom, as she read the card: *Take care of yourself and let's have dinner next week. I have a new joke for you.*

Ashburn was just what the doctor ordered. Catherine revisited childhood haunts with Tom, exploring the grounds in the early morning before breakfasting on the verandah. They swam in the huge swimming pool and had a hit of tennis, although Catherine wasn't physically up to playing her usual competitive game.

Tom had asked the chef to prepare all the dishes they'd most loved as children and was delighted at the look of pleasure on Catherine's face when he announced they were having pancakes for Sunday breakfast. Pancakes smothered with maple syrup and served with crispy bacon were a Walker family tradition.

'Tom, I haven't had pancakes for ages. Watch it, don't hog the maple syrup!' She covered her pancakes generously before she took a mouthful and pronounced them 'absolutely delicious'. They were so good she couldn't resist a second helping. 'Gosh, this brings back memories. Do you remember how Ma once tried to persuade us to have lemon and sugar on our pancakes instead of maple syrup?'

'We wouldn't even try it.' Tom laughed. 'And what about the time she suggested we have them rolled up in that blueberry sauce she had the cook make?'

'Poor Ma – she tried so hard to make us sample new things with our pancakes, didn't she?' Catherine laughed too but then a pensive look crossed her face. 'You know, I often think of her. Do you think she was ever happy, Tom? I've always thought so much of her life was wasted. She was so beautiful and gifted.'

He thought about it for a moment. 'I think she was as happy as she could be. I'm sure she'd have been happier if she hadn't loved Dad the way she did. It allowed him to dominate her to such an extent that in the end he crushed her spirit. She was a gentle creature, really, and she needed more nurturing than Dad was able to give her. Love shouldn't destroy a person, but the way Ma loved Dad was a soul-destroying kind of love.'

Over in his office, where he was catching up on some reading before the following week's board meeting, Huxley also had love on his mind. He wanted to tell Catherine about his feelings for her but knew the timing was wrong. She had to get Jack Clement out of her system before he could say anything. If he let slip the merest hint of anything it could scare her off completely and spell the end of their friendship. This meant as much to him as it did to her and he had no intention of doing anything that might harm it.

But it wasn't the easiest thing in the world, living with what he'd always thought of as unobtainable love. He'd managed because he'd never allowed himself to think he had a chance with her. But now destiny had intervened and changed the game plan, he was finding it harder then ever to keep his emotions under control. However, he steeled himself: even if it killed him, he would bide his time.

Being back in Australia suited him perfectly because he was ideally placed to see her more often, without anyone suspecting that he was anything more than just a friend. Friendship often developed into love, he knew that. There was no reason why it couldn't happen that way for him and Catherine. He just had to be patient.

Her colleagues at CW Publishing were pleased to see Catherine looking more like her old self when she returned to work. Her days with Tom at Ashburn had been beneficial in more ways than one. They'd spent a great deal of time talking about their parents and had been able to sort out their sentiments about them in a way that had never been possible before.

Tom confessed that he found his father impossible to figure out. 'He can be so cruel and crude and, at other times, so kind and helpful that it's hard to believe he's the same man. I always thought he was over-sexed when I was younger. Claudia seems to have soothed the beast in him – and thank heaven for that.'

'I think it's a combination of Claudia and age,' Catherine mused. 'I used to wonder about Dad too,' she went on. 'He cheated on Ma so often. I don't know how he could have lived here under the same roof with her and then, when she wasn't here, bring women home to the bed they shared together.'

They were sitting on Ashburn's verandah, admiring the view, and had never felt so close. 'But still there comes a time when you just have to accept your parents, warts and all. What you see is what you get – and that was certainly the case with our parents.'

'That's for sure,' Tom said. 'But Sis,' he looked at Catherine devotedly, 'I'm glad you've always been around.'

Catherine's first day back at the office was busier than usual. A press conference had been organised mid-morning to make the Webster Media announcement. Clare had rearranged the board-room so that the expected media would fit in but even then there'd been standing room only. Catherine was about to become a notable world figure and the media wanted to find out as much about her as possible. *MAUD* magazine had given her recognition outside of Australia but assuming the CEO's role at Webster Media would make her not only a powerful player but one of the most influential women in the world.

She'd just completed the last interview when Jack

arrived. Composing herself, she showed him into her office. 'What are you doing here, Jack?'

His reply was blunt. 'Why didn't you tell me about Webster Media when I spoke to you the other day?' he asked angrily.

'Why should I?' she said. 'You never discussed your business plans with me and what's more you never told me that you and Murdoch were cooking up something together for Webster Media either. You don't own me, Jack. Who the hell do you think you are?' Now she was angry. How dare he barge in and accuse her of having secrets. 'I do wish you'd stop standing there, glowering at me. Can't you sit down?'

'Let's not argue,' he said, sitting down opposite her.

'Suits me,' she replied, giving him a twisted smile. 'The irony of it all is that if you had married me you'd have got your hands on Webster Media with no trouble at all.'

'What do you mean?'

'You're going to find it difficult to believe,' she said, and quite matter-of-factly proceeded to tell him about the outcome of her dinner with Claudia and her father. 'They were truly happy that we were getting married and convinced that you and I would be an unbeatable team, professionally as well as personally. And we would have been, Jack, you know that as well as I do. Ultimately, they'd have allowed

542

us to acquire the rest of their shares and Webster Media would have been ours.'

She looked at him pityingly. 'What a shame you weren't prepared to take a gamble on me. For a man who prides himself on winning that came as a real surprise. Most winners I know take risks. But not you, it seems. If only you'd been brave enough to rock the boat.'

Jack was not only finding it difficult to take it all in, he was having trouble controlling his temper. Bugger that stupid cow Claudia Webster, he fumed. And bugger Sydney Walker as well. 'Is that all?' His tone was almost menacing.

'Don't lose your block with me, Jack. There's nothing to be gained by it.' She halted wearily. 'There is one more thing you need to know.' She couldn't stop the tears that came. She wiped them away before telling him about the miscarriage. As he got up and came towards her, all anger forgotten, she stopped him. 'It's too late for you to comfort me now. When I needed you most you weren't there for me.' Her voice trembled. 'We could have had the most tremendous time together. You were the love of my life.'

'*Were?*' Jack waved his arm dismissively. 'You don't mean that. You still love me, Catherine – you know you do.'

'How I feel is my business.' She was in control of herself now. 'But what we had is over. Your kind of love comes with a dollar value and now that I understand you're the kind of man who puts a price on love, let me tell you something . . .' She sat down behind her desk, before continuing decisively. 'You can't afford me, Jack. I'm way out of your price range.'

'You're making a big mistake,' he insisted.

'I'd be making a bigger one to ever believe in you again. You've caused me enough heartache – I wish you'd leave.' She picked up a letter from her in-tray and pretended to read it.

'You're mine, Catherine,' he said, as he left her office. 'Don't ever forget it.' His words lingered in the hush that filled the room.

Oh God! Catherine's heart was pounding. How did I manage to get through that? He was right – she did still love him, but it was pointless. There was no way he'd ever sacrifice his company for their happiness and she wasn't prepared to compromise. She was on her own now. Maybe it wouldn't be easy but life never was – she knew that better than most. If Jack had died unexpectedly I'd have had to get on with my life the best way I could.

The penny dropped. That's it, she thought. I'll think of him as dead. As far as she was concerned, Jack no longer existed. A bittersweet expression swept over her face. A more resolute one quickly replaced it. Don't look back, Catherine, she told herself sternly.

She got up from her desk and walked towards the window. The sunset had turned the sky into a spectacular kaleidoscope of pinks and crimsons. In spite of herself, she laughed. *Trust nature to bring down the curtain on my doomed love affair in such a memorable way.* She mockingly saluted the brilliant display before marching purposefully back to her desk.

She would chart a new course for herself. Webster Media would test her but so what? She liked challenges. They kept her on her toes. She was excited at the thought of what lay ahead. Her adrenaline was bubbling again and she was raring to go. The knockers would be ready to pounce at the first sign of an error of judgement but she had no intention of ever giving them that satisfaction.

She was Catherine Walker, very much her own woman, determined and ambitious – and proud of it, too. The innovative strategies she had in mind for Webster Media and CW Publishing would give her a position of authority on the world stage. People would remember her name!

There wasn't a moment to waste. She took some papers out of a drawer and, humming a happy tune, for what seemed like the first time in ages, made her way to the boardroom. *The best is yet to be, that's for sure, but my happy ending depends entirely on me.*

There was nothing she couldn't do. Anything was possible and she was in the mood to climb mountains, the bigger the better. Nothing and no one was going to stop her.